FOUR SISTERS

EuroComics.us

Editor Dean Mullaney • Art Director Lorraine Turner
Translation Edward Gauvin

EuroComics is an imprint of IDW Publishing
a Division of Idea and Design Works, LLC
2765 Truxtun Road • San Diego, CA 92106
www.idwpublishing.com

Distributed to the book trade by Penguin Random House
Distributed to the comic book trade by Diamond Book Distributors

ISBN: 978-1-68405-433-6
First Printing, April 2019

Four Sisters: Hortense, Volume 2 (original French title: *Quatre soeurs: Hortense, volume 2*)
© 2014 Rue de Sèvres
English translation © 2019 Library of American Comics LLC. All rights reserved.

IDW Publishing
Chris Ryall, President, Publisher, and Chief Creative Officer
John Barber, Editor-in-Chief
Robbie Robbins, EVP/Sr. Art Director
Cara Morrison, Chief Financial Officer
Matt Ruzicka, Chief Accounting Officer
Anita Frazier, SVP of Sales and Marketing
David Hedgecock, Associate Publisher
Jerry Bennington, VP of New Product Development
Lorelei Bunjes, VP of Digital Services
Justin Eisinger, Editorial Director, Graphic Novels & Collections
Eric Moss, Senior Director, Licensing and Business Development

Ted Adams, IDW Founder

Special thanks to Justin Eisinger and Alonzo Simon,
and Marija Gaudry of Rue de Sèvres.

Four Sisters

2. Hortense

Written and Illustrated by Cati Baur

Colors by Élodie Balandras

Based on the novel by Malika Ferdjoukh

EURO COMICS

ENGLISH EDITION · GRAPHIC NOVELS

An imprint of IDW PUBLISHING

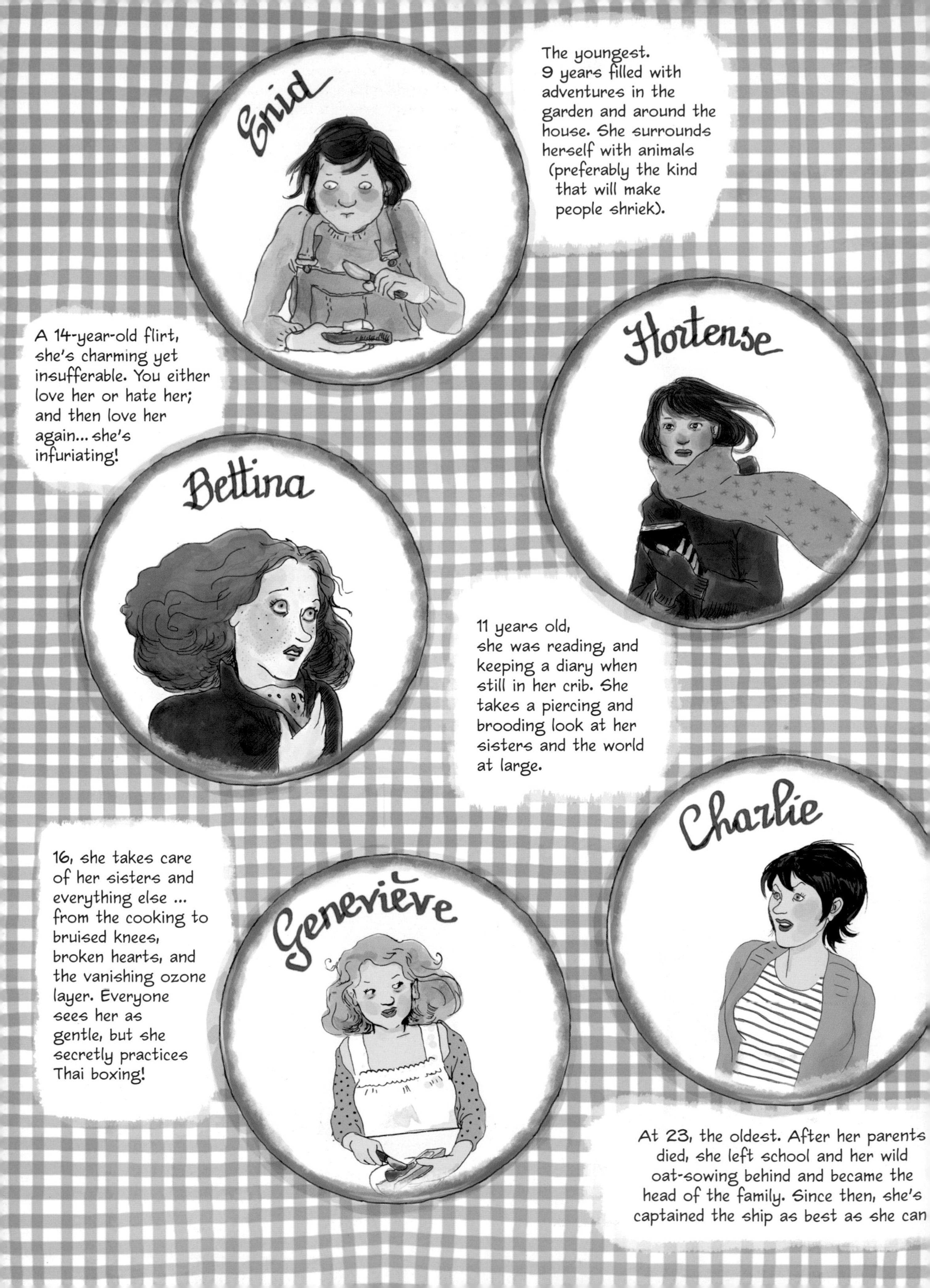
Enid
The youngest. 9 years filled with adventures in the garden and around the house. She surrounds herself with animals (preferably the kind that will make people shriek).
Hortense
A 14-year-old flirt, she's charming yet insufferable. You either love her or hate her; and then love her again... she's infuriating!
Bettina
11 years old, she was reading, and keeping a diary when still in her crib. She takes a piercing and brooding look at her sisters and the world at large.
Charlie
16, she takes care of her sisters and everything else ... from the cooking to bruised knees, broken hearts, and the vanishing ozone layer. Everyone sees her as gentle, but she secretly practices Thai boxing!
Geneviève
At 23, the oldest. After her parents died, she left school and her wild oat-sowing behind and became the head of the family. Since then, she's captained the ship as best as she can

cats of the
use.

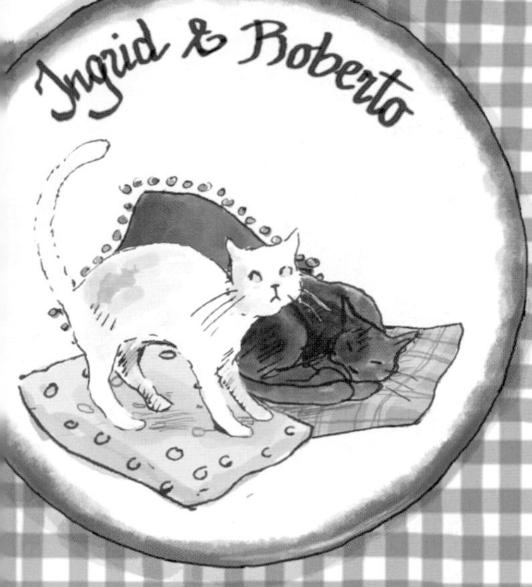
Ingrid & Roberto

Ghosts ever since their car accident, they watch over their daughters, appearing now and then, whenever they feel like it, dressed according to their mood, without a care for the weather.

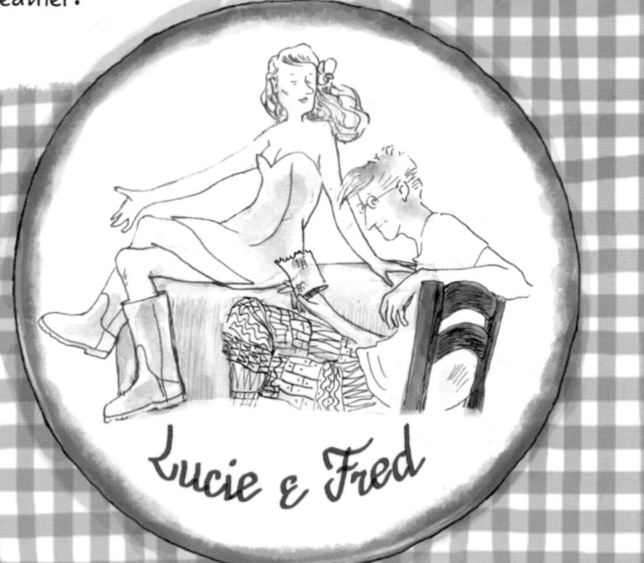
Lucie & Fred

Bettina's girlfriends. Together they are the DB&B: "Denise, Bettina, Behoteguy," or, according to Enid, "Dimwit, Bonehead, and Blockhead."

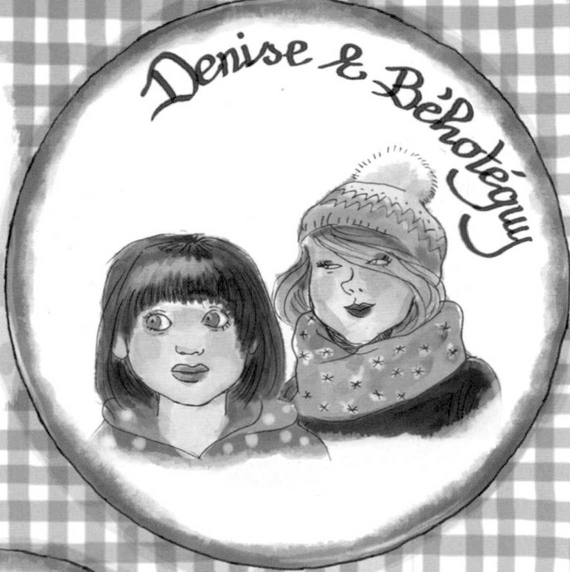
Denise & Béhotéguy

Their father's aunt, she's the girls' legal co-guardian. She likes orderliness, her dog Delmer, and the singer Engelbert Humperdinck. She provides the girls with a measly check every month.

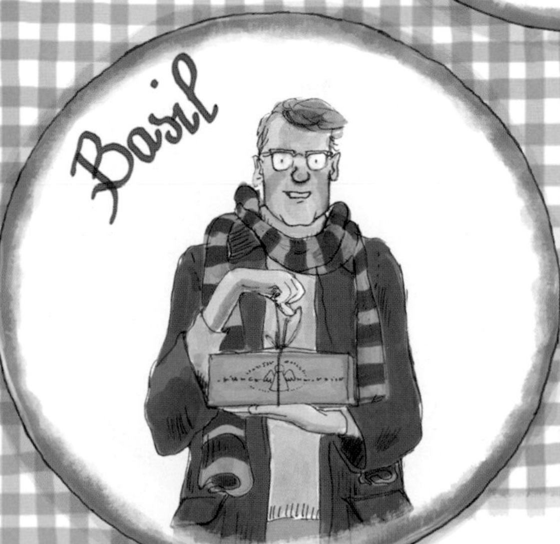
Basil

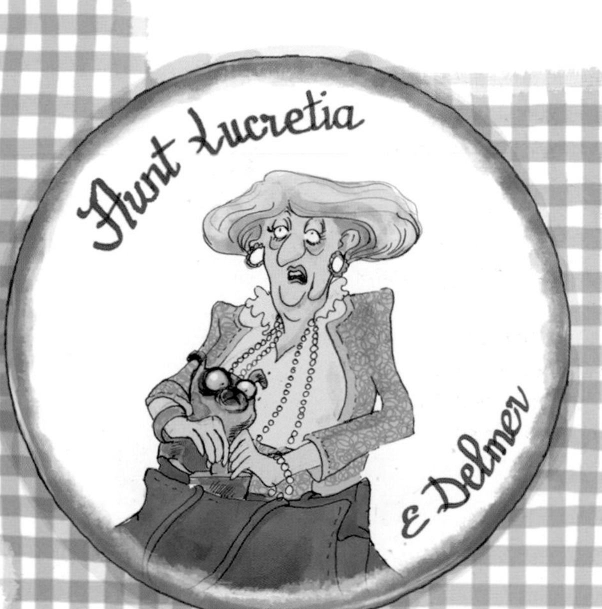
Aunt Lucretia
& Delmer

A young doctor, friend of the family, and Charlie's official boyfriend.

I would like to thank my Mom, Jean-François, Dad, and, of course, Nicolas
for their help and precious support day after day.

Malika for her kind and enlightening read-through.

All my readers, editors, and colleagues, as well as booksellers
for their trust and above all, their patience.

And, at last, special thanks to Thierry Joor, who with great talent and
involvement assisted with bringing this series into being.

This book is dedicated to my darlings: Siméon, Olympe and Honoré, Béryl and Soren.

And in memory of Tom.

— Cati Baur

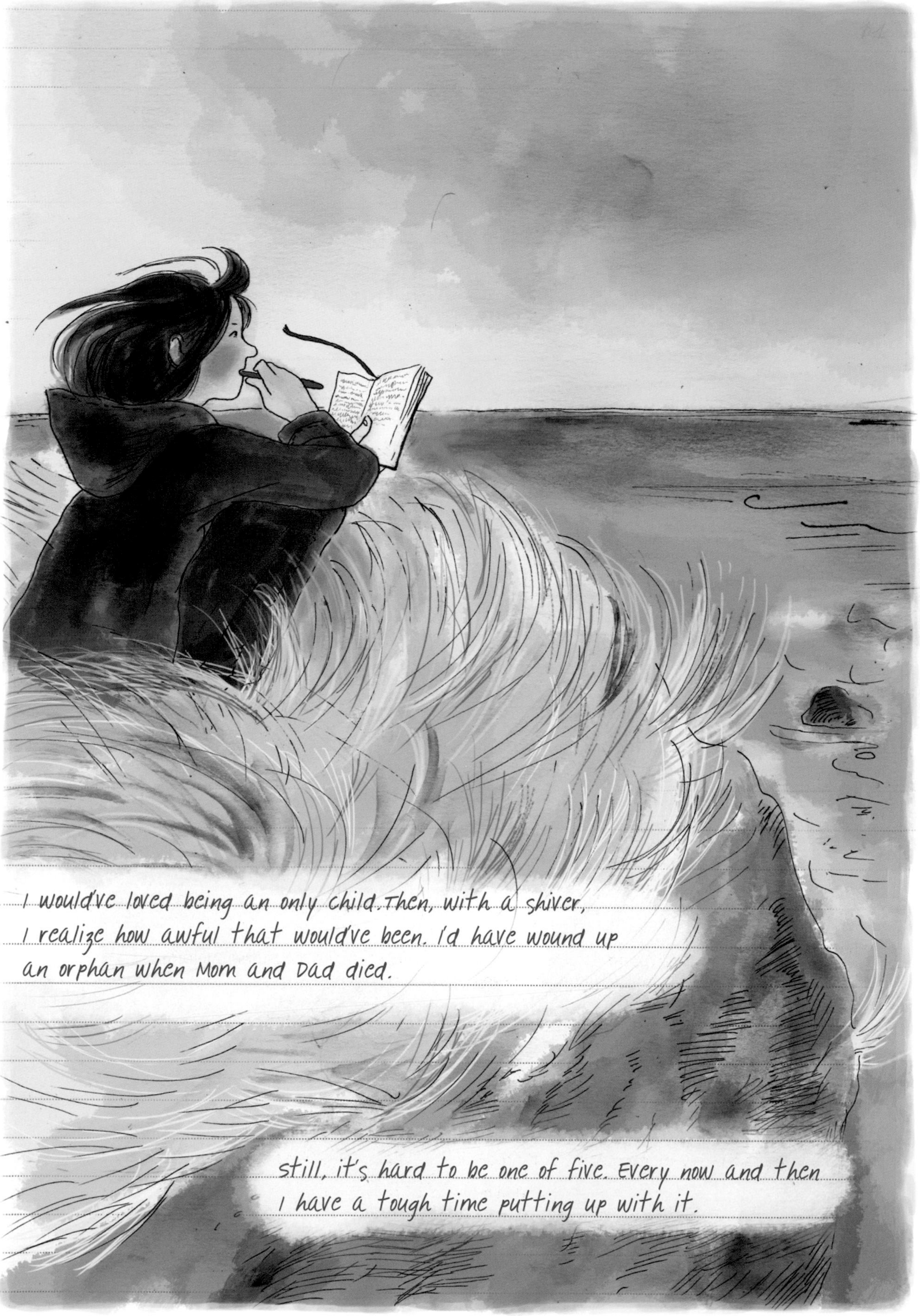
I would've loved being an only child. Then, with a shiver, I realize how awful that would've been. I'd have wound up an orphan when Mom and Dad died.
Still, it's hard to be one of five. Every now and then I have a tough time putting up with it.

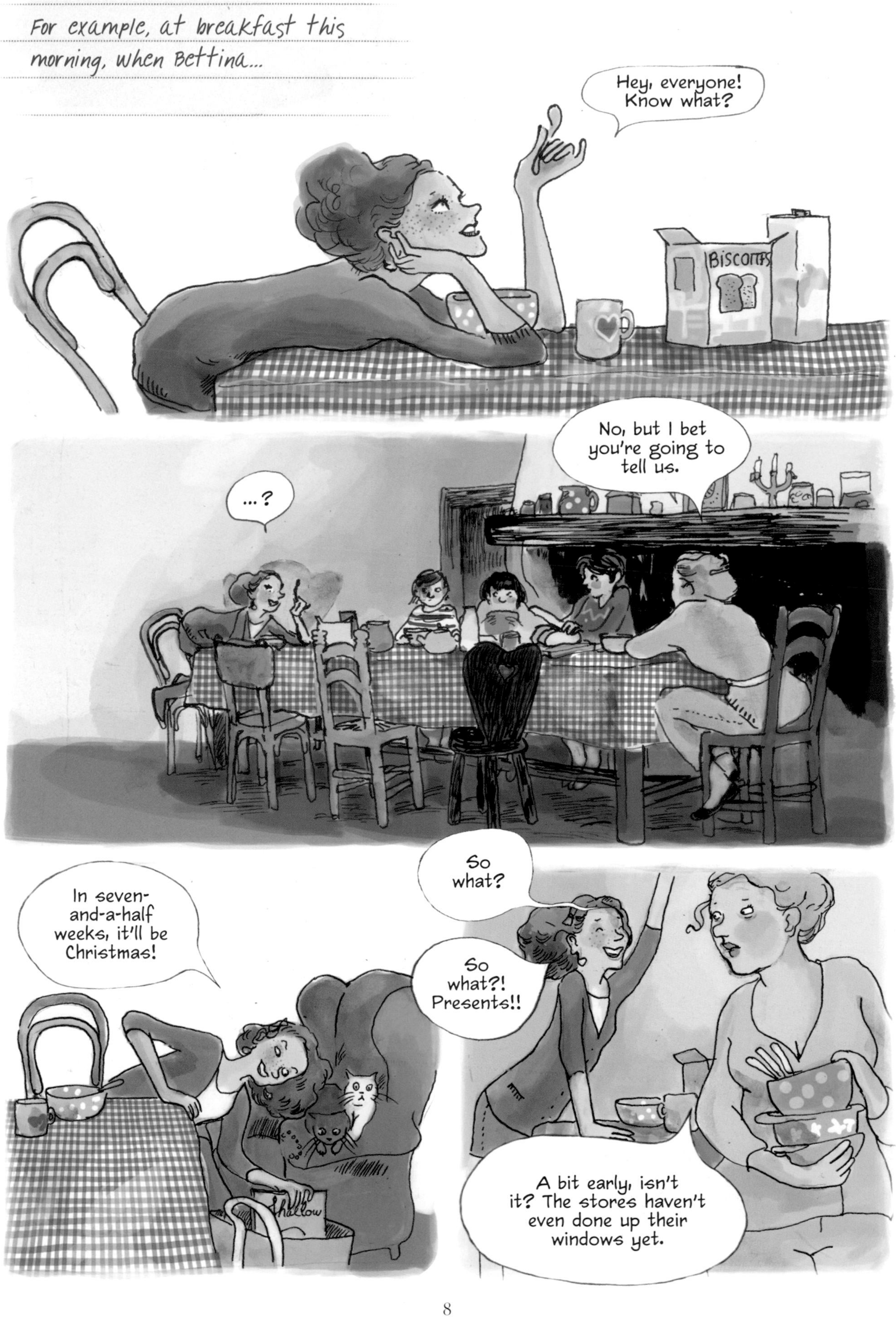
For example, at breakfast this morning, when Bettina...
Hey, everyone! Know what?
...?
No, but I bet you're going to tell us.
In seven-and-a-half weeks, it'll be Christmas!
So what?
So what?! Presents!!
A bit early, isn't it? The stores haven't even done up their windows yet.

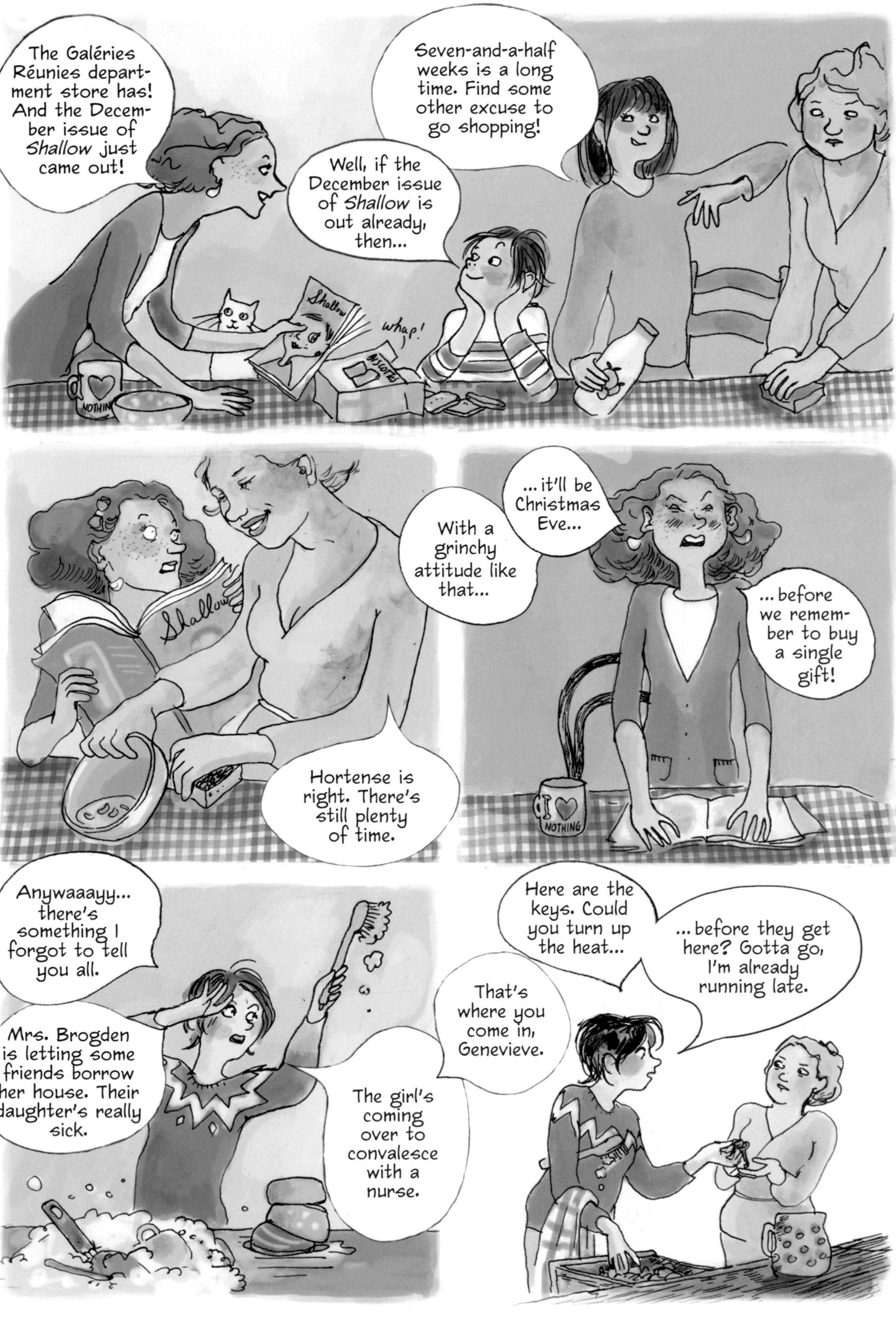

The Galéries Réunies department store has! And the December issue of *Shallow* just came out!
Seven-and-a-half weeks is a long time. Find some other excuse to go shopping!
Well, if the December issue of *Shallow* is out already, then...
Shallow
whap!
With a grinchy attitude like that...
...it'll be Christmas Eve...
...before we remember to buy a single gift!
Shallow
Hortense is right. There's still plenty of time.
I ♥ NOTHING
Anywaaayy... there's something I forgot to tell you all.
Mrs. Brogden is letting some friends borrow her house. Their daughter's really sick.
The girl's coming over to convalesce with a nurse.
That's where you come in, Genevieve.
Here are the keys. Could you turn up the heat...
...before they get here? Gotta go, I'm already running late.

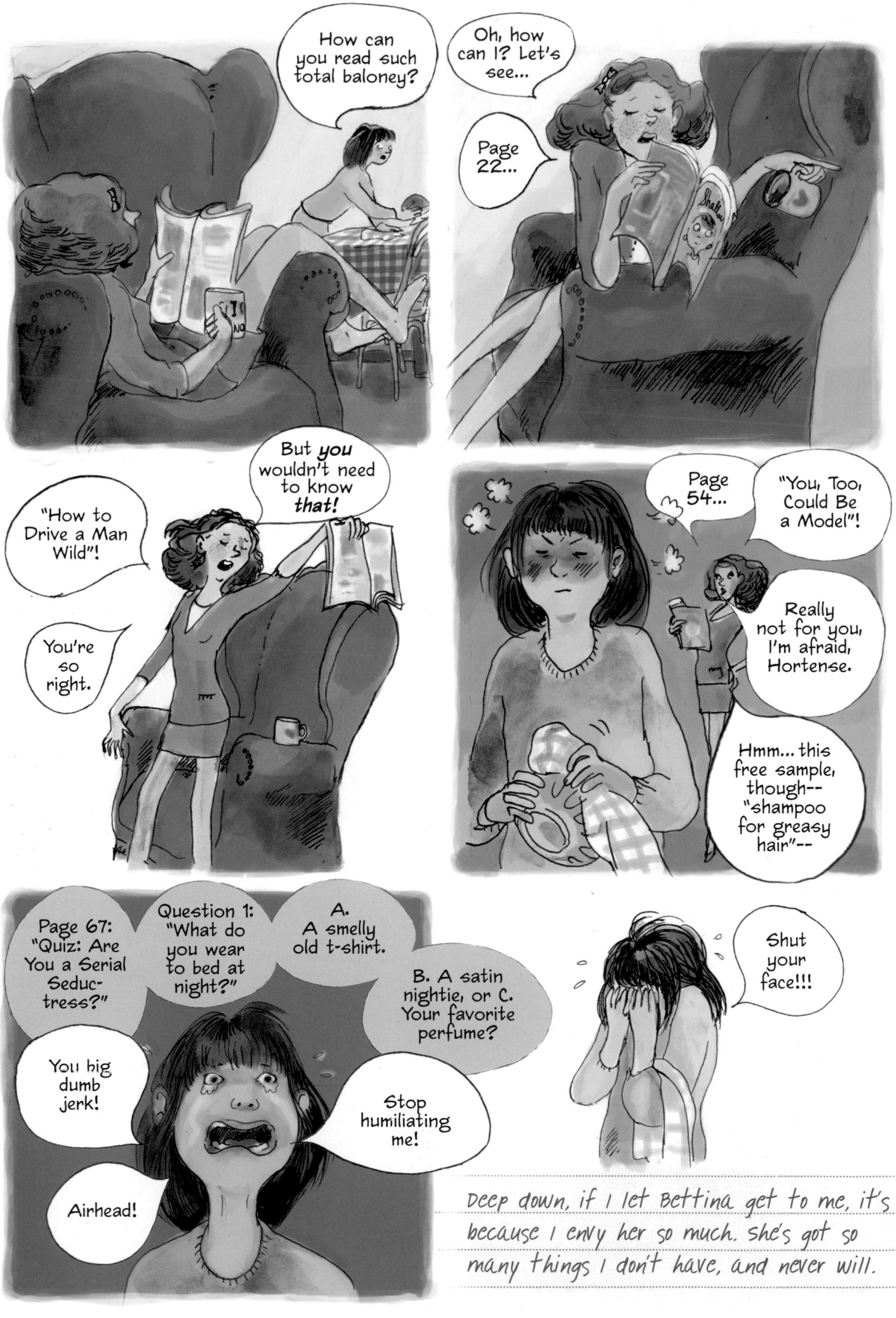
How can you read such total baloney?
Oh, how can I? Let's see...
Page 22...
"How to Drive a Man Wild"!
But *you* wouldn't need to know *that!*
You're so right.
Page 54...
"You, Too, Could Be a Model"!
Really not for you, I'm afraid, Hortense.
Hmm... this free sample, though-- "shampoo for greasy hair"--
Page 67: "Quiz: Are You a Serial Seductress?"
Question 1: "What do you wear to bed at night?"
A. A smelly old t-shirt.
B. A satin nightie, or C. Your favorite perfume?
You big dumb jerk!
Stop humiliating me!
Airhead!
Shut your face!!!
Deep down, if I let Bettina get to me, it's because I envy her so much. She's got so many things I don't have, and never will.

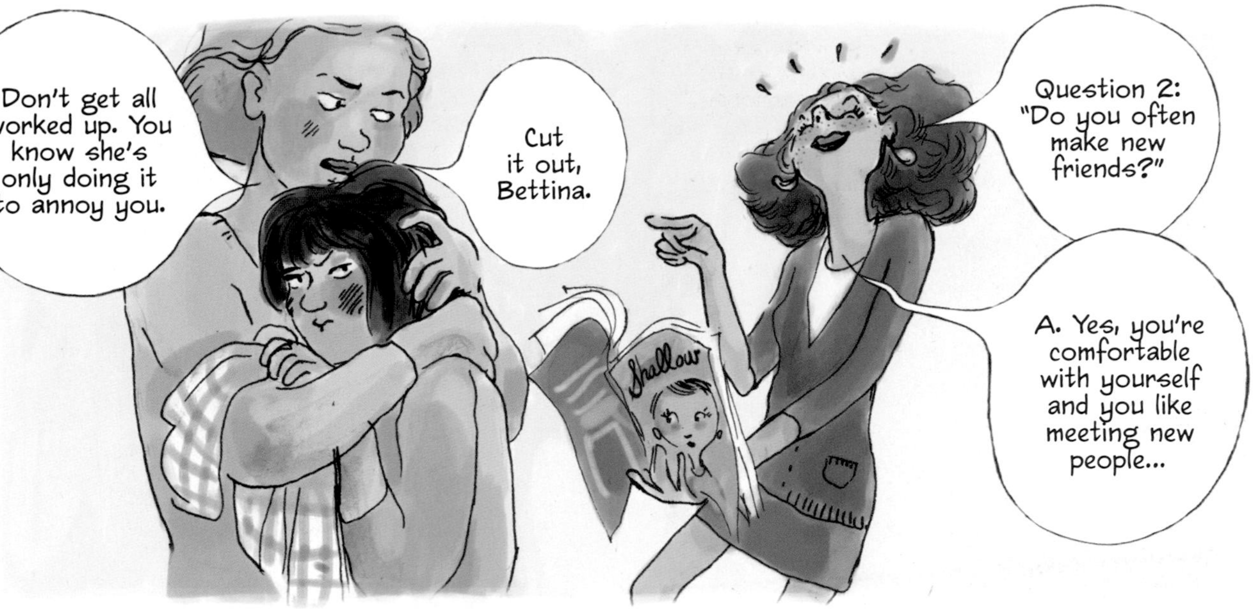
Don't get all worked up. You know she's only doing it to annoy you.
Cut it out, Bettina.
Question 2: "Do you often make new friends?"
A. Yes, you're comfortable with yourself and you like meeting new people...
Shallow

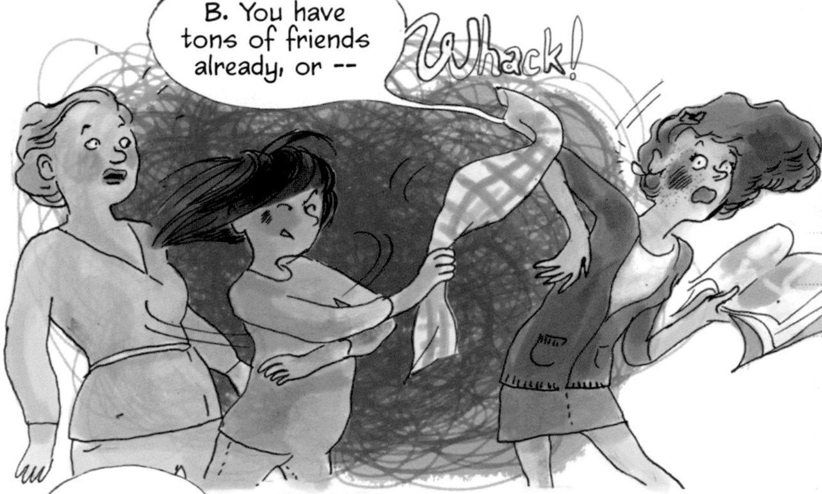
B. You have tons of friends already, or --
Whack!

She's not the prettiest among us. No, Bettina has a lively face and a sharp eye. She reminds you of pointy, sparkly things, like a needle, a dagger. Polished, seductive, very "watch out! Here I come!"

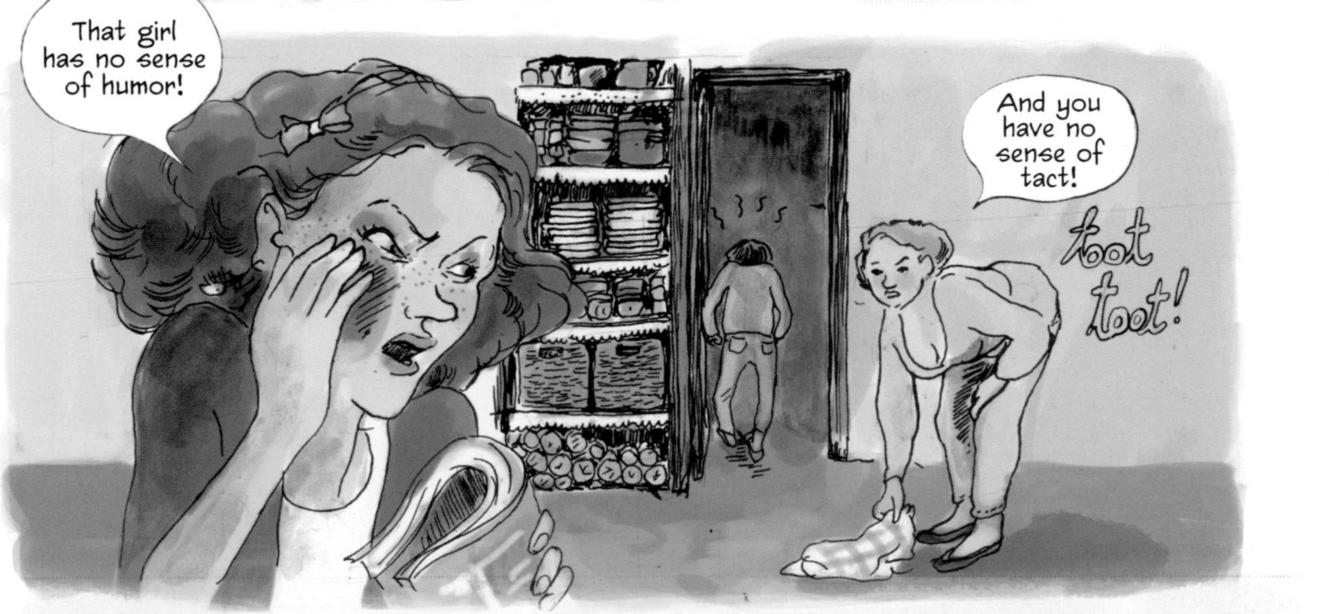
That girl has no sense of humor!
And you have no sense of tact!
toot toot!

She can be nice when she's not busy trying to be mean.

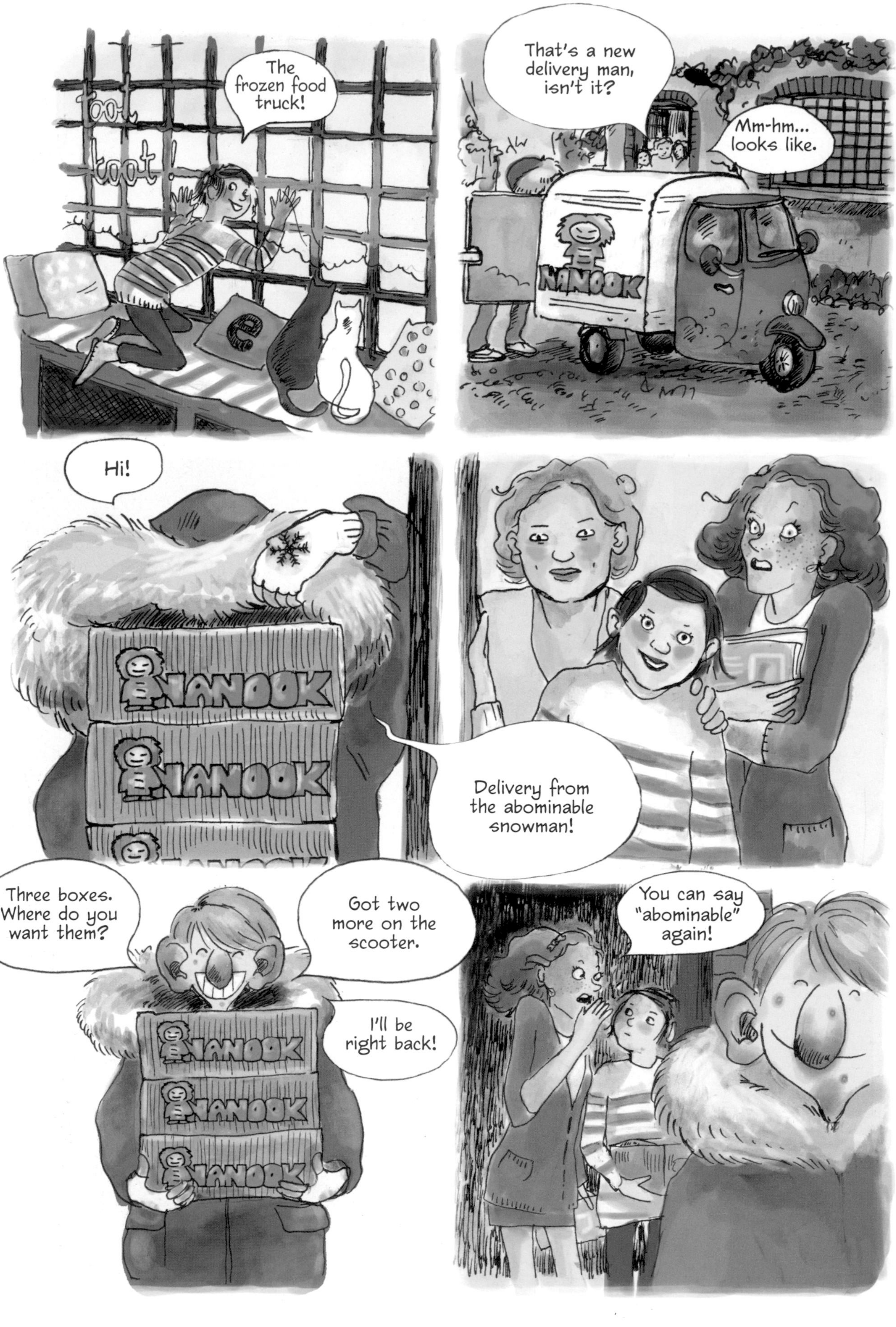
toot
toot!
The frozen food truck!
That's a new delivery man, isn't it?
Mm-hm... looks like.
NANOOK
Hi!
NANOOK
NANOOK
Delivery from the abominable snowman!
Three boxes. Where do you want them?
Got two more on the scooter.
I'll be right back!
NANOOK
NANOOK
NANOOK
You can say "abominable" again!

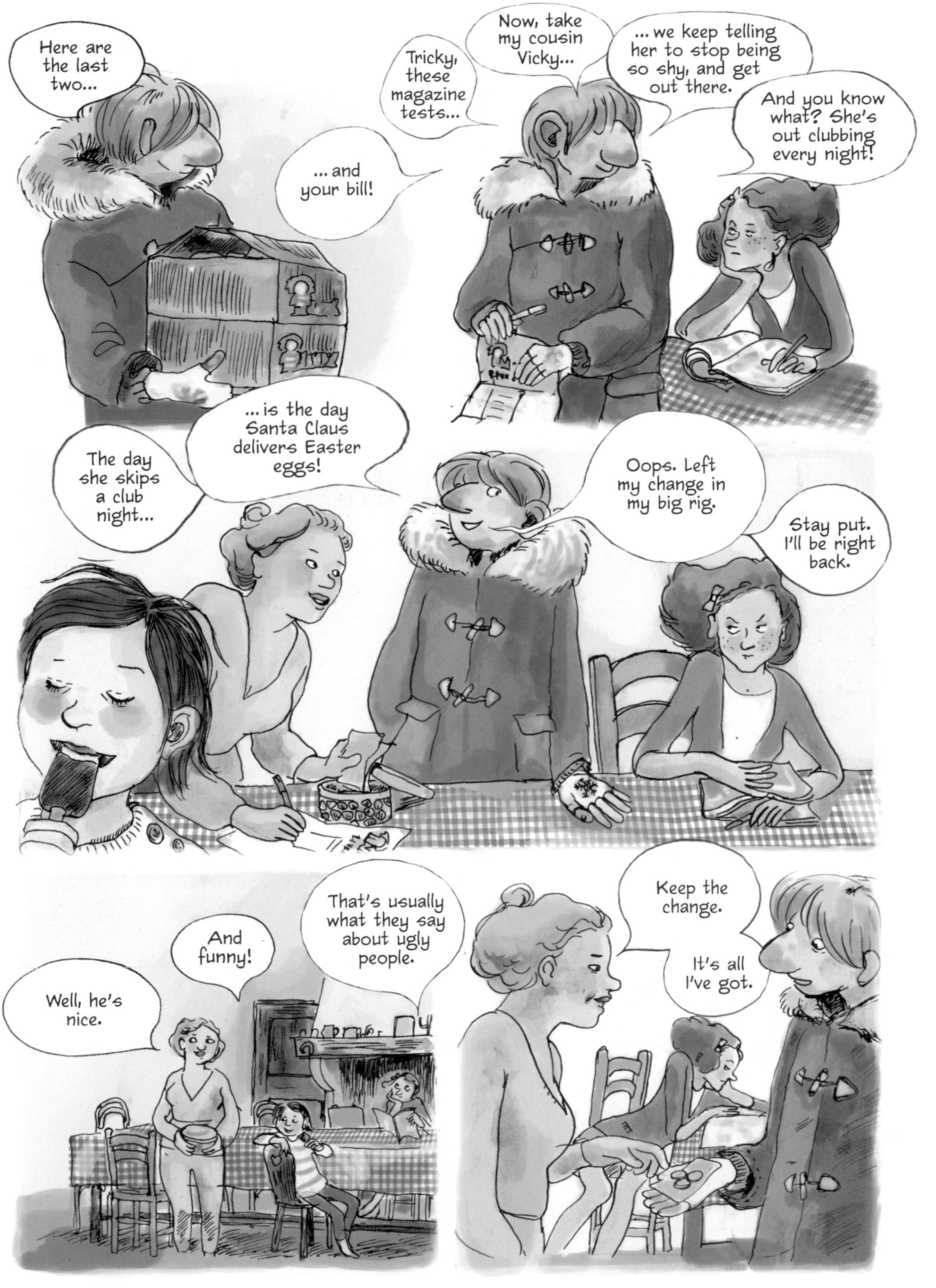
Here are the last two...
...and your bill!
Tricky, these magazine tests...
Now, take my cousin Vicky...
...we keep telling her to stop being so shy, and get out there.
And you know what? She's out clubbing every night!
The day she skips a club night...
...is the day Santa Claus delivers Easter eggs!
Oops. Left my change in my big rig.
Stay put. I'll be right back.
Well, he's nice.
And funny!
That's usually what they say about ugly people.
Keep the change.
It's all I've got.

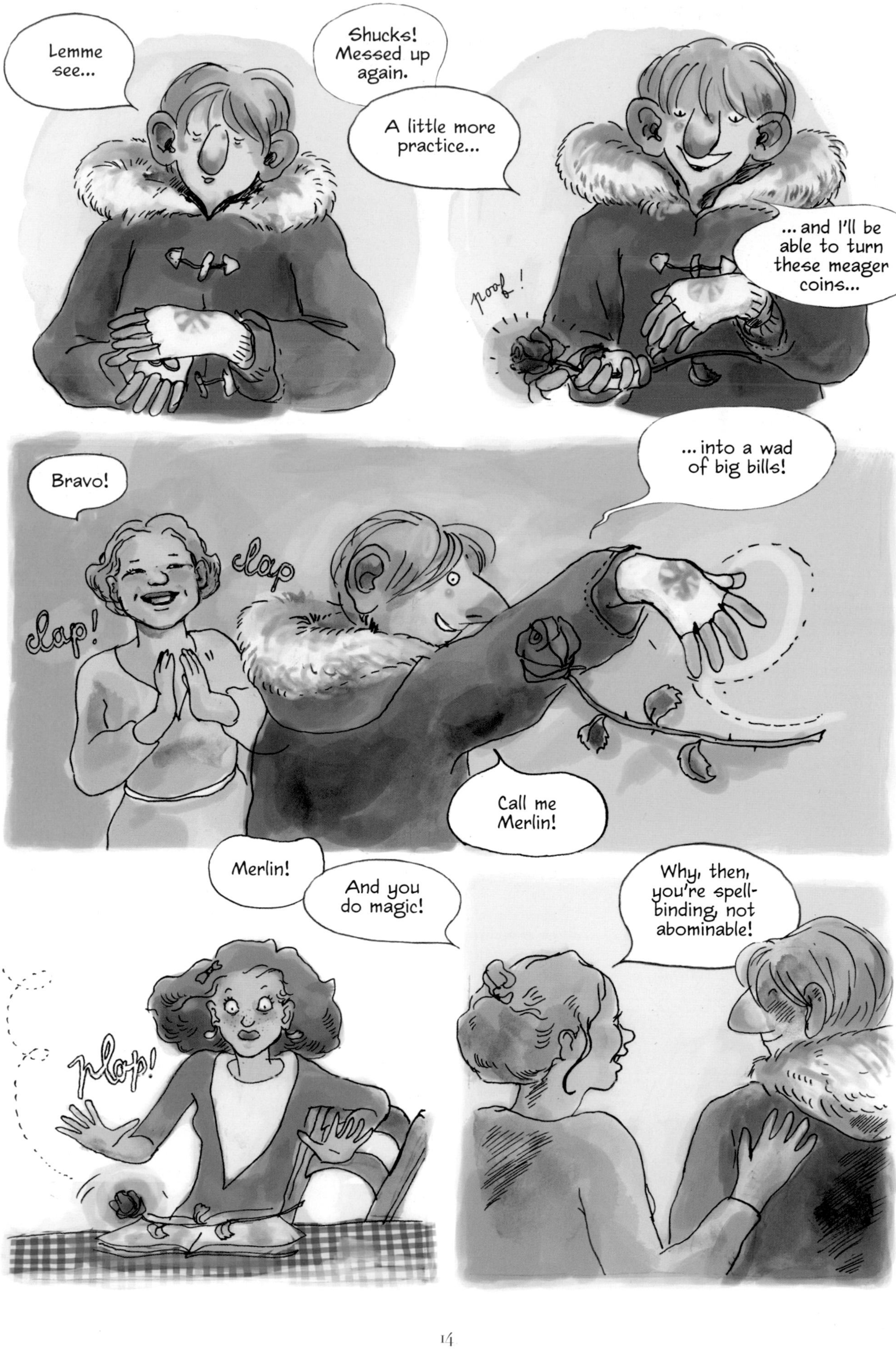
Lemme see...
Shucks! Messed up again.
A little more practice...
poof!
...and I'll be able to turn these meager coins...
Bravo!
...into a wad of big bills!
clap
clap!
Call me Merlin!
Merlin!
And you do magic!
Why, then, you're spell-binding, not abominable!
plop!

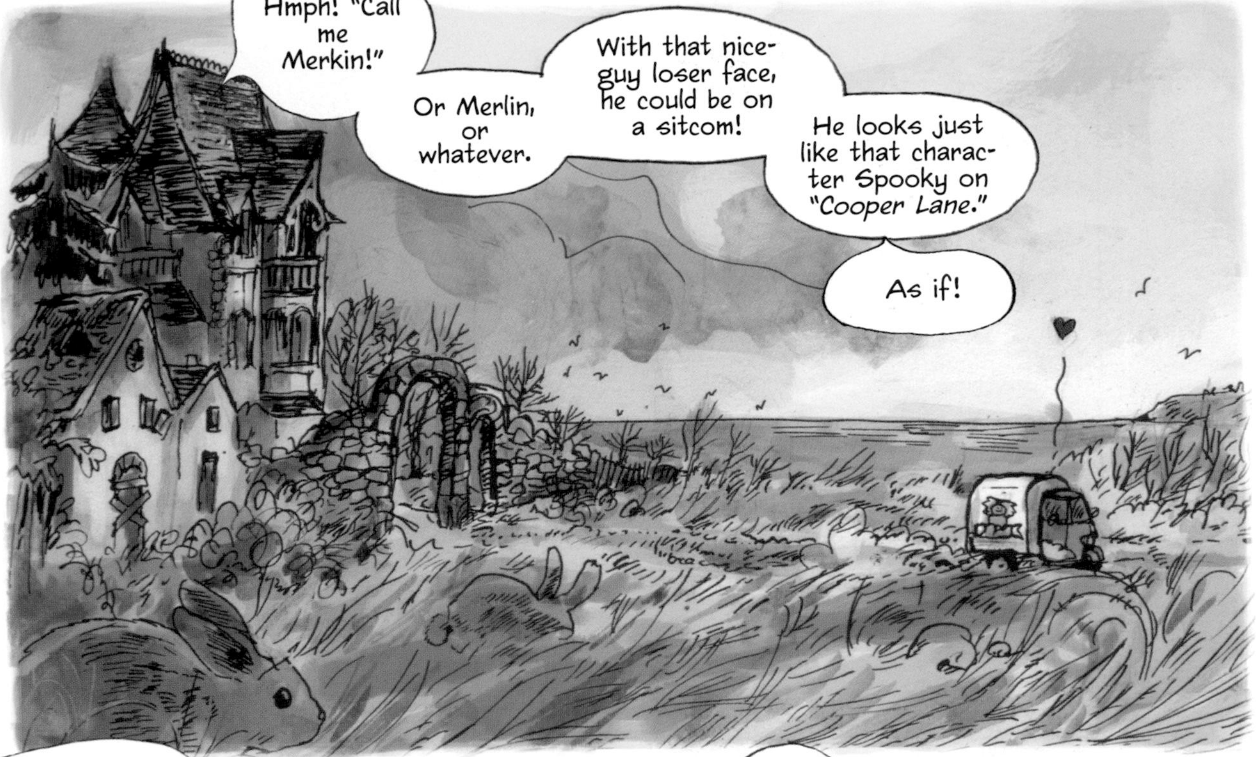
Hmph! "Call me Merkin!"
Or Merlin, or whatever.
With that nice-guy loser face, he could be on a sitcom!
He looks just like that charac-ter Spooky on "Cooper Lane."
As if!

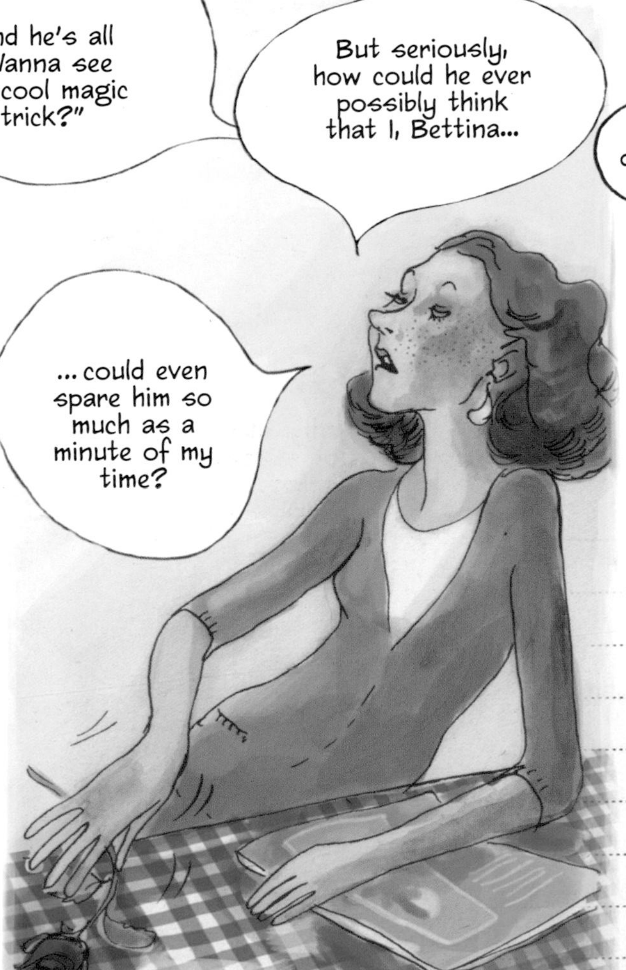
And he's all "Wanna see my cool magic trick?"
But seriously, how could he ever possibly think that I, Bettina...
... could even spare him so much as a minute of my time?

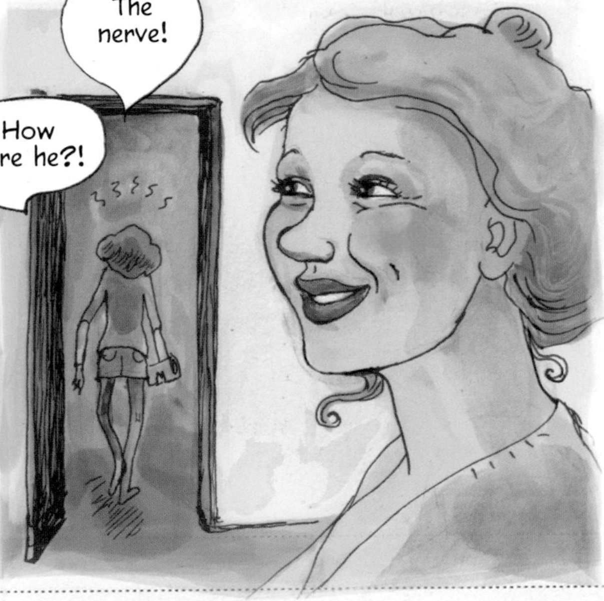
The nerve!
How dare he?!

Genevieve's the prettiest sister. She's very ladylike, the only blonde in the family (except for Mom, but she doesn't count anymore). She's got jet black eyes like the prince in the tower from that poem of Nerval's we studied in school last year, "El Desdichado." Dark eyes and light hair look so lovely together.

But actually, I am Nerval's wretched one: El Desdichado, the one who's lost it all. I don't know who I'm like. Not Mom. She was cheerful, with her cute little feet in ballet flats. Her pants with their humongous flowers. Her ringlets and her big dresses.

Instead, I should say: I don't know what I'm like. I'm not like anyone at all. Not Dad. He always wondered why people never built cities by the shore, where the air was cleaner. Dad, who loved people so much...

I don't care for people that much. Well, it depends who, I guess. If Bettina weren't my sister, I wouldn't give her a second glance; she'd be as boring to me as those other airheads at school. (Ursula Mourletatier, for example.) Except she is my sister.

I'm writing this on my cliff.

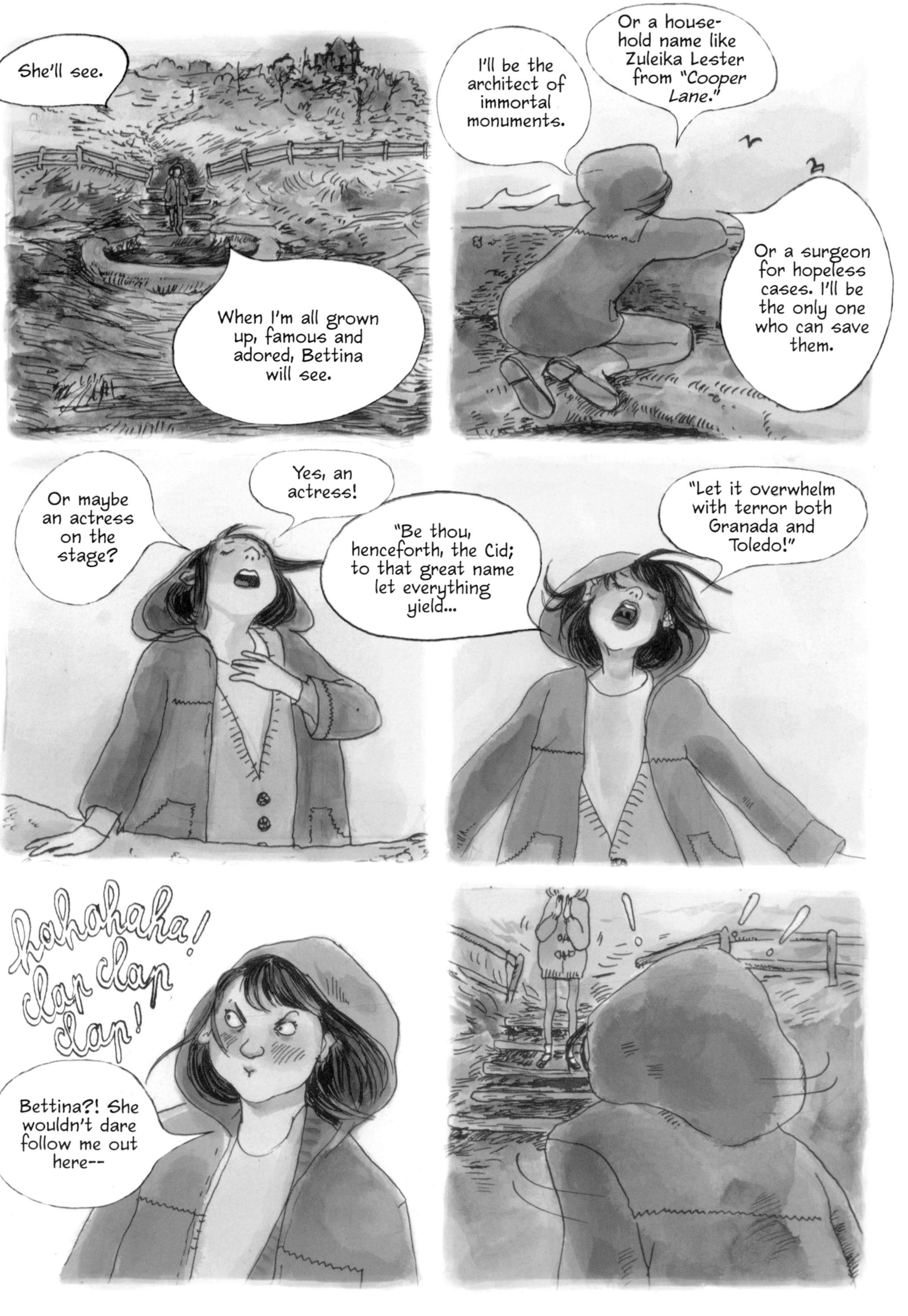
She'll see.
When I'm all grown up, famous and adored, Bettina will see.
I'll be the architect of immortal monuments.
Or a household name like Zuleika Lester from "Cooper Lane."
Or a surgeon for hopeless cases. I'll be the only one who can save them.
Or maybe an actress on the stage?
Yes, an actress!
"Be thou, henceforth, the Cid; to that great name let everything yield...
"Let it overwhelm with terror both Granada and Toledo!"
hahahaha! clap clap clap!
Bettina?! She wouldn't dare follow me out here--
!
!
!

Hi!

Don't stop! That was pretty good!

I was just giggling 'cause I was like: No way! She's...

...reciting Corneille's "Le Cid"!

This is actually the perfect spot for it. On top of the world. Corneille on the cliffs with the gulls in the sky...

It's so totally my favorite 17th Century tragedy!

hahaha!

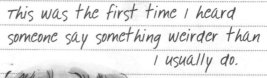

This was the first time I heard someone say something weirder than I usually do.

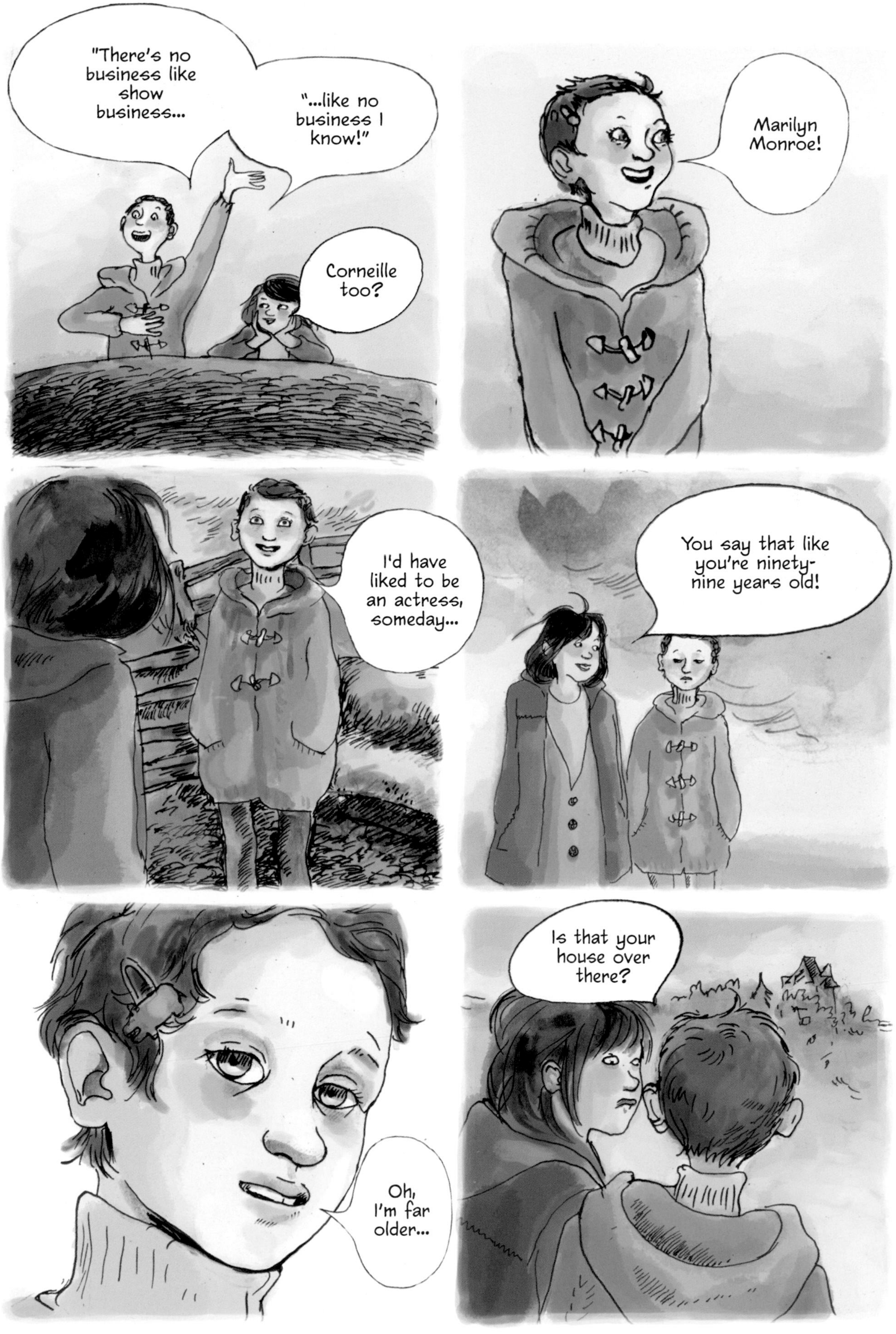
"There's no business like show business...
"...like no business I know!"
Corneille too?
Marilyn Monroe!
I'd have liked to be an actress, someday...
You say that like you're ninety-nine years old!
Oh, I'm far older...
Is that your house over there?

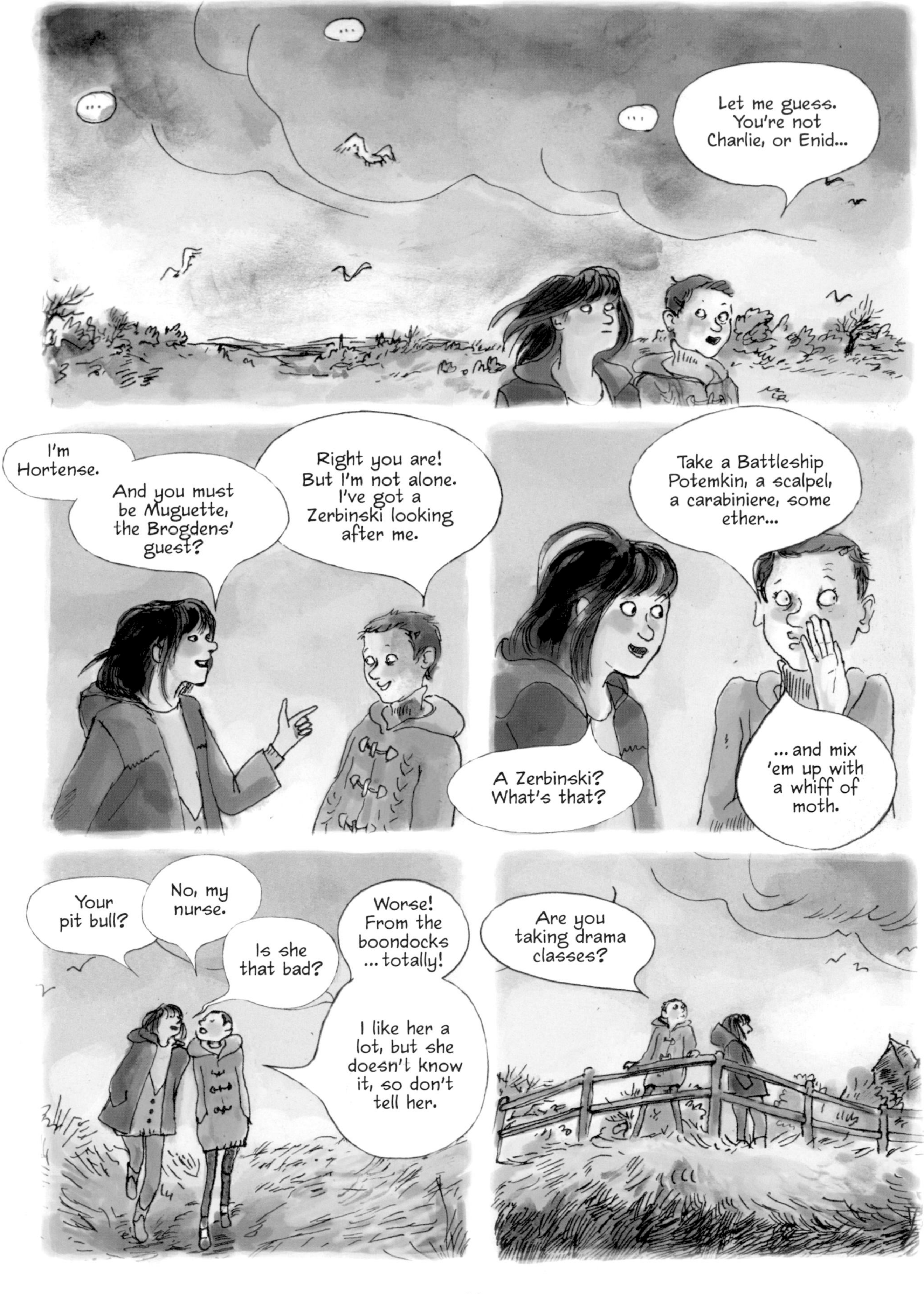
...
...
...
Let me guess. You're not Charlie, or Enid...
I'm Hortense.
And you must be Muguette, the Brogdens' guest?
Right you are! But I'm not alone. I've got a Zerbinski looking after me.
A Zerbinski? What's that?
Take a Battleship Potemkin, a scalpel, a carabiniere, some ether...
...and mix 'em up with a whiff of moth.
Your pit bull?
No, my nurse.
Is she that bad?
Worse! From the boondocks ...totally!
I like her a lot, but she doesn't know it, so don't tell her.
Are you taking drama classes?

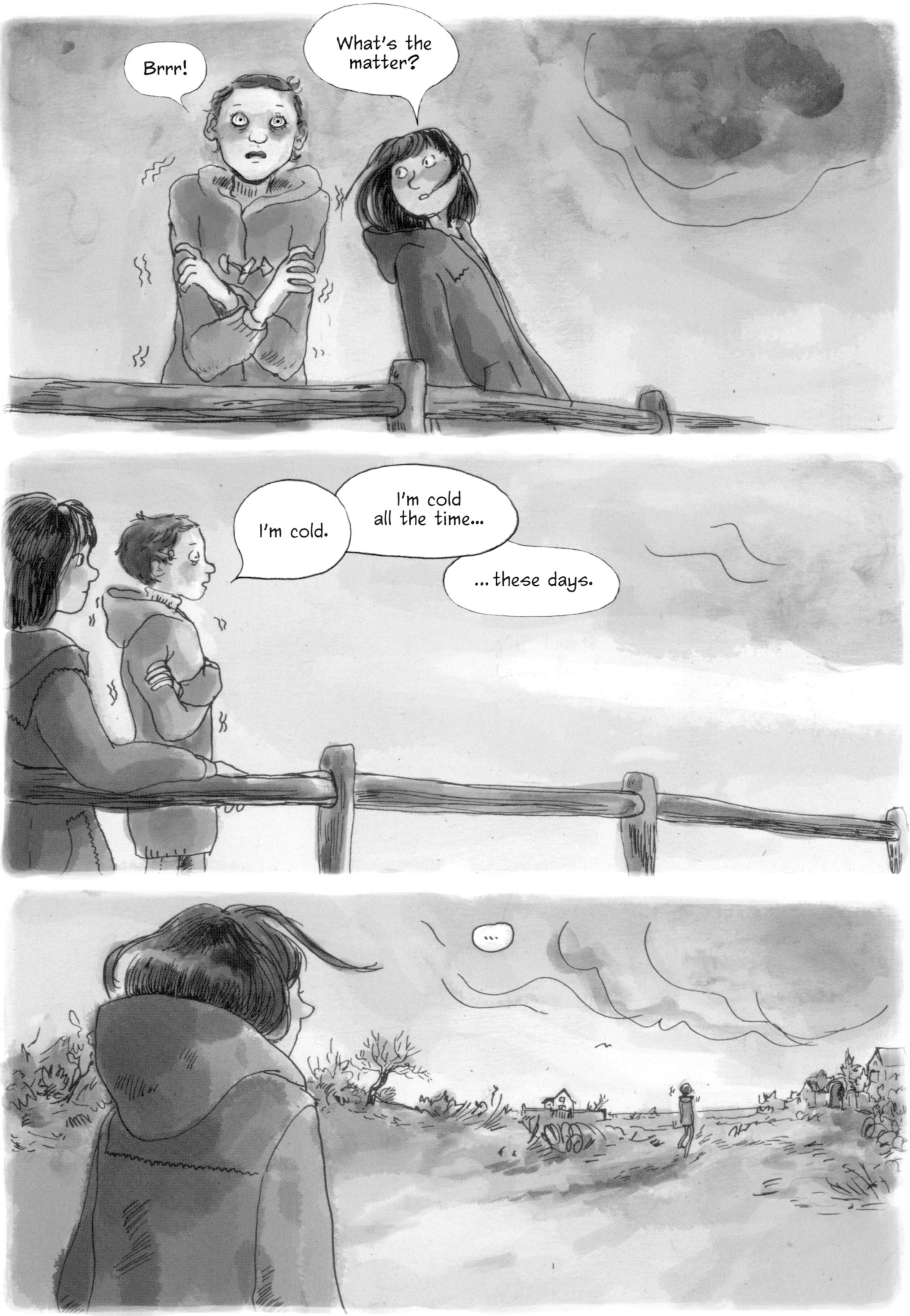
Brrr!
What's the matter?
I'm cold.
I'm cold all the time...
... these days.
...

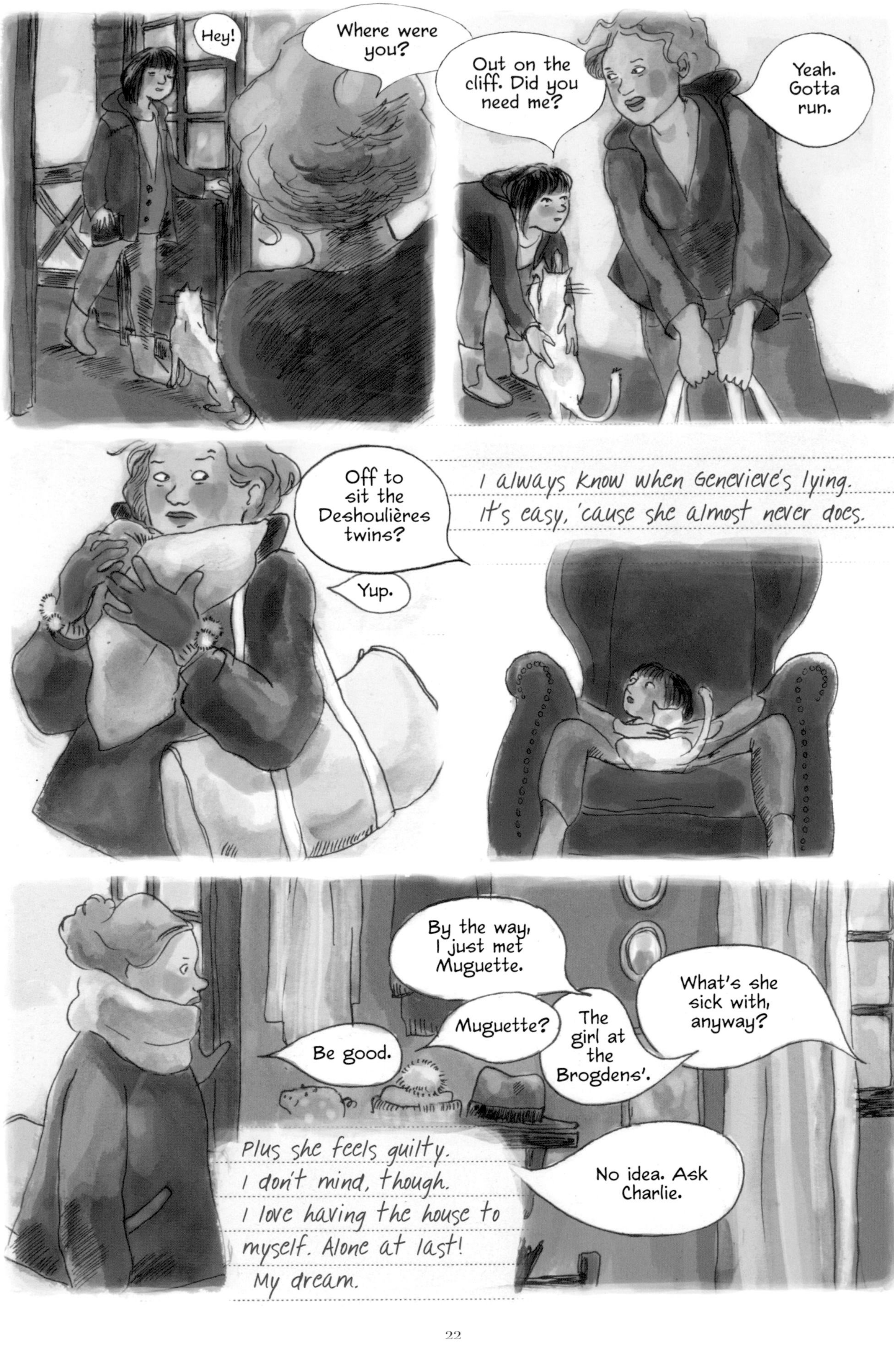
Hey!
Where were you?
Out on the cliff. Did you need me?
Yeah. Gotta run.
Off to sit the Deshoulières twins?
Yup.
I always know when Genevieve's lying.
It's easy, 'cause she almost never does.
By the way, I just met Muguette.
Muguette?
The girl at the Brogdens'.
What's she sick with, anyway?
Be good.
No idea. Ask Charlie.
Plus she feels guilty.
I don't mind, though.
I love having the house to myself. Alone at last!
My dream.

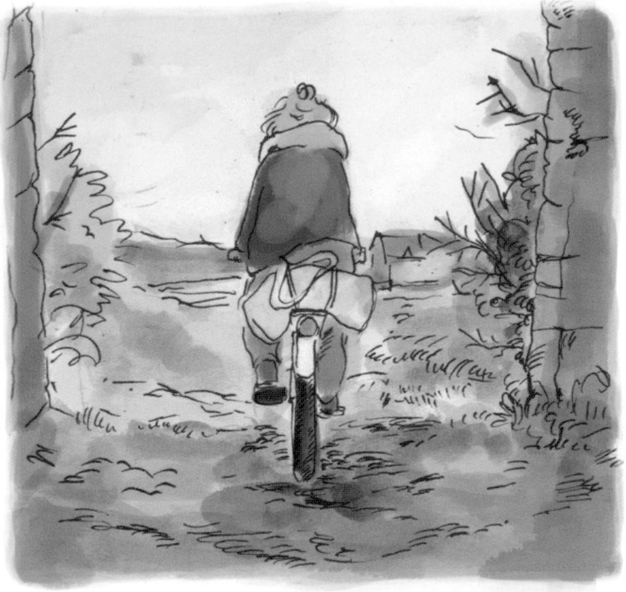

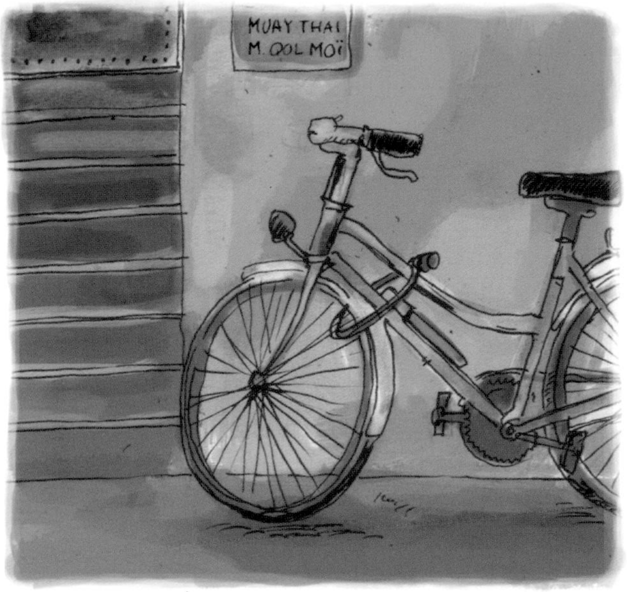
MUAY THAI
M. OOL MOÏ

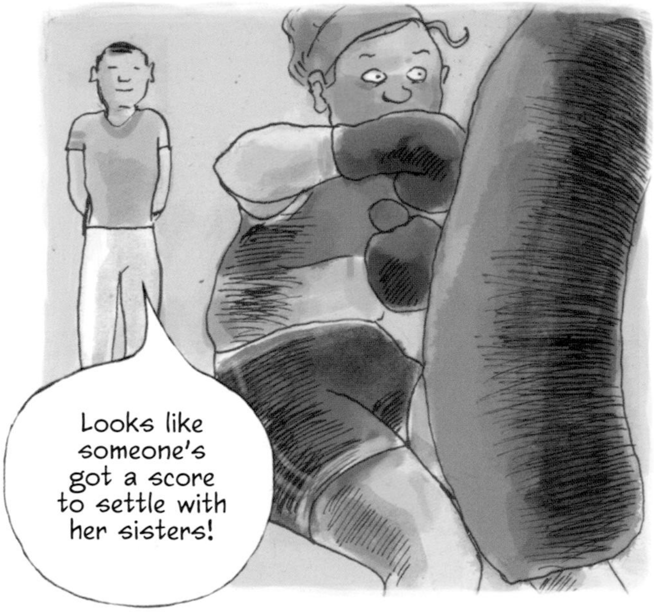
Looks like someone's got a score to settle with her sisters!

Obviously, there were no Deshoulières twins. Genevieve stole the name from a brand of soup tureens.

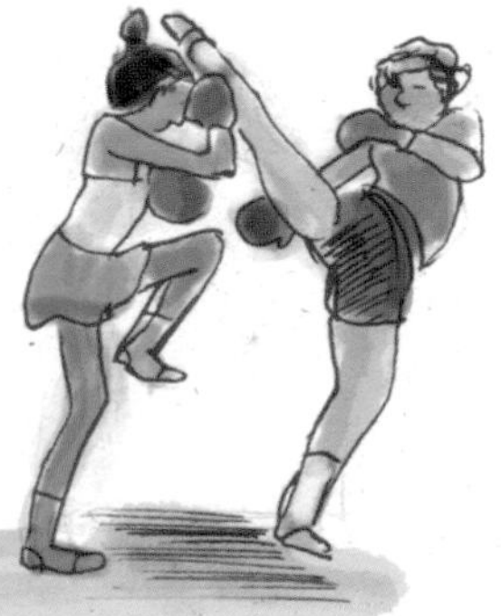

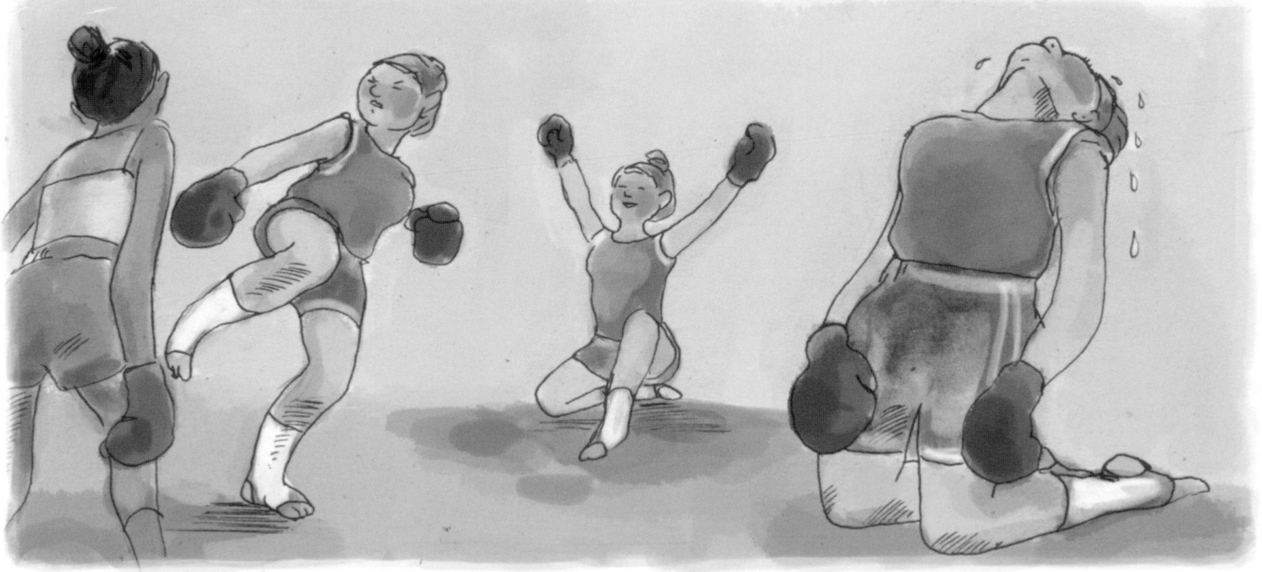

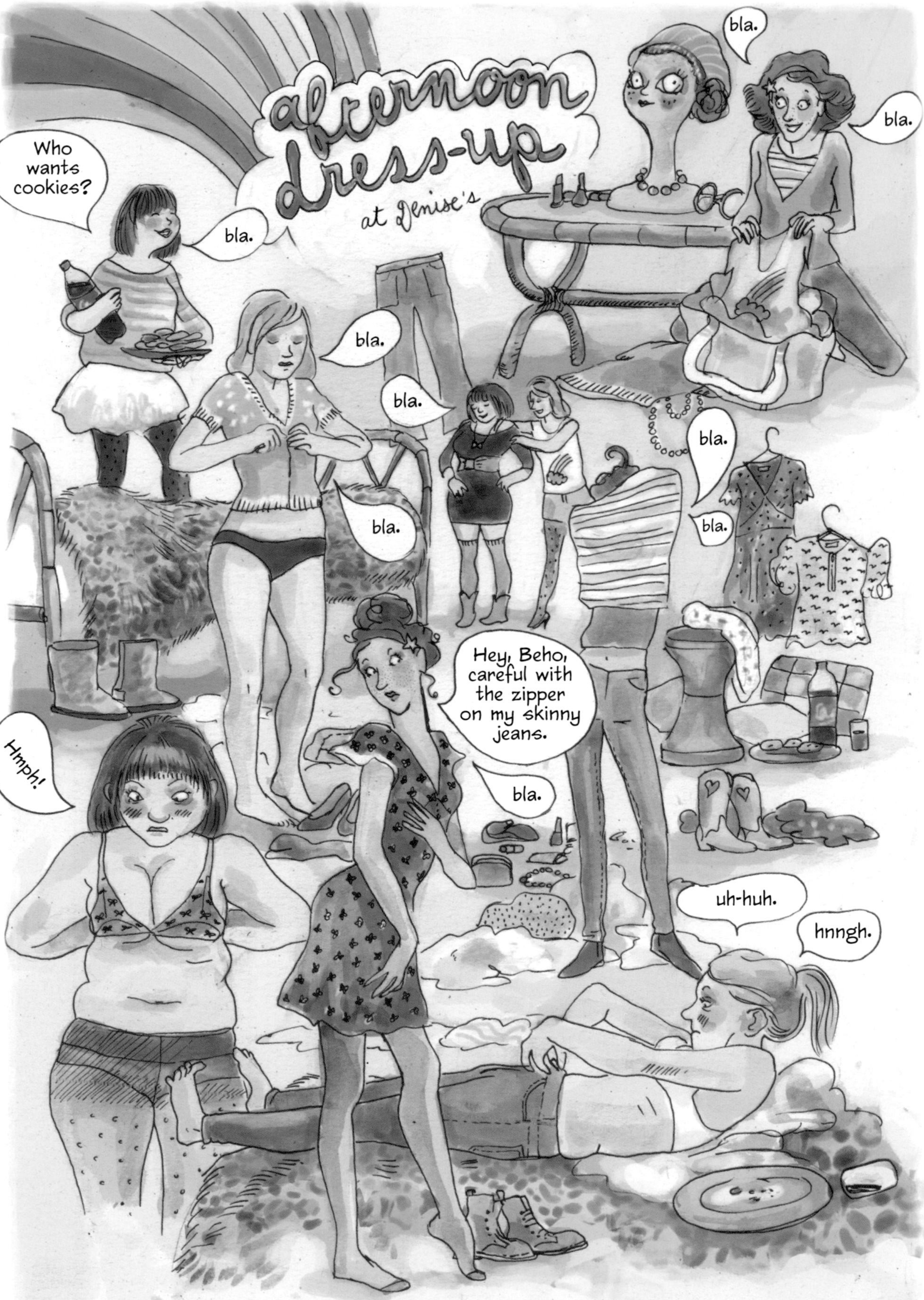

afternoon dress-up
at Denise's
Who wants cookies?
bla.
bla.
bla.
bla.
bla.
bla.
bla.
bla.
bla.
Hey, Beho, careful with the zipper on my skinny jeans.
Hmph!
bla.
uh-huh.
hnngh.

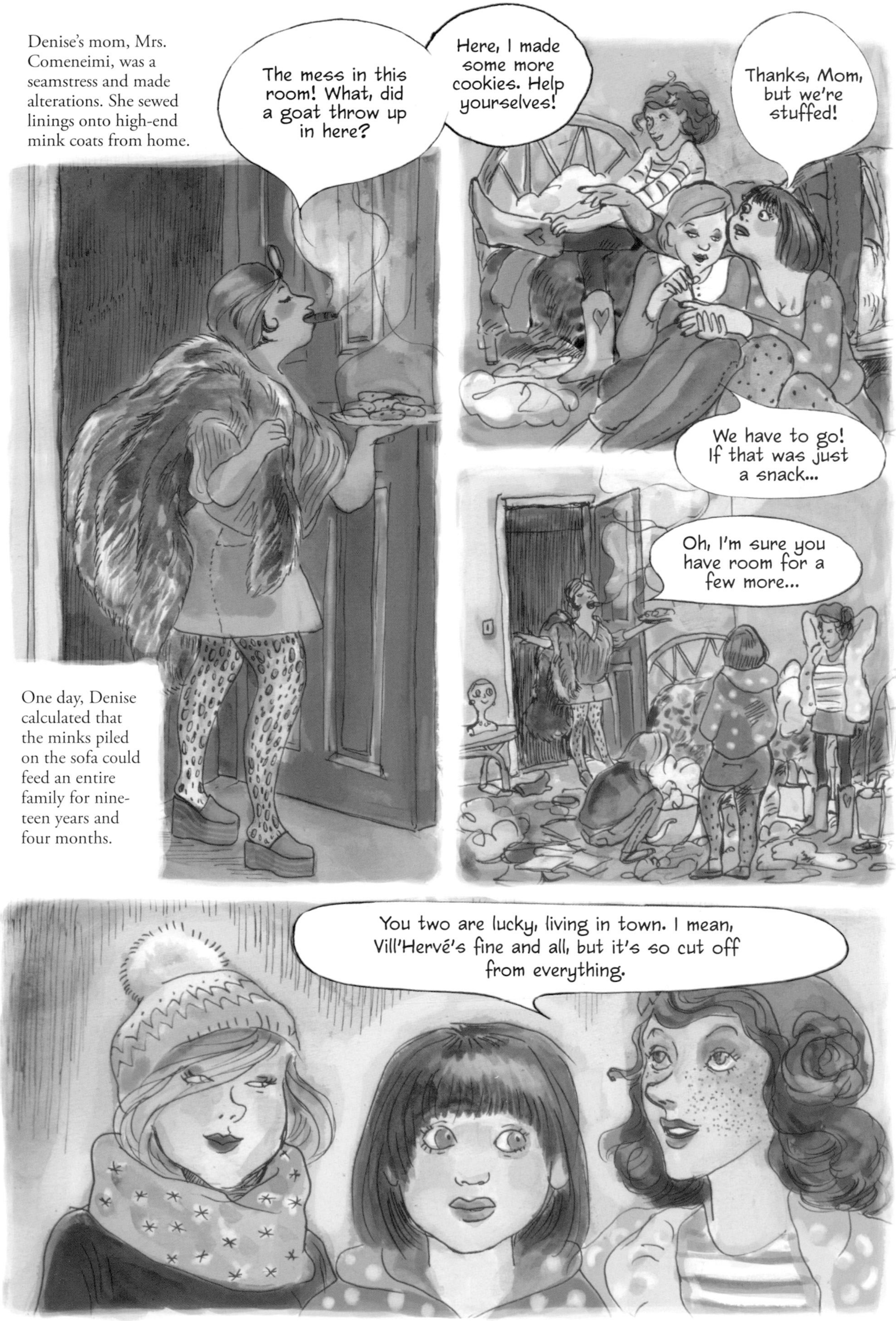
Denise's mom, Mrs. Comeneimi, was a seamstress and made alterations. She sewed linings onto high-end mink coats from home.
The mess in this room! What, did a goat throw up in here?
One day, Denise calculated that the minks piled on the sofa could feed an entire family for nineteen years and four months.
Here, I made some more cookies. Help yourselves!
Thanks, Mom, but we're stuffed!
We have to go! If that was just a snack...
Oh, I'm sure you have room for a few more...
You two are lucky, living in town. I mean, Vill'Hervé's fine and all, but it's so cut off from everything.

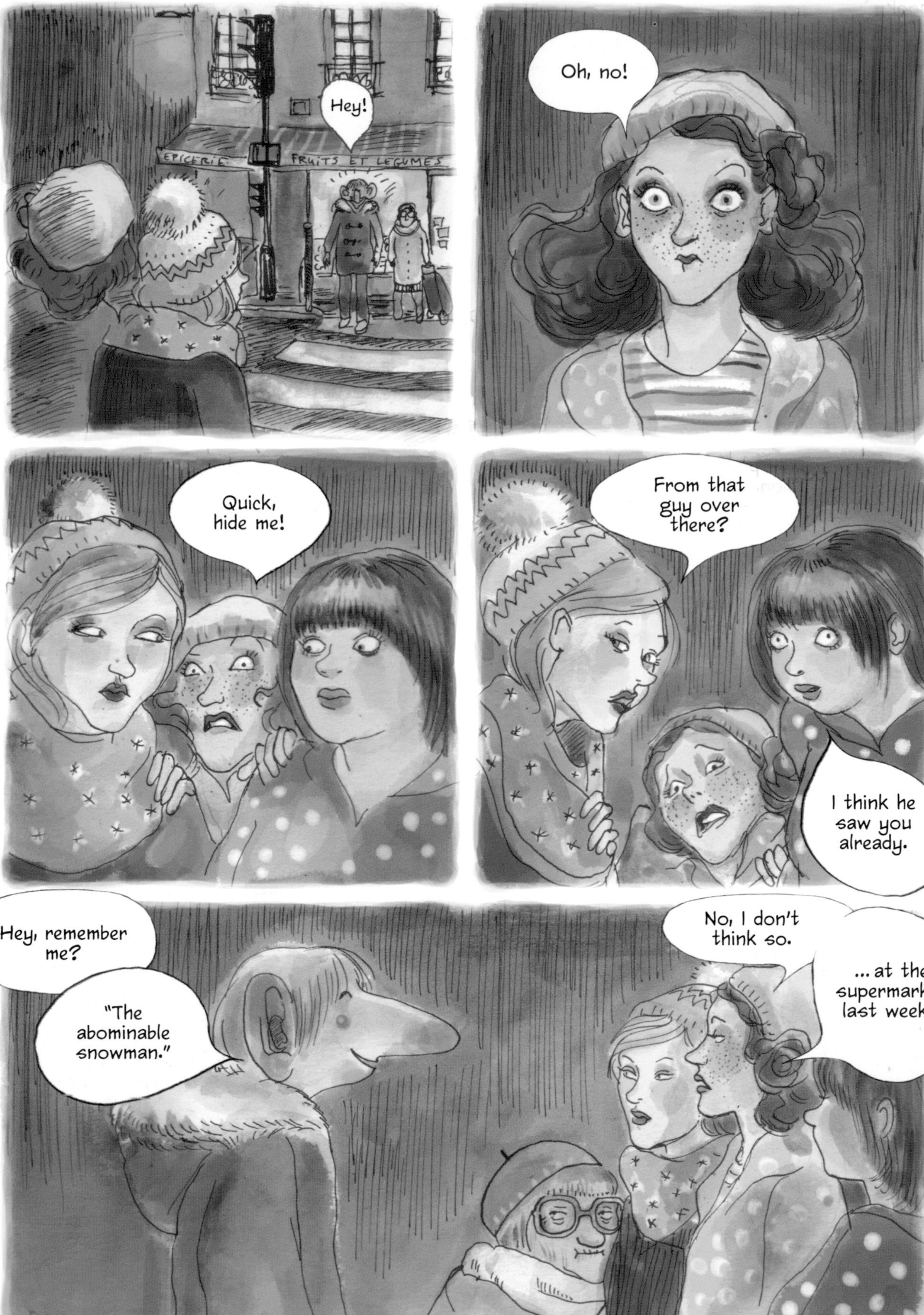
EPICERIE
FRUITS ET LEGUMES
Hey!
Oh, no!
Quick, hide me!
From that guy over there?
I think he saw you already.
Hey, remember me?
"The abominable snowman."
No, I don't think so.
...at the supermarket last week?

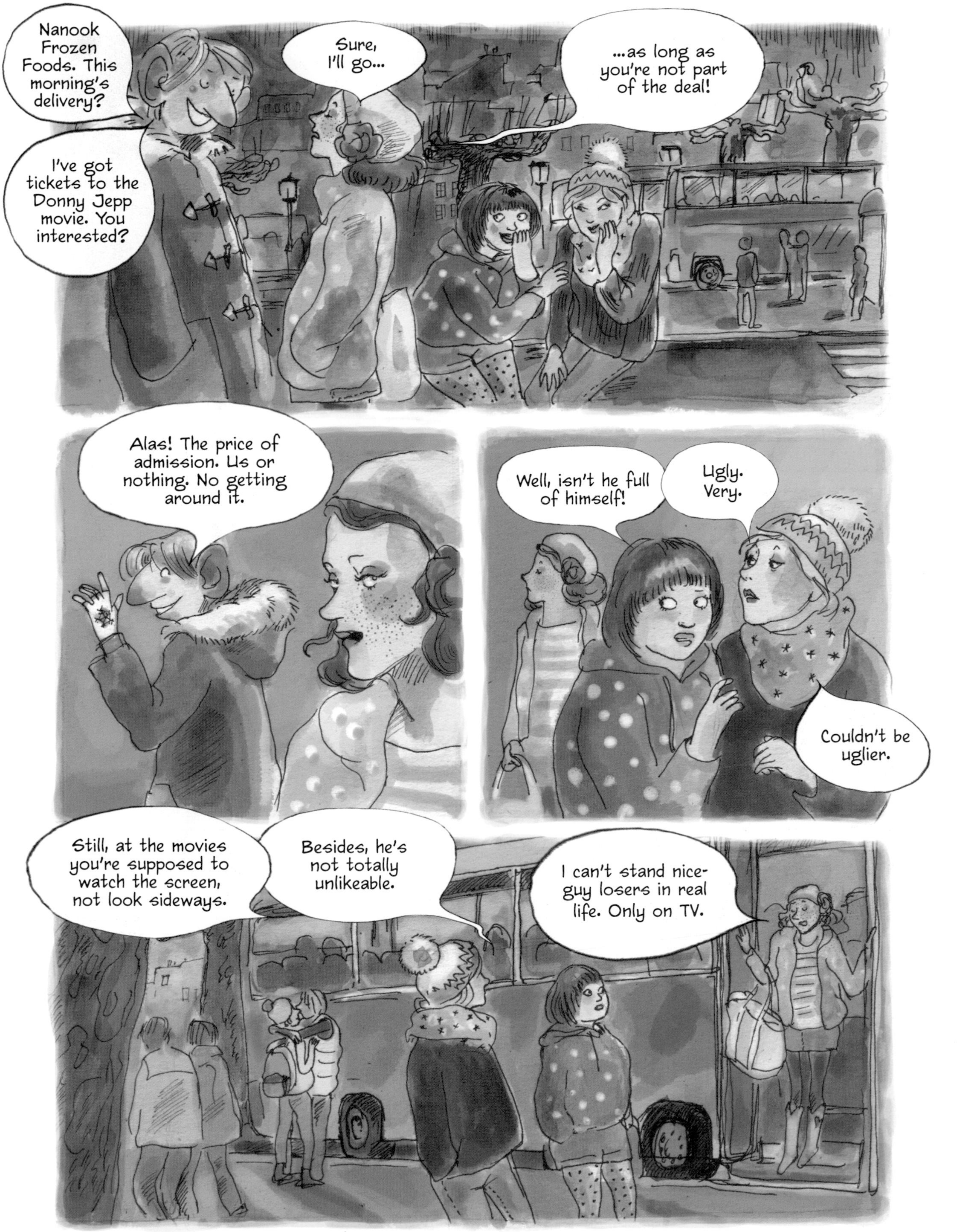
Nanook Frozen Foods. This morning's delivery?
I've got tickets to the Donny Jepp movie. You interested?
Sure, I'll go...
...as long as you're not part of the deal!
Alas! The price of admission. Us or nothing. No getting around it.
Well, isn't he full of himself!
Ugly. Very.
Couldn't be uglier.
Still, at the movies you're supposed to watch the screen, not look sideways.
Besides, he's not totally unlikeable.
I can't stand nice-guy losers in real life. Only on TV.

The French teacher pulled a dirty trick today. Made us read a passage from Leon Garfield's "The Sound of Coaches" in pairs. First up were Aramis Paradonche with Audrey, and then me, with guess who? Ursula Mourletatier! The queen bitch. Obviously, Madame Latour-Destours didn't do it on purpose, but it got me so worked up as usual, I mean having to stand up in front of everyone, with Mourletatier, of all people! So of course I lost my place, though I'd been following along till then. Madame got upset, which made me even more nervous.

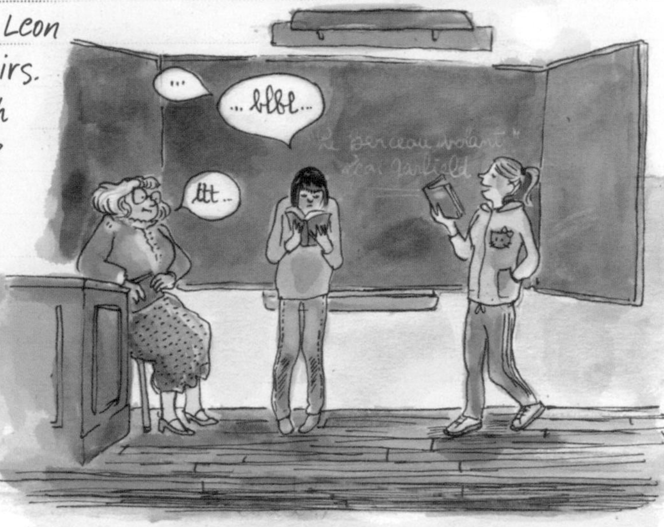

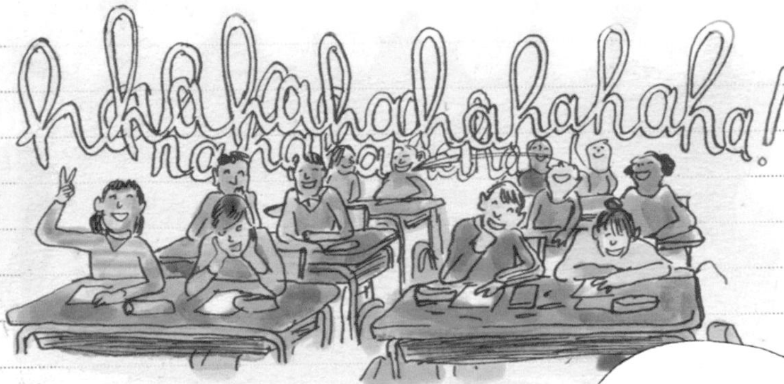

I messed up the first line (I said "serpette" instead of "civette"). Everyone laughed for a whole week (well, for at least five minutes!).

Then Madame said:

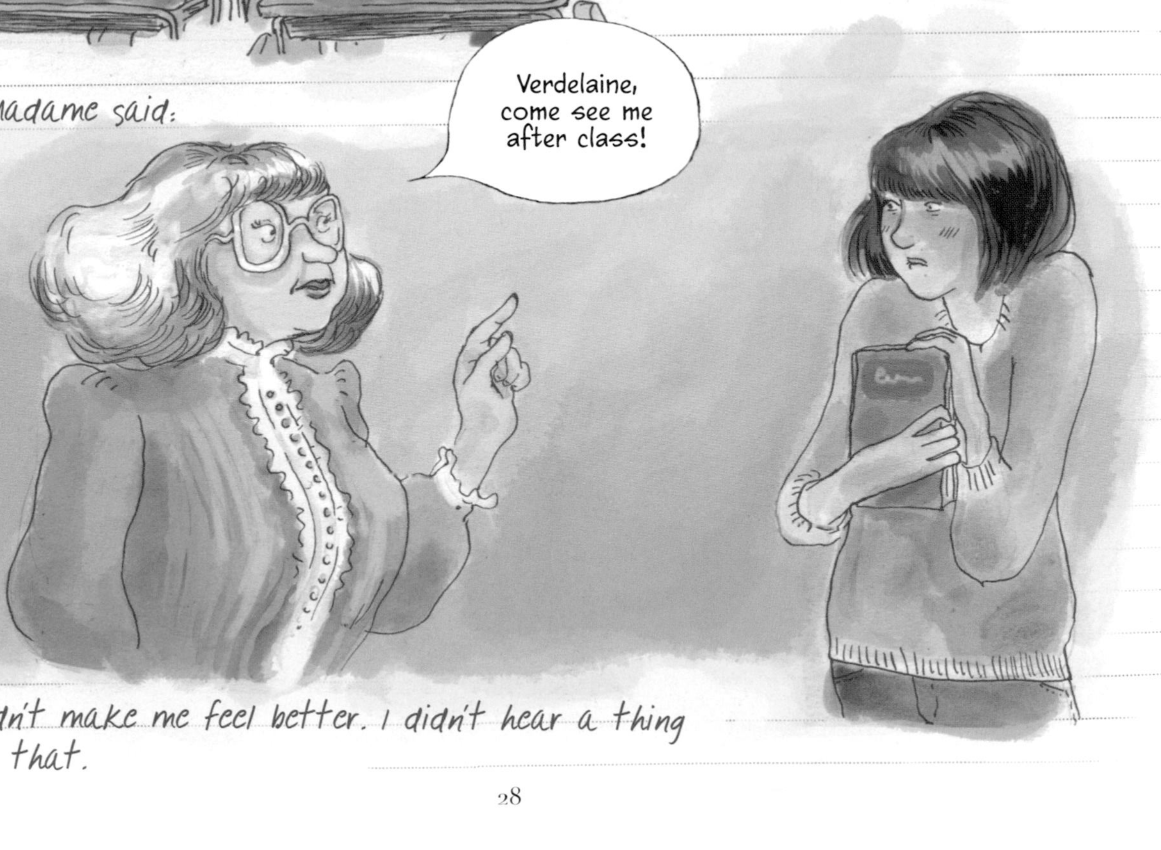
Verdelaine, come see me after class!

Which didn't make me feel better. I didn't hear a thing after that.

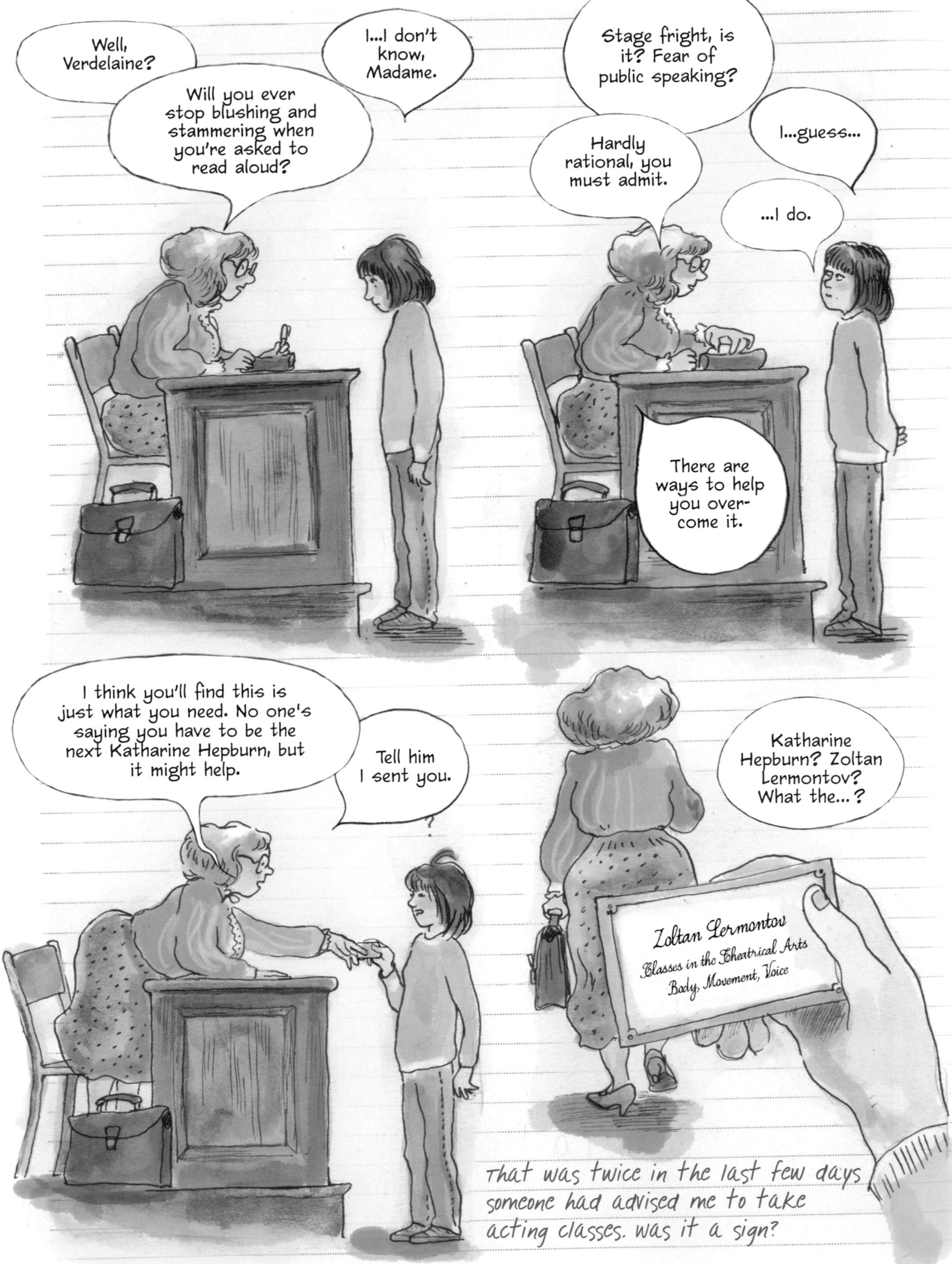
Well, Verdelaine?
Will you ever stop blushing and stammering when you're asked to read aloud?
I...I don't know, Madame.
Stage fright, is it? Fear of public speaking?
Hardly rational, you must admit.
I...guess...
...I do.
There are ways to help you over-come it.
I think you'll find this is just what you need. No one's saying you have to be the next Katharine Hepburn, but it might help.
Tell him I sent you.
Katharine Hepburn? Zoltan Lermontov? What the...?
Zoltan Lermontov
Classes in the Theatrical Arts
Body, Movement, Voice
That was twice in the last few days someone had advised me to take acting classes. Was it a sign?

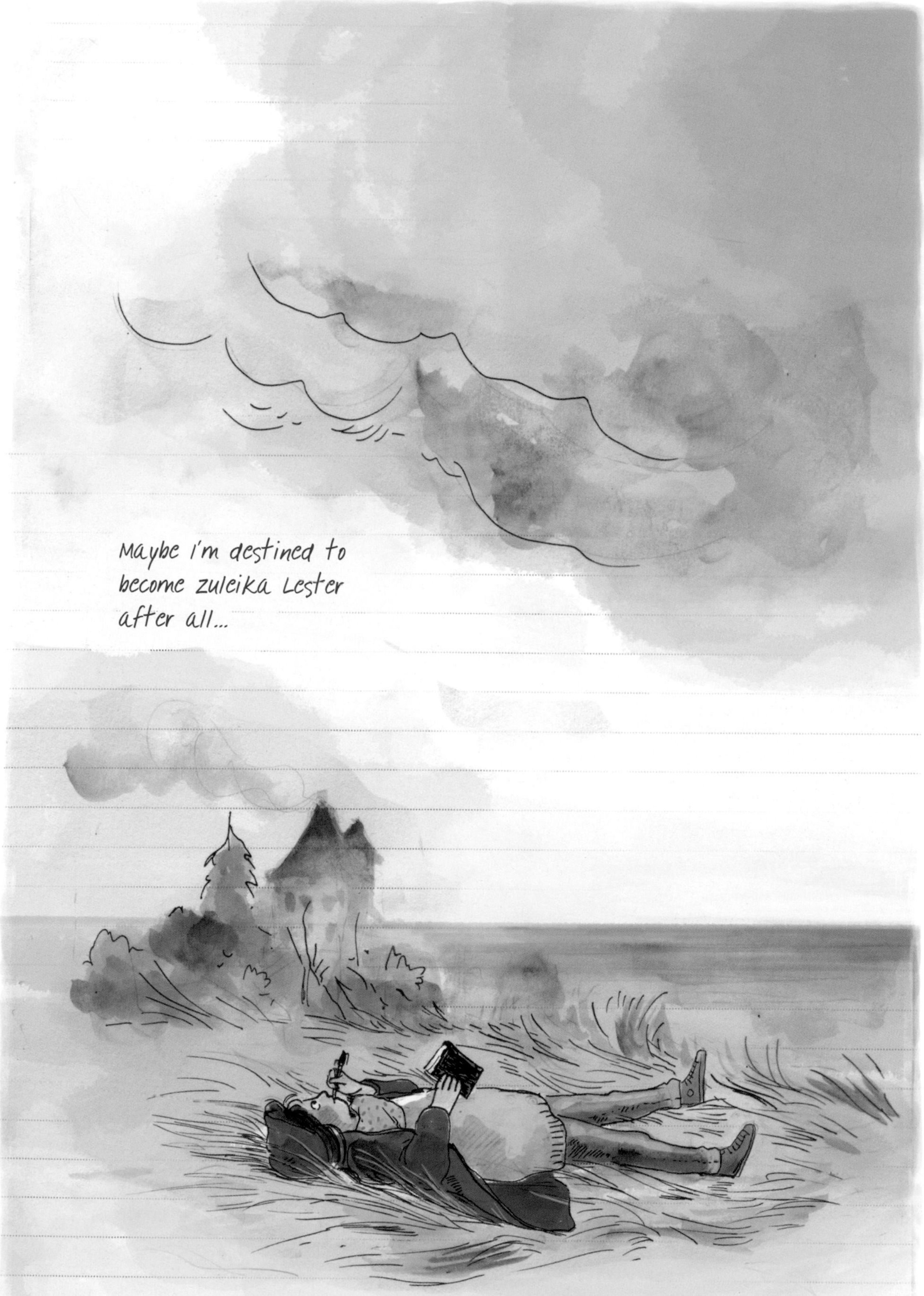
Maybe I'm destined to become Zuleika Lester after all...

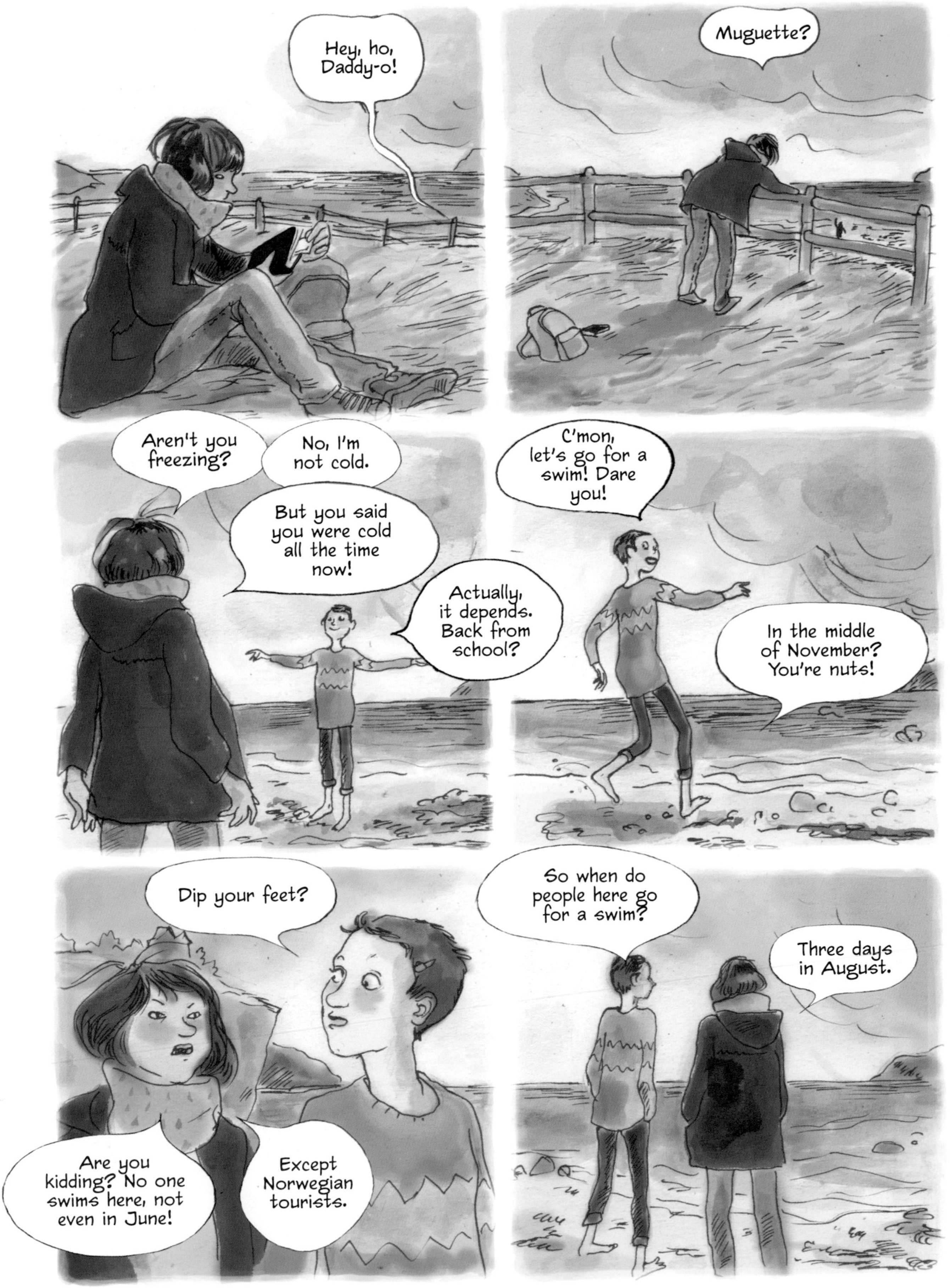
Hey, ho, Daddy-o!
Muguette?
Aren't you freezing?
No, I'm not cold.
But you said you were cold all the time now!
Actually, it depends. Back from school?
C'mon, let's go for a swim! Dare you!
In the middle of November? You're nuts!
Dip your feet?
Are you kidding? No one swims here, not even in June!
Except Norwegian tourists.
So when do people here go for a swim?
Three days in August.

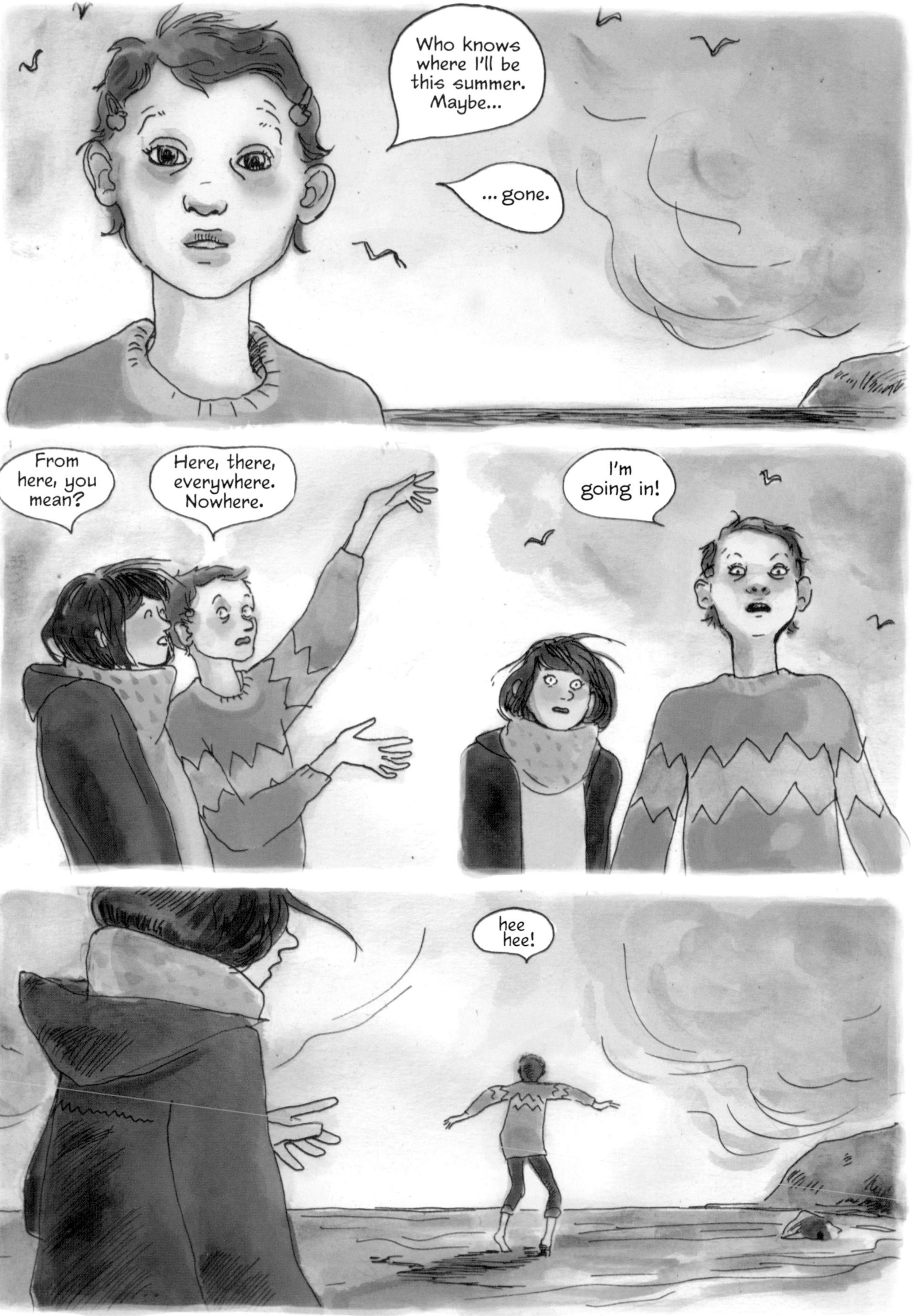
Who knows where I'll be this summer. Maybe...
...gone.
From here, you mean?
Here, there, everywhere. Nowhere.
I'm going in!
hee hee!

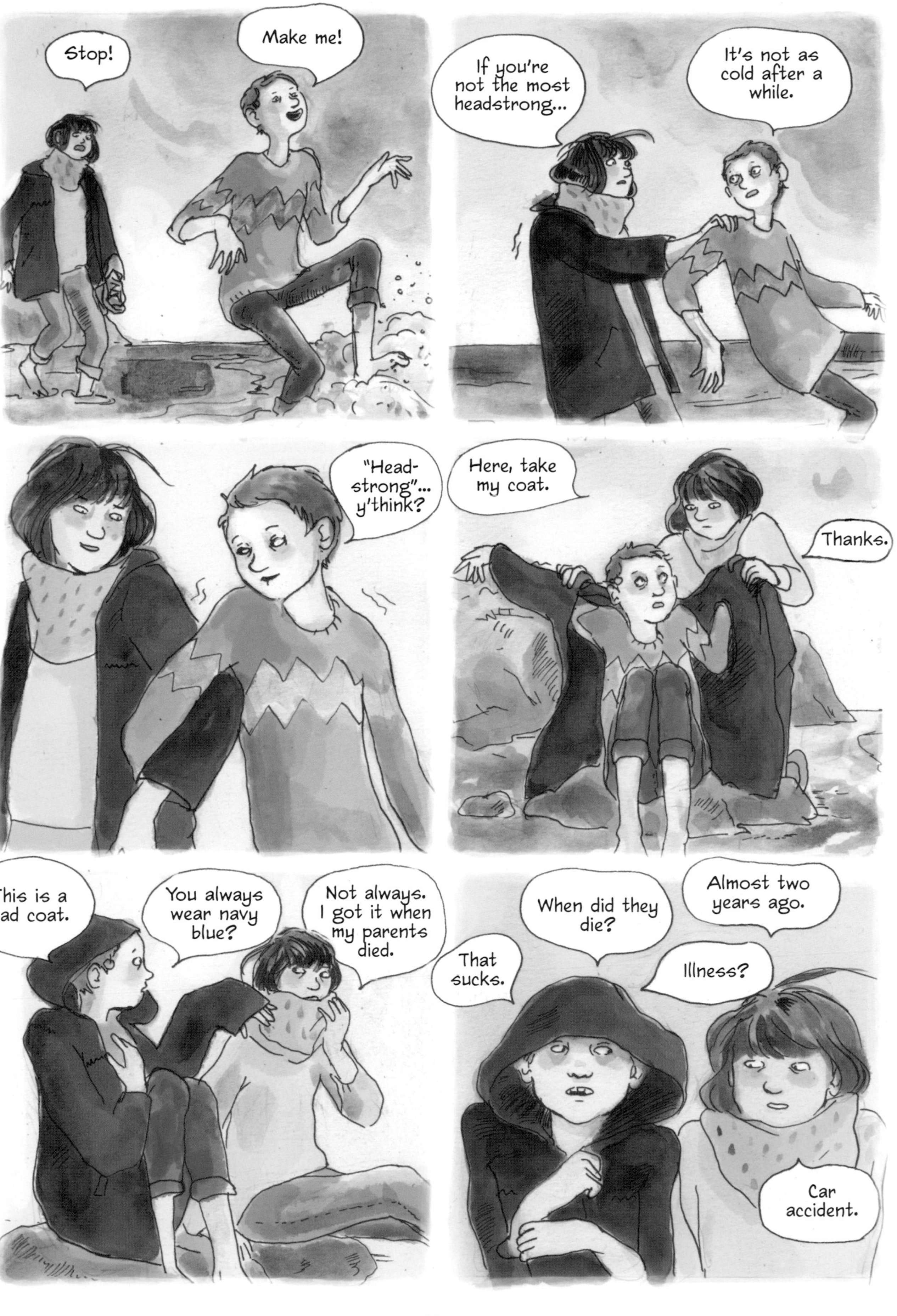

Stop!
Make me!
If you're not the most headstrong...
It's not as cold after a while.
"Head-strong"... y'think?
Here, take my coat.
Thanks.
This is a sad coat.
You always wear navy blue?
Not always. I got it when my parents died.
That sucks.
When did they die?
Almost two years ago.
Illness?
Car accident.

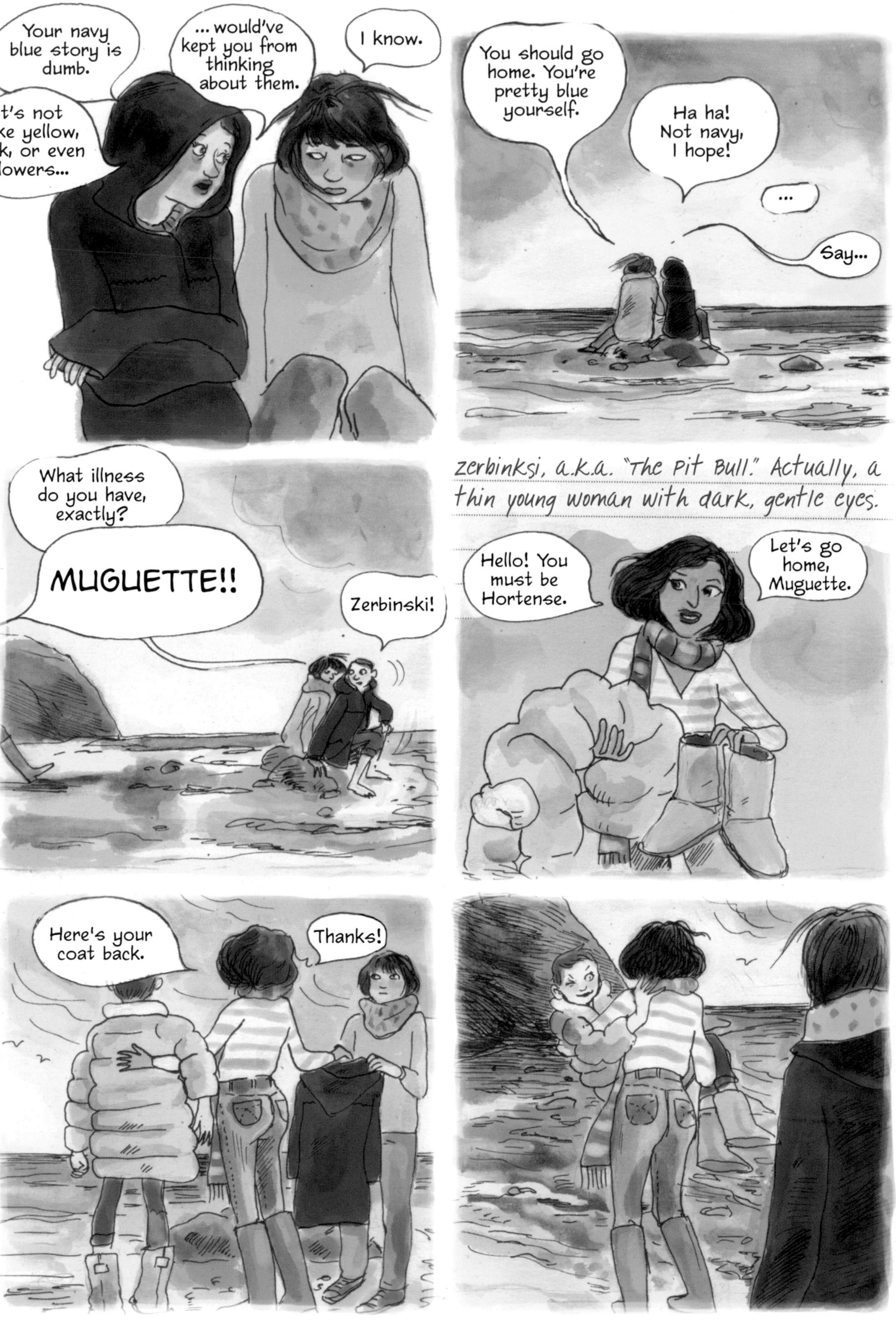
Your navy blue story is dumb.
It's not like yellow, pink, or even flowers...
... would've kept you from thinking about them.
I know.
You should go home. You're pretty blue yourself.
Ha ha! Not navy, I hope!
...
Say...
What illness do you have, exactly?
MUGUETTE!!
Zerbinski!
zerbinksi, a.k.a. "The Pit Bull." Actually, a thin young woman with dark, gentle eyes.
Hello! You must be Hortense.
Let's go home, Muguette.
Here's your coat back.
Thanks!

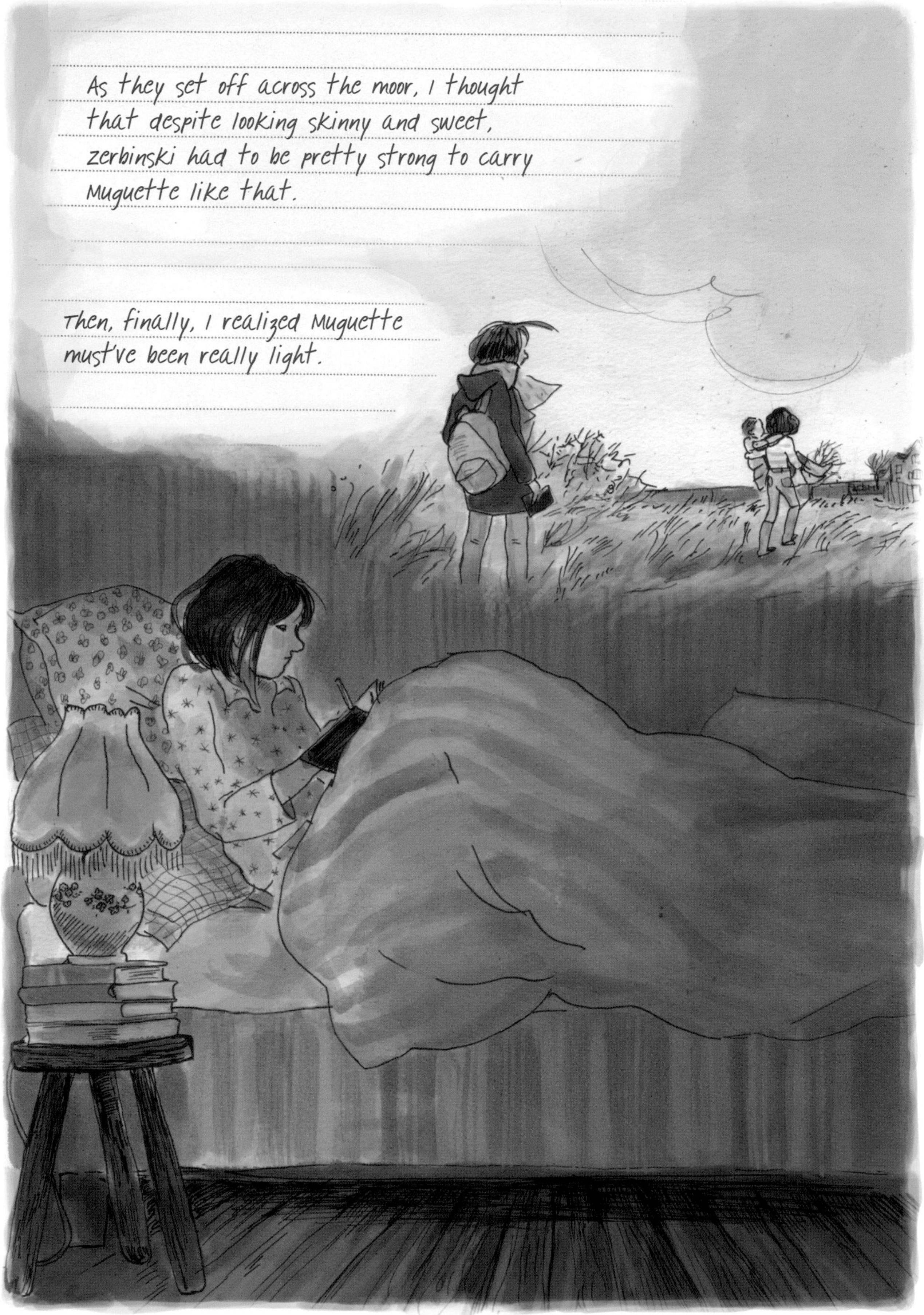
As they set off across the moor, I thought that despite looking skinny and sweet, Zerbinski had to be pretty strong to carry Muguette like that.
Then, finally, I realized Muguette must've been really light.

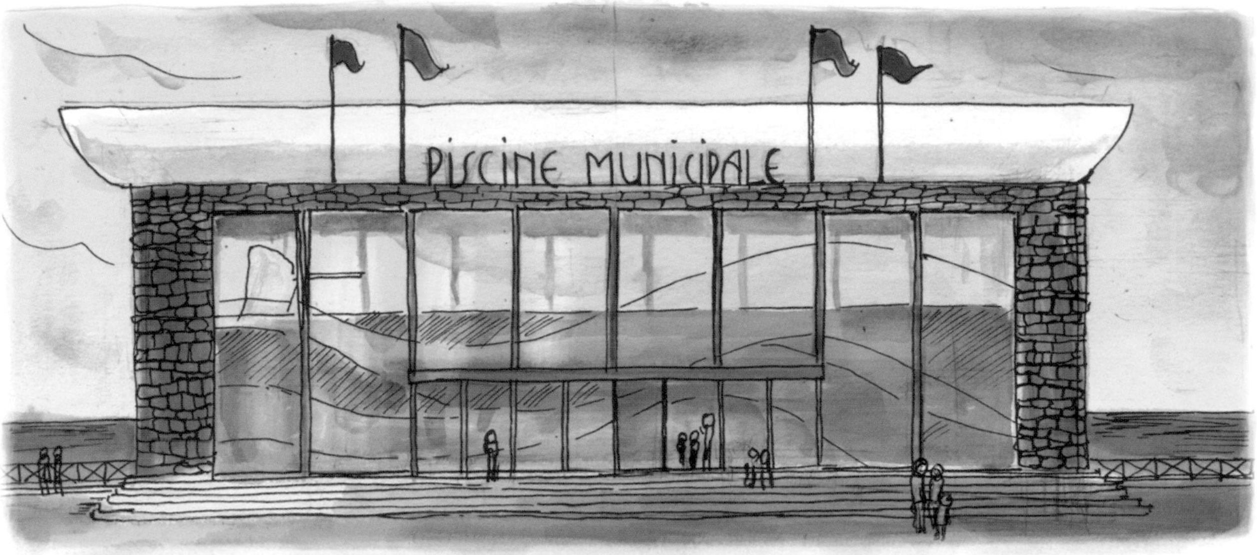
PISCINE MUNICIPALE

Wednesday was Bettina's turn to take Enid to the pool.

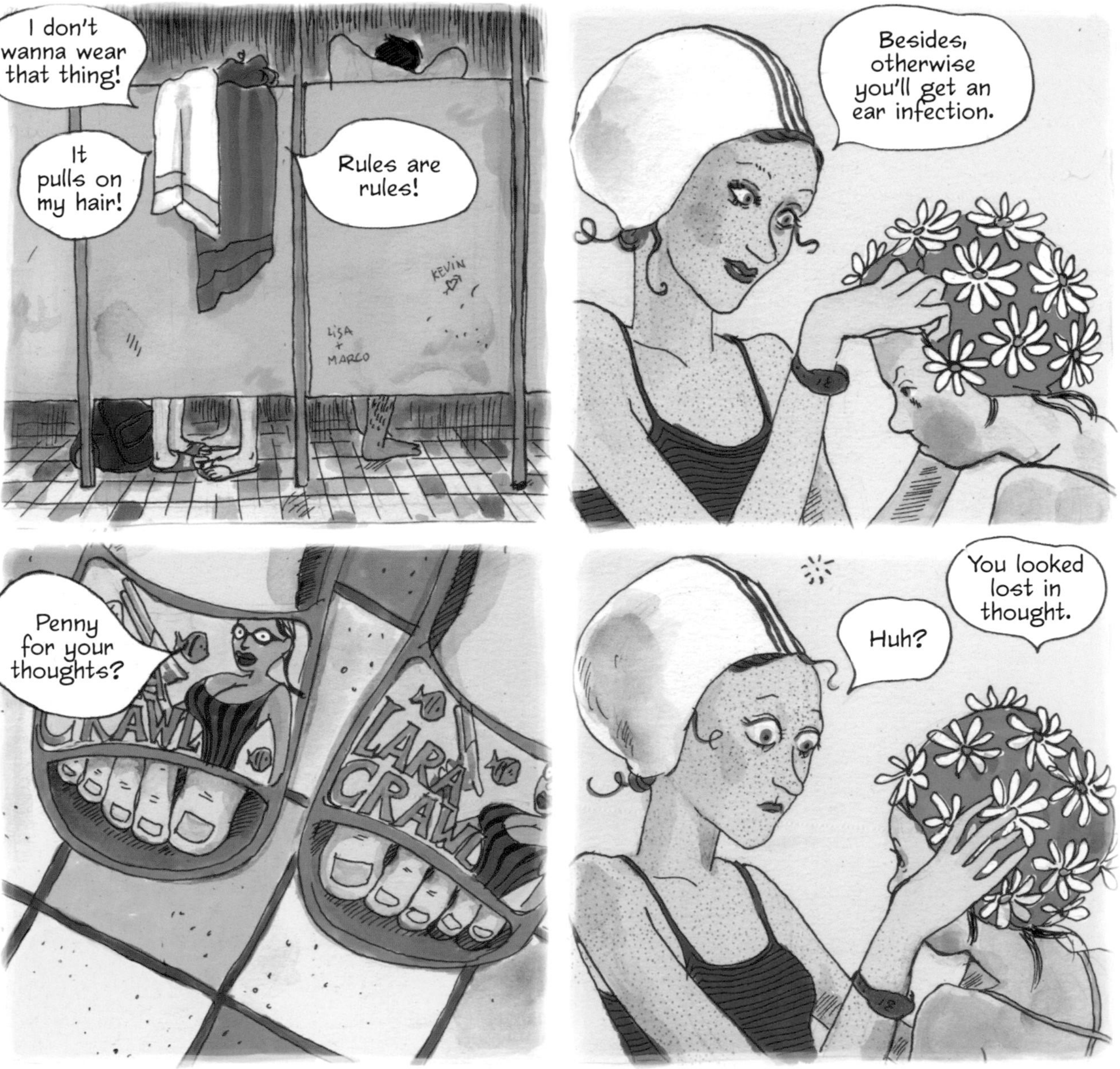
I don't wanna wear that thing!
It pulls on my hair!
Rules are rules!
KEVIN
LISA + MARCO
Besides, otherwise you'll get an ear infection.
Penny for your thoughts?
LARA CRAWL
LARA CRAWL
Huh?
You looked lost in thought.

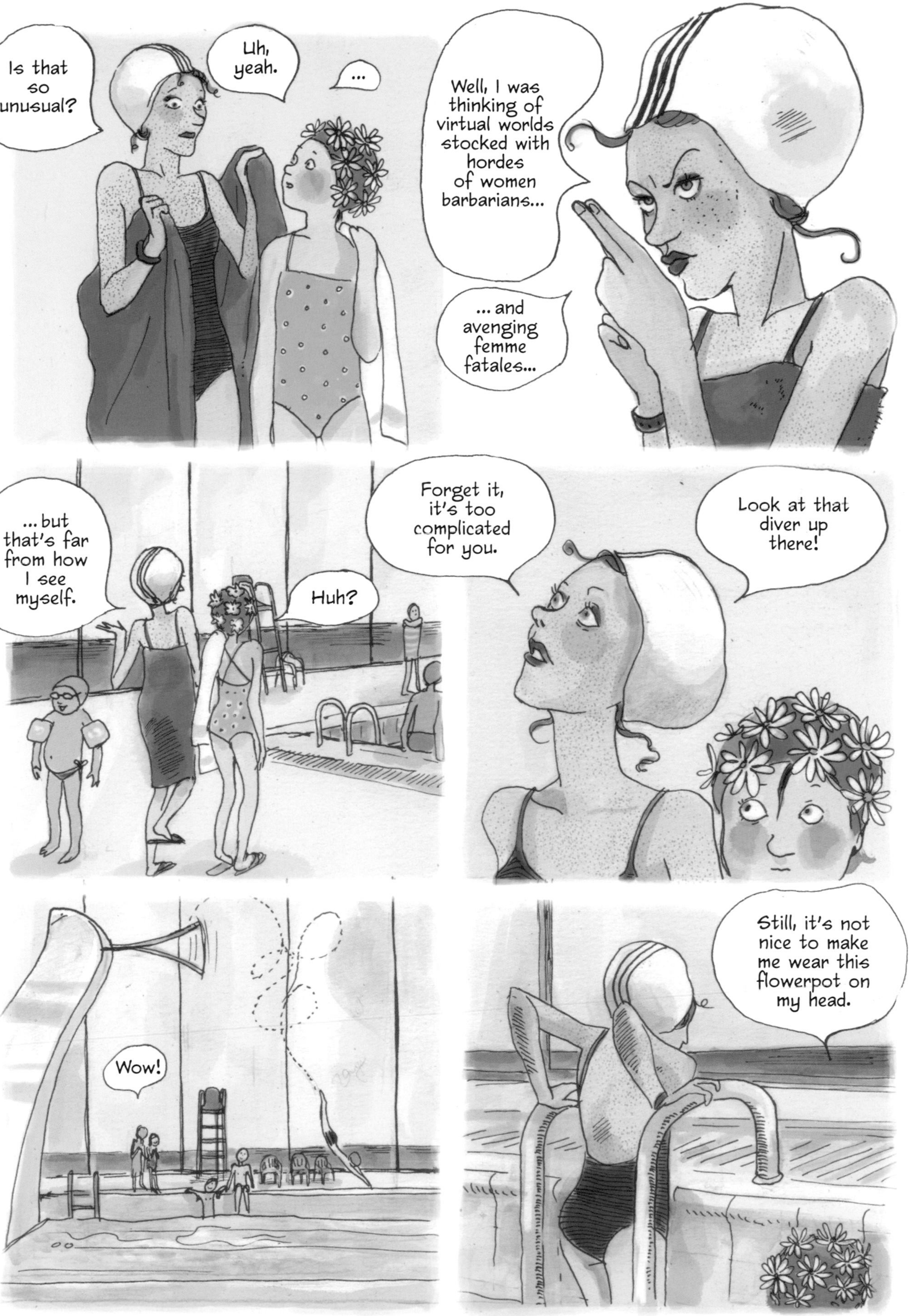
Is that so unusual?
Uh, yeah.
...
Well, I was thinking of virtual worlds stocked with hordes of women barbarians...
... and avenging femme fatales...
... but that's far from how I see myself.
Huh?
Forget it, it's too complicated for you.
Look at that diver up there!
Wow!
Still, it's not nice to make me wear this flowerpot on my head.

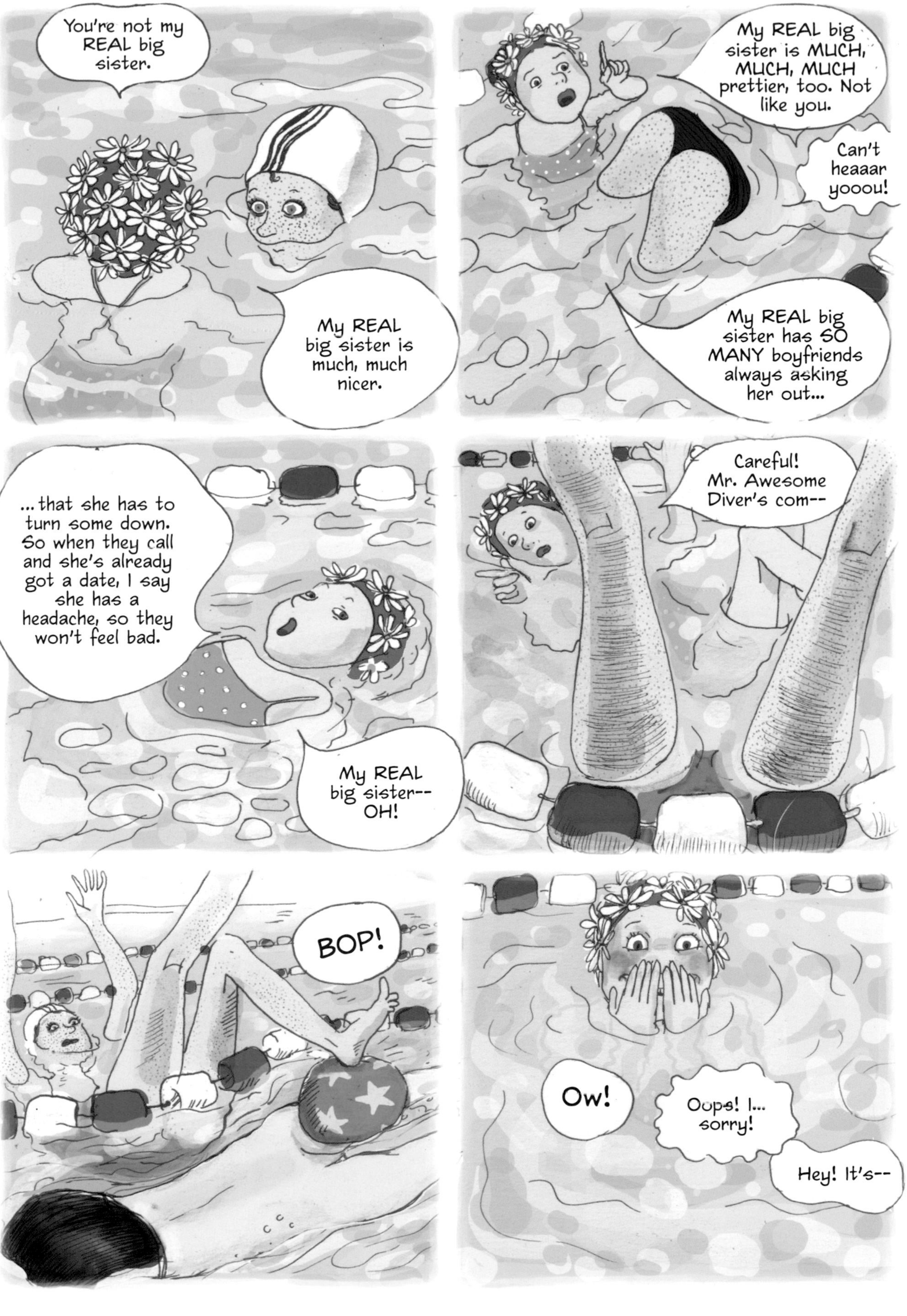

You're not my REAL big sister.
My REAL big sister is much, much nicer.
My REAL big sister is MUCH, MUCH, MUCH prettier, too. Not like you.
Can't heaaar yooou!
My REAL big sister has SO MANY boyfriends always asking her out...
...that she has to turn some down. So when they call and she's already got a date, I say she has a headache, so they won't feel bad.
My REAL big sister-- OH!
Careful! Mr. Awesome Diver's com--
BOP!
Ow!
Oops! I... sorry!
Hey! It's--

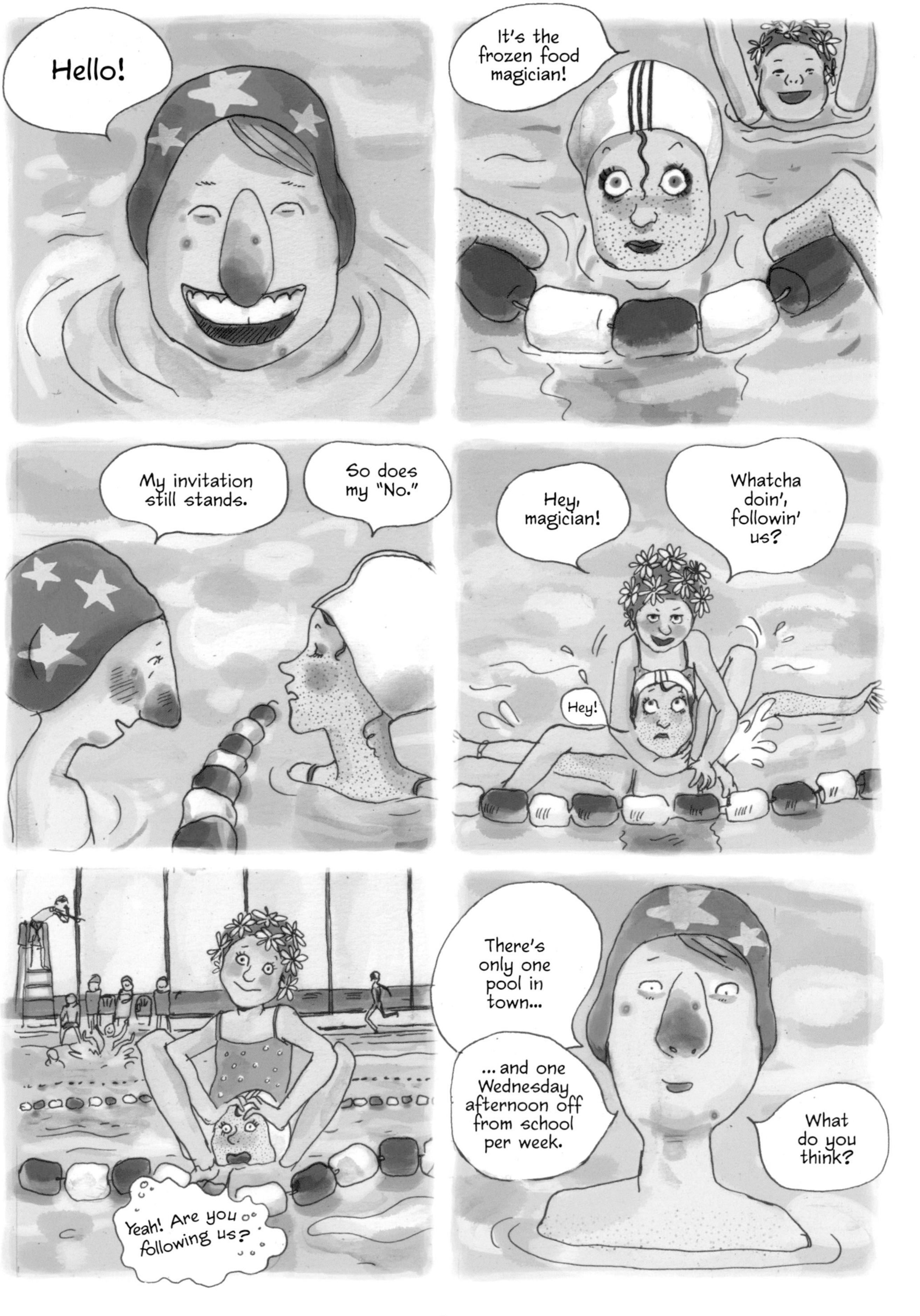
Hello!
It's the frozen food magician!
My invitation still stands.
So does my "No."
Hey, magician!
Whatcha doin', followin' us?
Hey!
Yeah! Are you following us?
There's only one pool in town...
... and one Wednesday afternoon off from school per week.
What do you think?

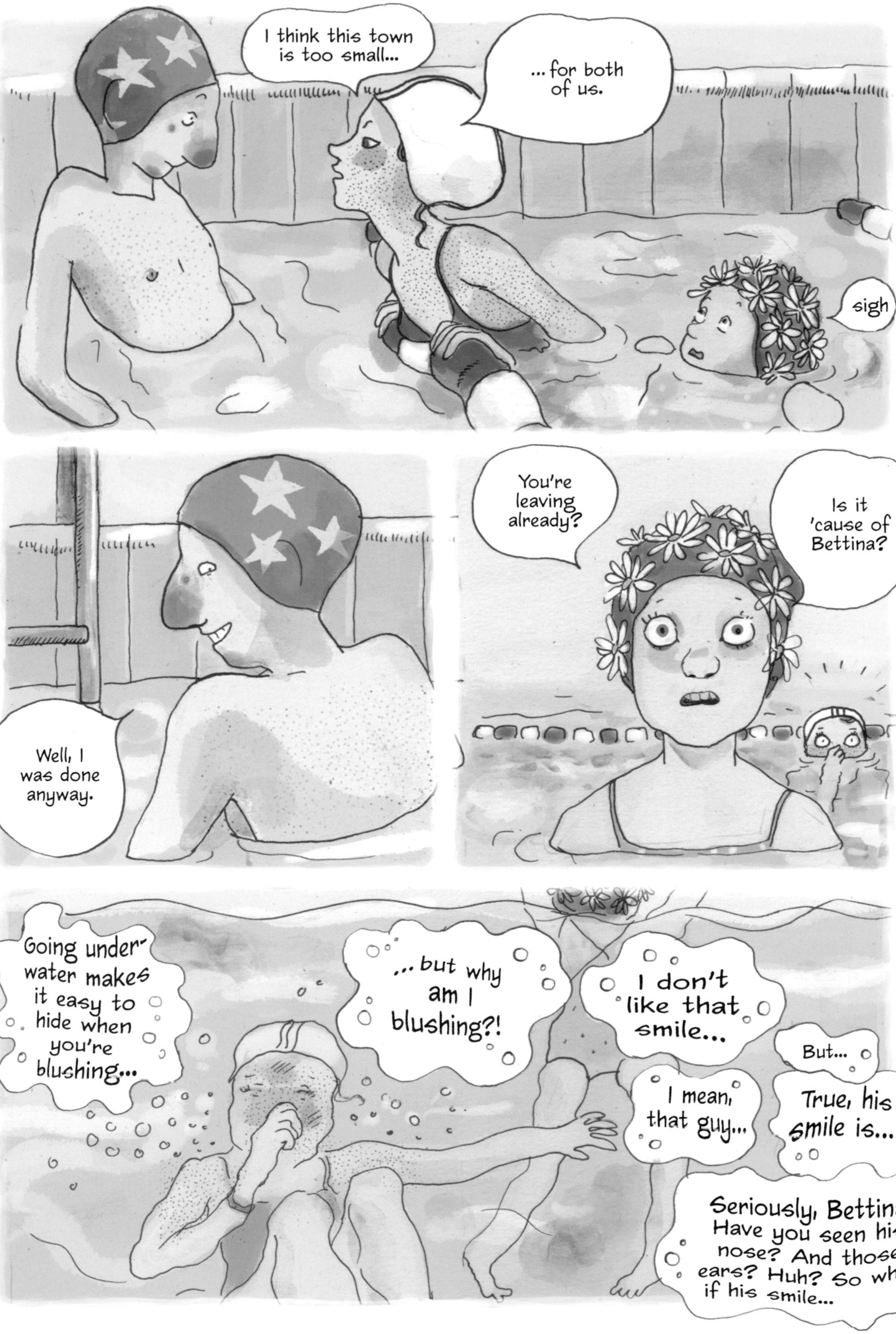
I think this town is too small...
... for both of us.
sigh
You're leaving already?
Is it 'cause of Bettina?
Well, I was done anyway.
Going underwater makes it easy to hide when you're blushing...
... but why am I blushing?!
I don't like that smile...
I mean, that guy...
But...
True, his smile is...
Seriously, Bettina! Have you seen his nose? And those ears? Huh? So what if his smile...

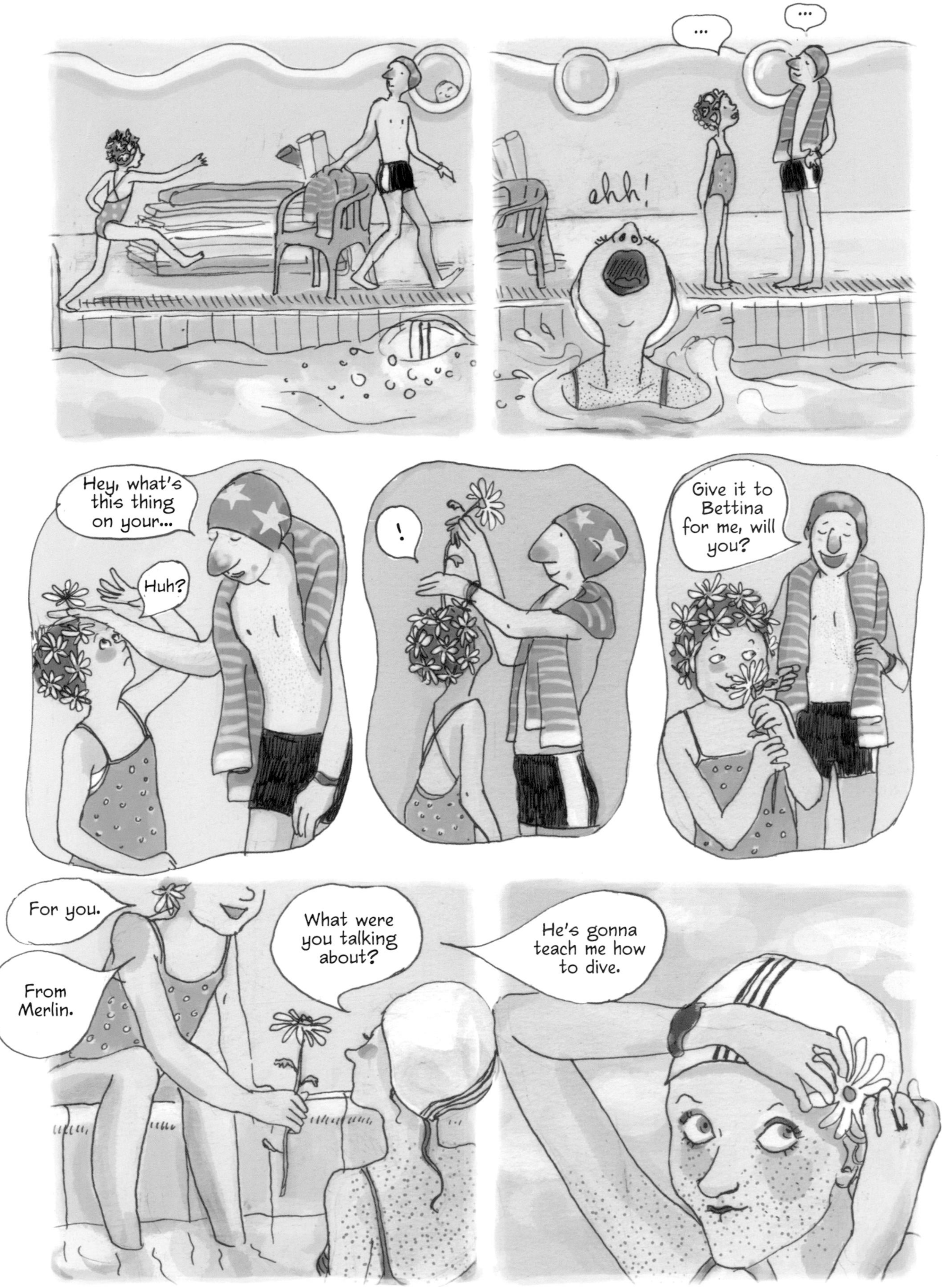
...
...
ahh!
Hey, what's this thing on your...
Huh?
!
Give it to Bettina for me, will you?
For you.
From Merlin.
What were you talking about?
He's gonna teach me how to dive.

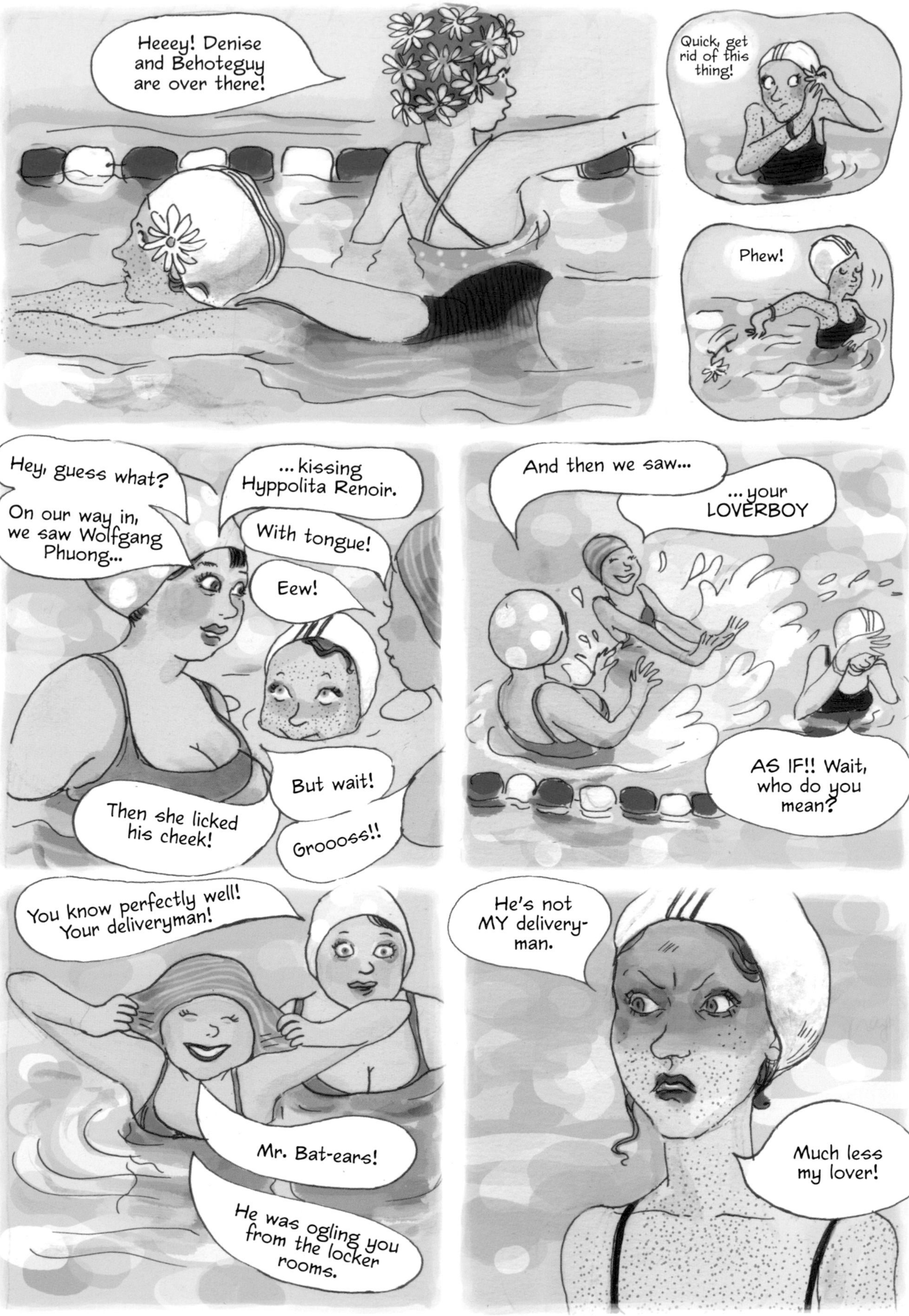
Heeey! Denise and Behoteguy are over there!
Quick, get rid of this thing!
Phew!
Hey, guess what?
On our way in, we saw Wolfgang Phuong...
...kissing Hyppolita Renoir.
With tongue!
Eew!
Then she licked his cheek!
But wait!
Grooooss!!
And then we saw...
...your LOVERBOY
AS IF!! Wait, who do you mean?
You know perfectly well! Your deliveryman!
Mr. Bat-ears!
He was ogling you from the locker rooms.
He's not MY delivery-man.
Much less my lover!

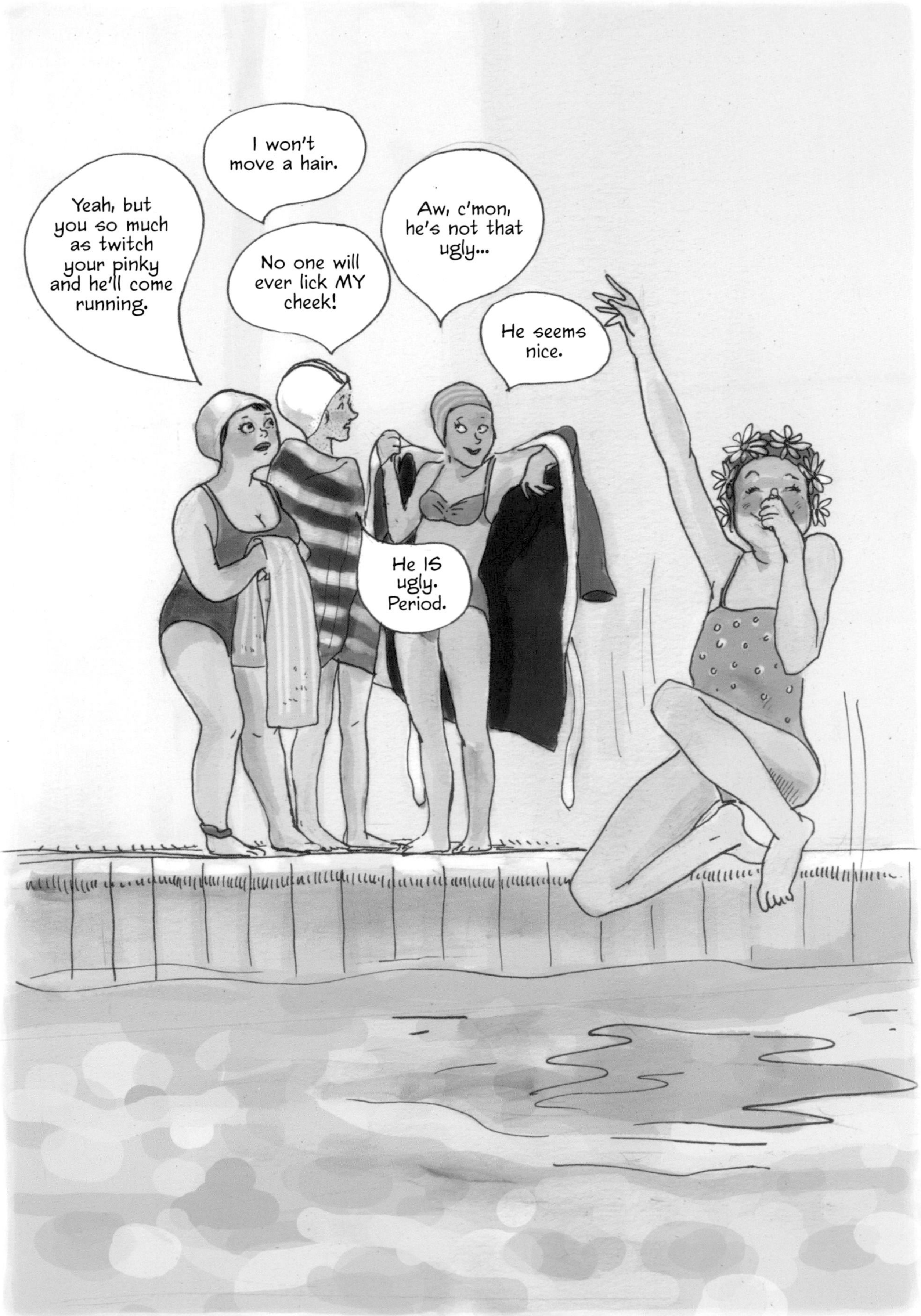
Yeah, but you so much as twitch your pinky and he'll come running.
I won't move a hair.
No one will ever lick MY cheek!
Aw, c'mon, he's not that ugly...
He seems nice.
He IS ugly. Period.

At that very moment, a few hundred yards away, Hortense was pushing open the heavy wooden door to an old apartment building downtown, whose address was on the little piece of dogeared cardstock that never left her pocket.

3, rue Alphonse Tabouret, 1st Floor Right: Lermontov's lair.

Apprehension. Excitement.

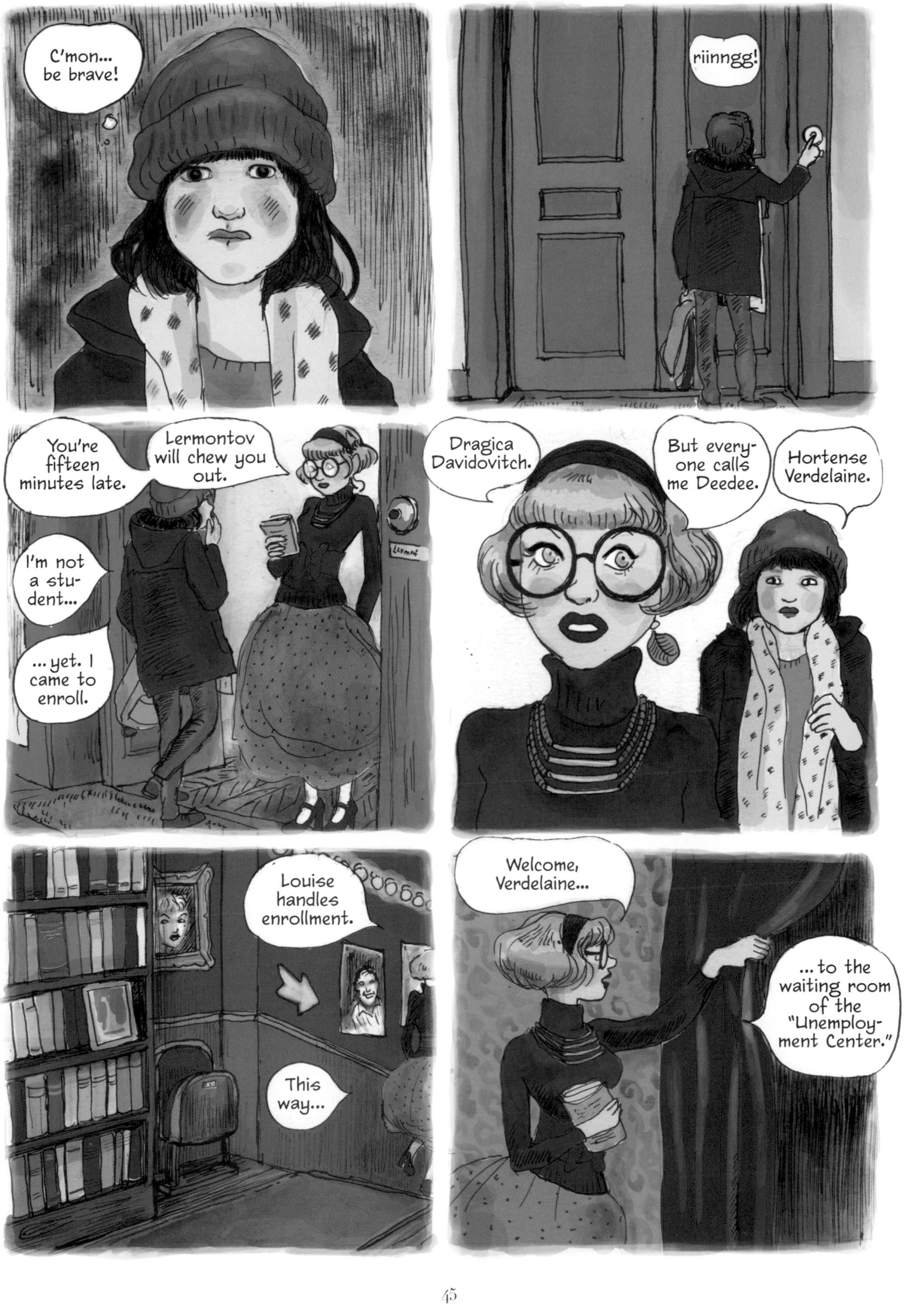
C'mon... be brave!
riinngg!
You're fifteen minutes late.
Lermontov will chew you out.
I'm not a student...
...yet. I came to enroll.
Dragica Davidovitch.
But everyone calls me Deedee.
Hortense Verdelaine.
Louise handles enrollment.
This way...
Welcome, Verdelaine...
...to the waiting room of the "Unemployment Center."

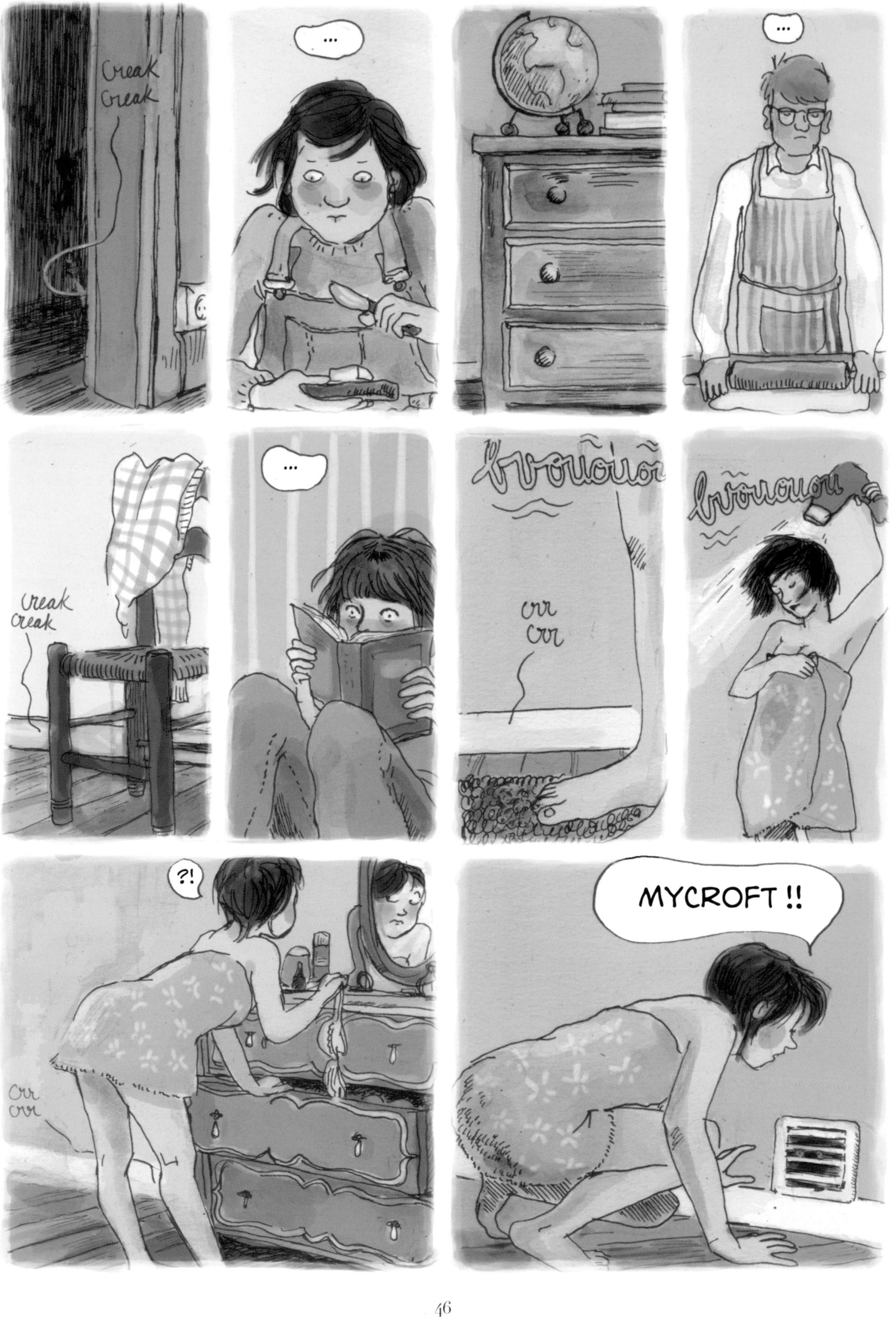
Creak
Creak
...
...
creak
creak
...
crr
crr
brououou
?!
crr
crr
MYCROFT !!

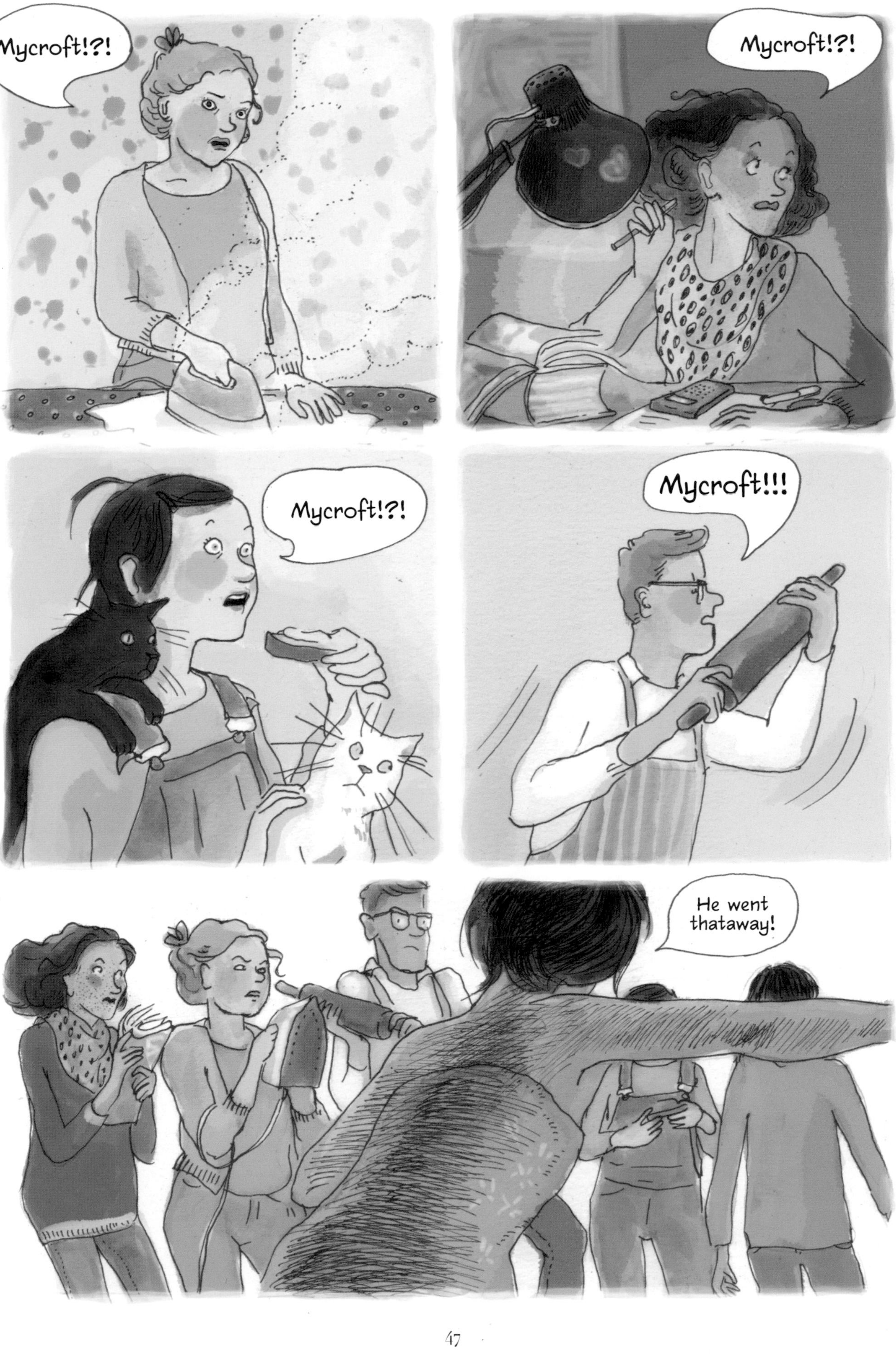
Mycroft!?!
Mycroft!?!
Mycroft!?!
Mycroft!!!
He went thataway!

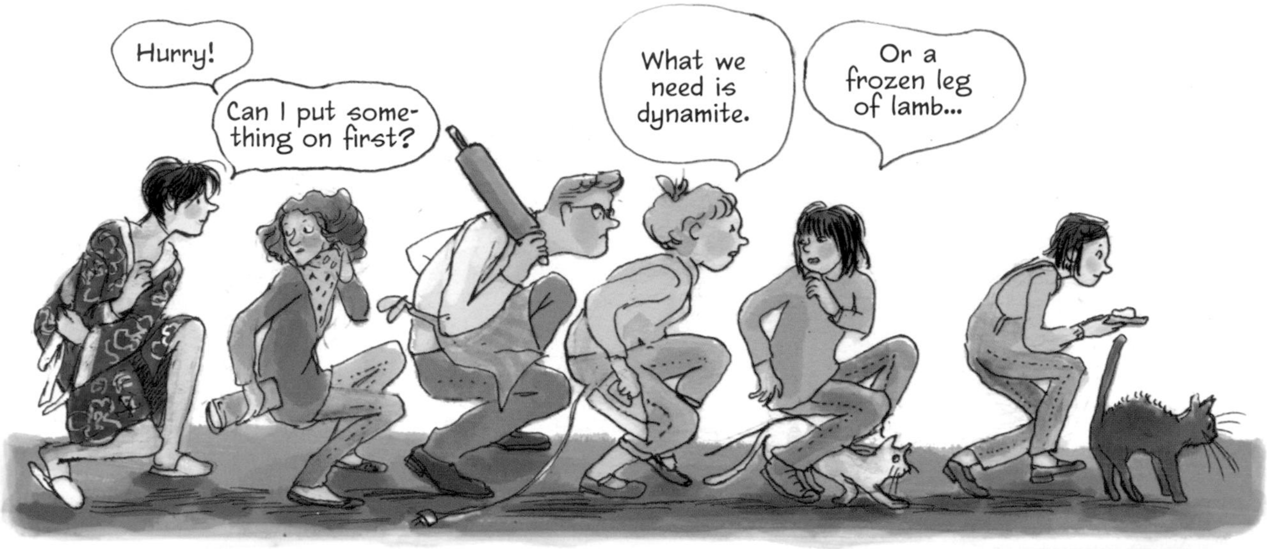
Hurry!
Can I put some-thing on first?
What we need is dynamite.
Or a frozen leg of lamb...

Mycroft was a high-flying, daredevil escape artist.

Mycroft was a rat. So crafty, and of such superior intellect, that the residents of Vill'Hervé christened him Mycroft Holmes, after Sherlock's older brother.

He was a diva, only making appearances when it suited him. Sometimes no one would see him for months, and then, without warning, he'd stick out his little snout again.

In short, Mycroft was an outlaw.

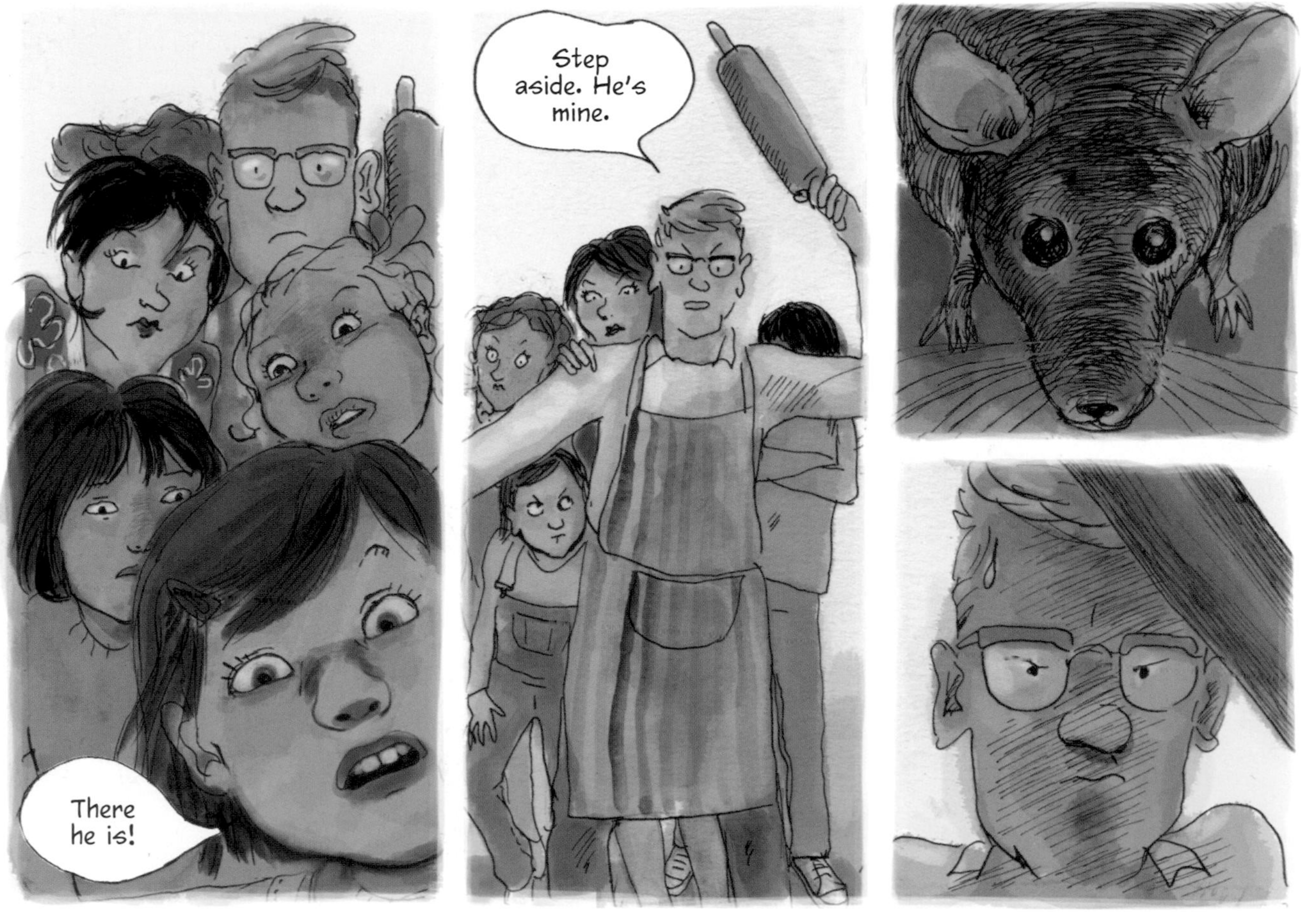
There he is!
Step aside. He's mine.

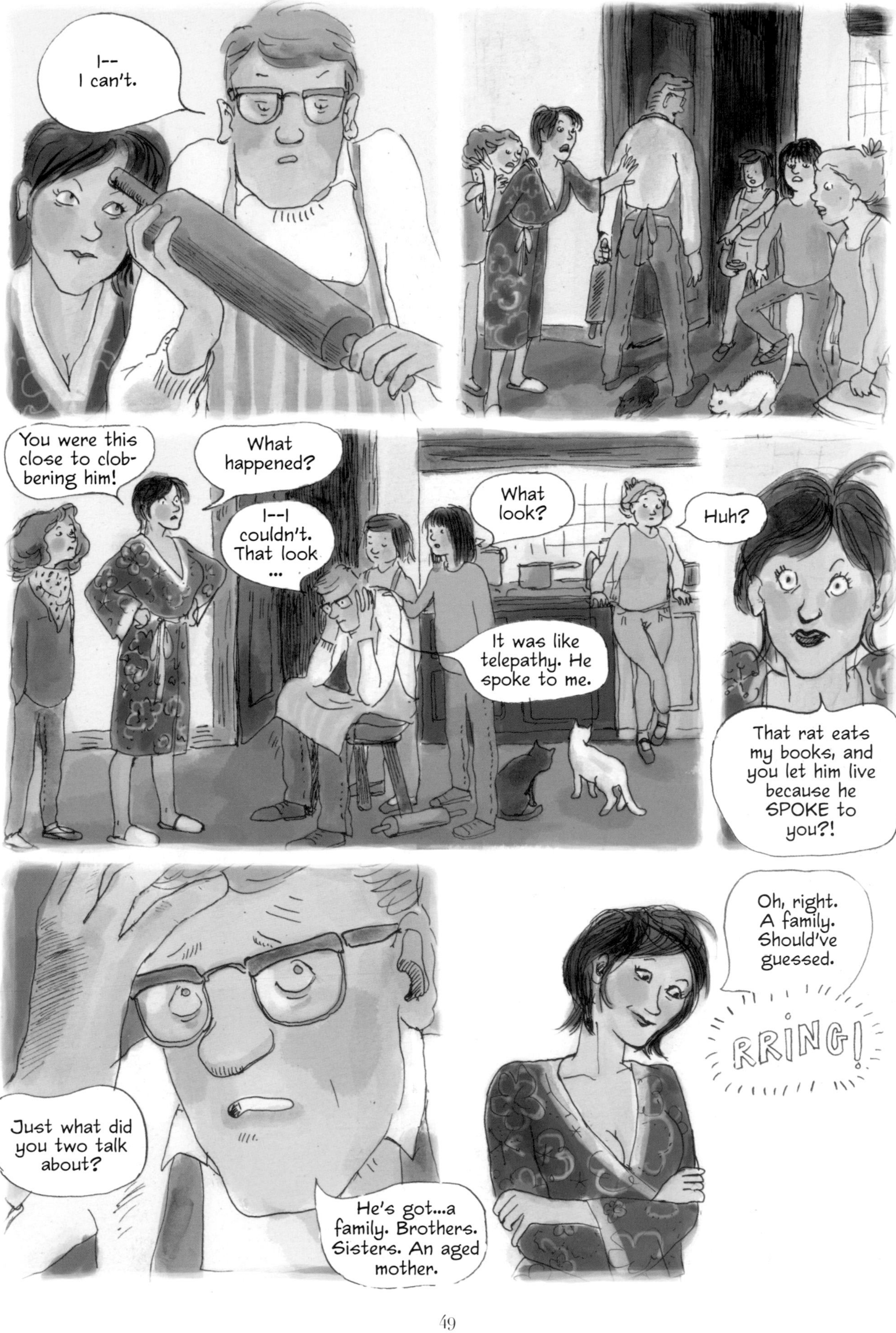
I--
I can't.
You were this close to clobbering him!
What happened?
I--I couldn't. That look ...
What look?
It was like telepathy. He spoke to me.
Huh?
That rat eats my books, and you let him live because he SPOKE to you?!
Just what did you two talk about?
He's got...a family. Brothers. Sisters. An aged mother.
Oh, right. A family. Should've guessed.
RRING!

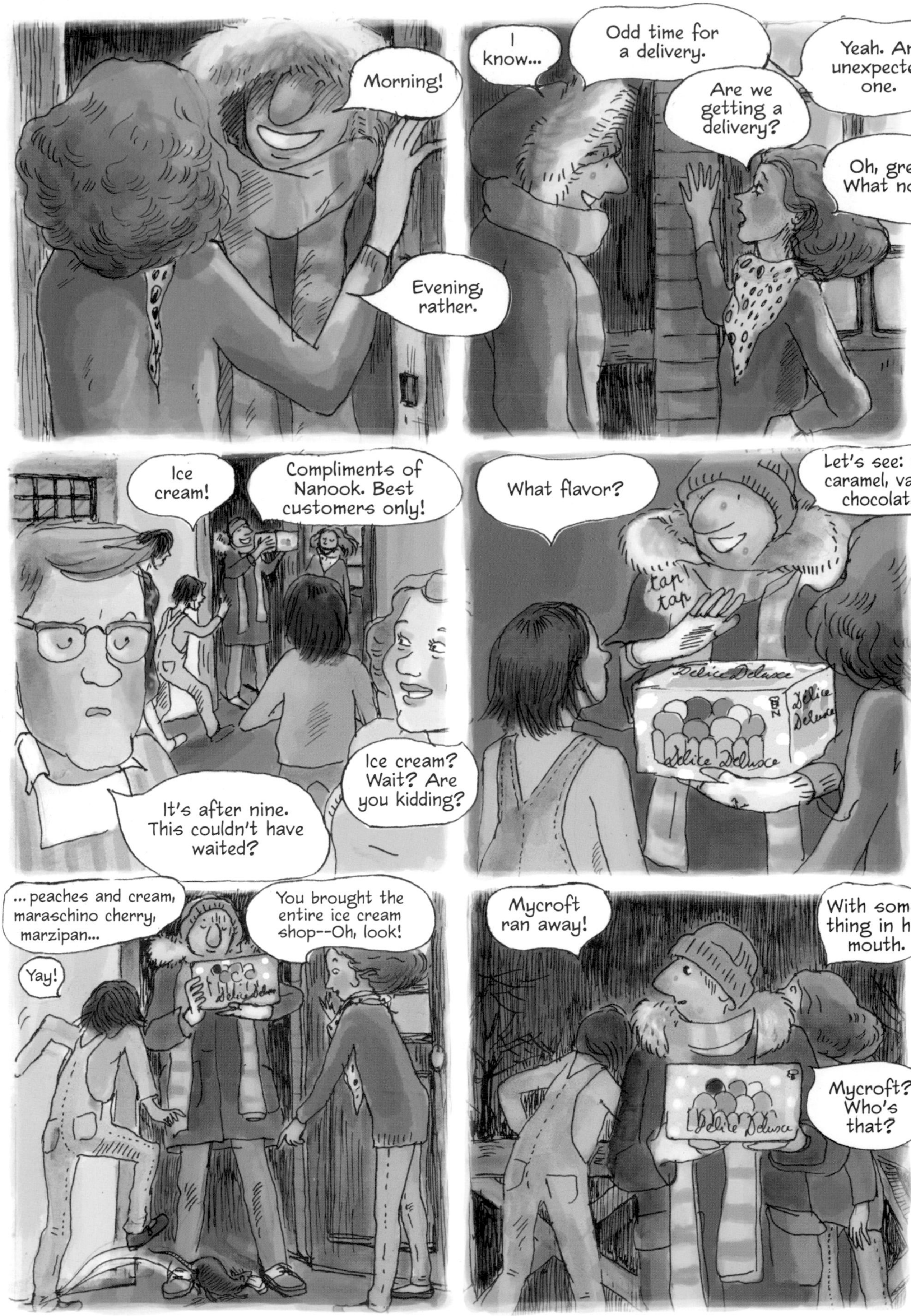

Morning!
Evening, rather.
I know...
Odd time for a delivery.
Yeah. An unexpected one.
Are we getting a delivery?
Oh, great. What now?
Ice cream!
Compliments of Nanook. Best customers only!
It's after nine. This couldn't have waited?
Ice cream? Wait? Are you kidding?
What flavor?
Let's see: mint, caramel, vanilla, chocolate...
tap tap
Delice Deluxe
...peaches and cream, maraschino cherry, marzipan...
Yay!
You brought the entire ice cream shop--Oh, look!
Mycroft ran away!
With something in his mouth.
Mycroft? Who's that?
Delice Deluxe

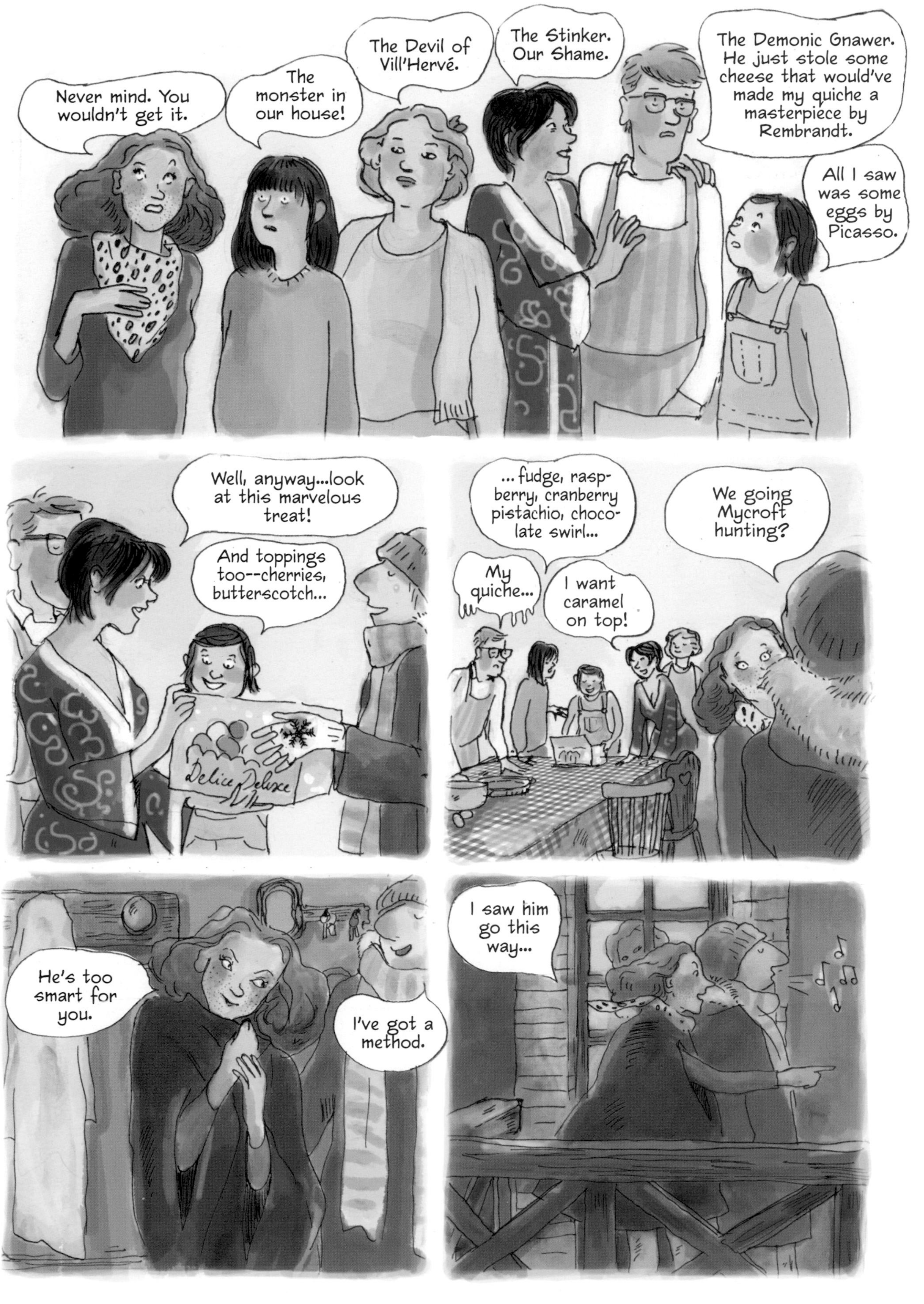
Never mind. You wouldn't get it.
The monster in our house!
The Devil of Vill'Hervé.
The Stinker. Our Shame.
The Demonic Gnawer. He just stole some cheese that would've made my quiche a masterpiece by Rembrandt.
All I saw was some eggs by Picasso.
Well, anyway...look at this marvelous treat!
And toppings too--cherries, butterscotch...
Delice Deluxe
...fudge, rasp-berry, cranberry pistachio, choco-late swirl...
My quiche...
I want caramel on top!
We going Mycroft hunting?
He's too smart for you.
I've got a method.
I saw him go this way...

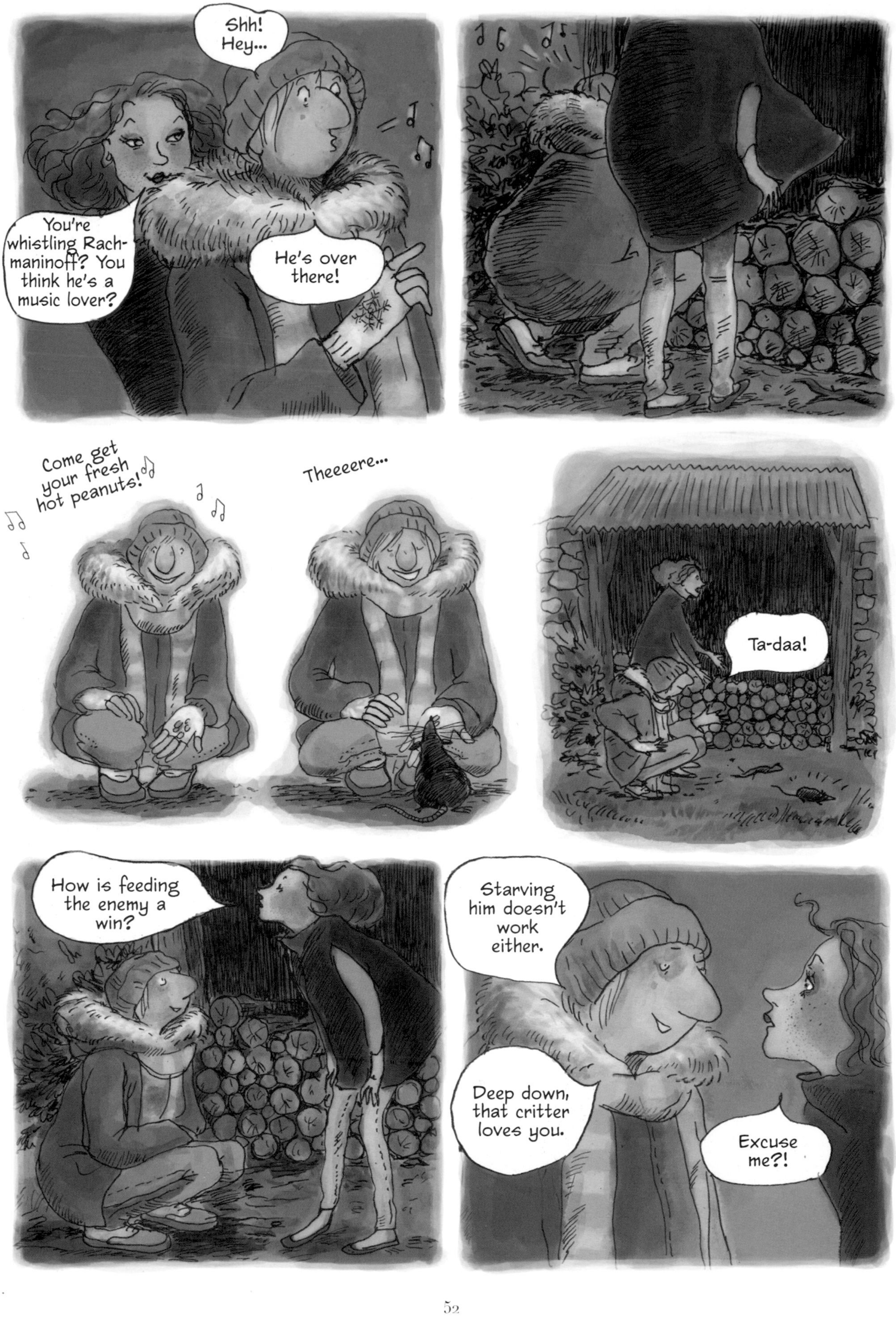
Shh! Hey...
You're whistling Rachmaninoff? You think he's a music lover?
He's over there!
Come get your fresh hot peanuts!
Theeeere...
Ta-daa!
How is feeding the enemy a win?
Starving him doesn't work either.
Deep down, that critter loves you.
Excuse me?!

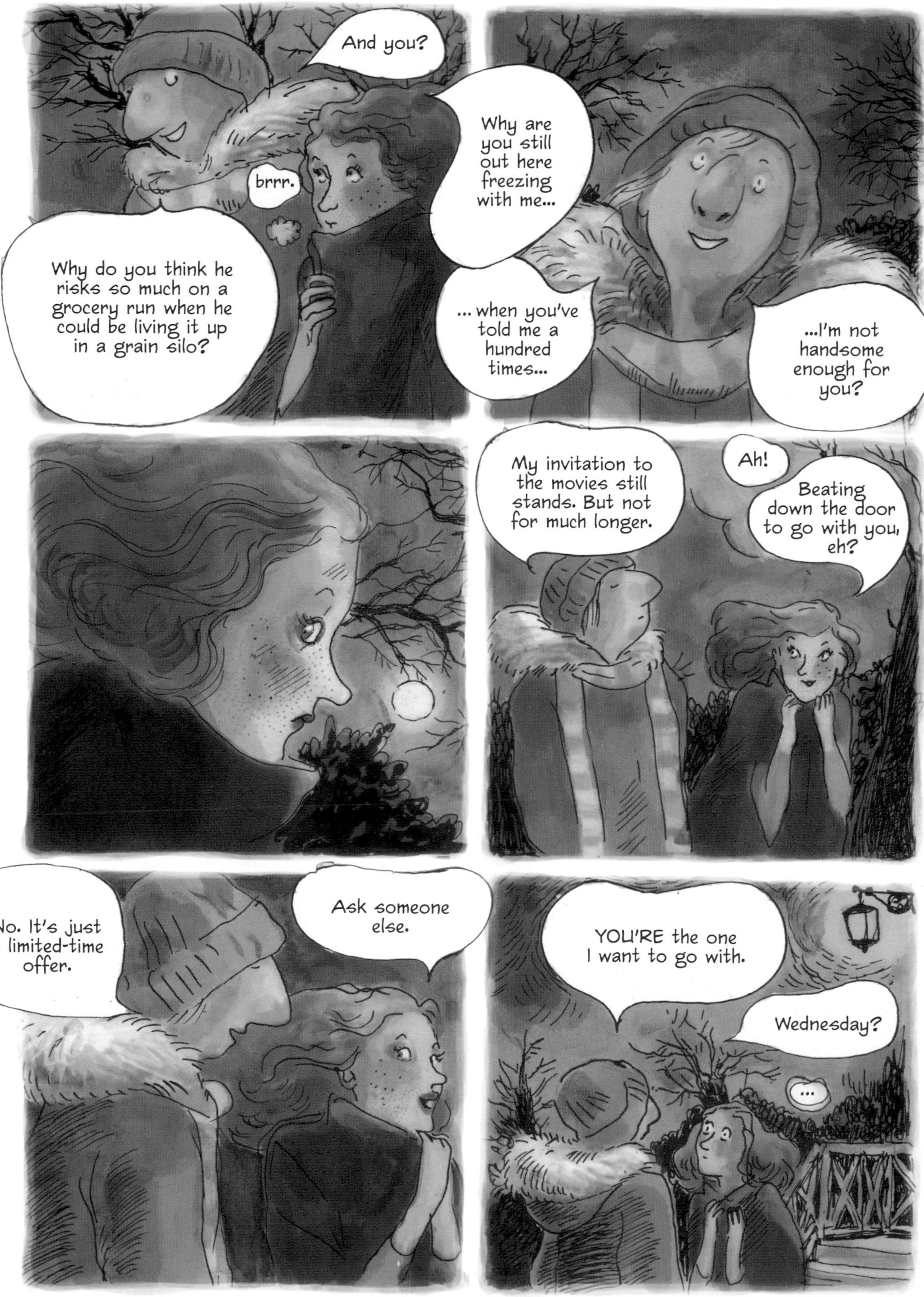
And you?
brrr.
Why do you think he risks so much on a grocery run when he could be living it up in a grain silo?
Why are you still out here freezing with me...
... when you've told me a hundred times...
...I'm not handsome enough for you?
My invitation to the movies still stands. But not for much longer.
Ah!
Beating down the door to go with you, eh?
No. It's just a limited-time offer.
Ask someone else.
YOU'RE the one I want to go with.
Wednesday?
...

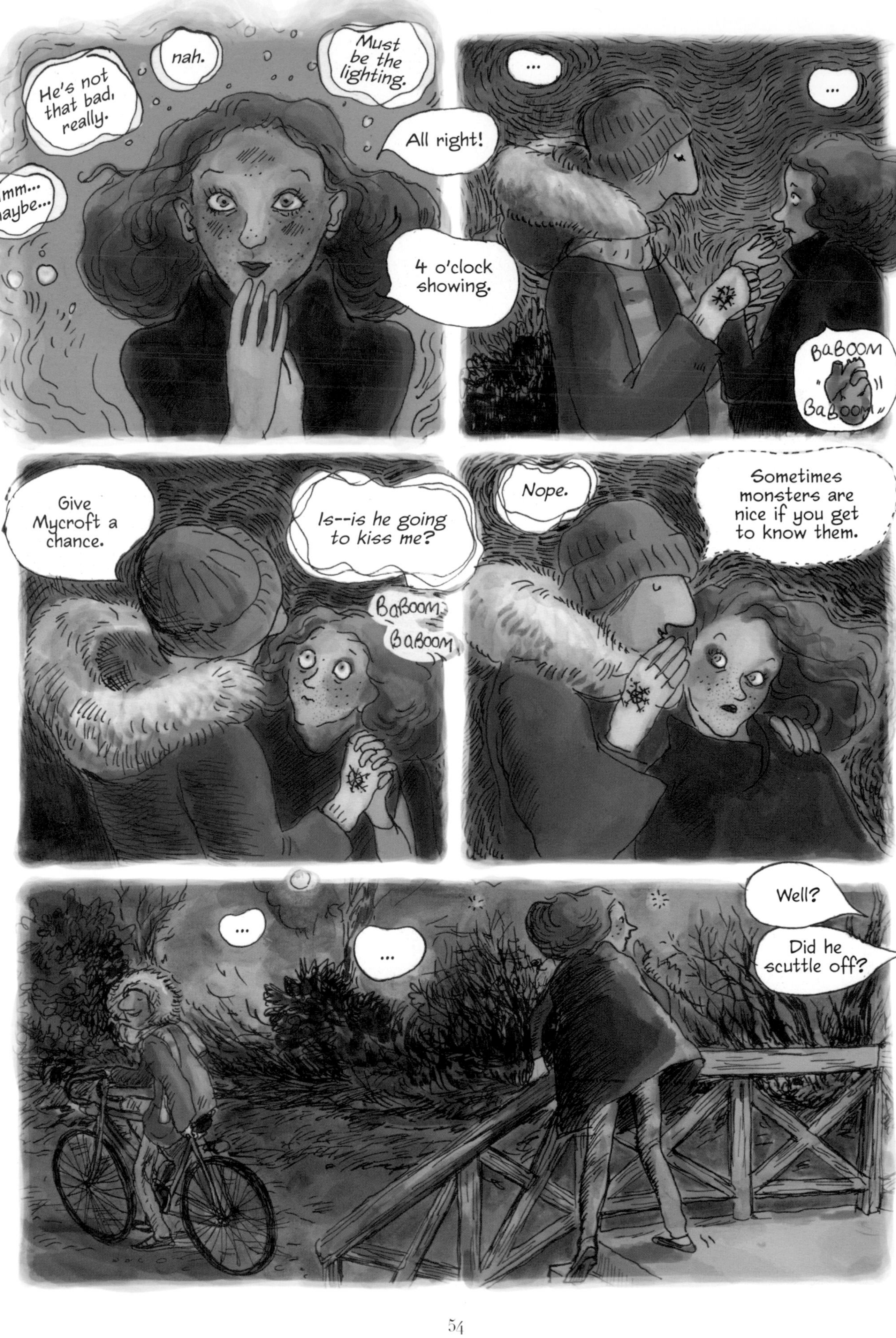
He's not that bad, really.
nah.
Must be the lighting.
All right!
Hmm... maybe...
4 o'clock showing.
...
...
BaBOOM
BaBOOM
Give Mycroft a chance.
Is--is he going to kiss me?
BaBOOM
BaBOOM
Nope.
Sometimes monsters are nice if you get to know them.
...
...
Well?
Did he scuttle off?

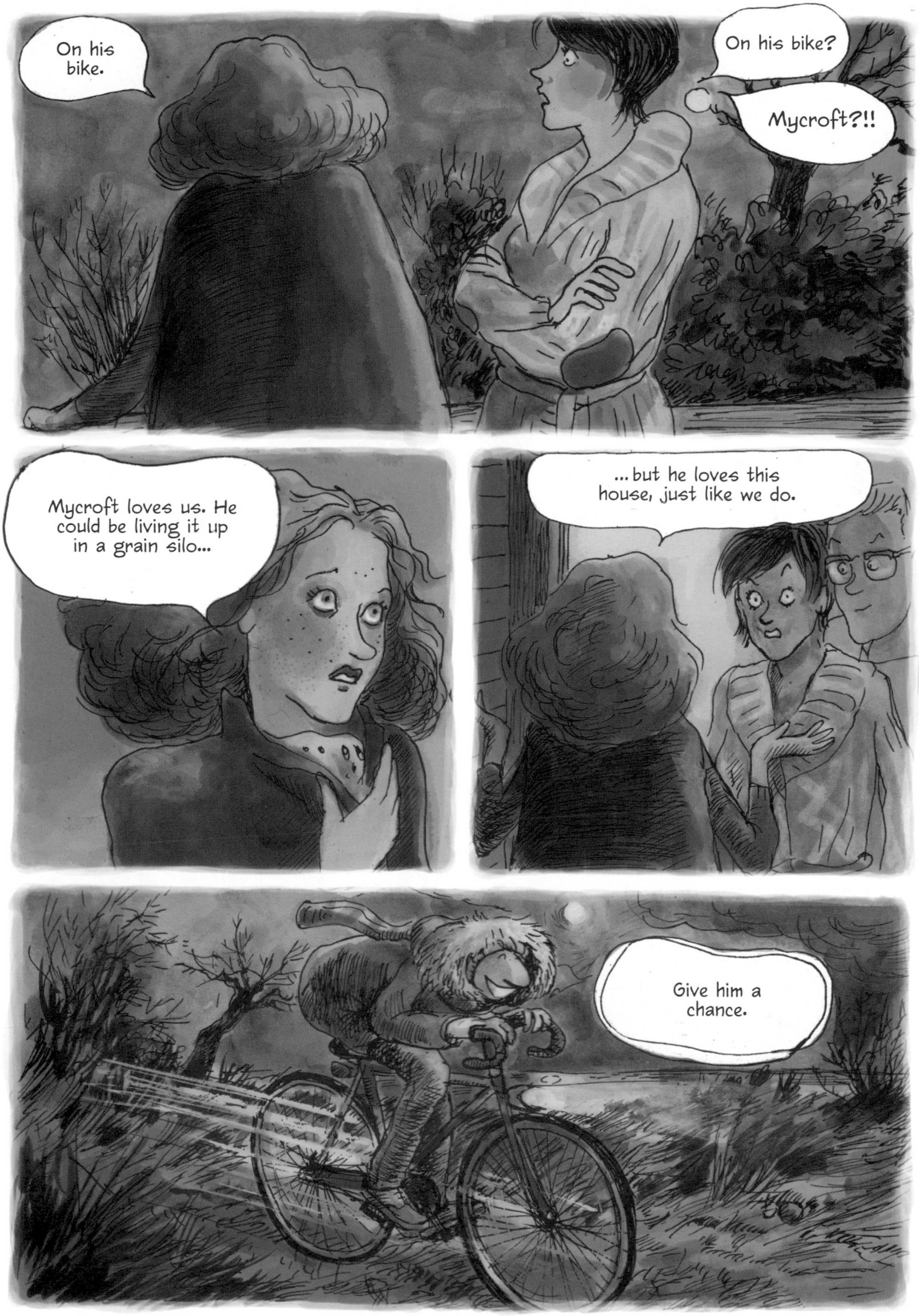
On his bike.
On his bike?
Mycroft?!!
Mycroft loves us. He could be living it up in a grain silo...
...but he loves this house, just like we do.
Give him a chance.

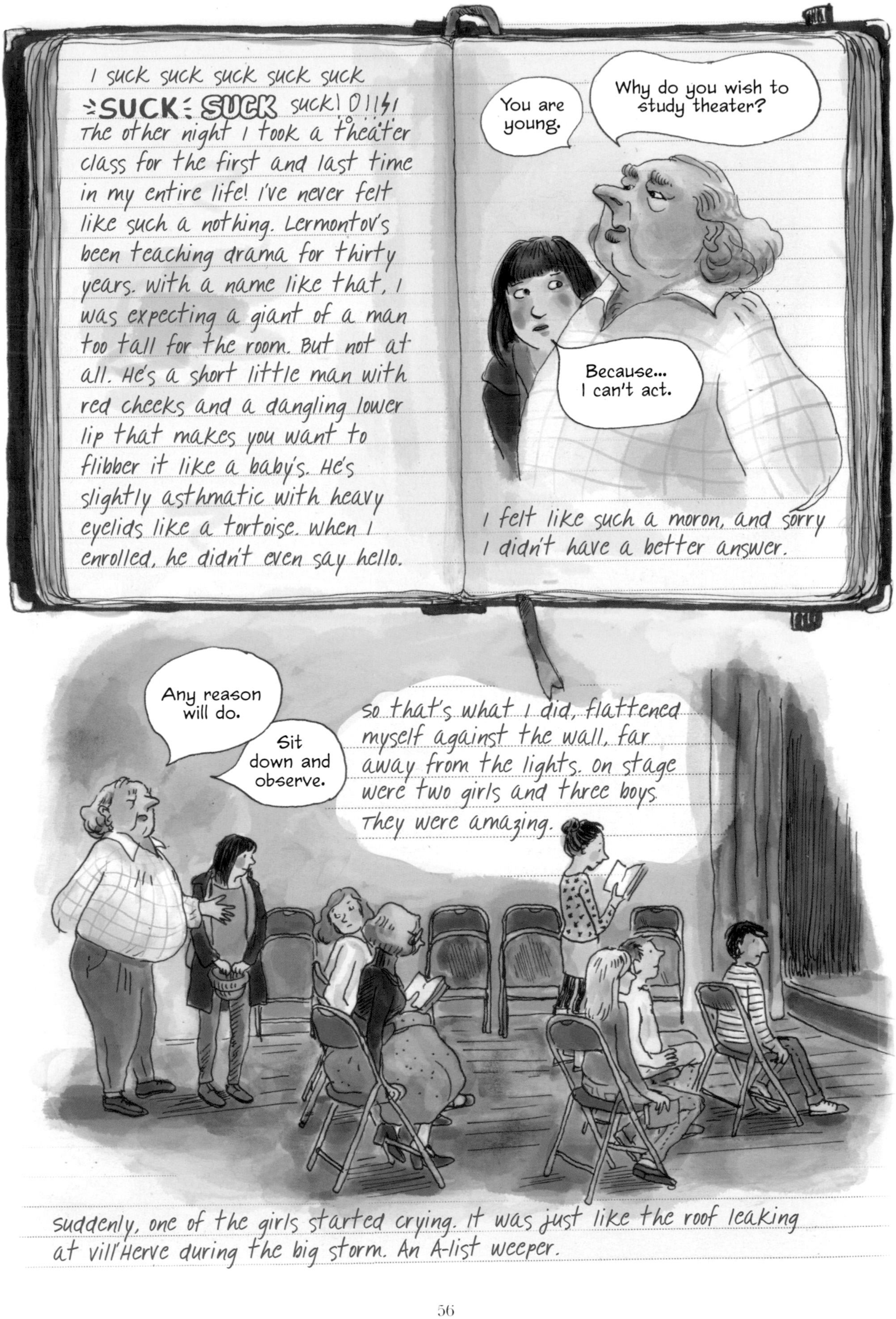
I suck suck suck suck suck
SUCK SUCK suck! 0!!ϟ!
The other night I took a theater class for the first and last time in my entire life! I've never felt like such a nothing. Lermontov's been teaching drama for thirty years. With a name like that, I was expecting a giant of a man too tall for the room. But not at all. He's a short little man with red cheeks and a dangling lower lip that makes you want to flibber it like a baby's. He's slightly asthmatic with heavy eyelids like a tortoise. When I enrolled, he didn't even say hello.
You are young.
Why do you wish to study theater?
Because... I can't act.
I felt like such a moron, and sorry I didn't have a better answer.
Any reason will do.
Sit down and observe.
So that's what I did, flattened myself against the wall, far away from the lights. On stage were two girls and three boys. They were amazing.
Suddenly, one of the girls started crying. It was just like the roof leaking at Vill'Herve during the big storm. An A-list weeper.

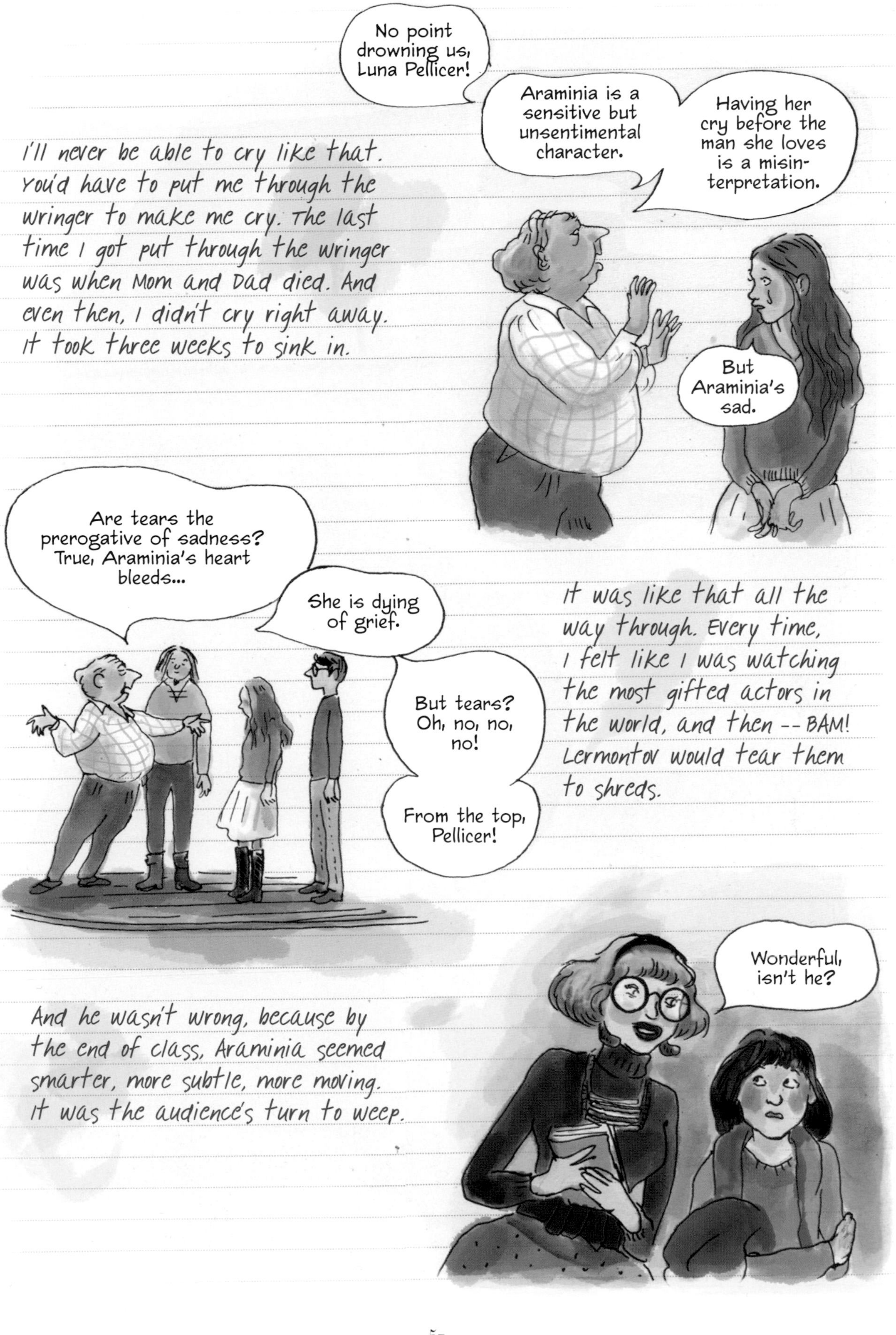
I'll never be able to cry like that. You'd have to put me through the wringer to make me cry. The last time I got put through the wringer was when Mom and Dad died. And even then, I didn't cry right away. It took three weeks to sink in.
No point drowning us, Luna Pellicer!
Araminia is a sensitive but unsentimental character.
Having her cry before the man she loves is a misinterpretation.
But Araminia's sad.
Are tears the prerogative of sadness? True, Araminia's heart bleeds...
She is dying of grief.
But tears? Oh, no, no, no!
From the top, Pellicer!
It was like that all the way through. Every time, I felt like I was watching the most gifted actors in the world, and then --BAM! Lermontov would tear them to shreds.
And he wasn't wrong, because by the end of class, Araminia seemed smarter, more subtle, more moving. It was the audience's turn to weep.
Wonderful, isn't he?

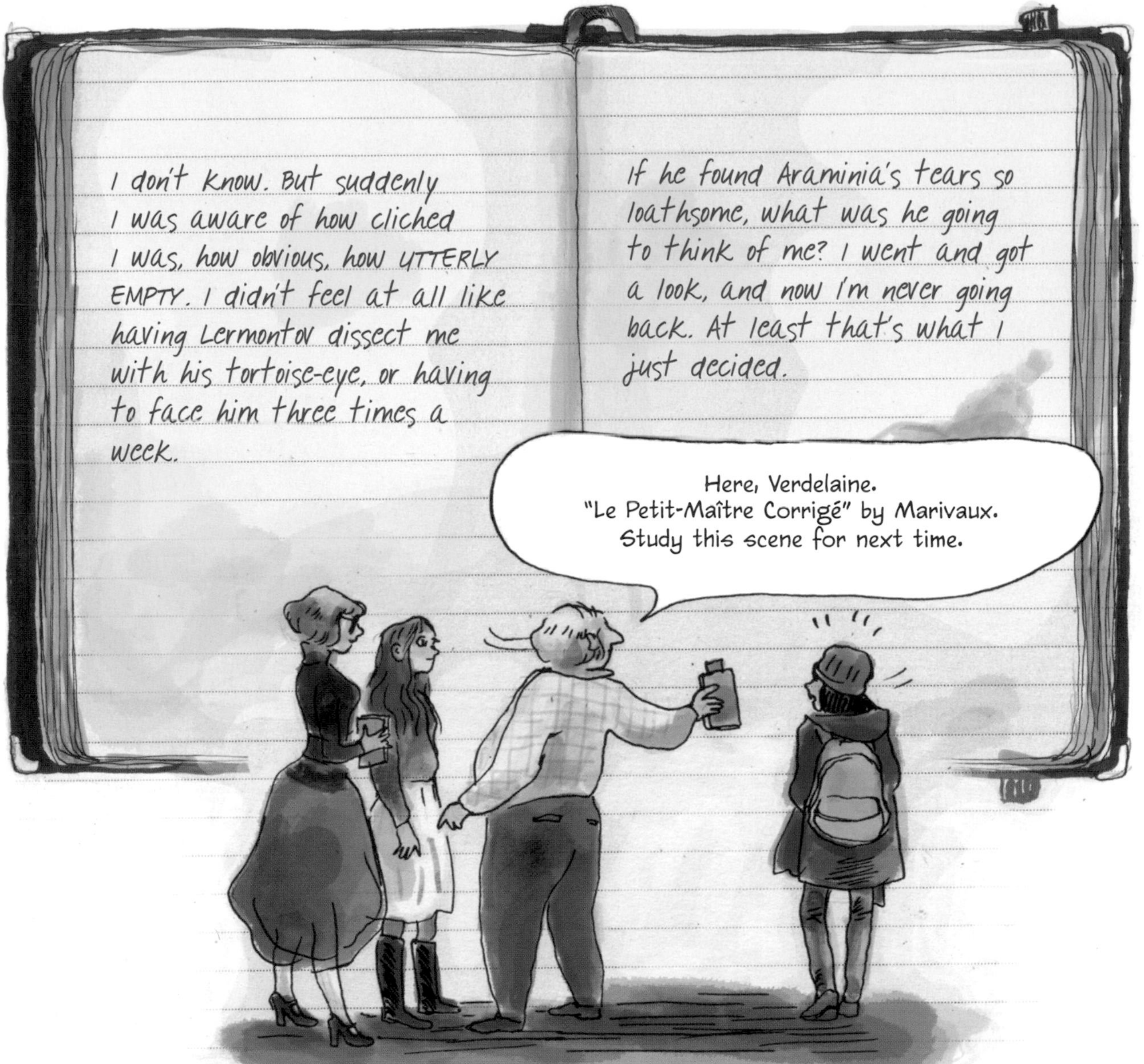
I don't know. But suddenly I was aware of how cliched I was, how obvious, how UTTERLY EMPTY. I didn't feel at all like having Lermontov dissect me with his tortoise-eye, or having to face him three times a week.
If he found Araminia's tears so loathsome, what was he going to think of me? I went and got a look, and now I'm never going back. At least that's what I just decided.
Here, Verdelaine. "Le Petit-Maître Corrigé" by Marivaux. Study this scene for next time.

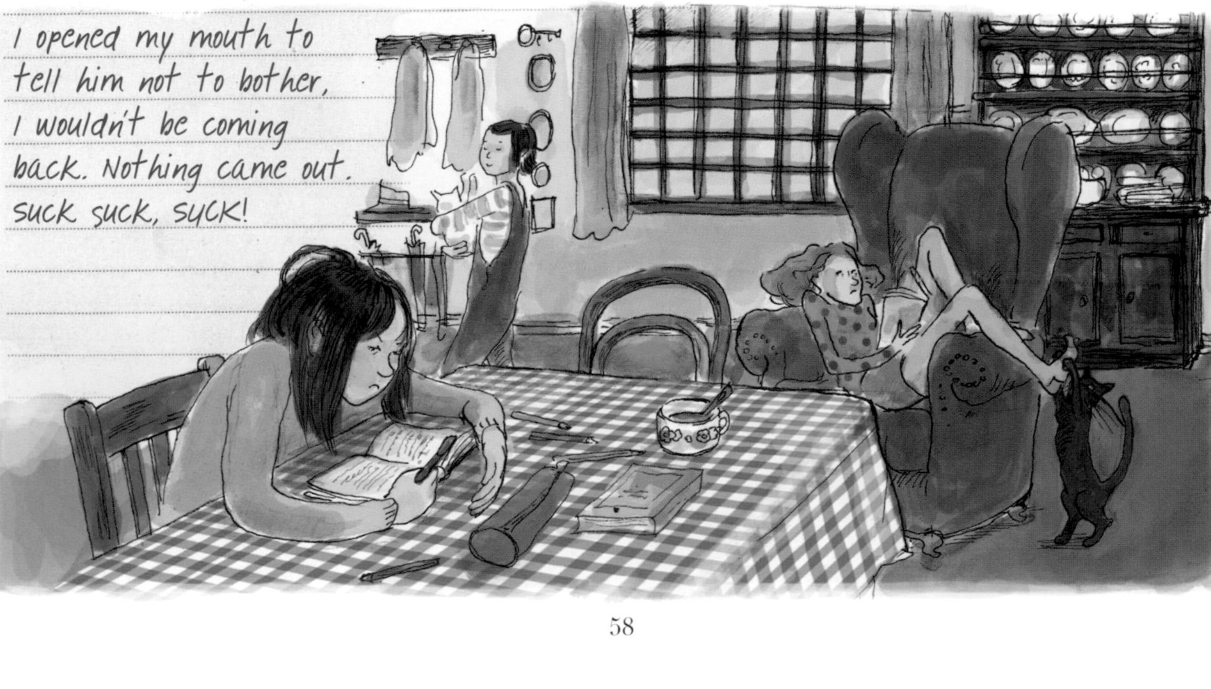
I opened my mouth to tell him not to bother, I wouldn't be coming back. Nothing came out. SUCK SUCK, SUCK!

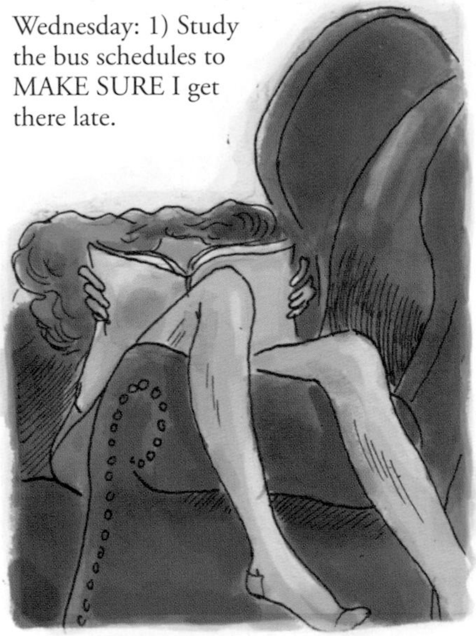
Wednesday: 1) Study the bus schedules to MAKE SURE I get there late.

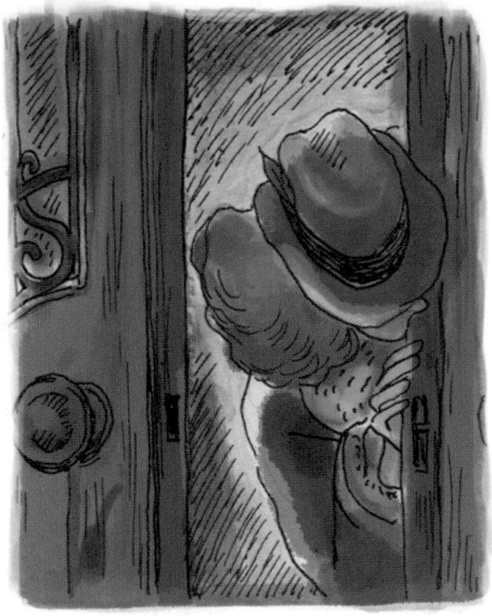

2) Sneak out of Vill'Hervé to avoid awkward questions.

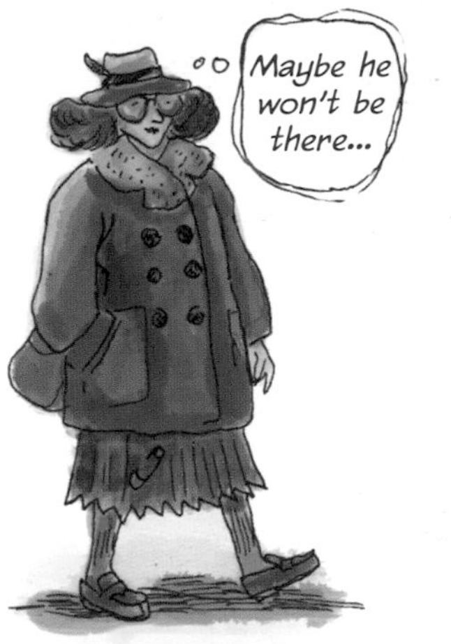
Maybe he won't be there...

3) Dress ugly. REALLY, REALLY UGLY!!

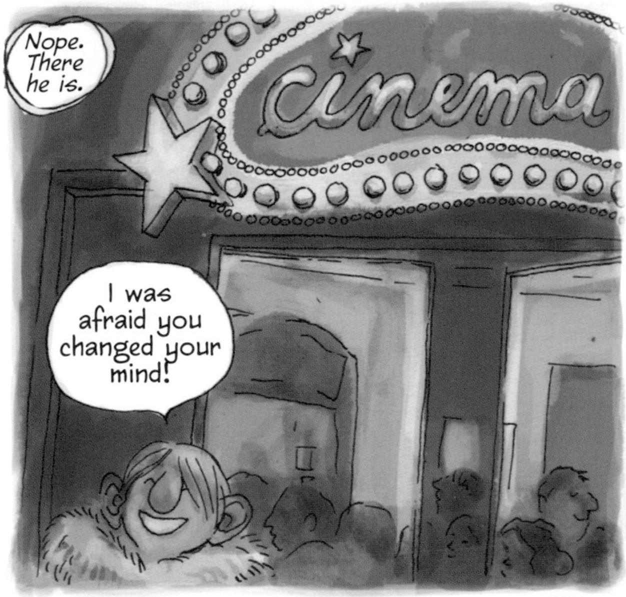
Nope. There he is.
cinema
I was afraid you changed your mind!

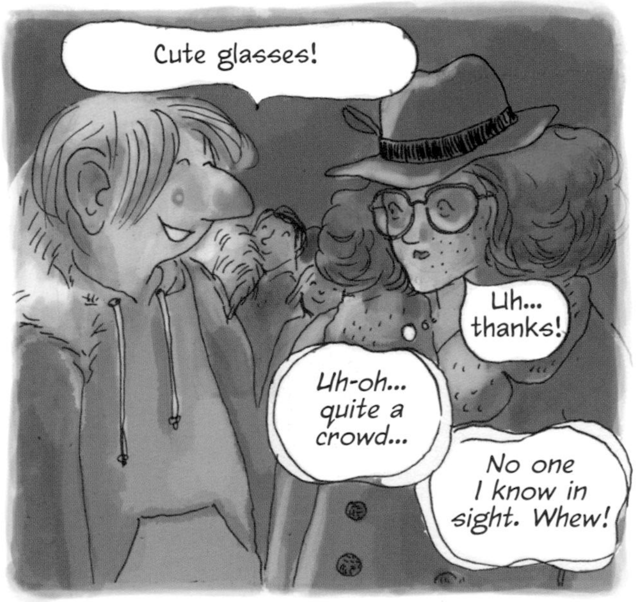
Cute glasses!
Uh... thanks!
Uh-oh... quite a crowd...
No one I know in sight. Whew!

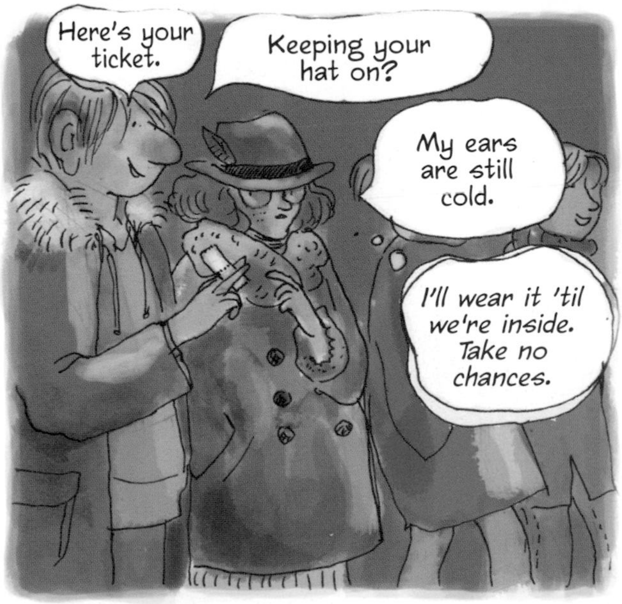
Here's your ticket.
Keeping your hat on?
My ears are still cold.
I'll wear it 'til we're inside. Take no chances.

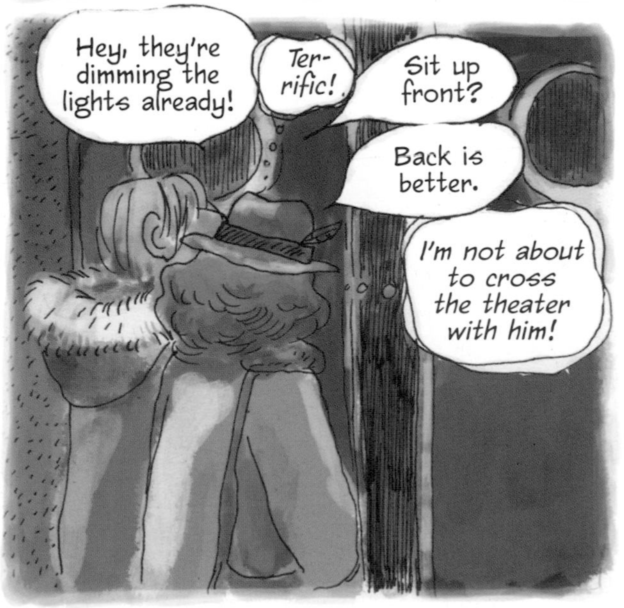
Hey, they're dimming the lights already!
Ter-rific!
Sit up front?
Back is better.
I'm not about to cross the theater with him!

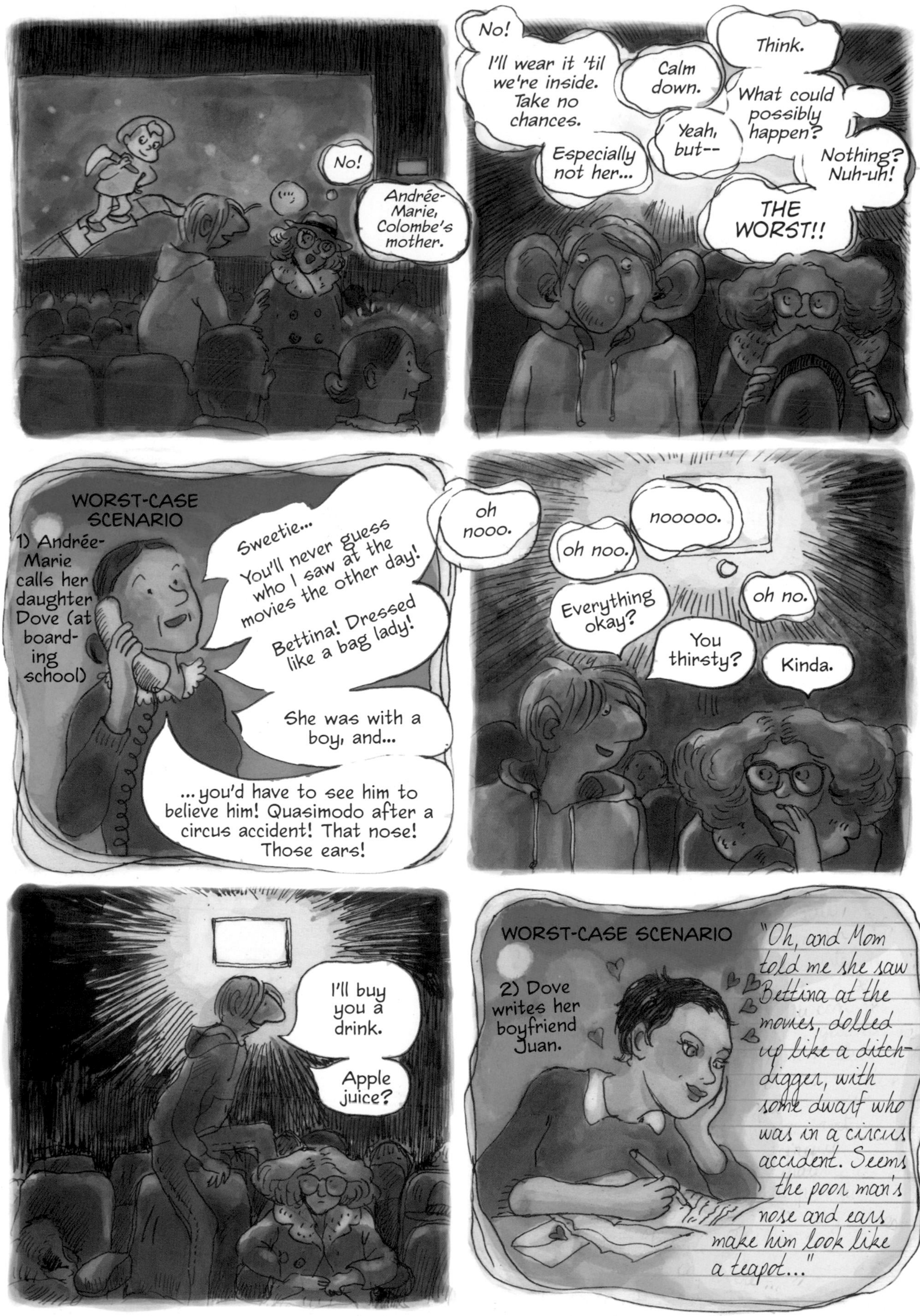
No!
Andrée-Marie, Colombe's mother.
No!
I'll wear it 'til we're inside. Take no chances.
Especially not her...
Calm down.
Yeah, but--
Think.
What could possibly happen?
Nothing? Nuh-uh!
THE WORST!!
WORST-CASE SCENARIO
1) Andrée-Marie calls her daughter Dove (at boarding school)
Sweetie... You'll never guess who I saw at the movies the other day!
Bettina! Dressed like a bag lady!
She was with a boy, and...
...you'd have to see him to believe him! Quasimodo after a circus accident! That nose! Those ears!
oh nooo.
oh noo.
nooooo.
oh no.
Everything okay?
You thirsty?
Kinda.
I'll buy you a drink.
Apple juice?
WORST-CASE SCENARIO
2) Dove writes her boyfriend Juan.
"Oh, and Mom told me she saw Bettina at the movies, dolled up like a ditch-digger, with some dwarf who was in a circus accident. Seems the poor man's nose and ears make him look like a teapot..."

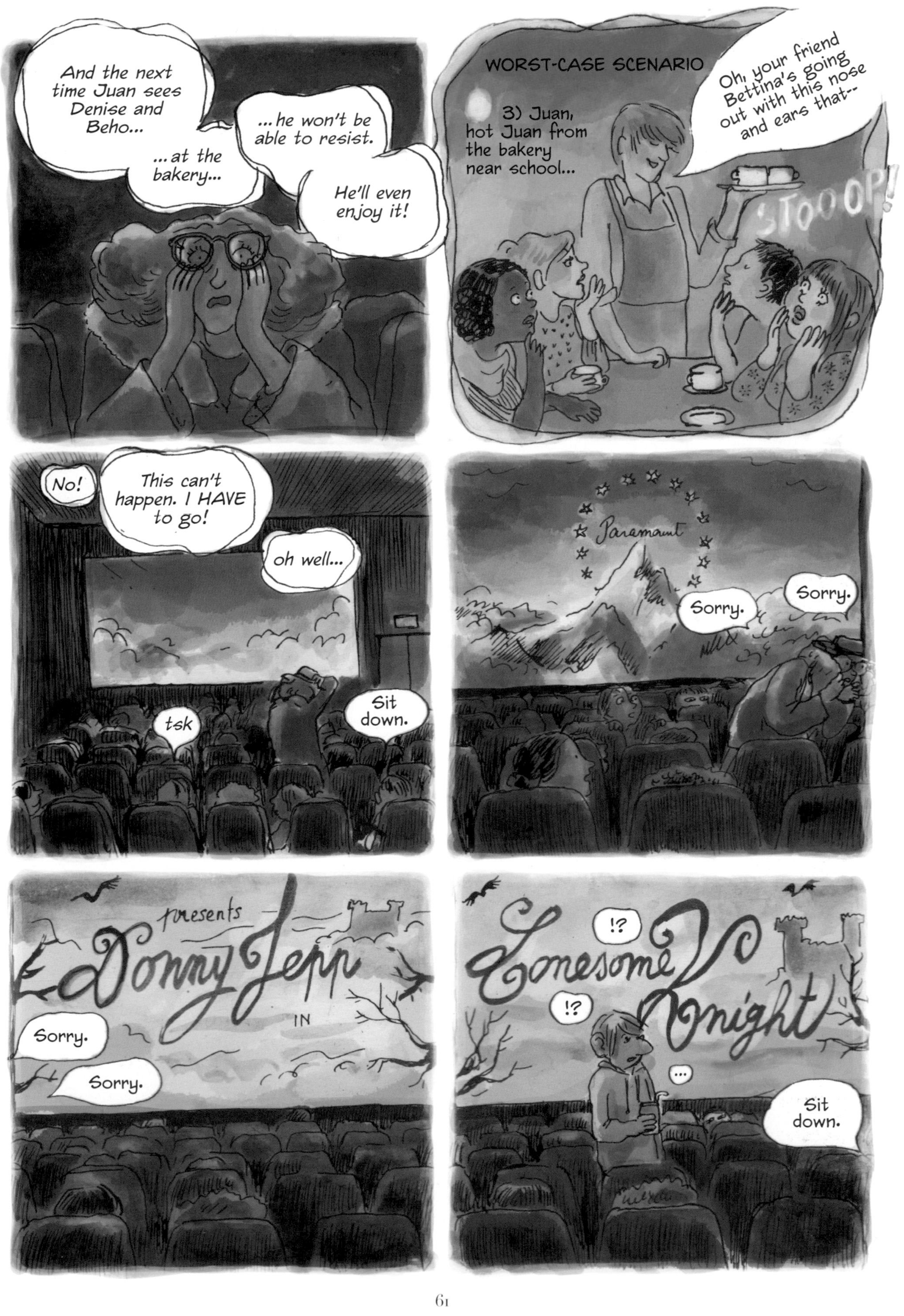
And the next time Juan sees Denise and Beho...
...at the bakery...
...he won't be able to resist.
He'll even enjoy it!
WORST-CASE SCENARIO
3) Juan, hot Juan from the bakery near school...
Oh, your friend Bettina's going out with this nose and ears that--
STOOOP!
No!
This can't happen. I HAVE to go!
oh well...
tsk
Sit down.
Paramount
Sorry.
Sorry.
presents
Donny Jepp
IN
Sorry.
Sorry.
Lonesome Knight
!?
!?
...
Sit down.

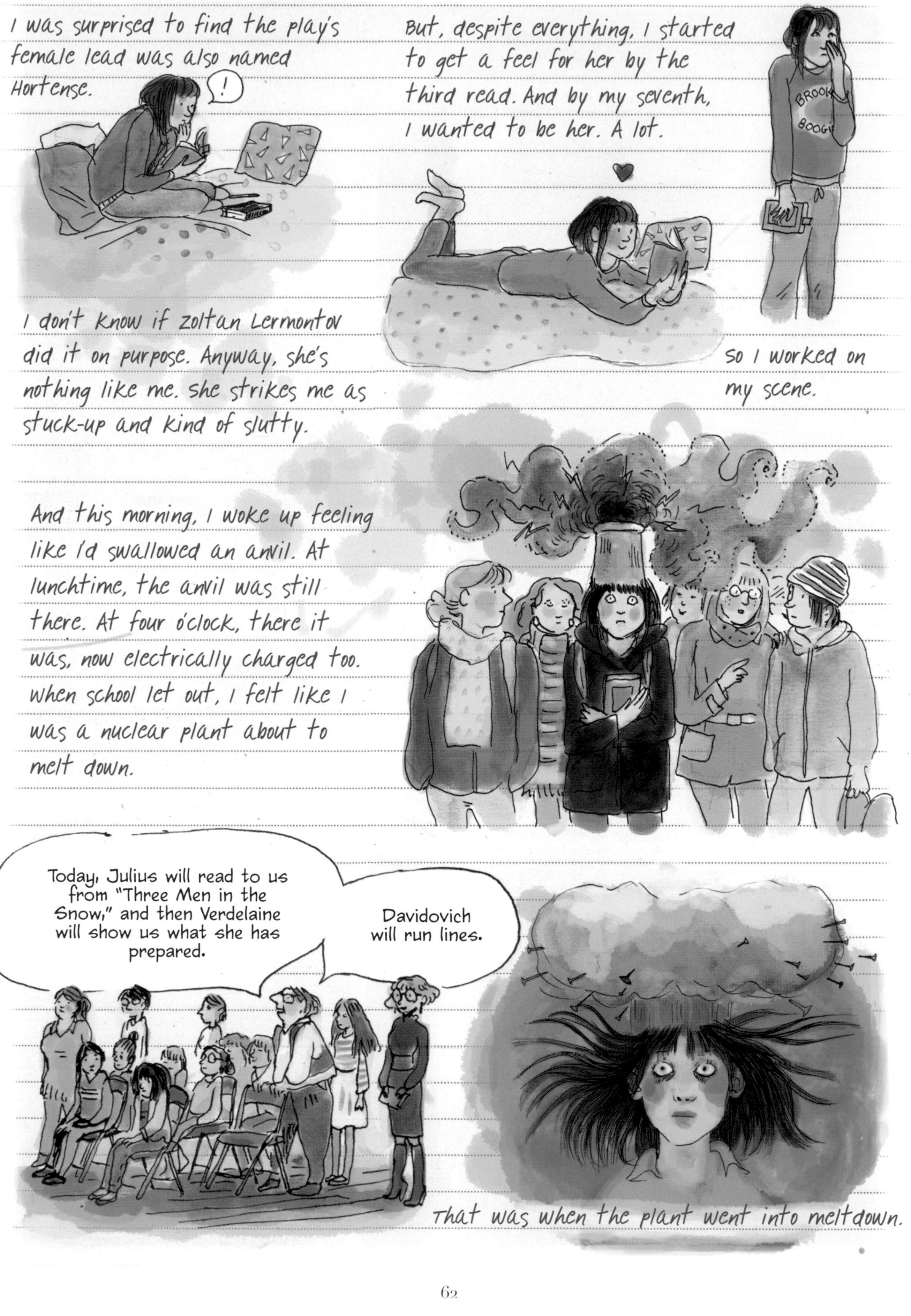
I was surprised to find the play's female lead was also named Hortense.
!
But, despite everything, I started to get a feel for her by the third read. And by my seventh, I wanted to be her. A lot.
I don't know if Zoltan Lermontov did it on purpose. Anyway, she's nothing like me. She strikes me as stuck-up and kind of slutty.
So I worked on my scene.
And this morning, I woke up feeling like I'd swallowed an anvil. At lunchtime, the anvil was still there. At four o'clock, there it was, now electrically charged too. When school let out, I felt like I was a nuclear plant about to melt down.
Today, Julius will read to us from "Three Men in the Snow," and then Verdelaine will show us what she has prepared.
Davidovich will run lines.
That was when the plant went into meltdown.

It's like everything was wiped from my mind and my muscles. I couldn't remember a thing. Not a word, not a gesture, even though I'd rehearsed them over and over.

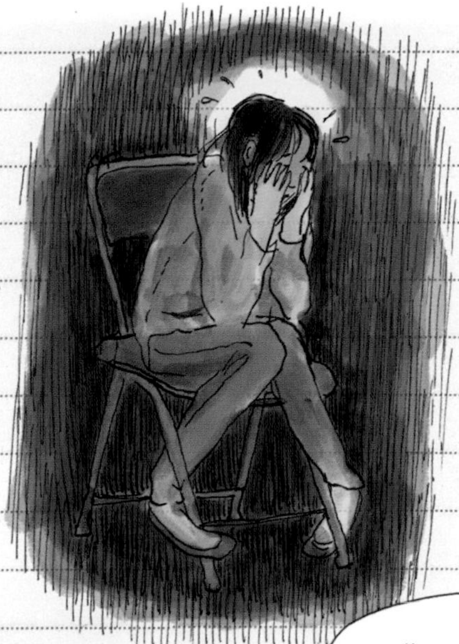

I sat there on my chair, limp as a mop, the whole time Julius was reading what sounded like Greek to me. When he was done, Lermontov beckoned me up on stage. Slowly, I unfolded myself. Everyone was staring at me.

I could feel all those curious gazes on my cheeks, like insect wings.

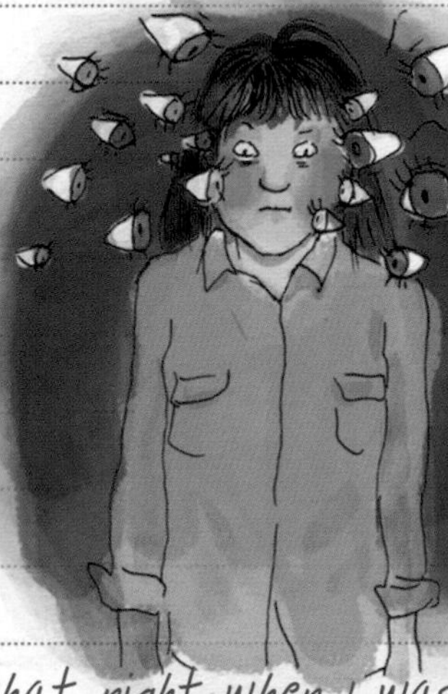

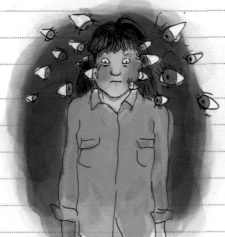

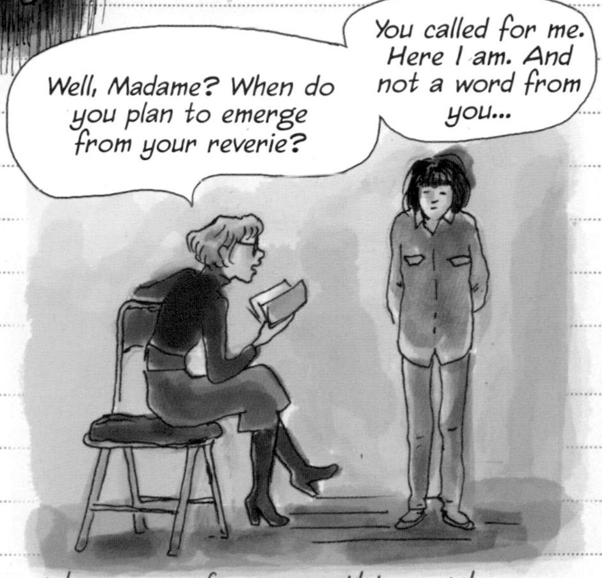
Well, Madame? When do you plan to emerge from your reverie?
You called for me. Here I am. And not a word from you...

Not a word from me either. Not one. Lips sealed. In the dark.

Like that night when I was going down the curvy and smushy staircase we call the Macaroni at Vill'Herve and someone upstairs turned out the lights. All I could think of was burrowing into the floorboards and hiding out like a clam in the sand.

A bell rang. Deedee got up to answer the door, and that saved me for two seconds, a tenth of a lifetime.

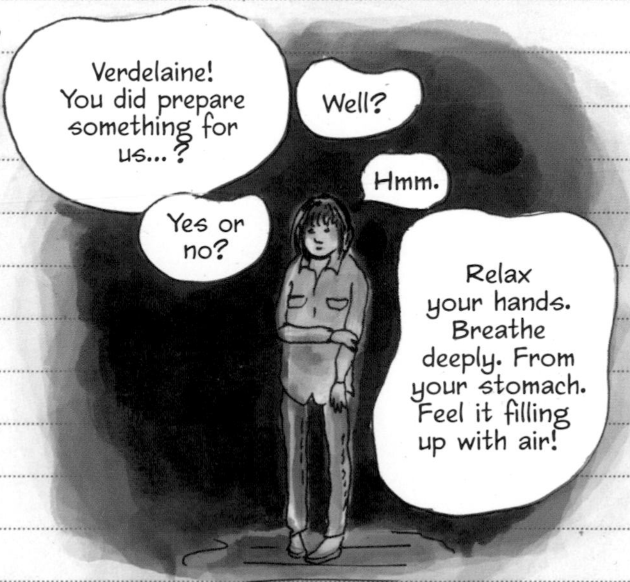
Verdelaine! You did prepare something for us...?
Well?
Hmm.
Yes or no?
Relax your hands. Breathe deeply. From your stomach. Feel it filling up with air!

I needed to pee...

Deedee came back from the foyer.
Someone was with her.

An audience member.

I didn't dare imagine what would
happen if I so much as twitched
anything around my stomach. Nothing
was filling up.

Muguette!

What's she doing here?

Why??

Everyone turned back to me.
Then something weird happened.
No more butterflies, no more anvil,
no more nuclear plant.
I saw my lines, dazzling as a
matador's cape. And I plunged, horns
lowered, in a kind of trance.

I can't explain what happened after
that. I saw Zoltan Lermontov's fiery
gaze. And Julius, and Deedee, and
Nina, all astonished.
And the others all silent.

And Muguette in the back, silently
clapping for me.

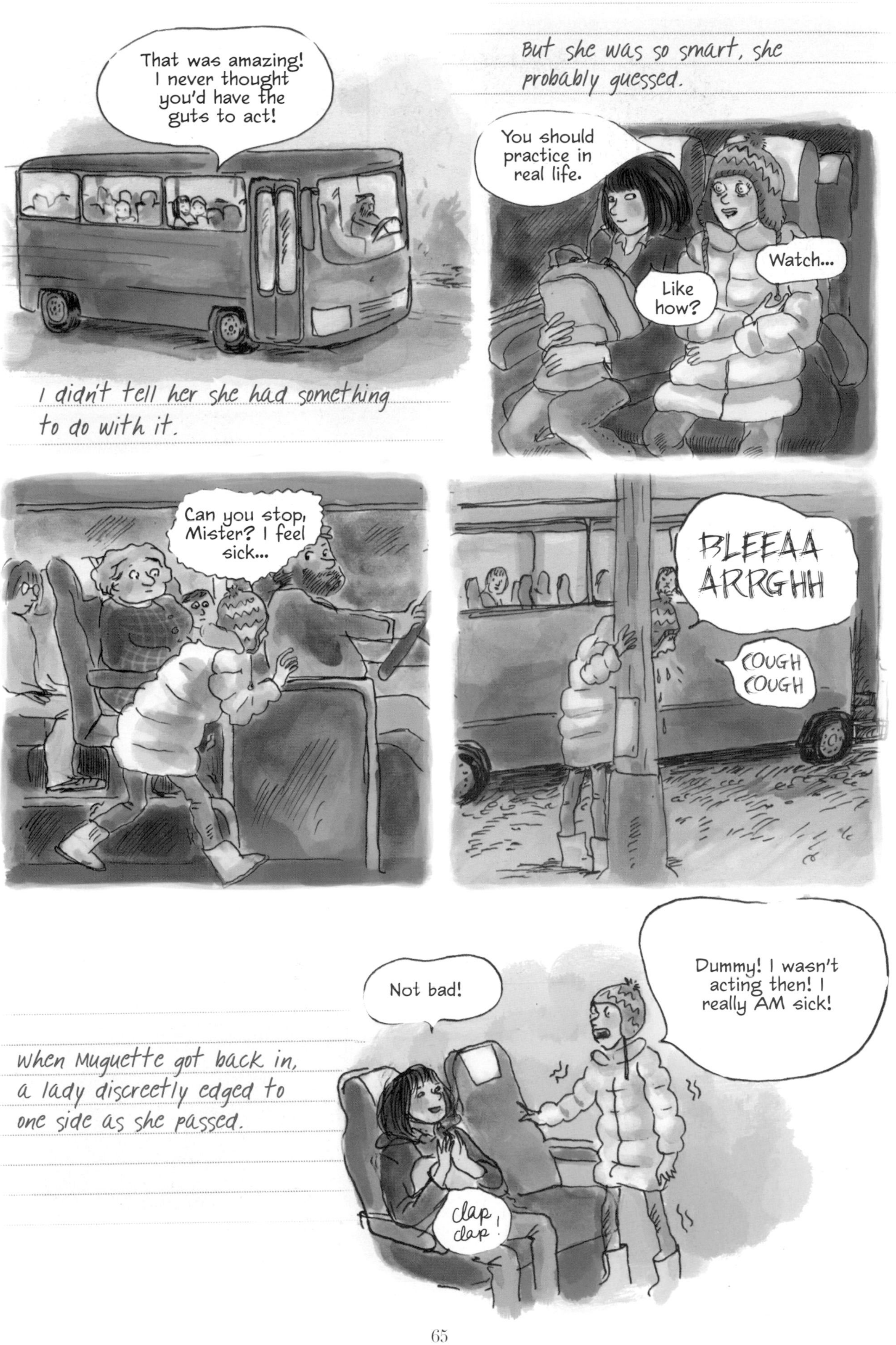
That was amazing! I never thought you'd have the guts to act!
I didn't tell her she had something to do with it.
But she was so smart, she probably guessed.
You should practice in real life.
Like how?
Watch...
Can you stop, Mister? I feel sick...
BLEEAA ARRGHH
COUGH COUGH
When Muguette got back in, a lady discreetly edged to one side as she passed.
Not bad!
Dummy! I wasn't acting then! I really AM sick!
clap, clap!

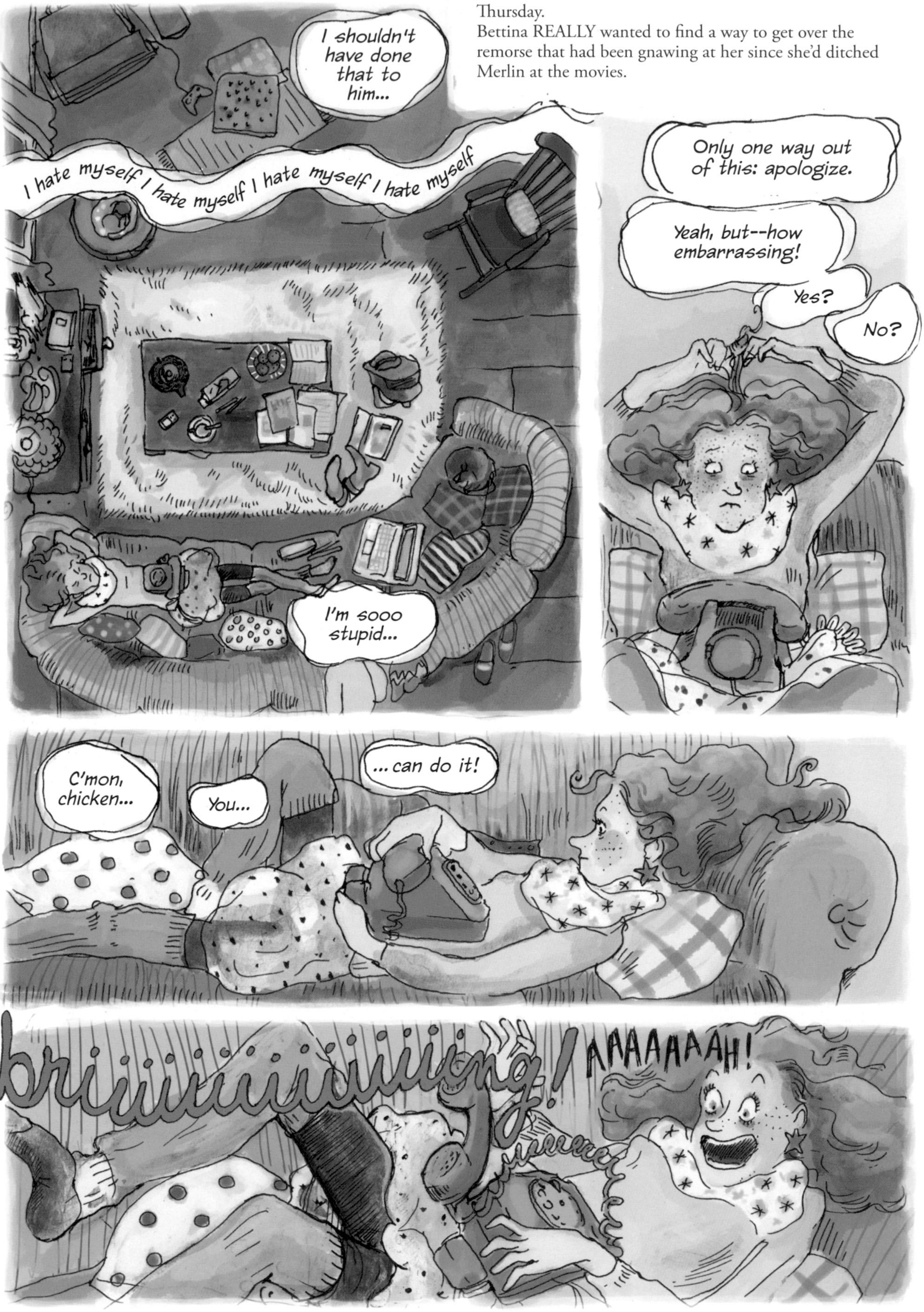
Thursday.
Bettina REALLY wanted to find a way to get over the remorse that had been gnawing at her since she'd ditched Merlin at the movies.
I shouldn't have done that to him...
I hate myself I hate myself I hate myself I hate myself
I'm sooo stupid...
Only one way out of this: apologize.
Yeah, but--how embarrassing!
Yes?
No?
C'mon, chicken...
You...
...can do it!
briiiiiiiiiiiing!
AAAAAAH!

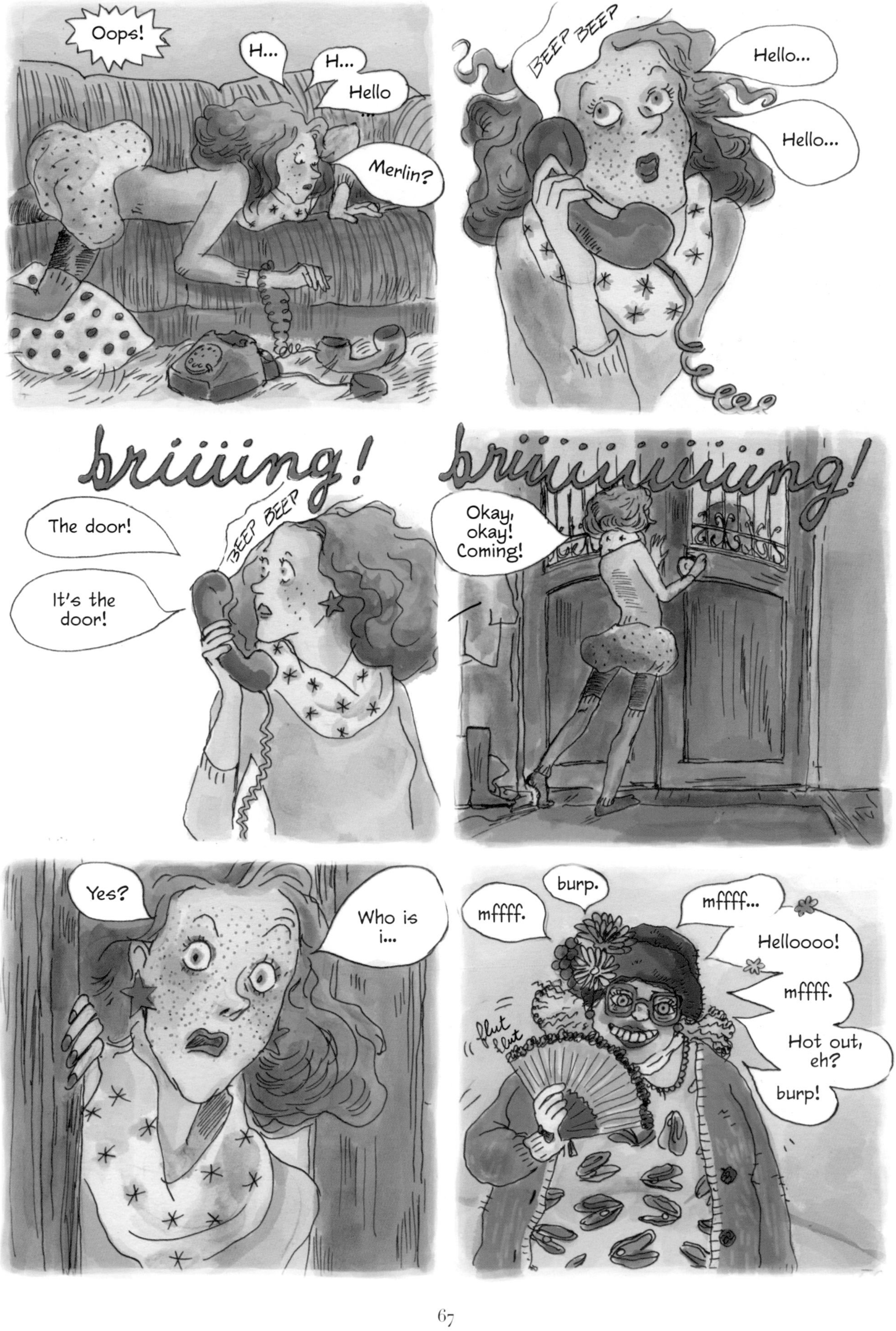
Oops!
H...
H...
Hello
...
Merlin?
BEEP BEEP
Hello...
Hello...
briiiing!
The door!
It's the door!
BEEP BEEP
briiiiiiiiing!
Okay, okay! Coming!
Yes?
Who is i...
mffff.
burp.
mffff...
Helloooo!
mffff.
Hot out, eh?
burp!
flut flut

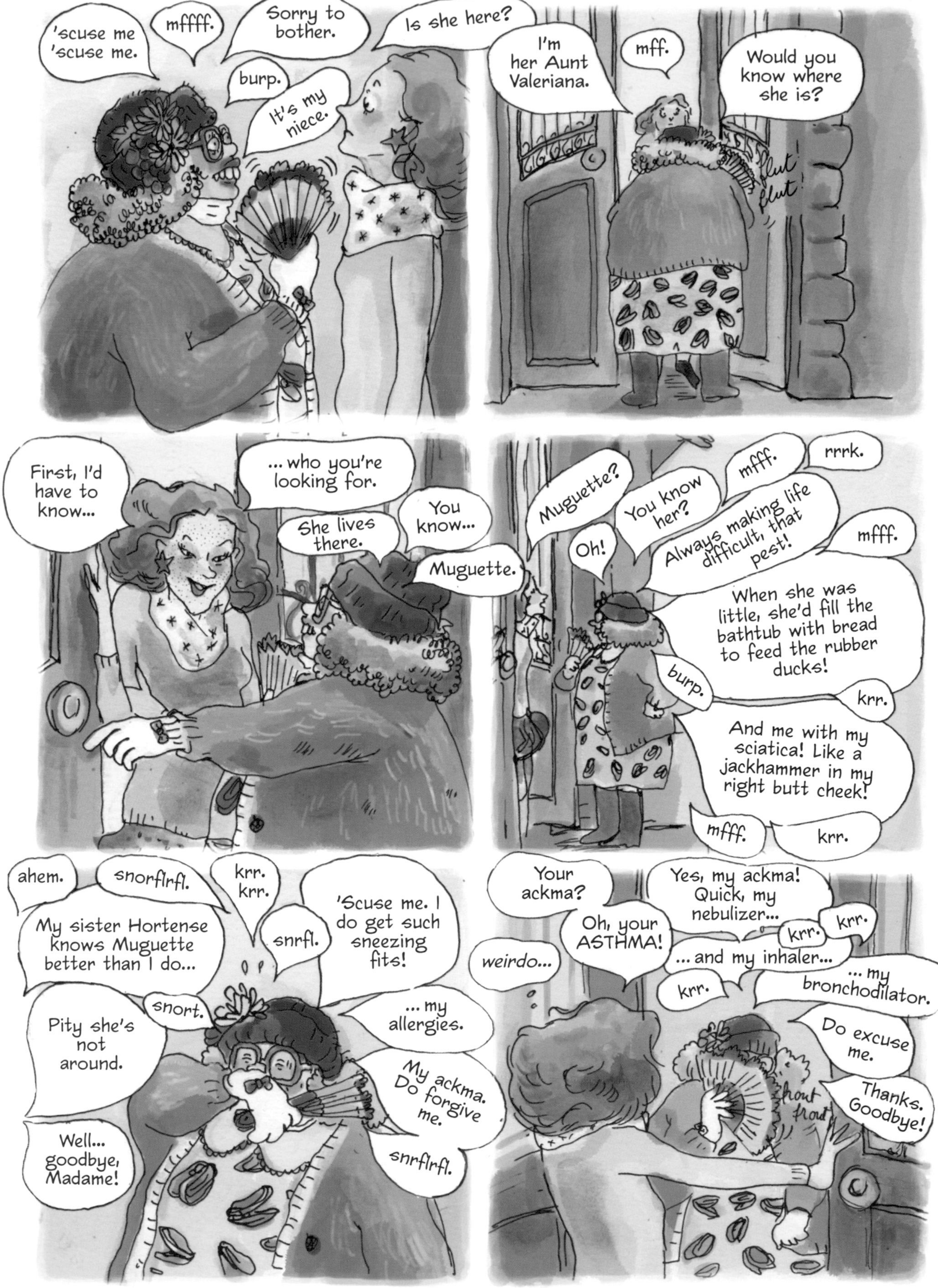
'scuse me 'scuse me.
mffff.
Sorry to bother.
Is she here?
burp.
It's my niece.
I'm her Aunt Valeriana.
mff.
Would you know where she is?
flut flut
First, I'd have to know...
... who you're looking for.
She lives there.
You know...
Muguette.
Muguette?
You know her?
mfff.
rrrk.
Oh!
Always making life difficult, that pest!
mfff.
When she was little, she'd fill the bathtub with bread to feed the rubber ducks!
burp.
krr.
And me with my sciatica! Like a jackhammer in my right butt cheek!
mfff.
krr.
ahem.
snorflrfl.
krr. krr.
My sister Hortense knows Muguette better than I do...
snrfl.
'Scuse me. I do get such sneezing fits!
snort.
Pity she's not around.
... my allergies.
My ackma. Do forgive me.
Well... goodbye, Madame!
snrflrfl.
Your ackma?
Yes, my ackma! Quick, my nebulizer...
Oh, your ASTHMA!
krr.
krr.
weirdo...
... and my inhaler...
krr.
... my bronchodilator.
Do excuse me.
frout frout
Thanks. Goodbye!

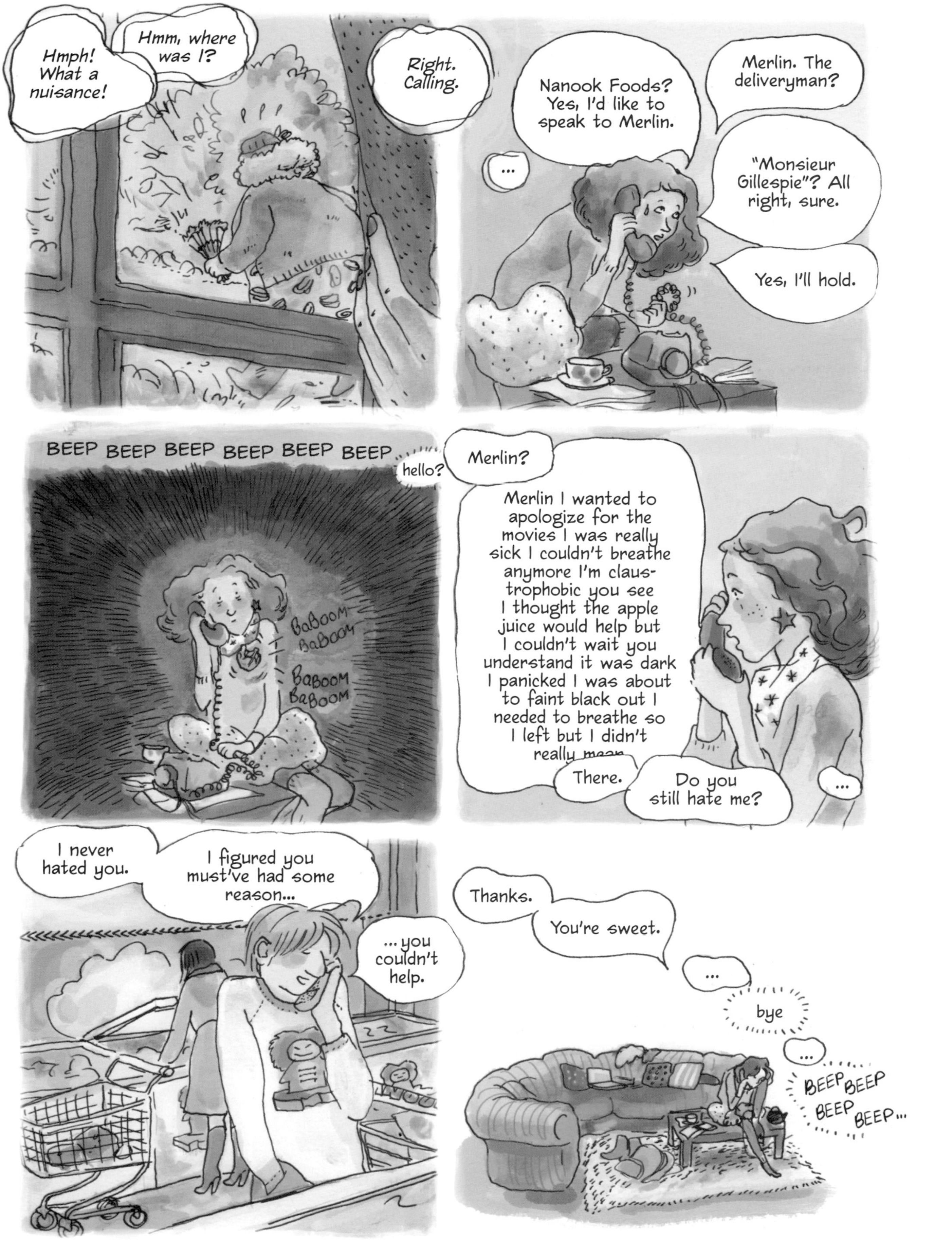
Hmph! What a nuisance!
Hmm, where was I?
Right. Calling.
Nanook Foods? Yes, I'd like to speak to Merlin.
Merlin. The deliveryman?
...
"Monsieur Gillespie"? All right, sure.
Yes, I'll hold.
BEEP BEEP BEEP BEEP BEEP BEEP
BaBOOM BaBOOM
BaBOOM BaBOOM
hello?
Merlin?
Merlin I wanted to apologize for the movies I was really sick I couldn't breathe anymore I'm claus-trophobic you see I thought the apple juice would help but I couldn't wait you understand it was dark I panicked I was about to faint black out I needed to breathe so I left but I didn't really mean
There.
Do you still hate me?
...
I never hated you.
I figured you must've had some reason...
...you couldn't help.
Thanks.
You're sweet.
...
bye
...
BEEP BEEP BEEP BEEP...

When Bettina hung up, she felt like a marathon runner crossing the finish line: relieved, exhausted, overjoyed...

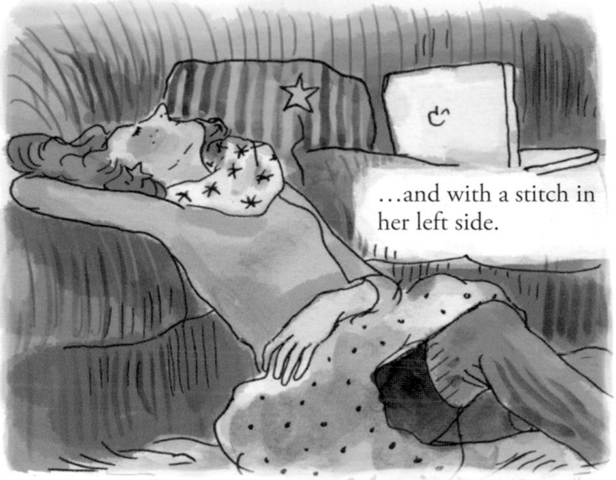
...and with a stitch in her left side.

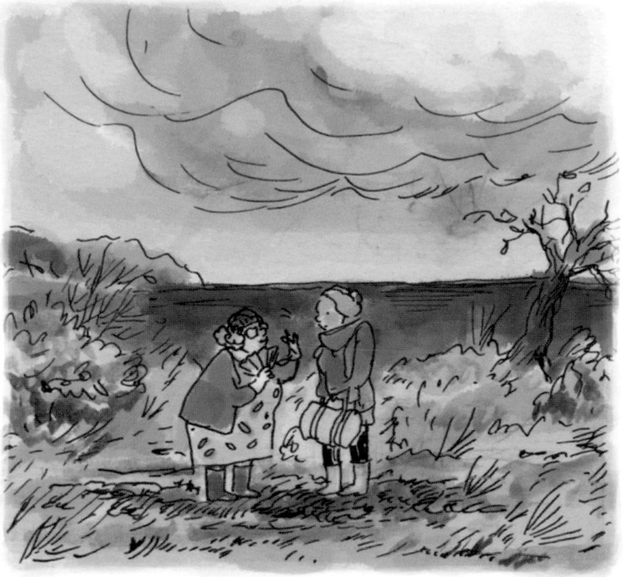

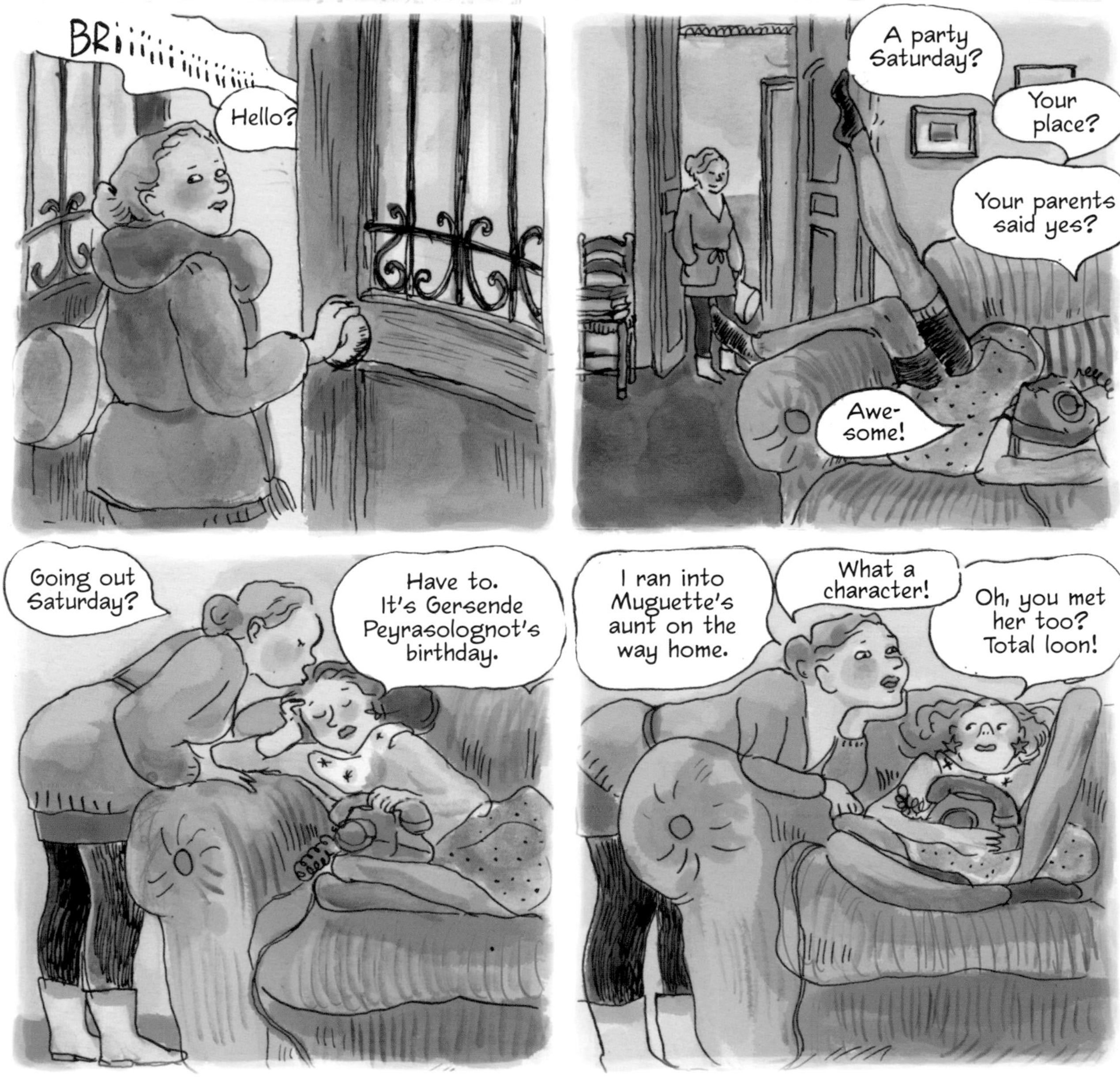
BRiiiiiiiiiiiiii
Hello?
A party Saturday?
Your place?
Your parents said yes?
Awe-some!
Going out Saturday?
Have to. It's Gersende Peyrasolognot's birthday.
I ran into Muguette's aunt on the way home.
What a character!
Oh, you met her too? Total loon!

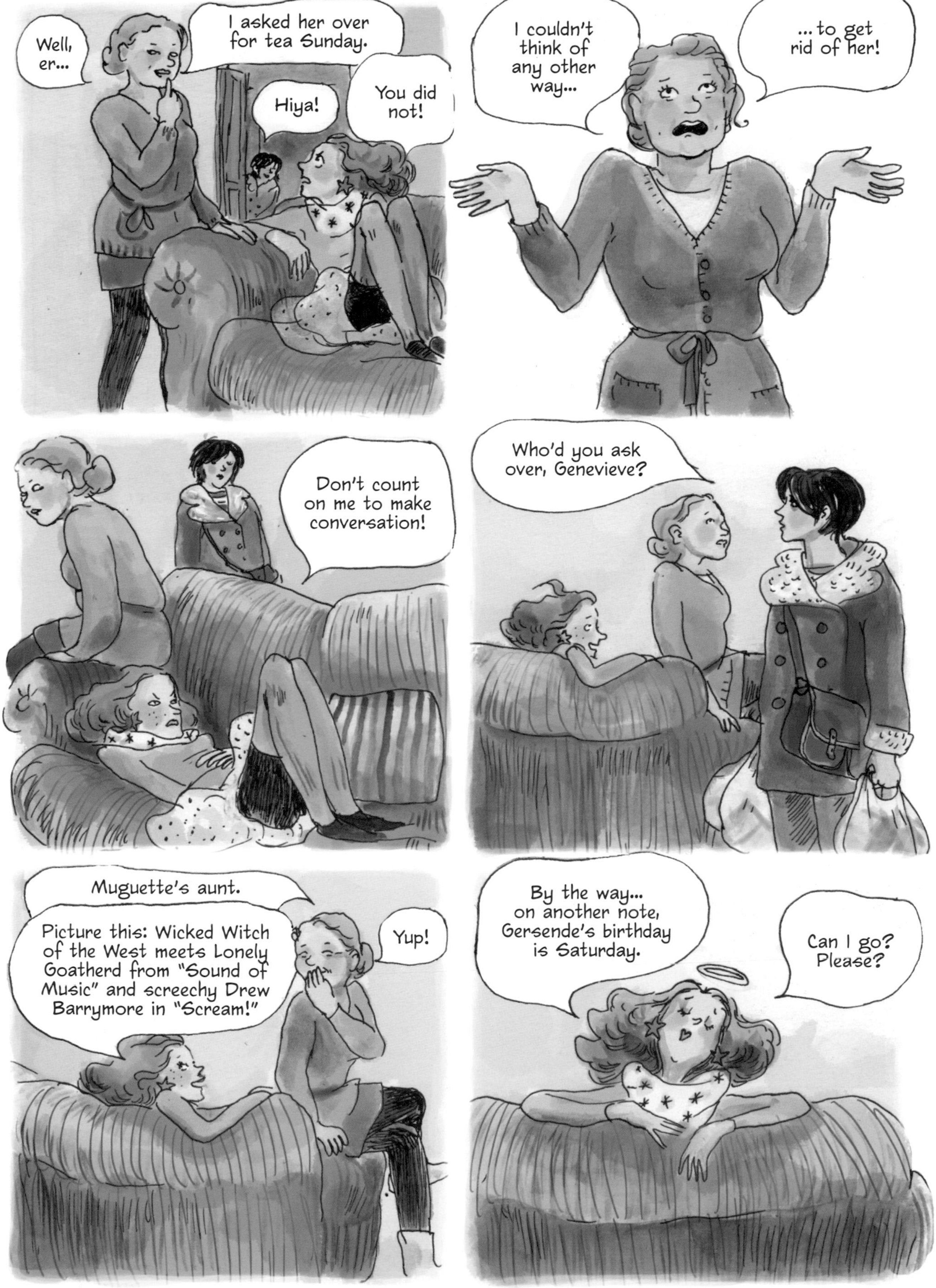

Well, er...
I asked her over for tea Sunday.
Hiya!
You did not!
I couldn't think of any other way...
... to get rid of her!
Don't count on me to make conversation!
Who'd you ask over, Genevieve?
Muguette's aunt.
Picture this: Wicked Witch of the West meets Lonely Goatherd from "Sound of Music" and screechy Drew Barrymore in "Scream!"
Yup!
By the way... on another note, Gersende's birthday is Saturday.
Can I go? Please?

Saturday.
Gersende's parents let her use their garage and rented two flashy fluorescent spotlights.

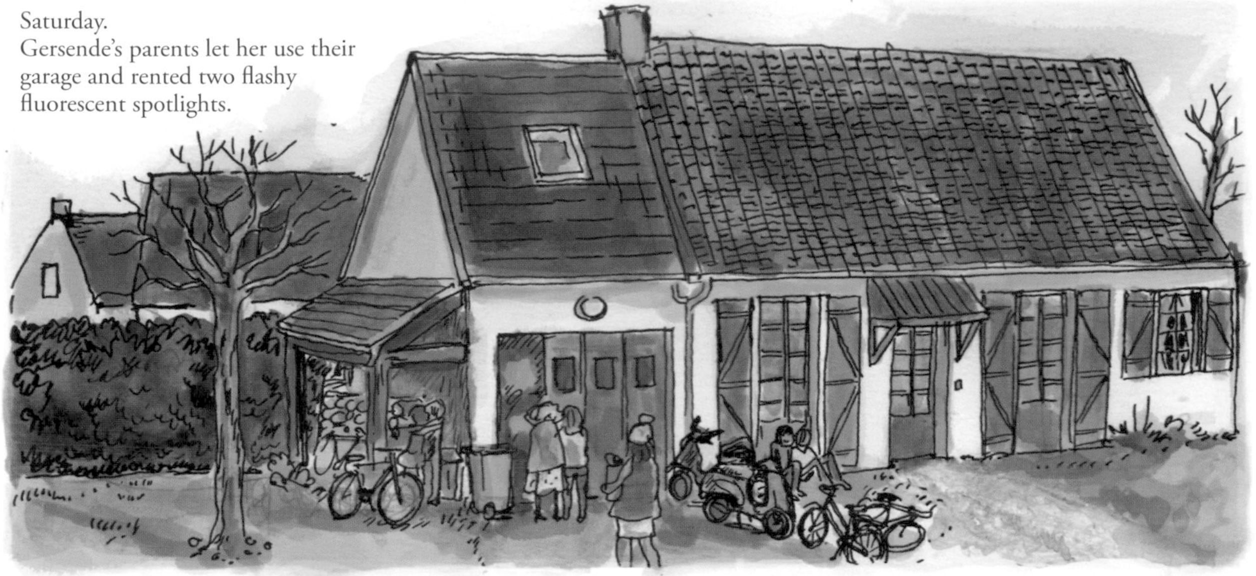

Gersende's oldest brother, Aurèle, was the DJ. There were about six pounds of chips and candy per person...

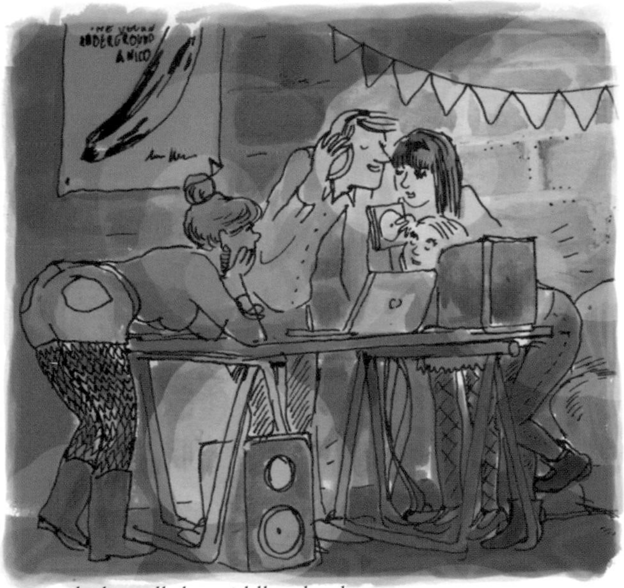

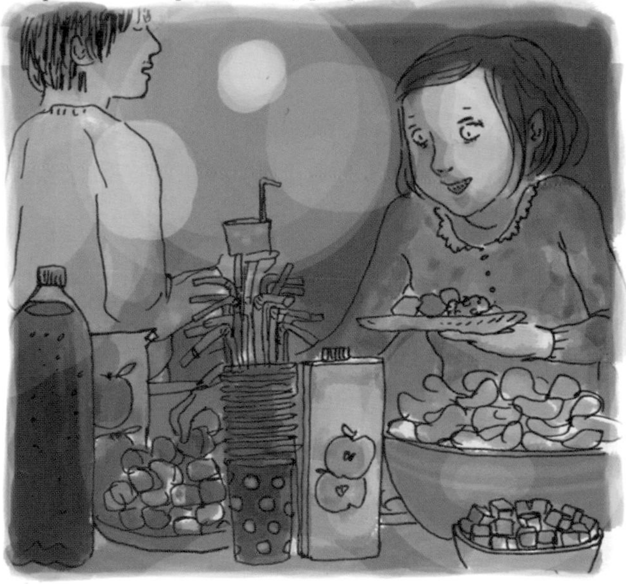

...including all the middle schoolers.

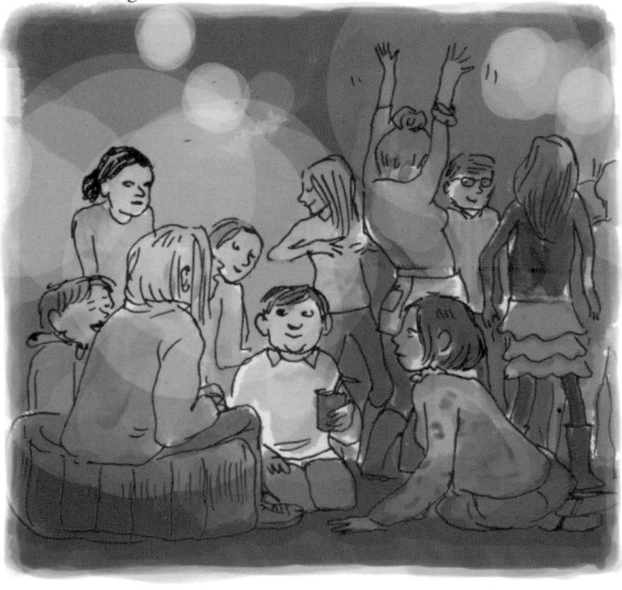

Among whom was Julianne: not a particularly interesting or popular girl, but today she had a juicy story to share:

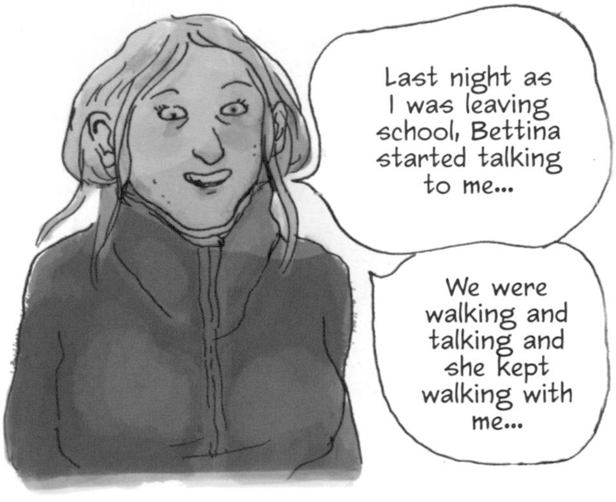
Last night as I was leaving school, Bettina started talking to me...
We were walking and talking and she kept walking with me...

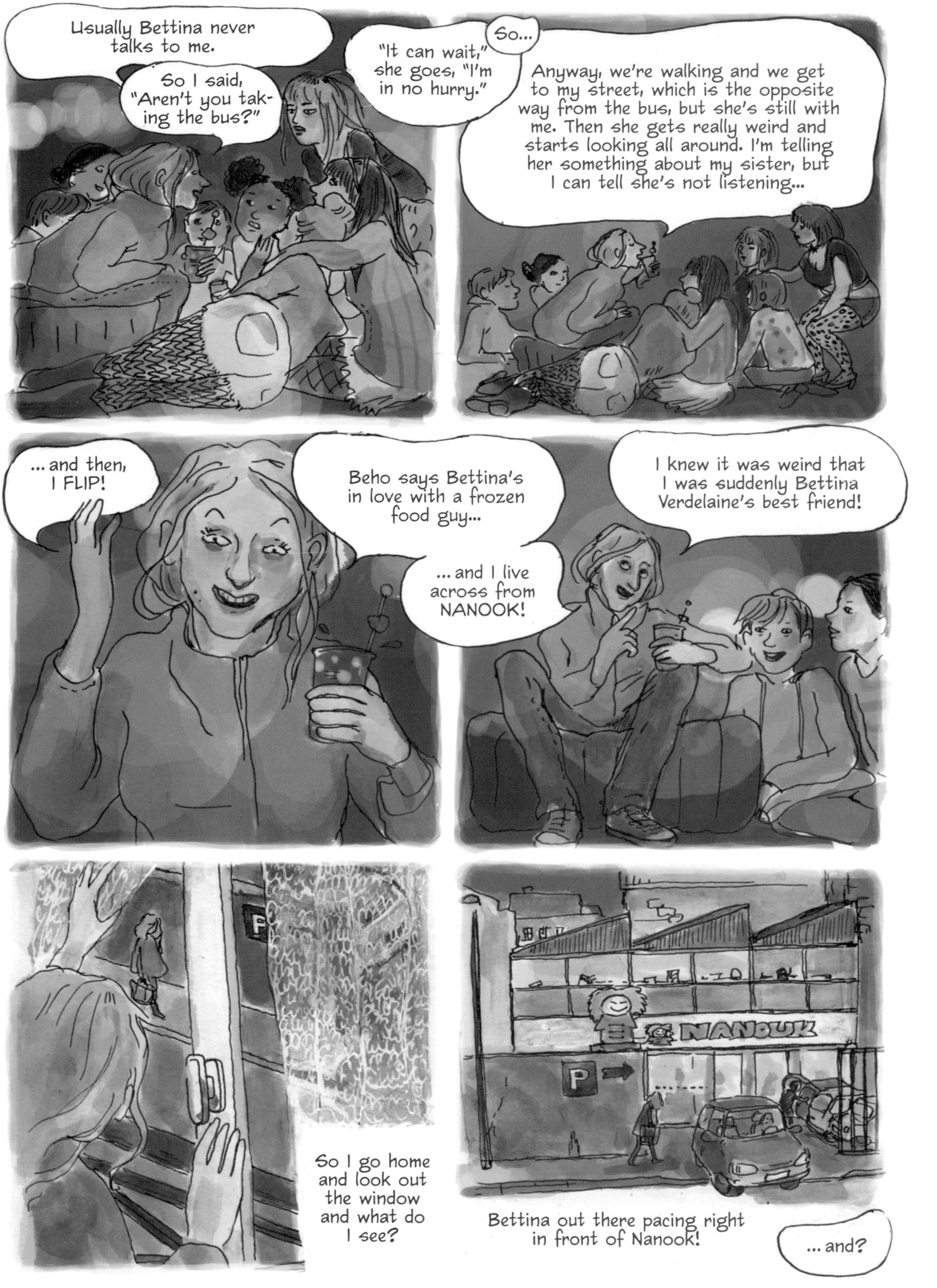
Usually Bettina never talks to me.
So I said, "Aren't you taking the bus?"
"It can wait," she goes, "I'm in no hurry."
So...
Anyway, we're walking and we get to my street, which is the opposite way from the bus, but she's still with me. Then she gets really weird and starts looking all around. I'm telling her something about my sister, but I can tell she's not listening...
... and then, I FLIP!
Beho says Bettina's in love with a frozen food guy...
... and I live across from NANOOK!
I knew it was weird that I was suddenly Bettina Verdelaine's best friend!
P
So I go home and look out the window and what do I see?
NANOUK
P
Bettina out there pacing right in front of Nanook!
... and?

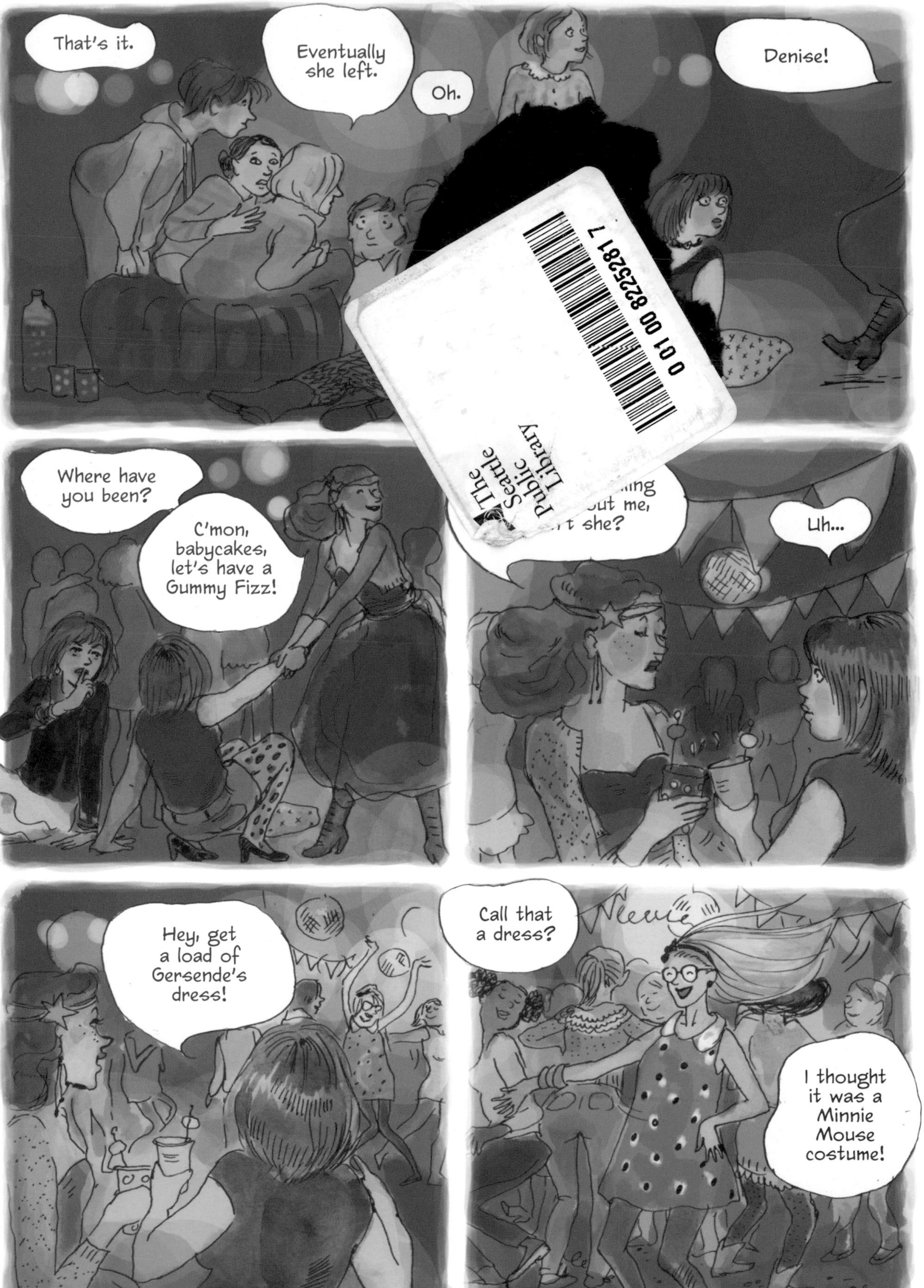
That's it.
Eventually she left.
Oh.
Denise!
Where have you been?
C'mon, babycakes, let's have a Gummy Fizz!
Uh...
Hey, get a load of Gersende's dress!
Call that a dress?
I thought it was a Minnie Mouse costume!

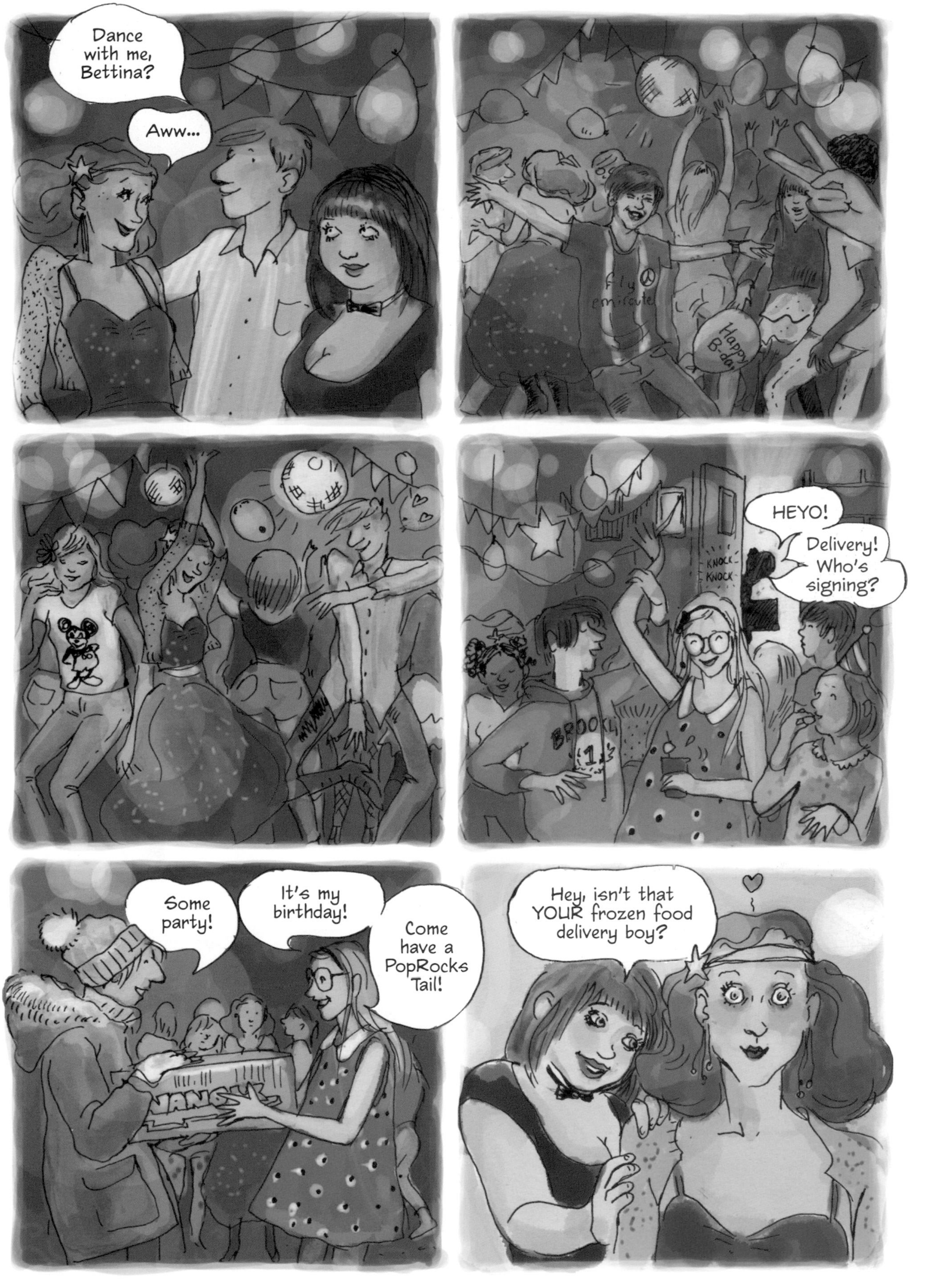

Dance with me, Bettina?
Aww...
fly emircute
Happy B-day
HEYO!
KNOCK KNOCK
Delivery! Who's signing?
BROOKL 1
Some party!
It's my birthday!
Come have a PopRocks Tail!
Hey, isn't that YOUR frozen food delivery boy?

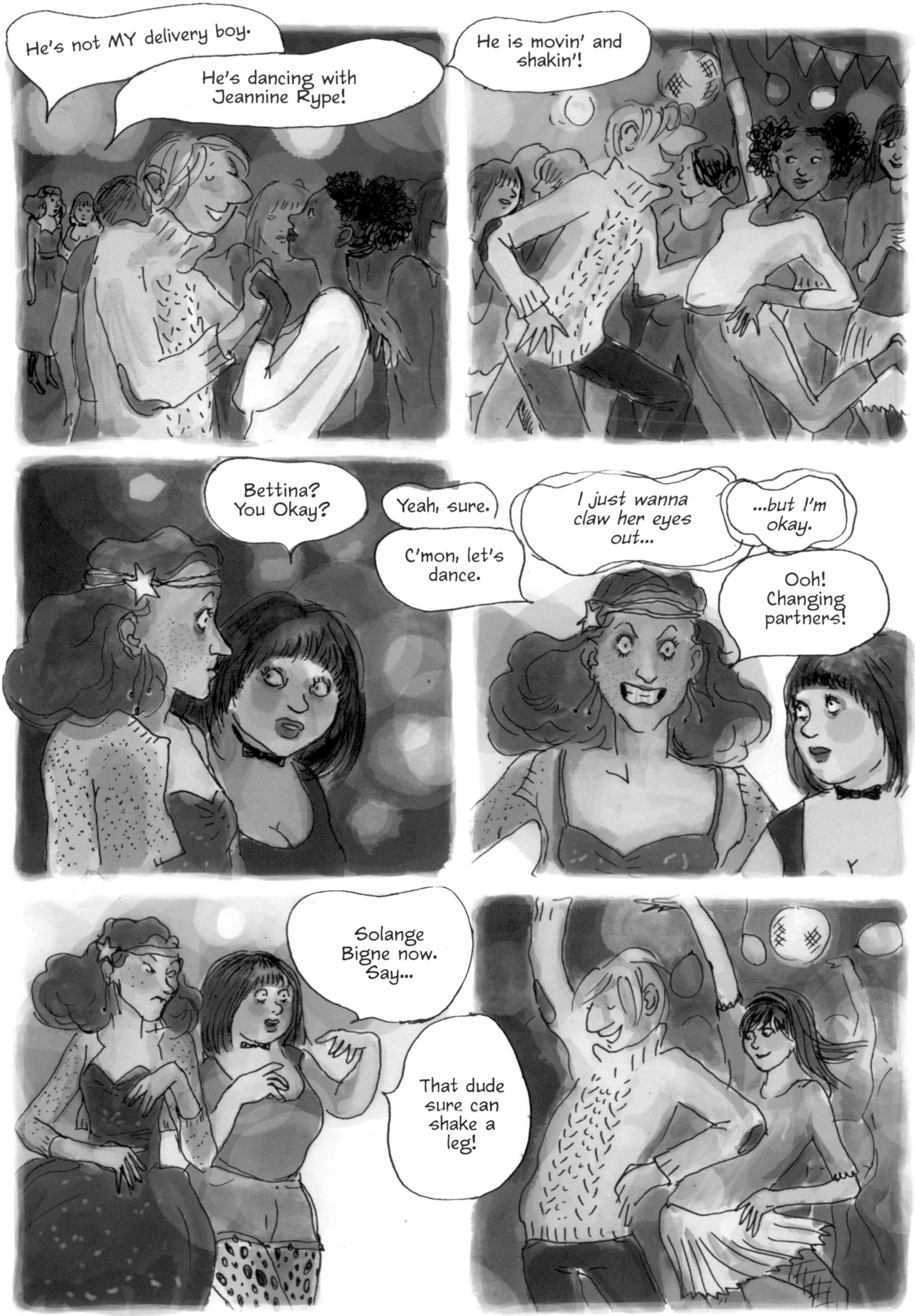
He's not MY delivery boy.
He's dancing with Jeannine Rype!
He is movin' and shakin'!
Bettina? You Okay?
Yeah, sure.
C'mon, let's dance.
I just wanna claw her eyes out...
...but I'm okay.
Ooh! Changing partners!
Solange Bigne now. Say...
That dude sure can shake a leg!

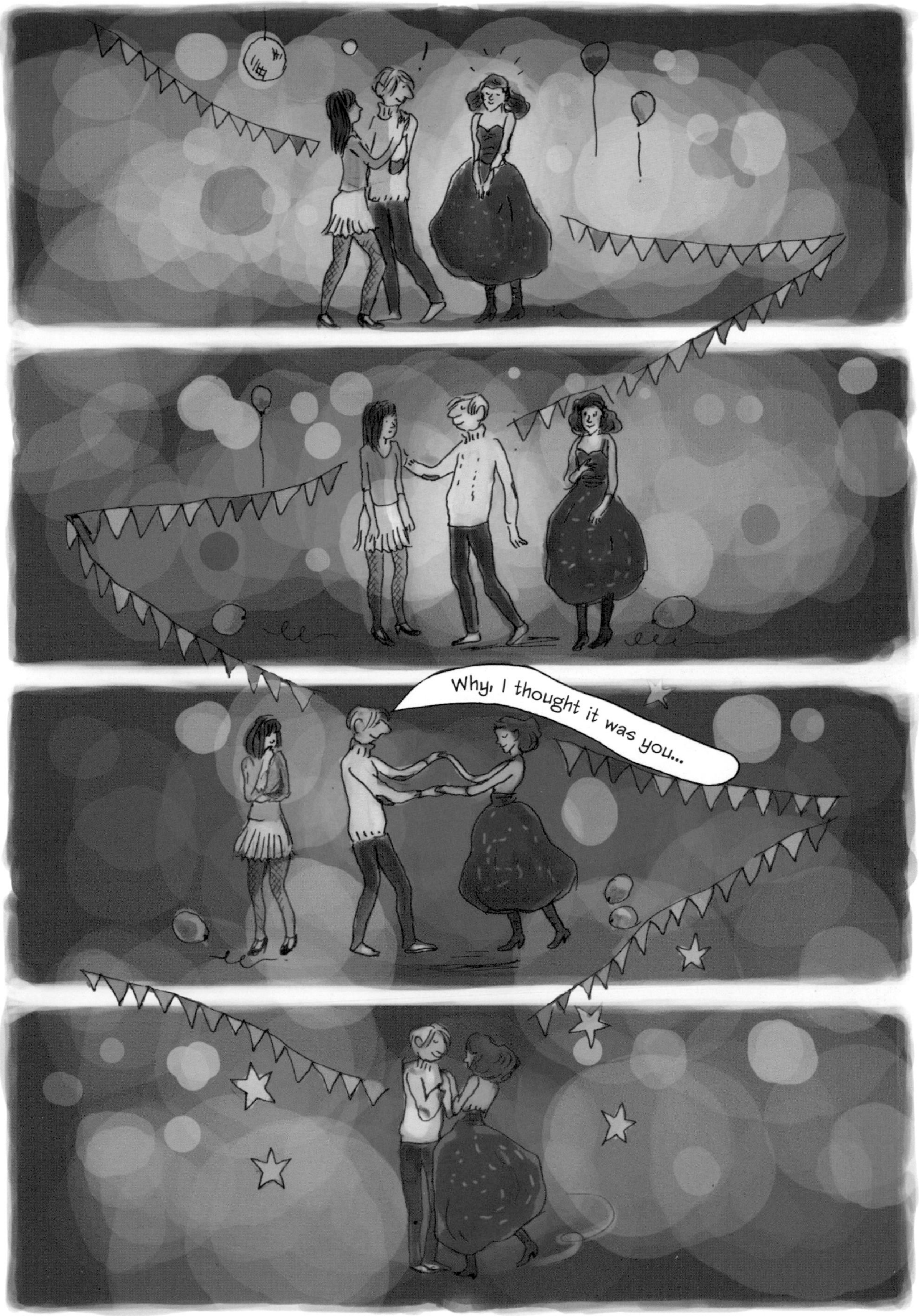
Why, I thought it was you...

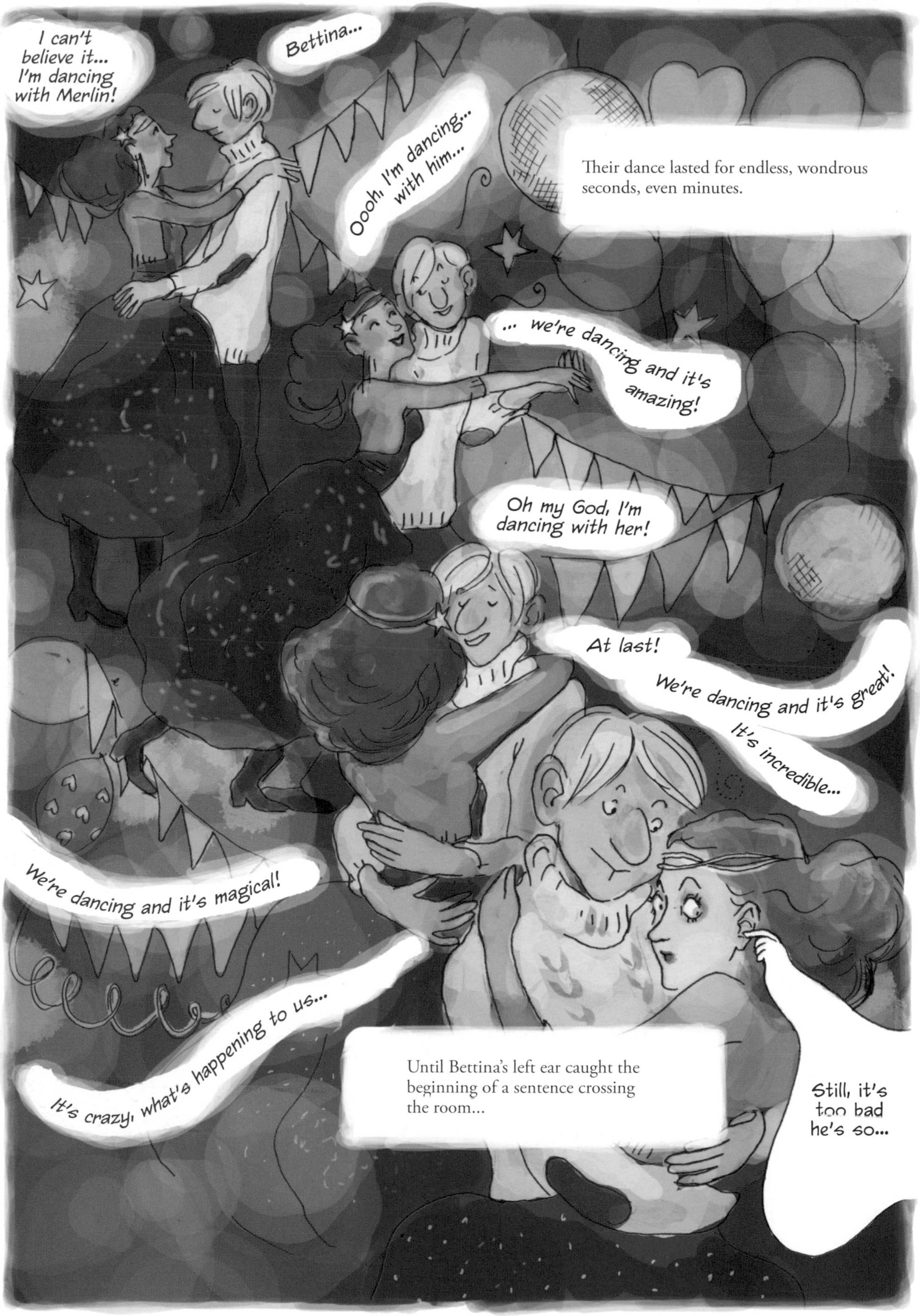
I can't believe it... I'm dancing with Merlin!
Bettina...
Oooh, I'm dancing... with him...
Their dance lasted for endless, wondrous seconds, even minutes.
... we're dancing and it's amazing!
Oh my God, I'm dancing with her!
At last!
We're dancing and it's great!
It's incredible...
We're dancing and it's magical!
It's crazy, what's happening to us...
Until Bettina's left ear caught the beginning of a sentence crossing the room...
Still, it's too bad he's so...

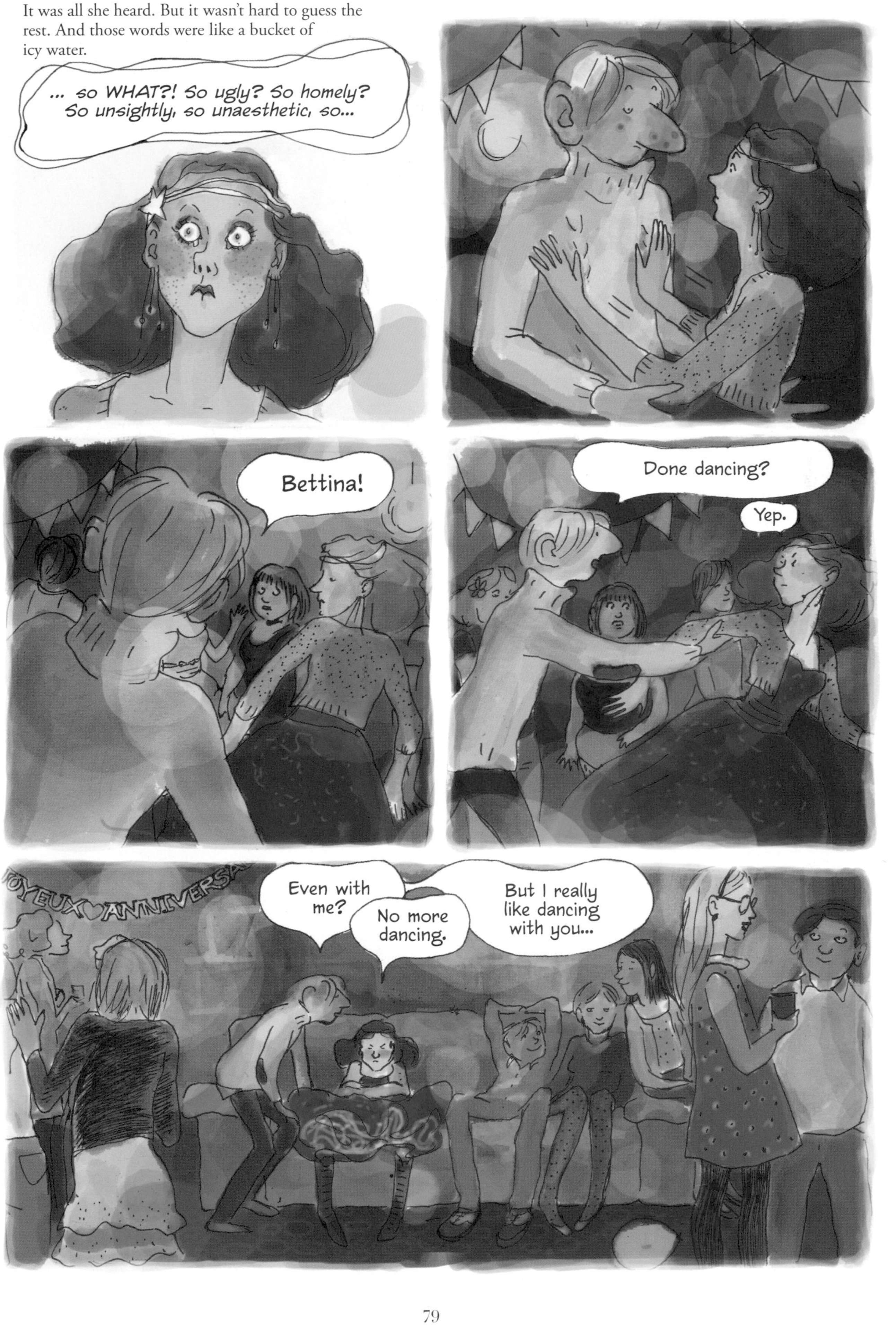
It was all she heard. But it wasn't hard to guess the rest. And those words were like a bucket of icy water.
... so WHAT?! So ugly? So homely? So unsightly, so unaesthetic, so...
Bettina!
Done dancing?
Yep.
Even with me?
No more dancing.
But I really like dancing with you...

Bettina felt terrible, angry. A pot boiling over with bitterness, hissing and spitting. And Merlin couldn't see a thing. She hated him even more for being so nice, for not getting it...

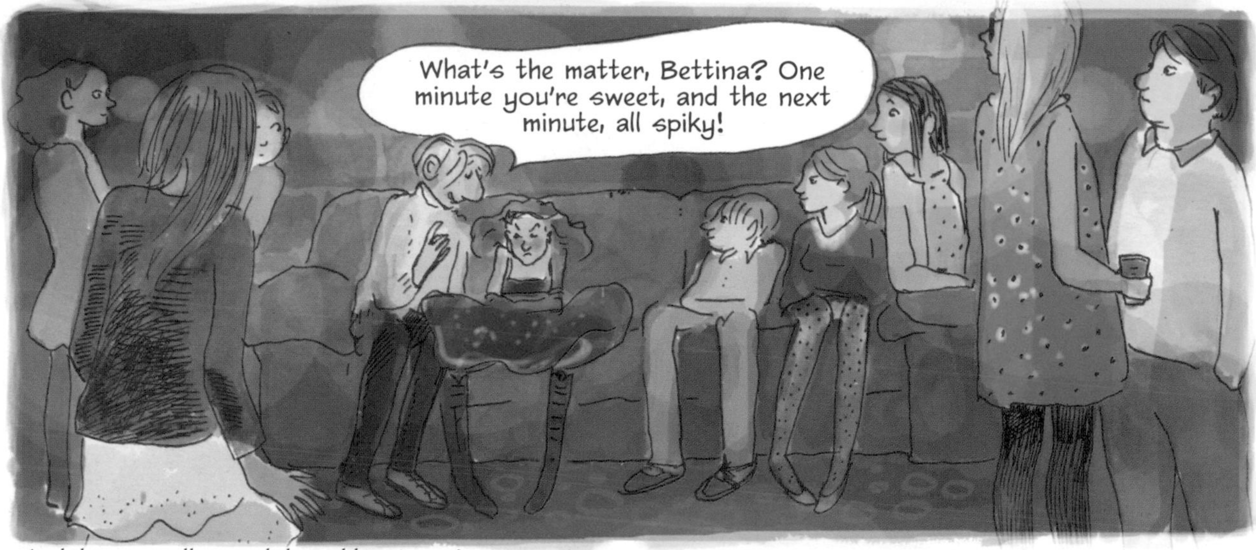
What's the matter, Bettina? One minute you're sweet, and the next minute, all spiky!

And those eyes all around them, like stingers!

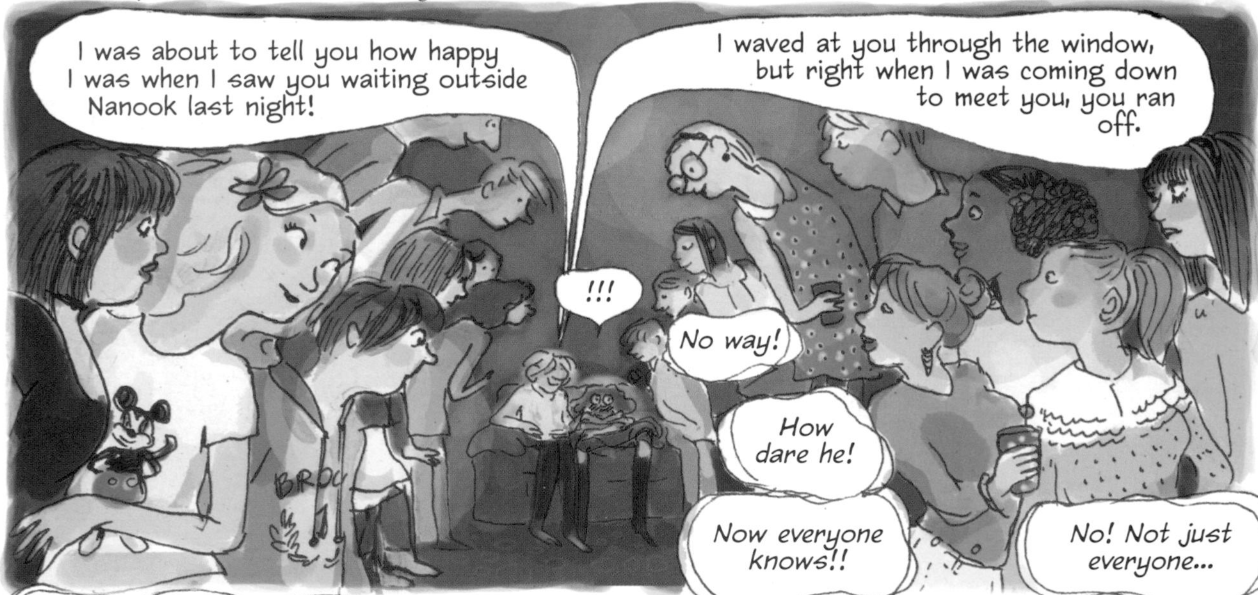
I was about to tell you how happy I was when I saw you waiting outside Nanook last night!
I waved at you through the window, but right when I was coming down to meet you, you ran off.
!!!
No way!
How dare he!
Now everyone knows!!
No! Not just everyone...

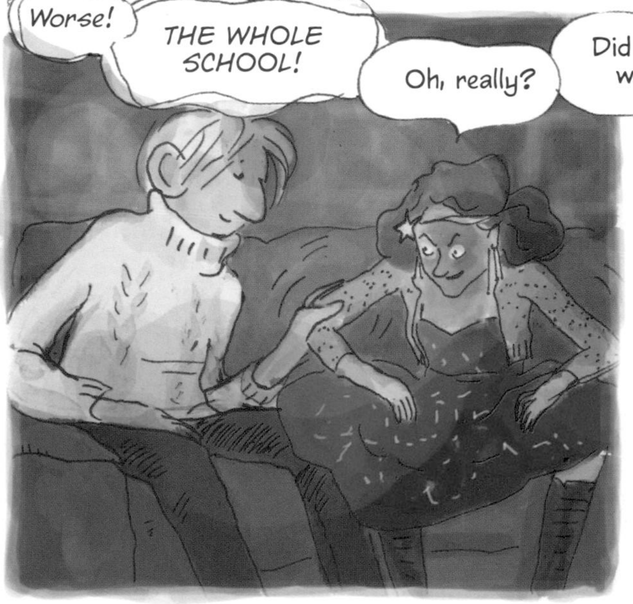
Worse!
THE WHOLE SCHOOL!
Oh, really?

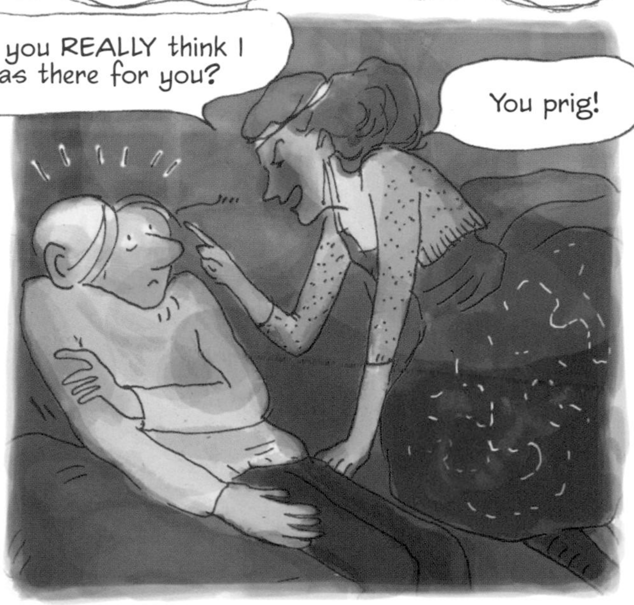
Did you REALLY think I was there for you?
You prig!

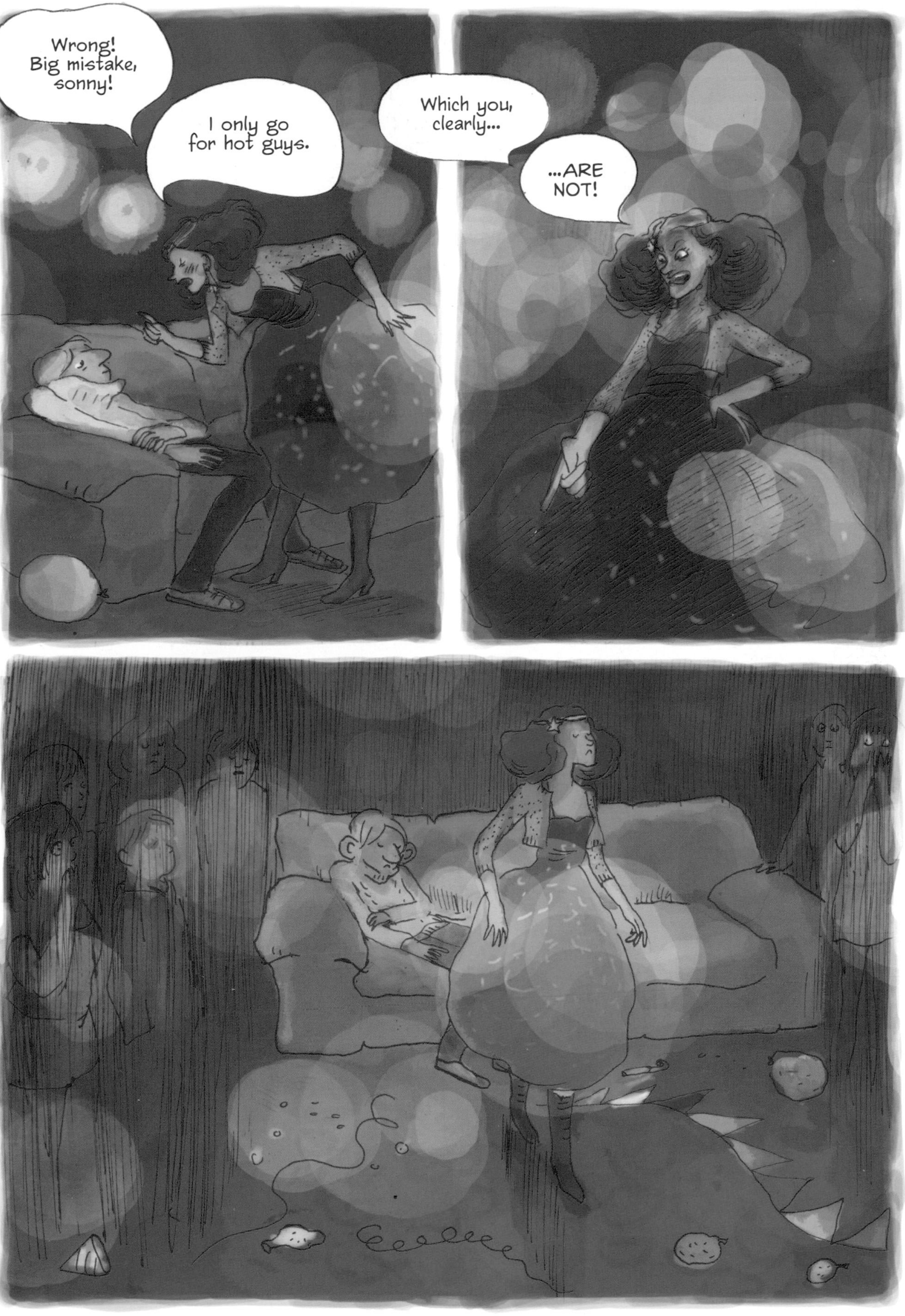

Wrong! Big mistake, sonny!
I only go for hot guys.
Which you, clearly...
...ARE NOT!

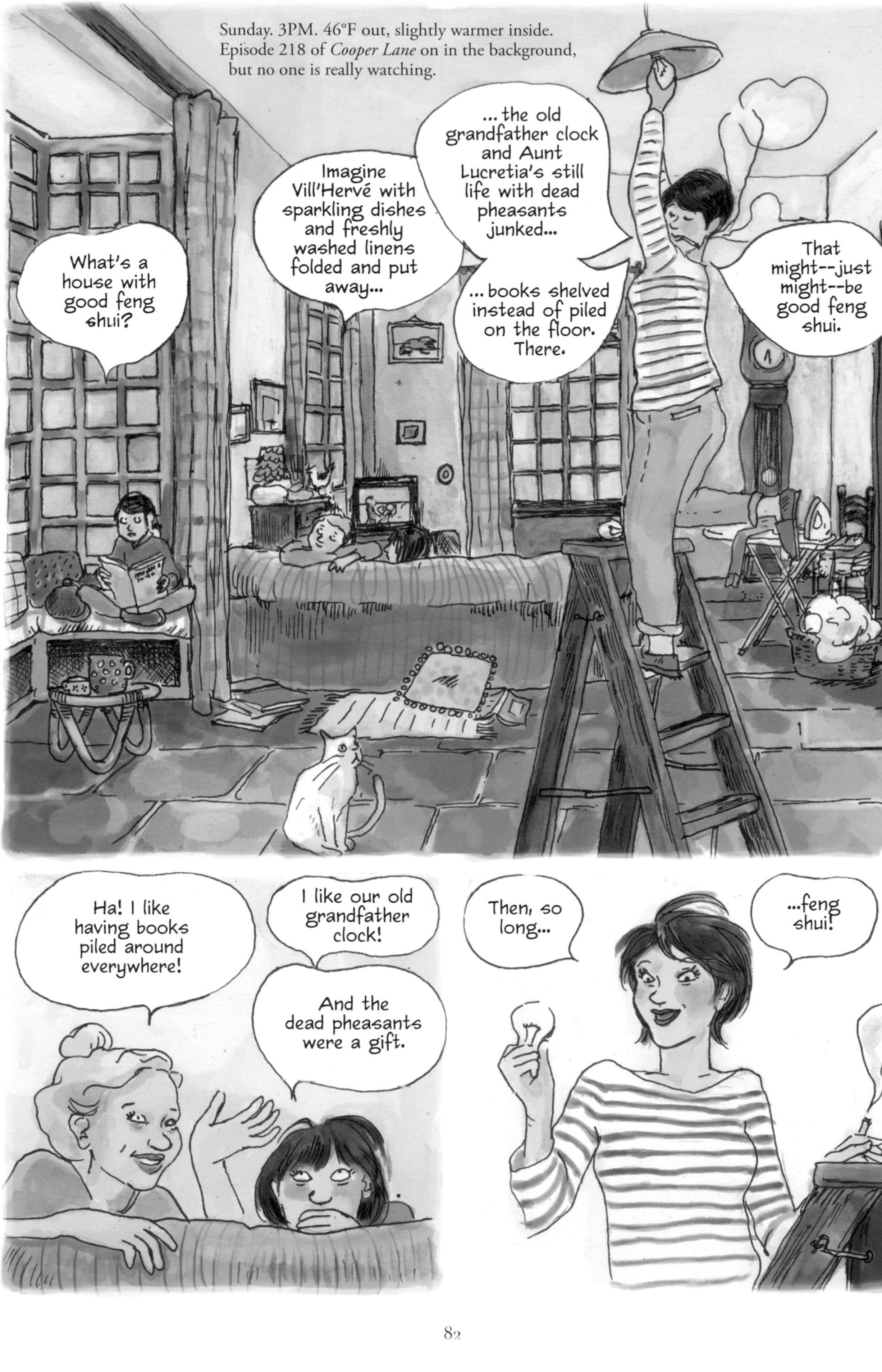

Sunday. 3PM. 46°F out, slightly warmer inside. Episode 218 of *Cooper Lane* on in the background, but no one is really watching.
What's a house with good feng shui?
Imagine Vill'Hervé with sparkling dishes and freshly washed linens folded and put away...
... the old grandfather clock and Aunt Lucretia's still life with dead pheasants junked...
... books shelved instead of piled on the floor. There.
That might--just might--be good feng shui.
Ha! I like having books piled around everywhere!
I like our old grandfather clock!
And the dead pheasants were a gift.
Then, so long...
...feng shui!

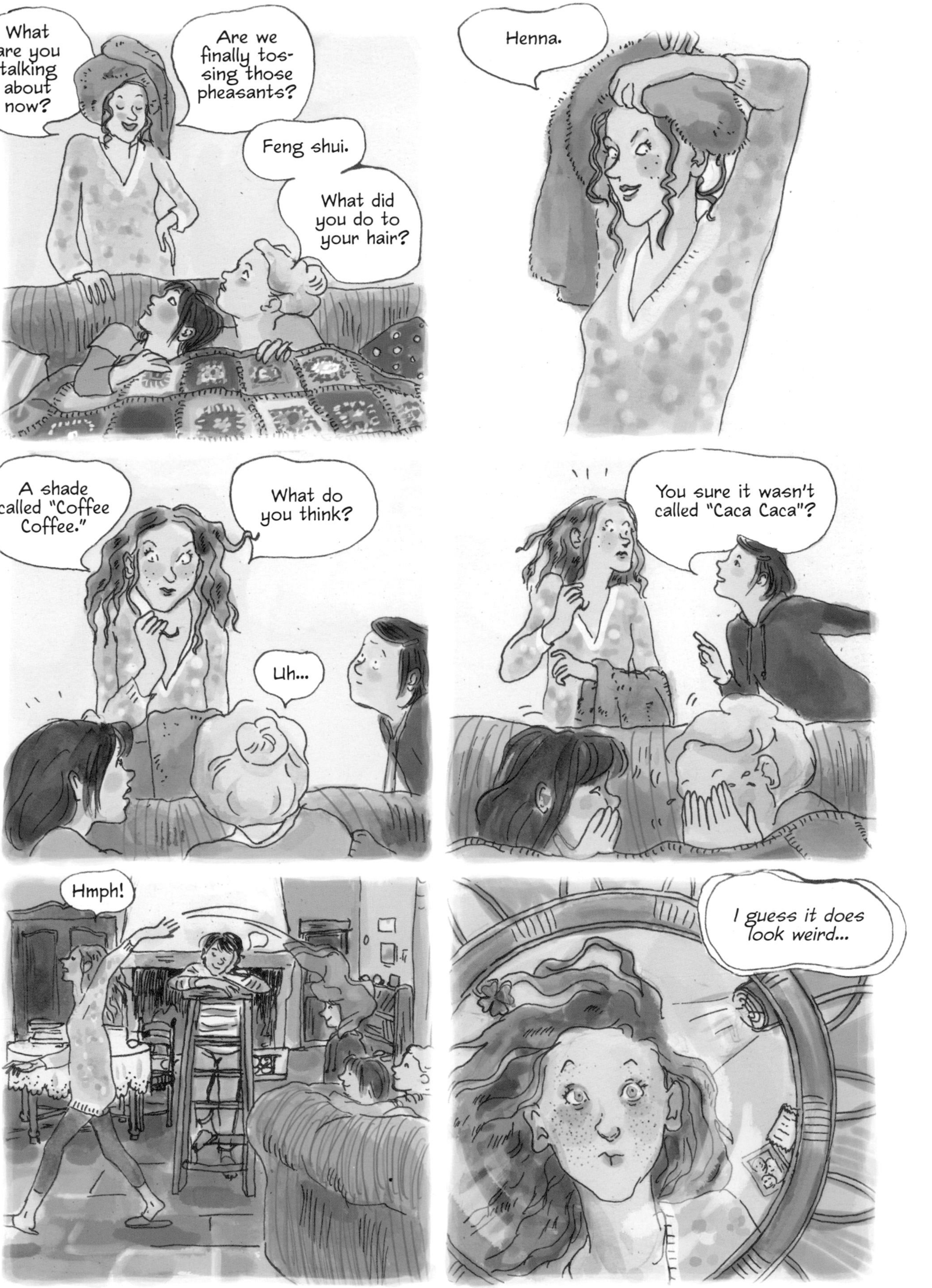
What are you talking about now?
Are we finally tossing those pheasants?
Feng shui.
What did you do to your hair?
Henna.
A shade called "Coffee Coffee."
What do you think?
Uh...
You sure it wasn't called "Caca Caca"?
Hmph!
I guess it does look weird...

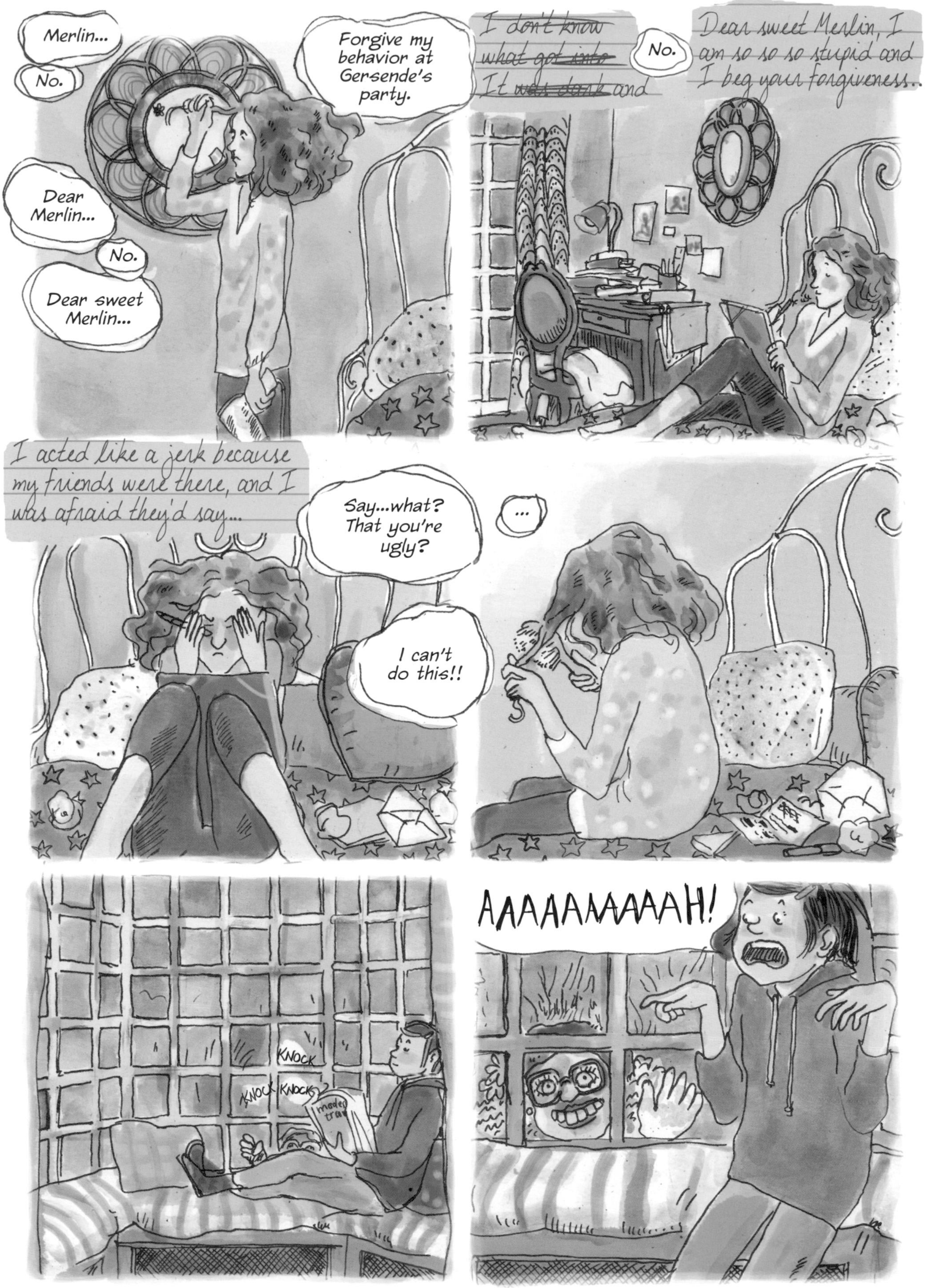
Merlin...
No.
Dear Merlin...
No.
Dear sweet Merlin...
Forgive my behavior at Gersende's party.
~~I don't know what got into~~
~~It was dark~~ and
No.
Dear sweet Merlin, I am so so so stupid and I beg your forgiveness...
I acted like a jerk because my friends were there, and I was afraid they'd say...
Say...what? That you're ugly?
I can't do this!!
...
KNOCK
KNOCK KNOCK
AAAAAAAAAAH!

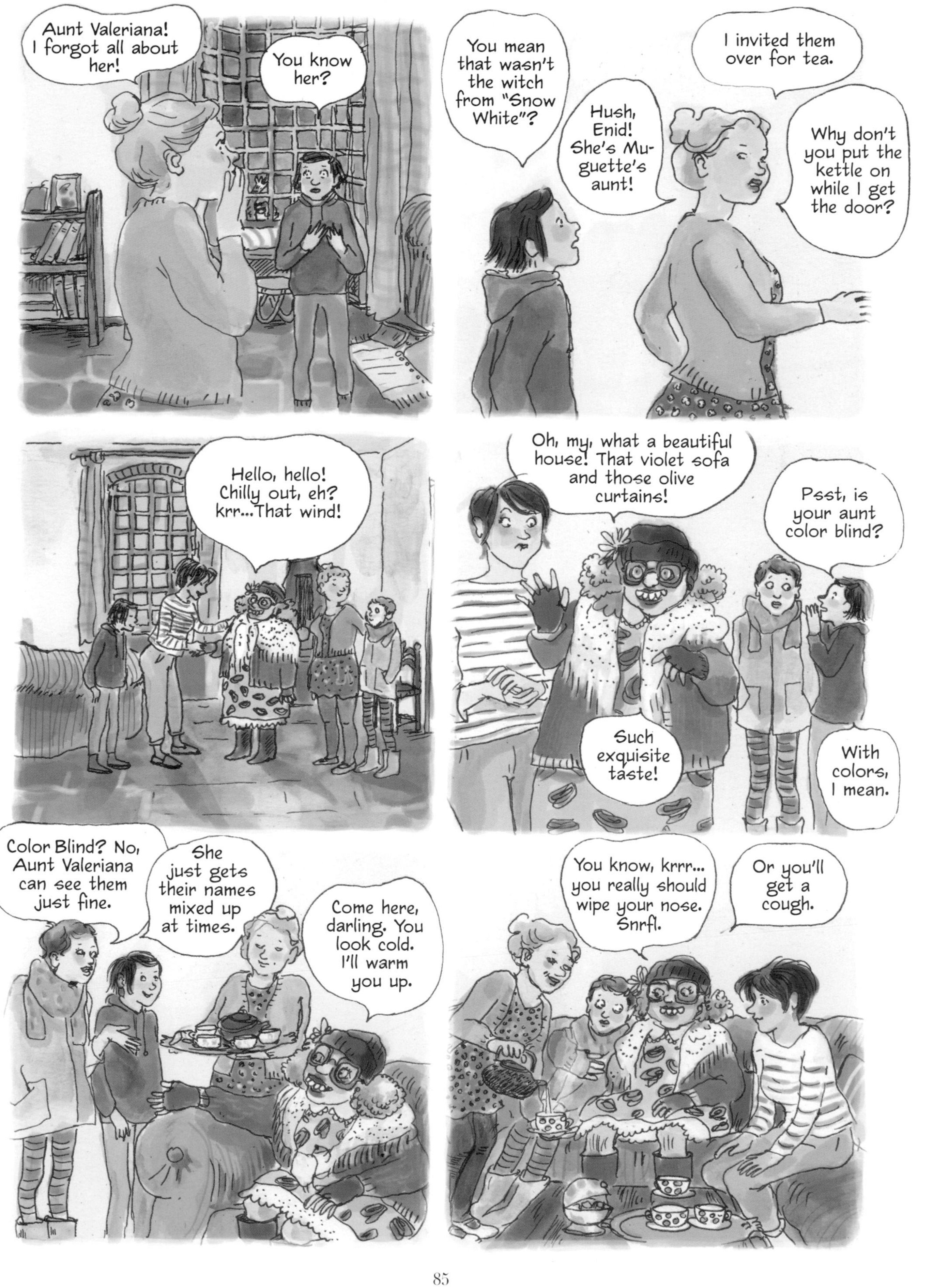
Aunt Valeriana! I forgot all about her!
You know her?
You mean that wasn't the witch from "Snow White"?
Hush, Enid! She's Muguette's aunt!
I invited them over for tea.
Why don't you put the kettle on while I get the door?
Hello, hello! Chilly out, eh? krr...That wind!
Oh, my, what a beautiful house! That violet sofa and those olive curtains!
Such exquisite taste!
Psst, is your aunt color blind?
With colors, I mean.
Color Blind? No, Aunt Valeriana can see them just fine.
She just gets their names mixed up at times.
Come here, darling. You look cold. I'll warm you up.
You know, krrr... you really should wipe your nose. Snrfl.
Or you'll get a cough.

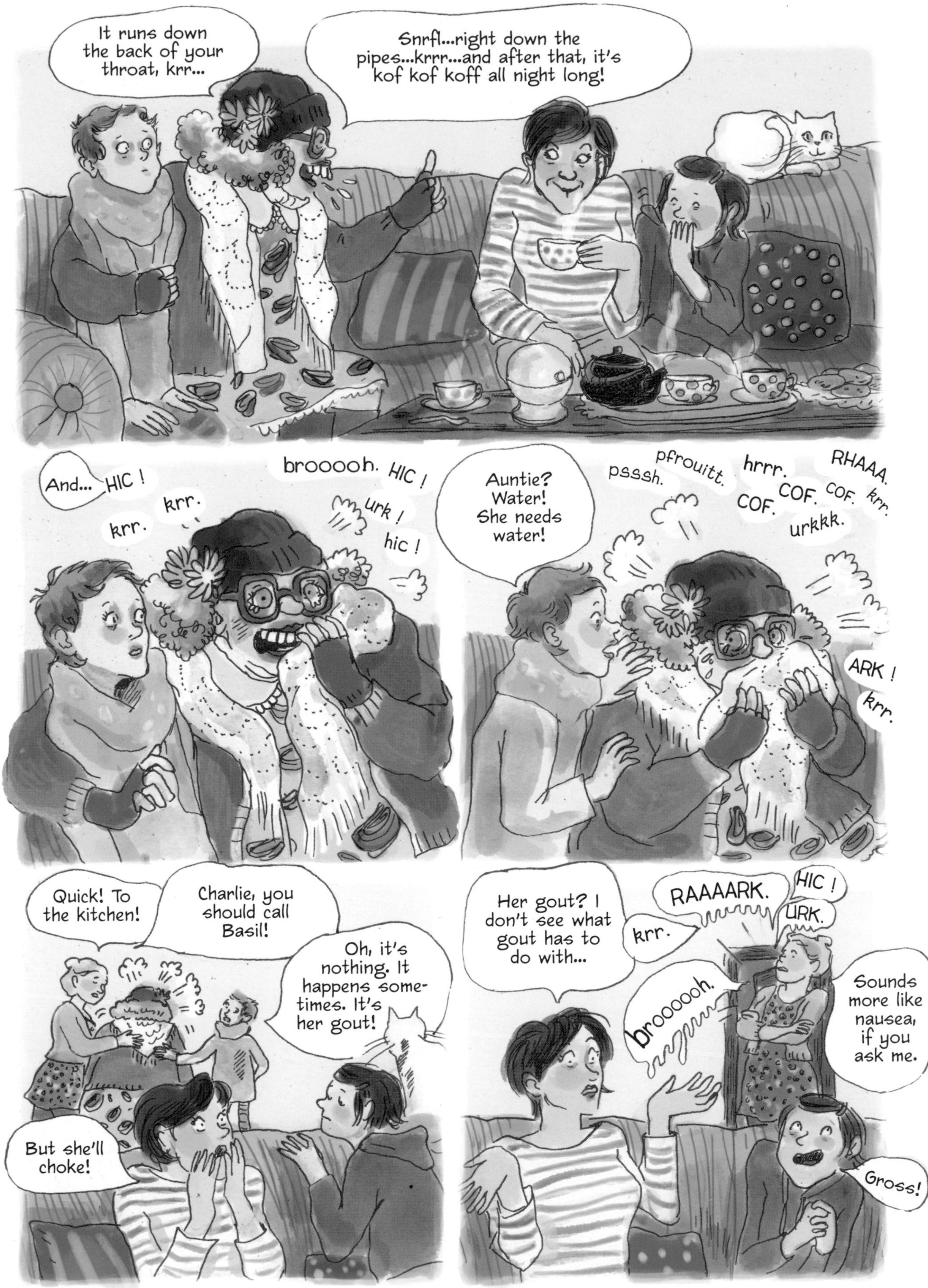

It runs down the back of your throat, krr...
Snrfl...right down the pipes...krrr...and after that, it's kof kof koff all night long!
And... HIC !
brooooh. HIC !
krr.
krr.
urk !
hic !
Auntie? Water! She needs water!
psssh.
pfrouitt.
hrrr.
RHAAA.
COF.
COF.
COF.
krr.
urkkk.
ARK !
krr.
Quick! To the kitchen!
Charlie, you should call Basil!
Oh, it's nothing. It happens some-times. It's her gout!
But she'll choke!
Her gout? I don't see what gout has to do with...
krr.
RAAAARK.
HIC !
URK.
brooooh.
Sounds more like nausea, if you ask me.
Gross!

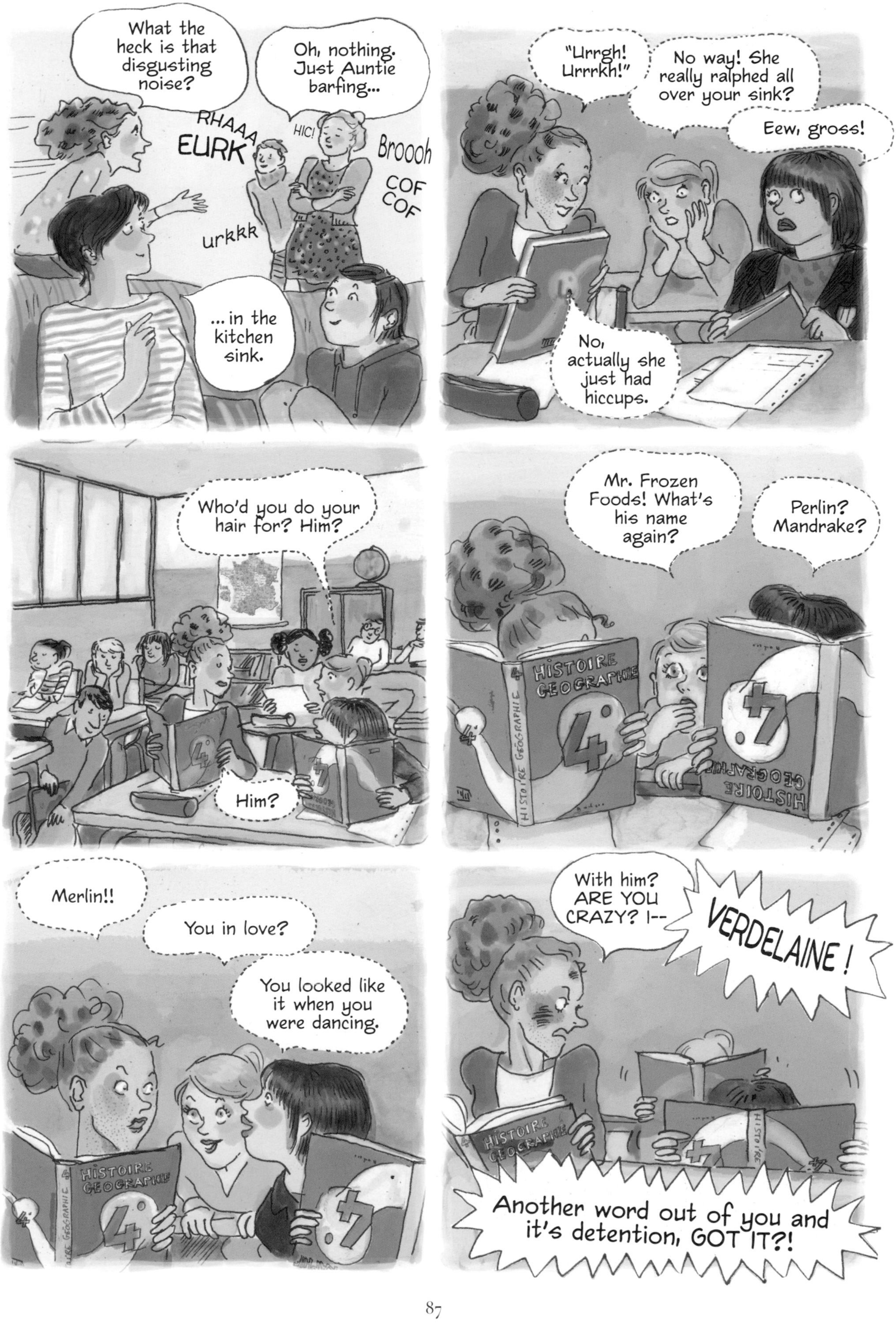
What the heck is that disgusting noise?
Oh, nothing. Just Auntie barfing...
RHAAA
EURK
HIC!
Broooh
COF COF
urkkk
... in the kitchen sink.
"Urrgh! Urrrkh!"
No way! She really ralphed all over your sink?
Eew, gross!
No, actually she just had hiccups.
Who'd you do your hair for? Him?
Him?
Mr. Frozen Foods! What's his name again?
Perlin? Mandrake?
HISTOIRE GEOGRAPHIE
Merlin!!
You in love?
You looked like it when you were dancing.
With him? ARE YOU CRAZY? I--
VERDELAINE !
Another word out of you and it's detention, GOT IT?!

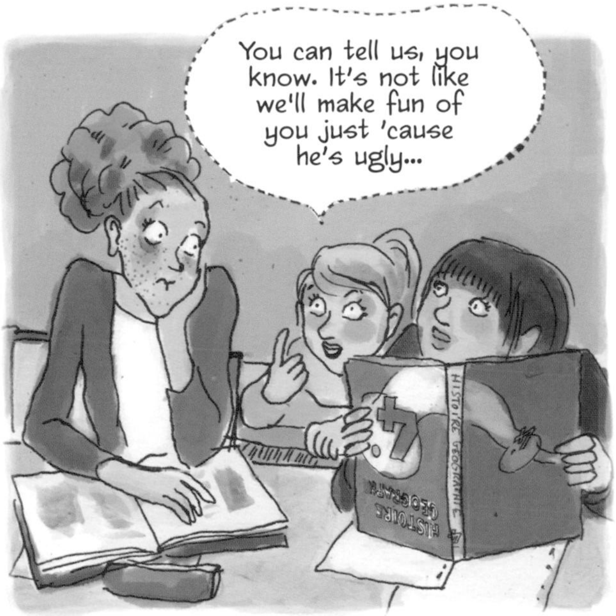
You can tell us, you know. It's not like we'll make fun of you just 'cause he's ugly...

Bettina's heart was tied in knots. It was the cruelest thing anyone had ever said to her. But it was about not losing face in front of her girlfriends.

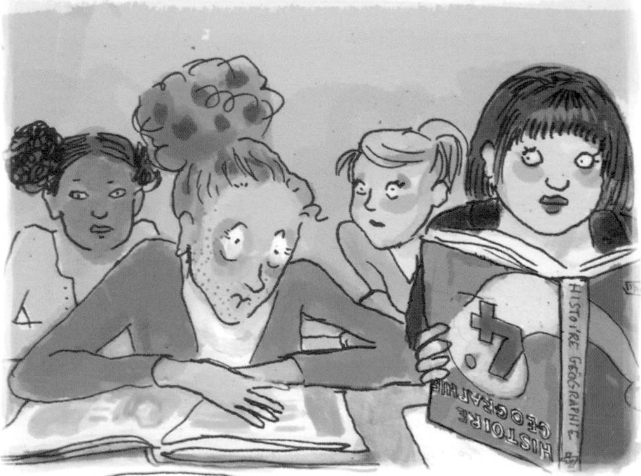

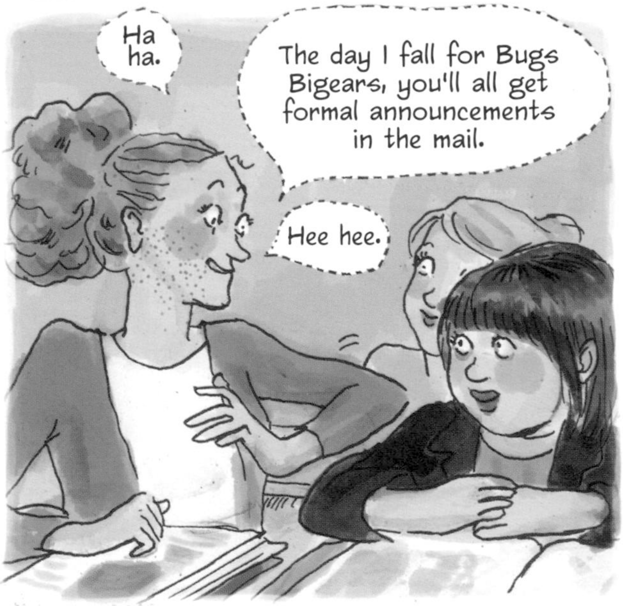
Ha ha.
The day I fall for Bugs Bigears, you'll all get formal announcements in the mail.
Hee hee.

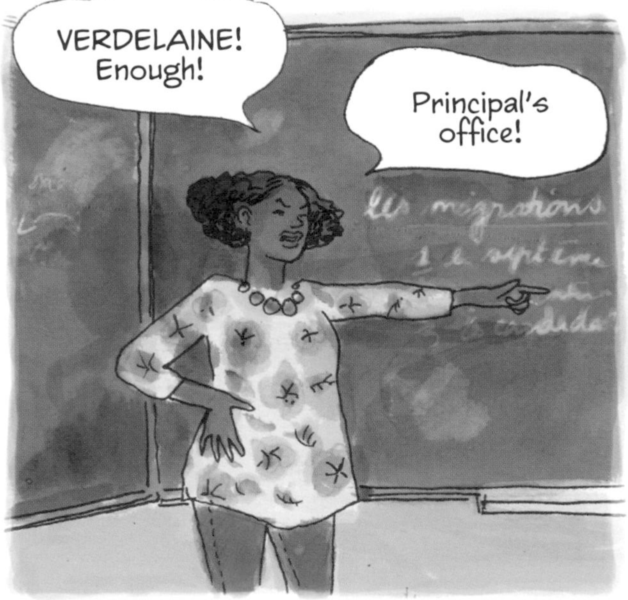
VERDELAINE! Enough!
Principal's office!

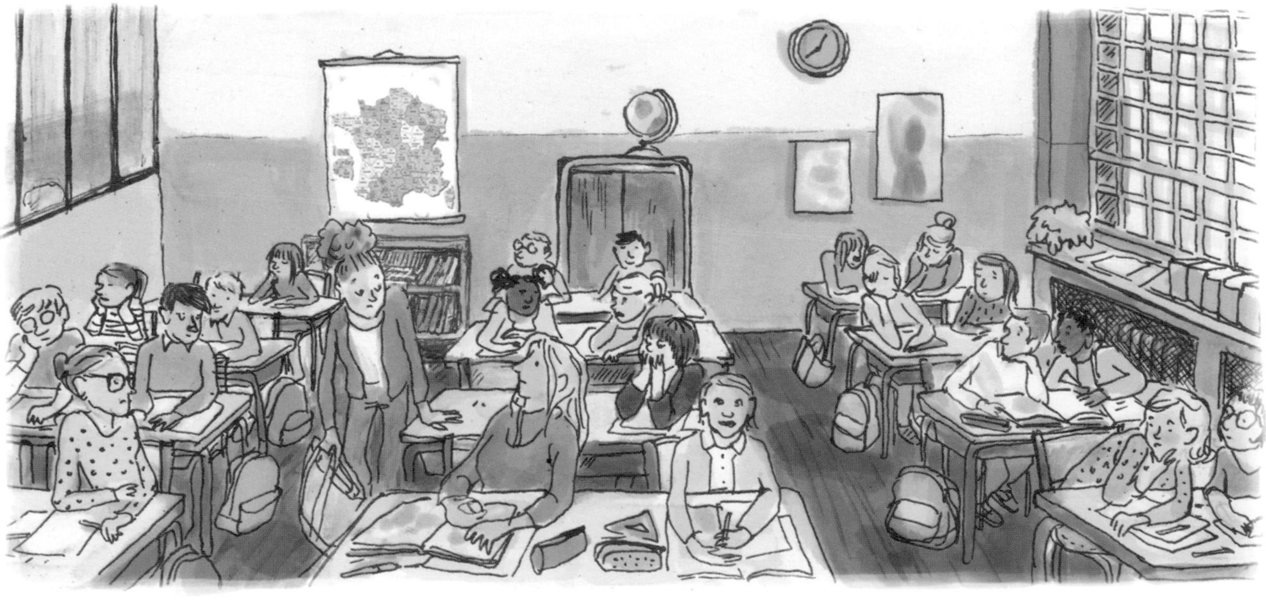

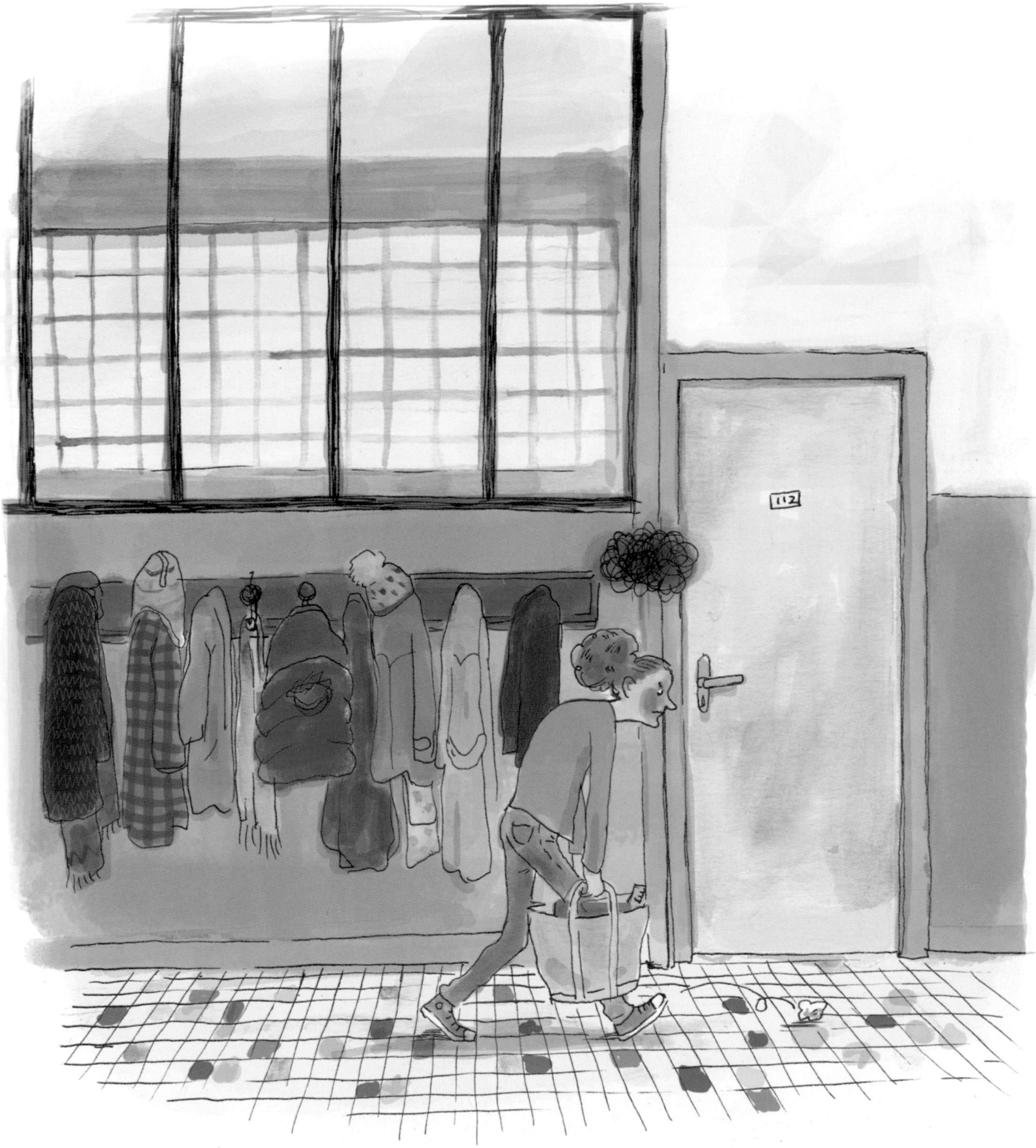
112

Bettina had never much liked Mondays, but she hated this one with all her heart.

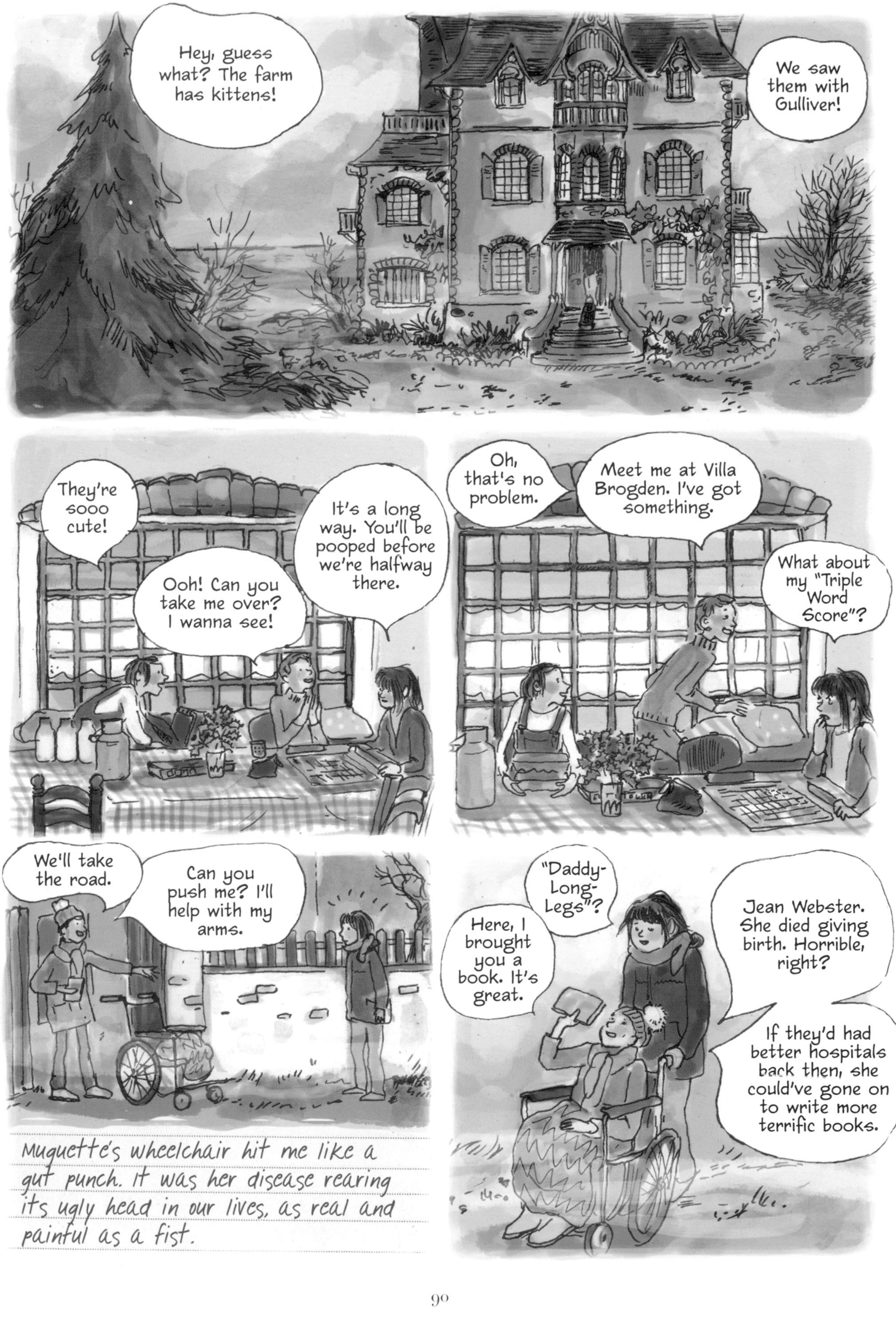
Hey, guess what? The farm has kittens!
We saw them with Gulliver!
They're sooo cute!
Ooh! Can you take me over? I wanna see!
It's a long way. You'll be pooped before we're halfway there.
Oh, that's no problem.
Meet me at Villa Brogden. I've got something.
What about my "Triple Word Score"?
We'll take the road.
Can you push me? I'll help with my arms.
Muguette's wheelchair hit me like a gut punch. It was her disease rearing its ugly head in our lives, as real and painful as a fist.
"Daddy-Long-Legs"?
Here, I brought you a book. It's great.
Jean Webster. She died giving birth. Horrible, right?
If they'd had better hospitals back then, she could've gone on to write more terrific books.

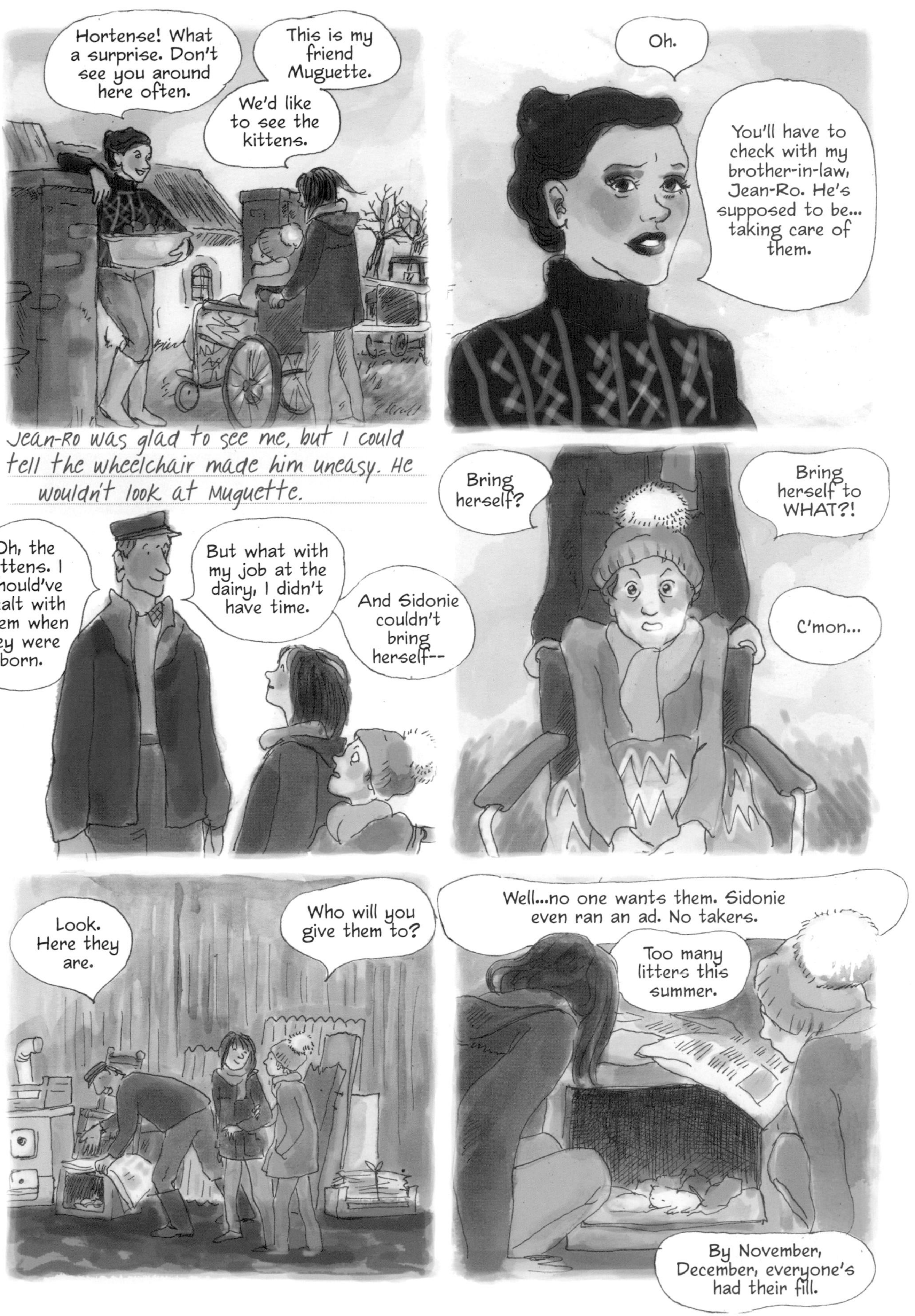
Hortense! What a surprise. Don't see you around here often.
This is my friend Muguette.
We'd like to see the kittens.
Oh.
You'll have to check with my brother-in-law, Jean-Ro. He's supposed to be... taking care of them.
Jean-Ro was glad to see me, but I could tell the wheelchair made him uneasy. He wouldn't look at Muguette.
Oh, the kittens. I should've dealt with them when they were born.
But what with my job at the dairy, I didn't have time.
And Sidonie couldn't bring herself--
Bring herself?
Bring herself to WHAT?!
C'mon...
Look. Here they are.
Who will you give them to?
Well...no one wants them. Sidonie even ran an ad. No takers.
Too many litters this summer.
By November, December, everyone's had their fill.

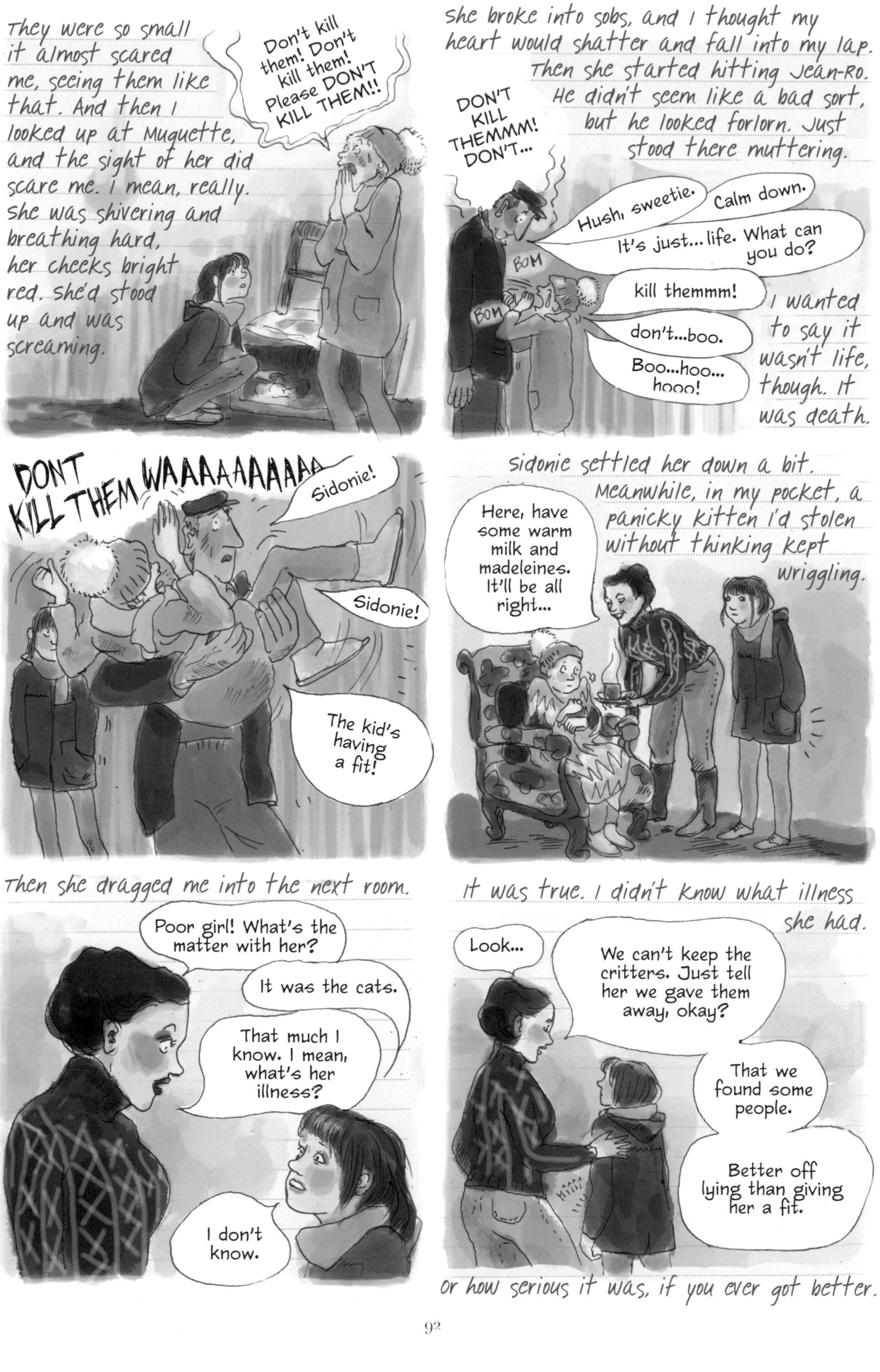
They were so small it almost scared me, seeing them like that. And then I looked up at Muguette, and the sight of her did scare me. I mean, really. She was shivering and breathing hard, her cheeks bright red. She'd stood up and was screaming.
Don't kill them! Don't kill them! Please DON'T KILL THEM!!
She broke into sobs, and I thought my heart would shatter and fall into my lap. Then she started hitting Jean-Ro. He didn't seem like a bad sort, but he looked forlorn. Just stood there muttering.
DON'T KILL THEMMM! DON'T...
Hush, sweetie.
Calm down.
It's just... life. What can you do?
BOM
BOM
kill themmm!
don't...boo.
Boo...hoo... hooo!
I wanted to say it wasn't life, though. It was death.
DONT KILL THEM WAAAAAAAAA
Sidonie!
Sidonie!
The kid's having a fit!
Sidonie settled her down a bit. Meanwhile, in my pocket, a panicky kitten I'd stolen without thinking kept wriggling.
Here, have some warm milk and madeleines. It'll be all right...
Then she dragged me into the next room.
Poor girl! What's the matter with her?
It was the cats.
That much I know. I mean, what's her illness?
I don't know.
It was true. I didn't know what illness she had.
Look...
We can't keep the critters. Just tell her we gave them away, okay?
That we found some people.
Better off lying than giving her a fit.
or how serious it was, if you ever got better.

When we came back to the room, Muguette was up, slightly out of breath, but better. She gave me a look like I'd betrayed her. But I knew when she saw the kitten...

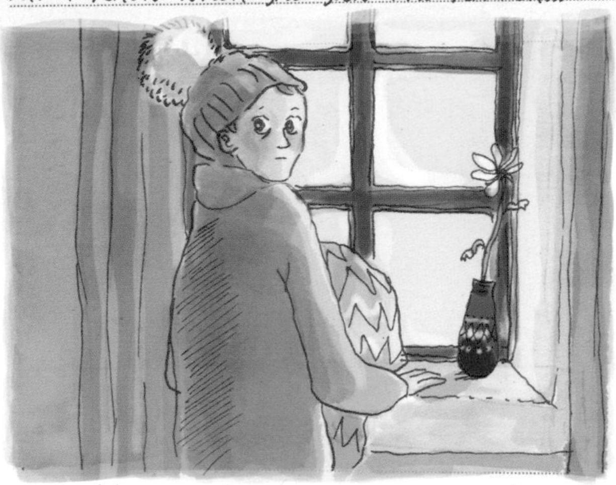

At least I'd saved one life.

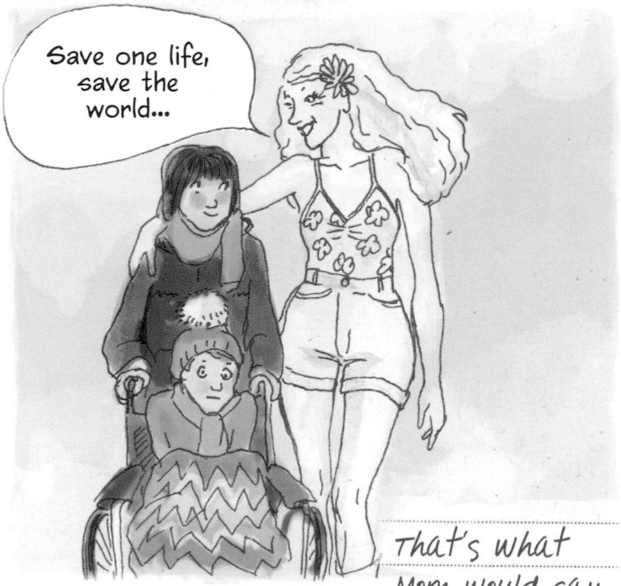
Save one life, save the world...

That's what Mom would say.

Muguette didn't say a word. I waited 'til we'd gone almost a quarter-mile, and then:

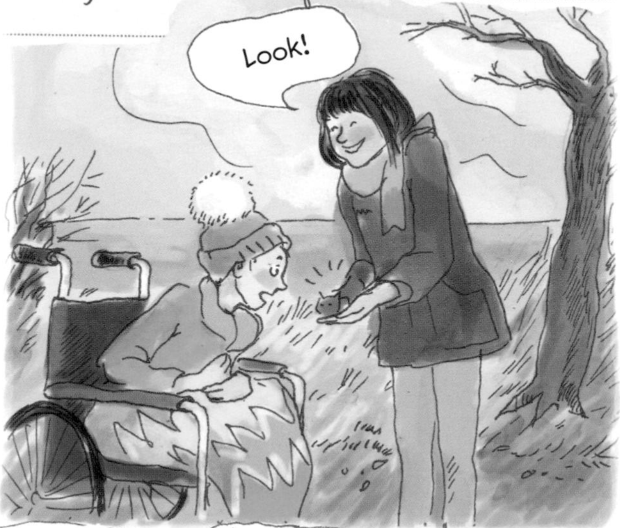
Look!

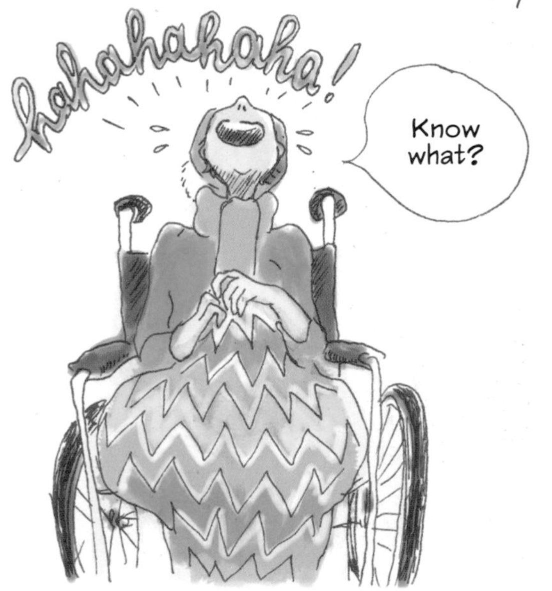
hahahaha!
Know what?

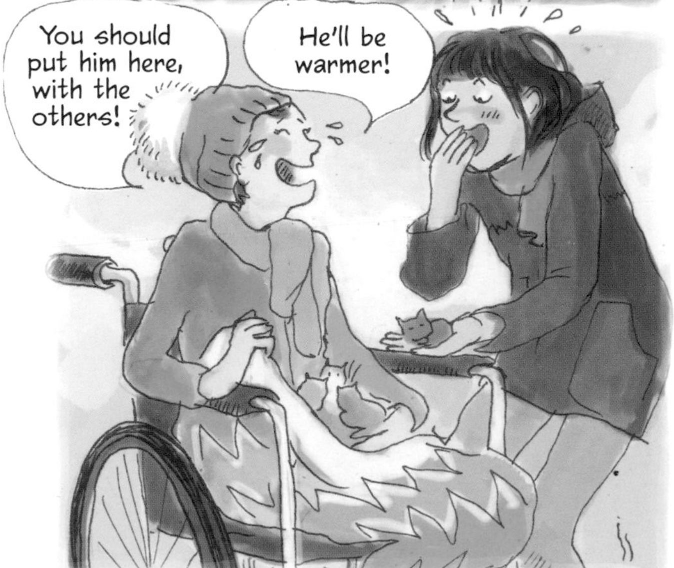
You should put him here, with the others!
He'll be warmer!

Muguette and I had a good long laugh...

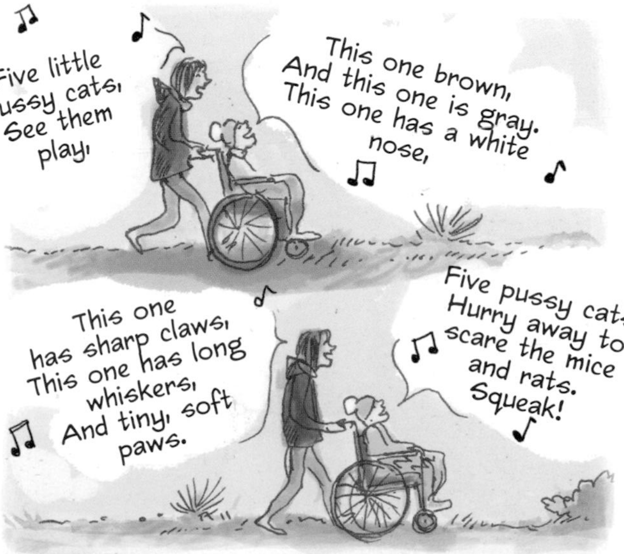
Five little pussy cats, See them play,
This one brown, And this one is gray. This one has a white nose,
This one has sharp claws, This one has long whiskers, And tiny, soft paws.
Five pussy cats, Hurry away to scare the mice and rats. Squeak!

...but our troubles weren't over yet.

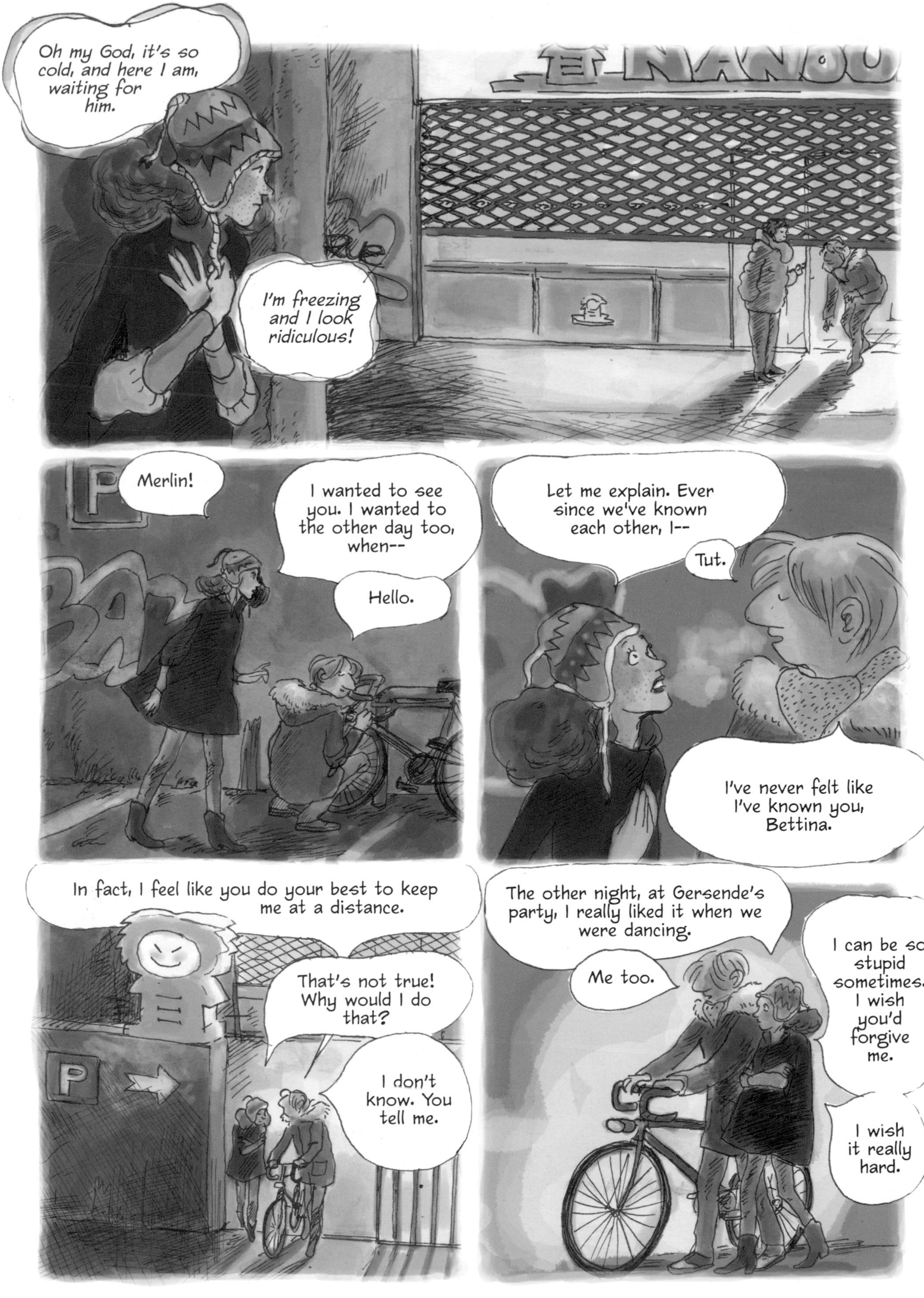
Oh my God, it's so cold, and here I am, waiting for him.
I'm freezing and I look ridiculous!
Merlin!
I wanted to see you. I wanted to the other day too, when--
Hello.
Let me explain. Ever since we've known each other, I--
Tut.
I've never felt like I've known you, Bettina.
In fact, I feel like you do your best to keep me at a distance.
That's not true! Why would I do that?
I don't know. You tell me.
The other night, at Gersende's party, I really liked it when we were dancing.
Me too.
I can be so stupid sometimes. I wish you'd forgive me.
I wish it really hard.

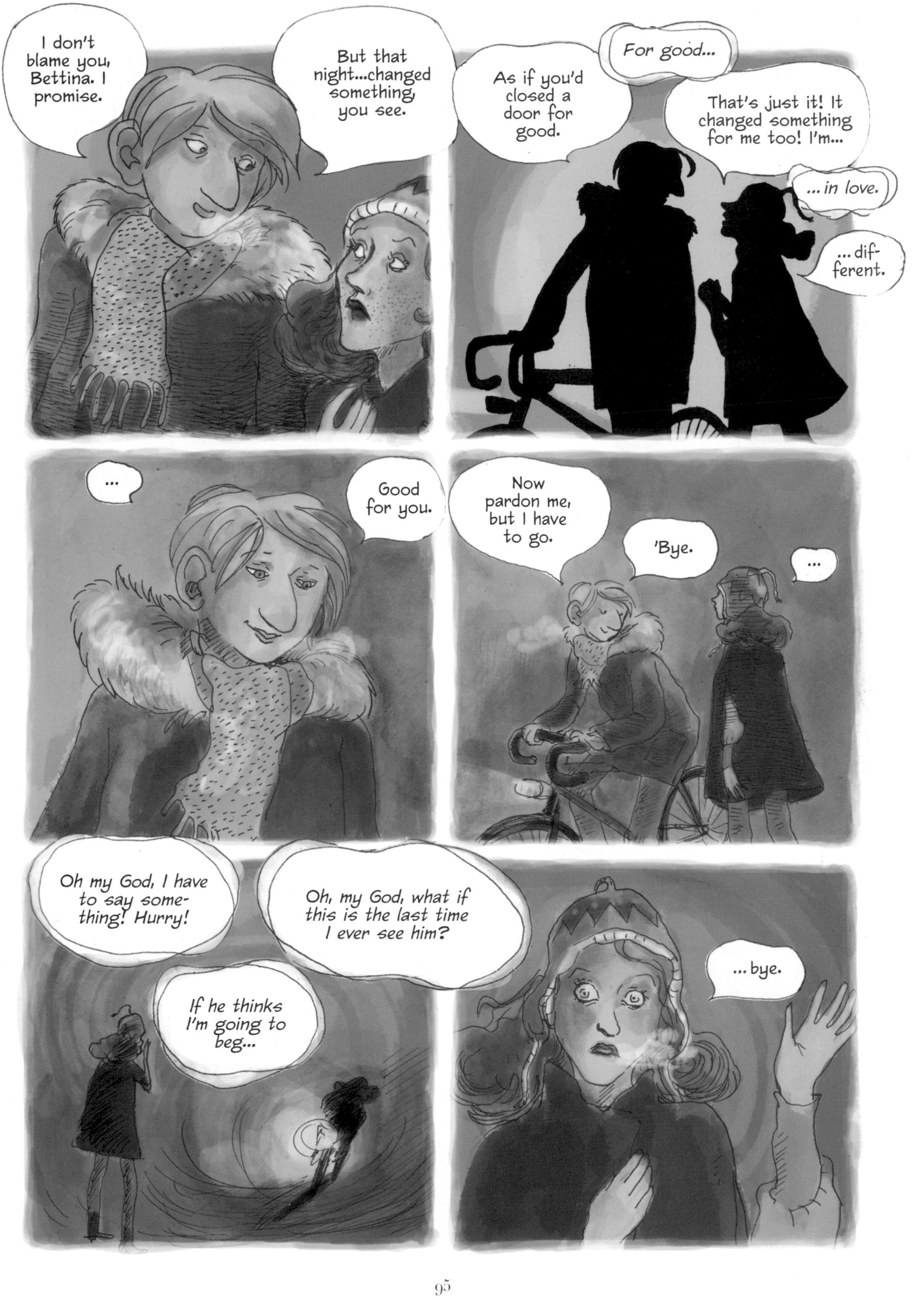
I don't blame you, Bettina. I promise.
But that night...changed something, you see.
As if you'd closed a door for good.
For good...
That's just it! It changed something for me too! I'm...
...in love.
...dif-ferent.
...
Good for you.
Now pardon me, but I have to go.
'Bye.
...
Oh my God, I have to say some-thing! Hurry!
Oh, my God, what if this is the last time I ever see him?
If he thinks I'm going to beg...
...bye.

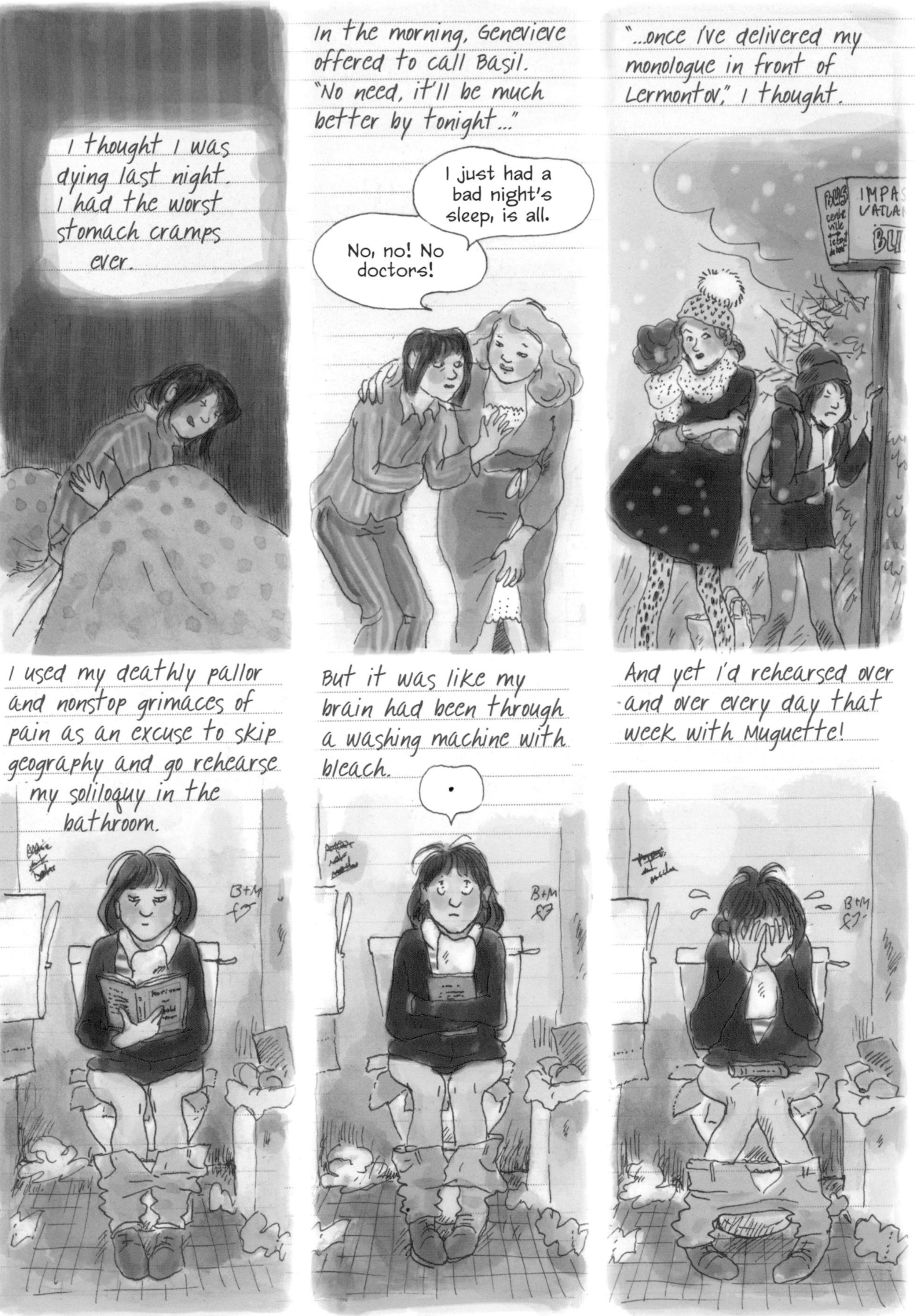
I thought I was dying last night. I had the worst stomach cramps ever.
In the morning, Genevieve offered to call Basil. "No need, it'll be much better by tonight..."
I just had a bad night's sleep, is all.
No, no! No doctors!
"...once I've delivered my monologue in front of Lermontov," I thought.
I used my deathly pallor and nonstop grimaces of pain as an excuse to skip geography and go rehearse my soliloquy in the bathroom.
B+M
But it was like my brain had been through a washing machine with bleach.
B+M
And yet I'd rehearsed over and over every day that week with Muguette!

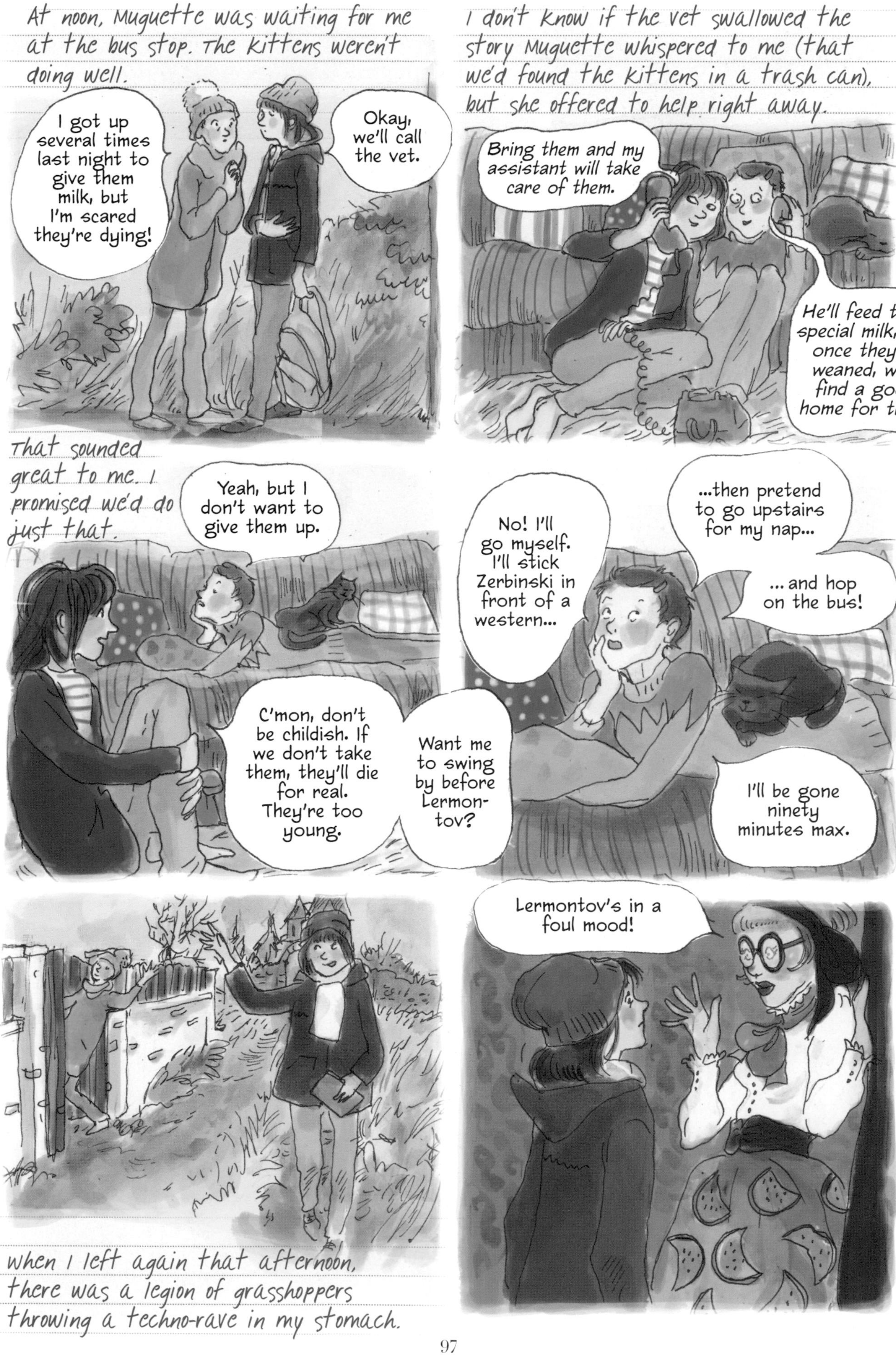
At noon, Muguette was waiting for me at the bus stop. The kittens weren't doing well.
I got up several times last night to give them milk, but I'm scared they're dying!
Okay, we'll call the vet.
I don't know if the vet swallowed the story Muguette whispered to me (that we'd found the kittens in a trash can), but she offered to help right away.
Bring them and my assistant will take care of them.
He'll feed them special milk, and once they're weaned, we'll find a good home for them.
That sounded great to me. I promised we'd do just that.
Yeah, but I don't want to give them up.
C'mon, don't be childish. If we don't take them, they'll die for real. They're too young.
Want me to swing by before Lermontov?
No! I'll go myself. I'll stick Zerbinski in front of a western...
...then pretend to go upstairs for my nap...
... and hop on the bus!
I'll be gone ninety minutes max.
When I left again that afternoon, there was a legion of grasshoppers throwing a techno-rave in my stomach.
Lermontov's in a foul mood!

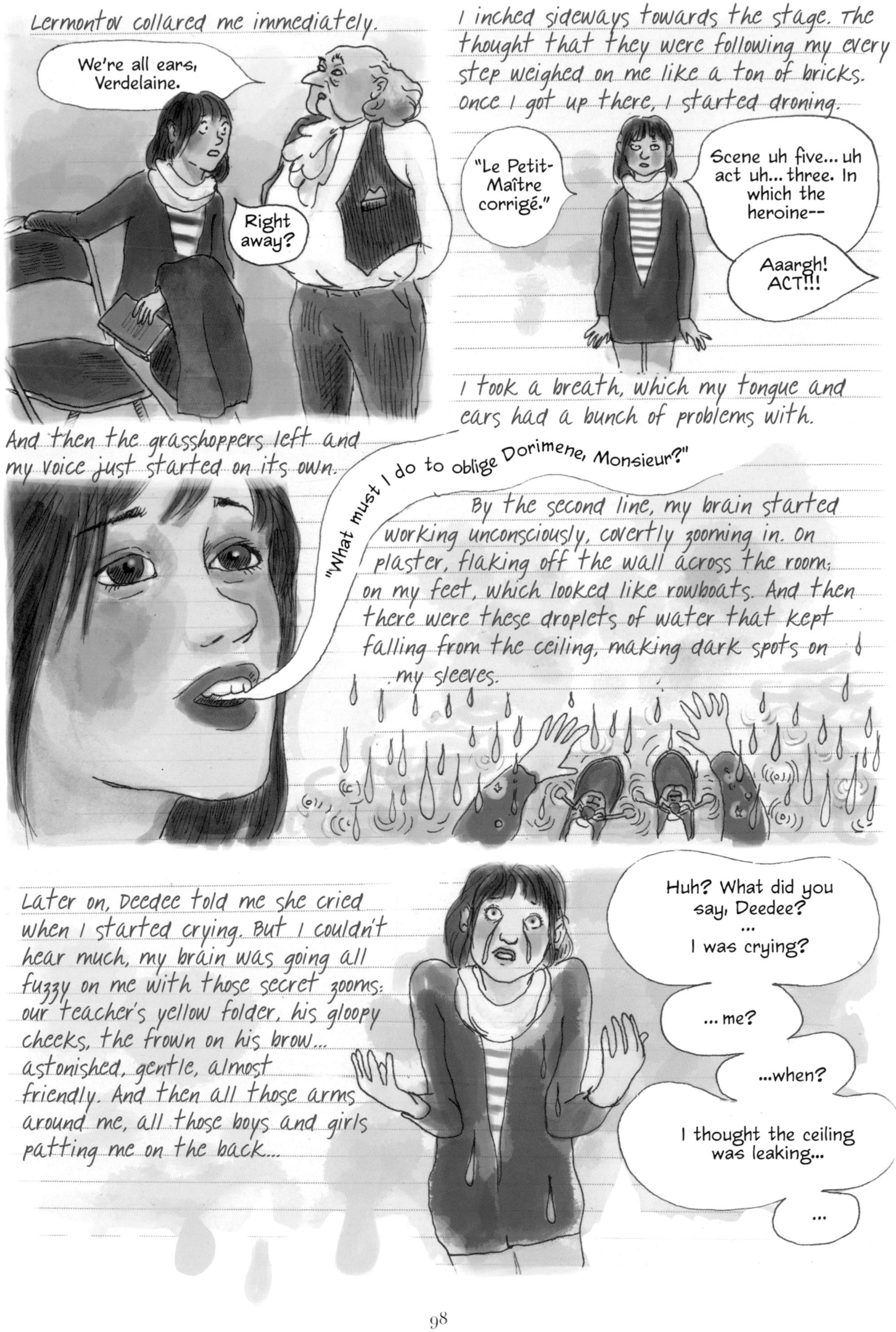
Lermontov collared me immediately.
We're all ears, Verdelaine.
Right away?
I inched sideways towards the stage. The thought that they were following my every step weighed on me like a ton of bricks. Once I got up there, I started droning.
"Le Petit-Maître corrigé."
Scene uh five... uh act uh... three. In which the heroine--
Aaargh! ACT!!!
I took a breath, which my tongue and ears had a bunch of problems with.
And then the grasshoppers left and my voice just started on its own.
"What must I do to oblige Dorimene, Monsieur?"
By the second line, my brain started working unconsciously, covertly zooming in. On plaster, flaking off the wall across the room; on my feet, which looked like rowboats. And then there were these droplets of water that kept falling from the ceiling, making dark spots on my sleeves.
Later on, Deedee told me she cried when I started crying. But I couldn't hear much, my brain was going all fuzzy on me with those secret zooms: our teacher's yellow folder, his gloopy cheeks, the frown on his brow... astonished, gentle, almost friendly. And then all those arms around me, all those boys and girls patting me on the back...
Huh? What did you say, Deedee? ... I was crying?
... me?
...when?
I thought the ceiling was leaking...
...

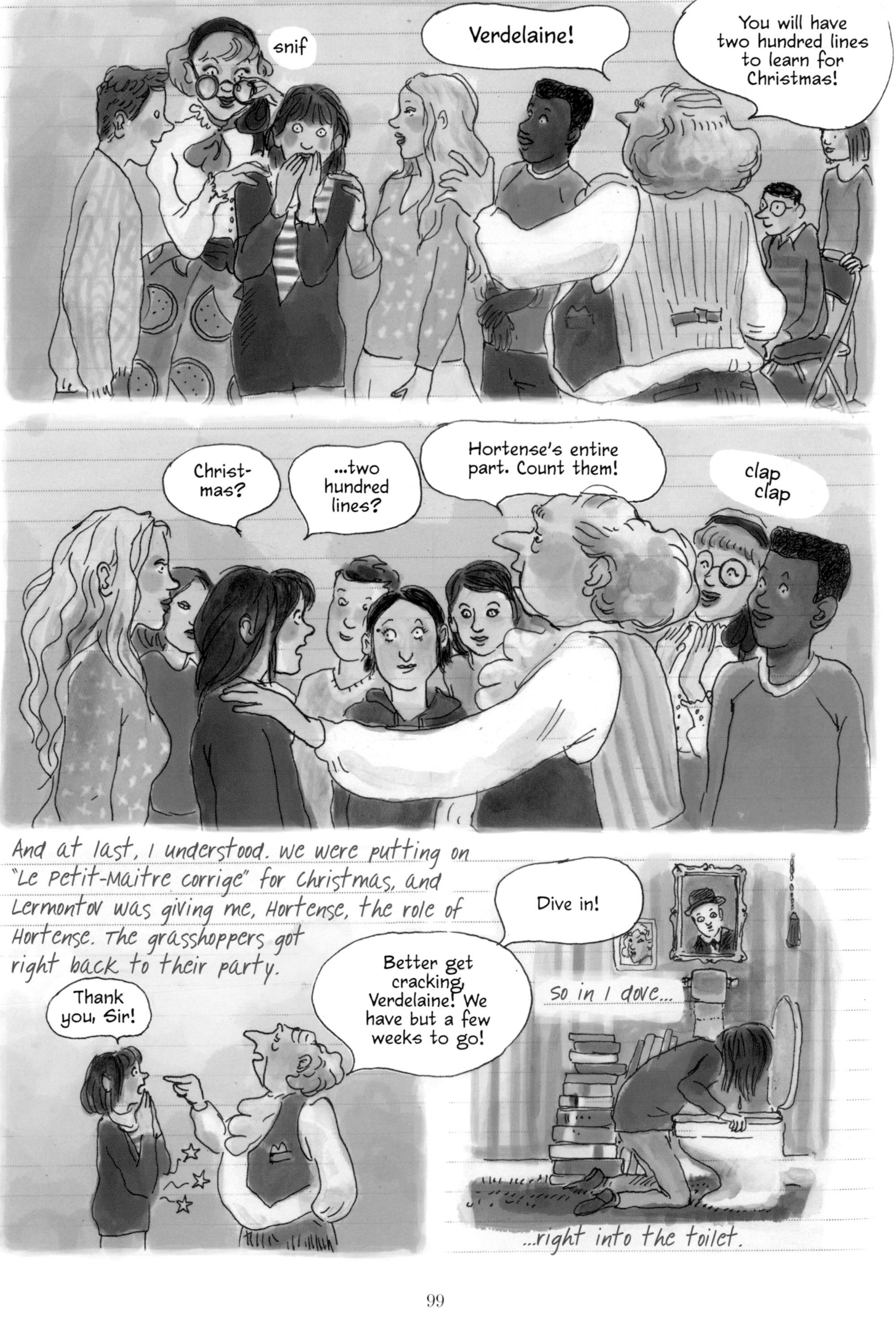
snif
Verdelaine!
You will have two hundred lines to learn for Christmas!
Christ-mas?
...two hundred lines?
Hortense's entire part. Count them!
clap clap
And at last, I understood. We were putting on "Le Petit-Maitre corrige" for Christmas, and Lermontov was giving me, Hortense, the role of Hortense. The grasshoppers got right back to their party.
Thank you, Sir!
Better get cracking, Verdelaine! We have but a few weeks to go!
Dive in!
So in I dove...
...right into the toilet.

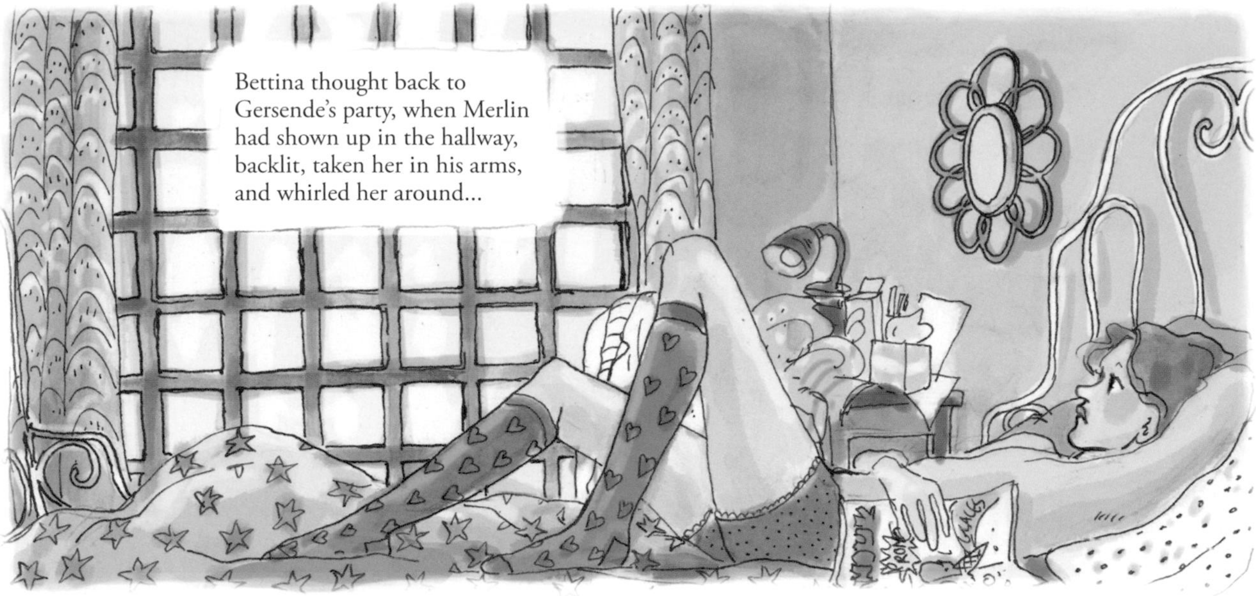
Bettina thought back to Gersende's party, when Merlin had shown up in the hallway, backlit, taken her in his arms, and whirled her around...

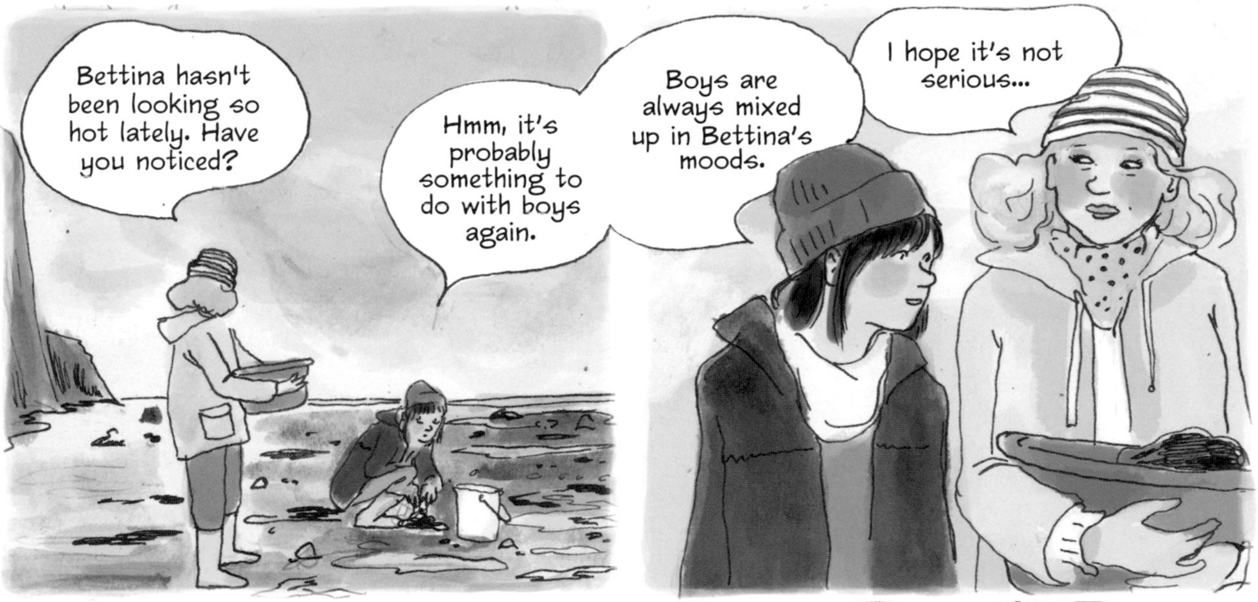
Bettina hasn't been looking so hot lately. Have you noticed?
Hmm, it's probably something to do with boys again.
Boys are always mixed up in Bettina's moods.
I hope it's not serious...

...his way of being funny, sweet, and helpful. At the pool, his lyrical dives, his poetic smiles...

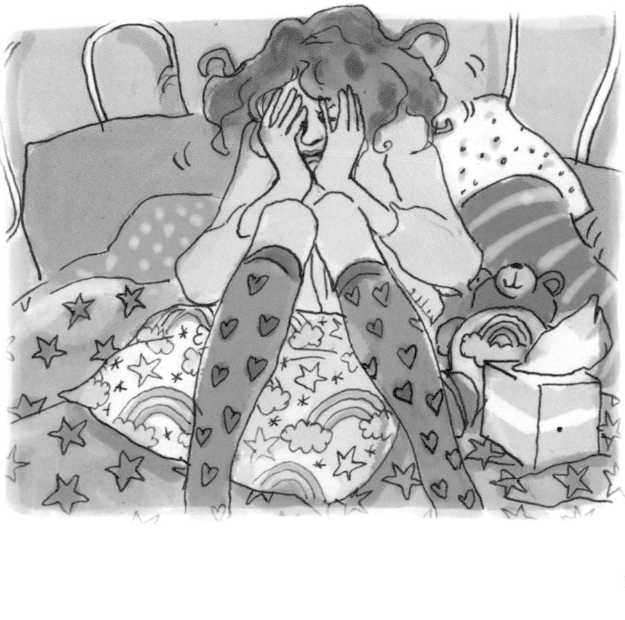

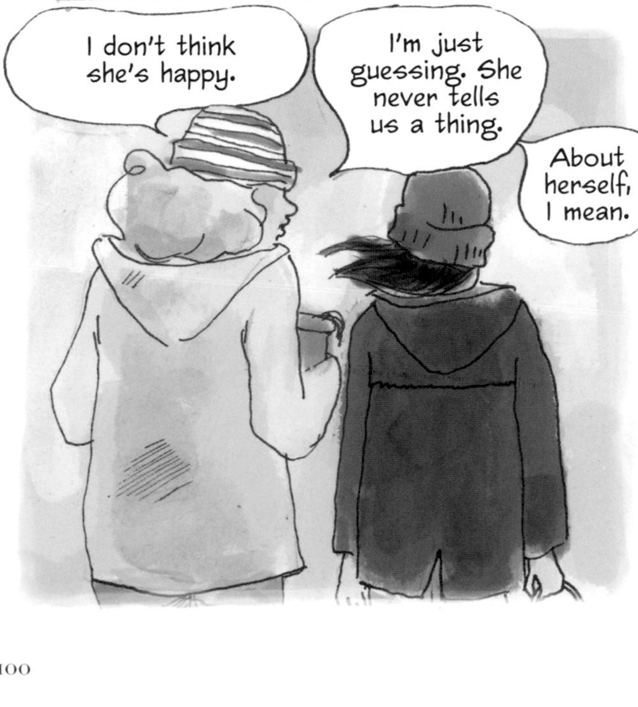
I don't think she's happy.
I'm just guessing. She never tells us a thing.
About herself, I mean.

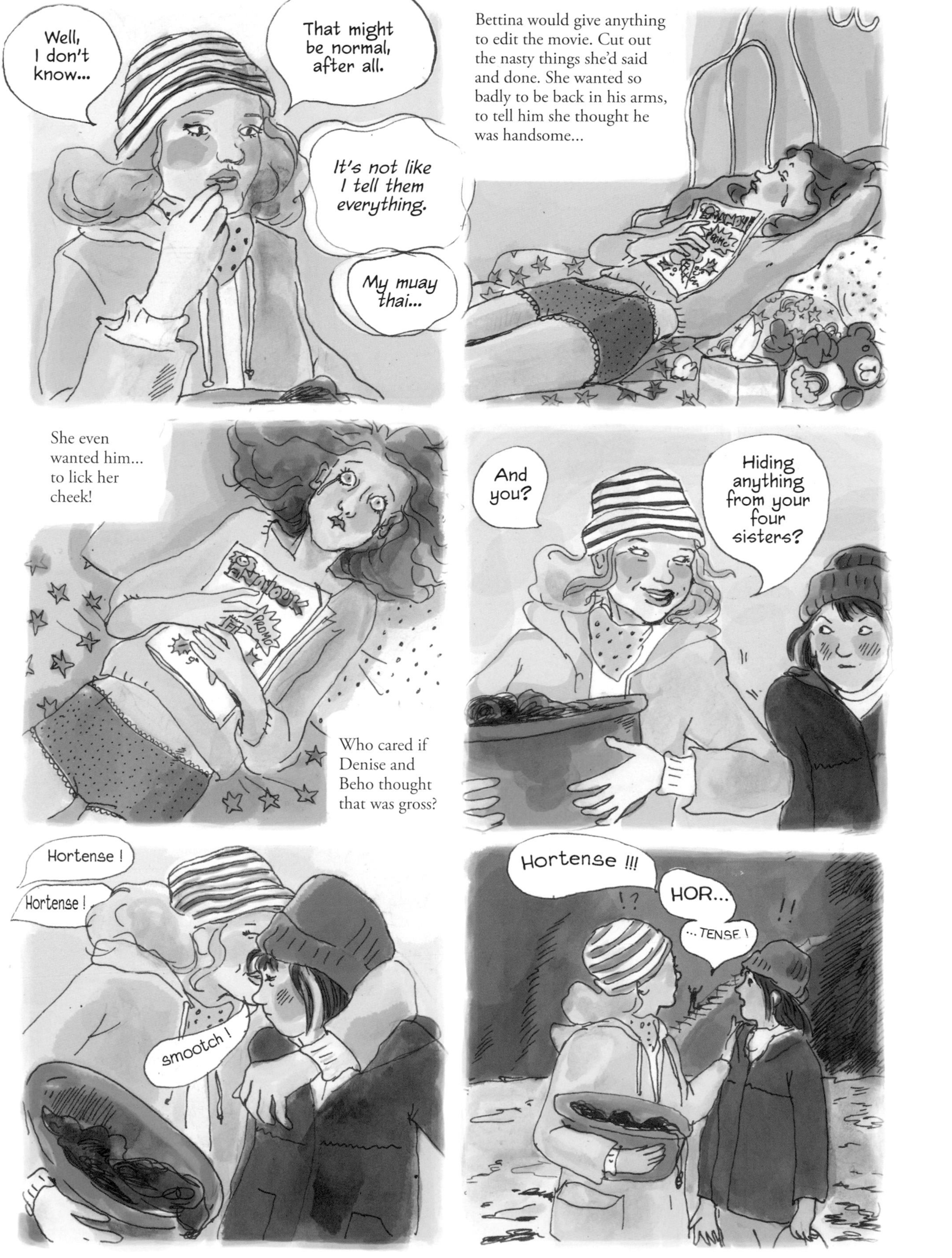
Well, I don't know...
That might be normal, after all.
It's not like I tell them everything.
My muay thai...
Bettina would give anything to edit the movie. Cut out the nasty things she'd said and done. She wanted so badly to be back in his arms, to tell him she thought he was handsome...
She even wanted him... to lick her cheek!
Who cared if Denise and Beho thought that was gross?
And you?
Hiding anything from your four sisters?
Hortense !
Hortense !
smootch !
Hortense !!!
!?
HOR...
...TENSE !
!!

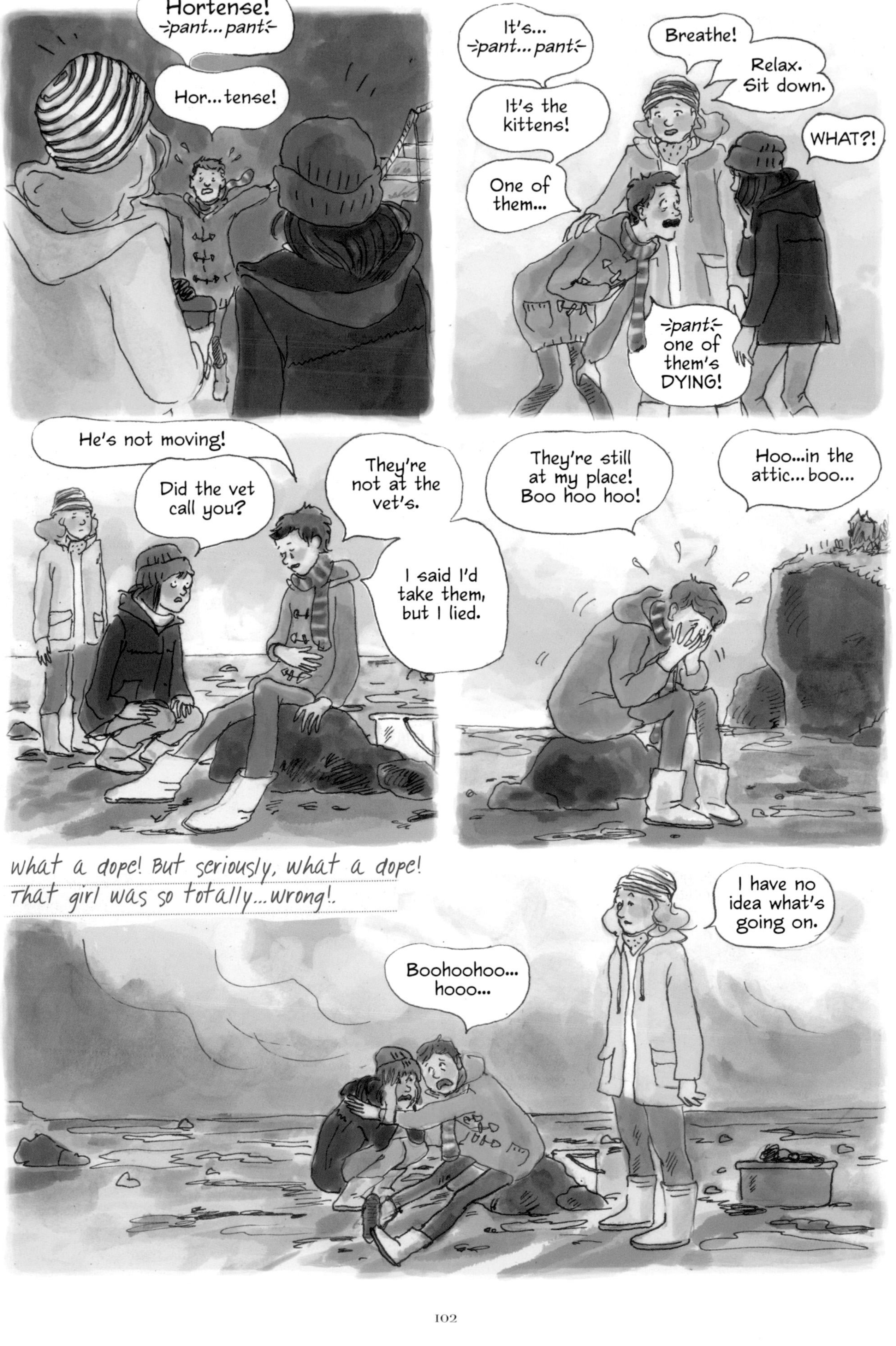
Hortense!
-pant... pant-
Hor...tense!
It's... -pant... pant-
It's the kittens!
One of them...
Breathe!
Relax. Sit down.
WHAT?!
-pant- one of them's DYING!
He's not moving!
Did the vet call you?
They're not at the vet's.
I said I'd take them, but I lied.
They're still at my place! Boo hoo hoo!
Hoo...in the attic... boo...
what a dope! But seriously, what a dope! That girl was so totally...wrong!.
Boohoohoo... hooo...
I have no idea what's going on.

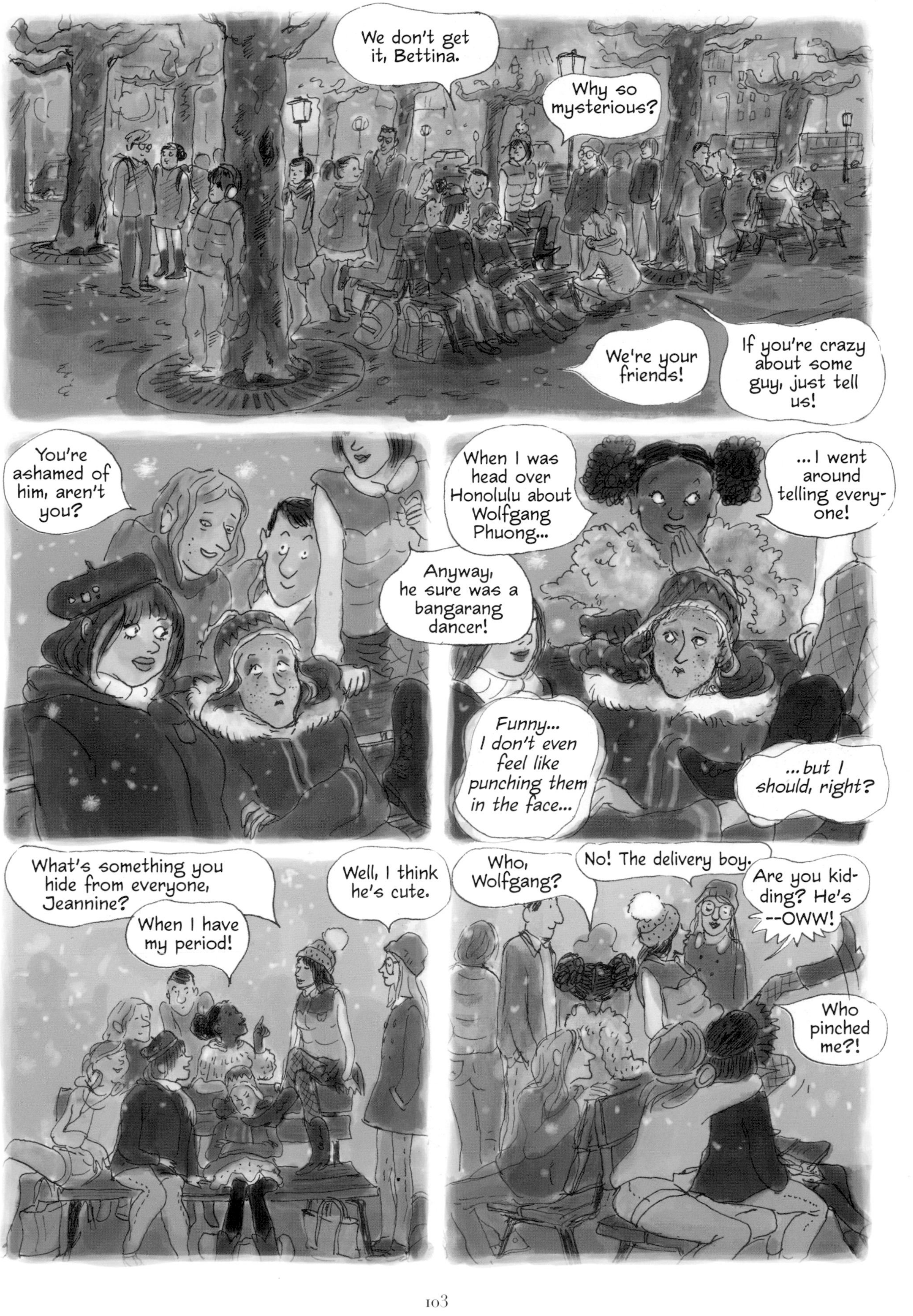
We don't get it, Bettina.
Why so mysterious?
We're your friends!
If you're crazy about some guy, just tell us!
You're ashamed of him, aren't you?
When I was head over Honolulu about Wolfgang Phuong...
...I went around telling every-one!
Anyway, he sure was a bangarang dancer!
Funny... I don't even feel like punching them in the face...
...but I should, right?
What's something you hide from everyone, Jeannine?
When I have my period!
Well, I think he's cute.
Who, Wolfgang?
No! The delivery boy.
Are you kid-ding? He's --OWW!
Who pinched me?!

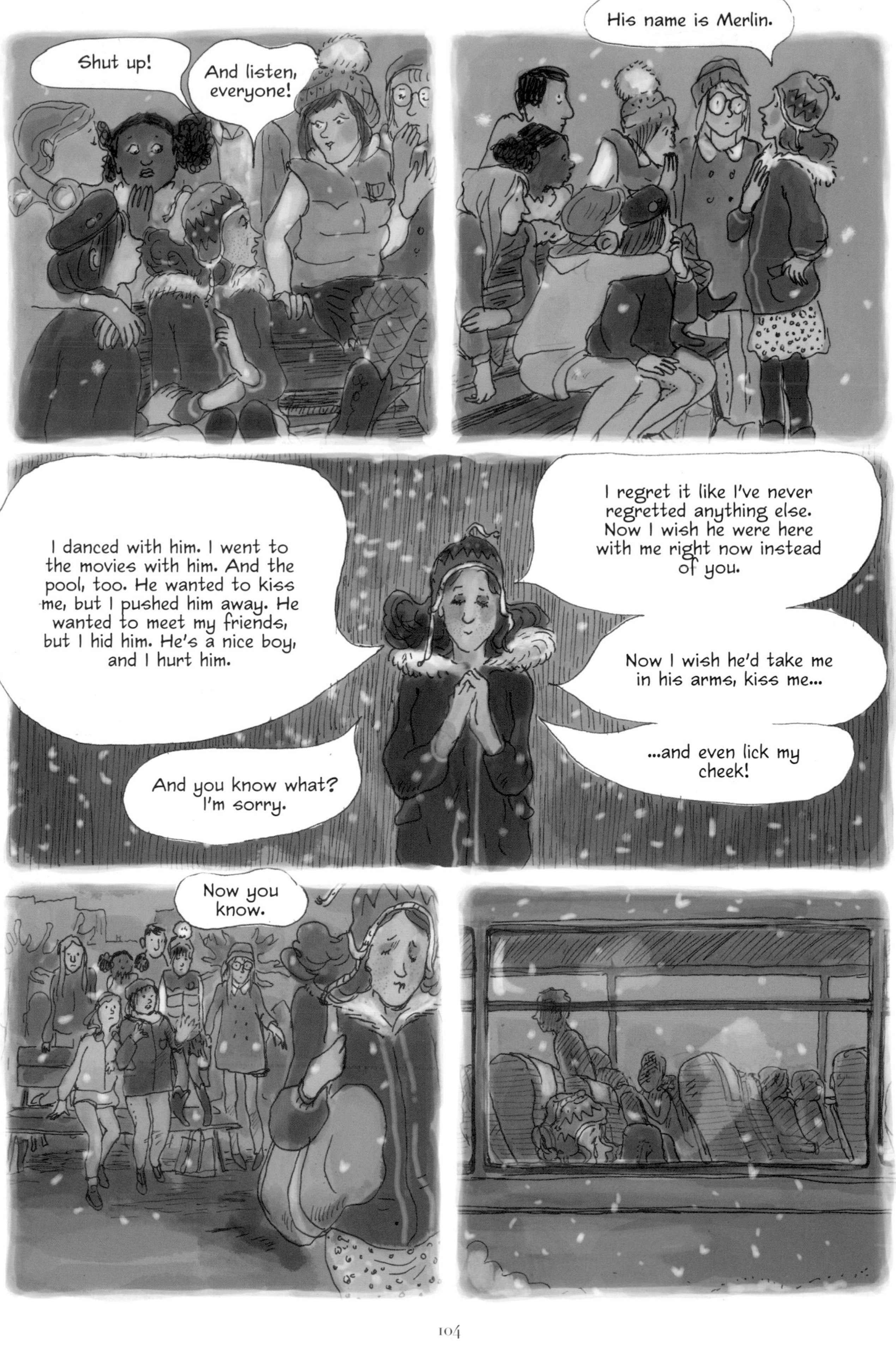
Shut up!
And listen, everyone!
His name is Merlin.
I danced with him. I went to the movies with him. And the pool, too. He wanted to kiss me, but I pushed him away. He wanted to meet my friends, but I hid him. He's a nice boy, and I hurt him.
And you know what? I'm sorry.
I regret it like I've never regretted anything else. Now I wish he were here with me right now instead of you.
Now I wish he'd take me in his arms, kiss me...
...and even lick my cheek!
Now you know.

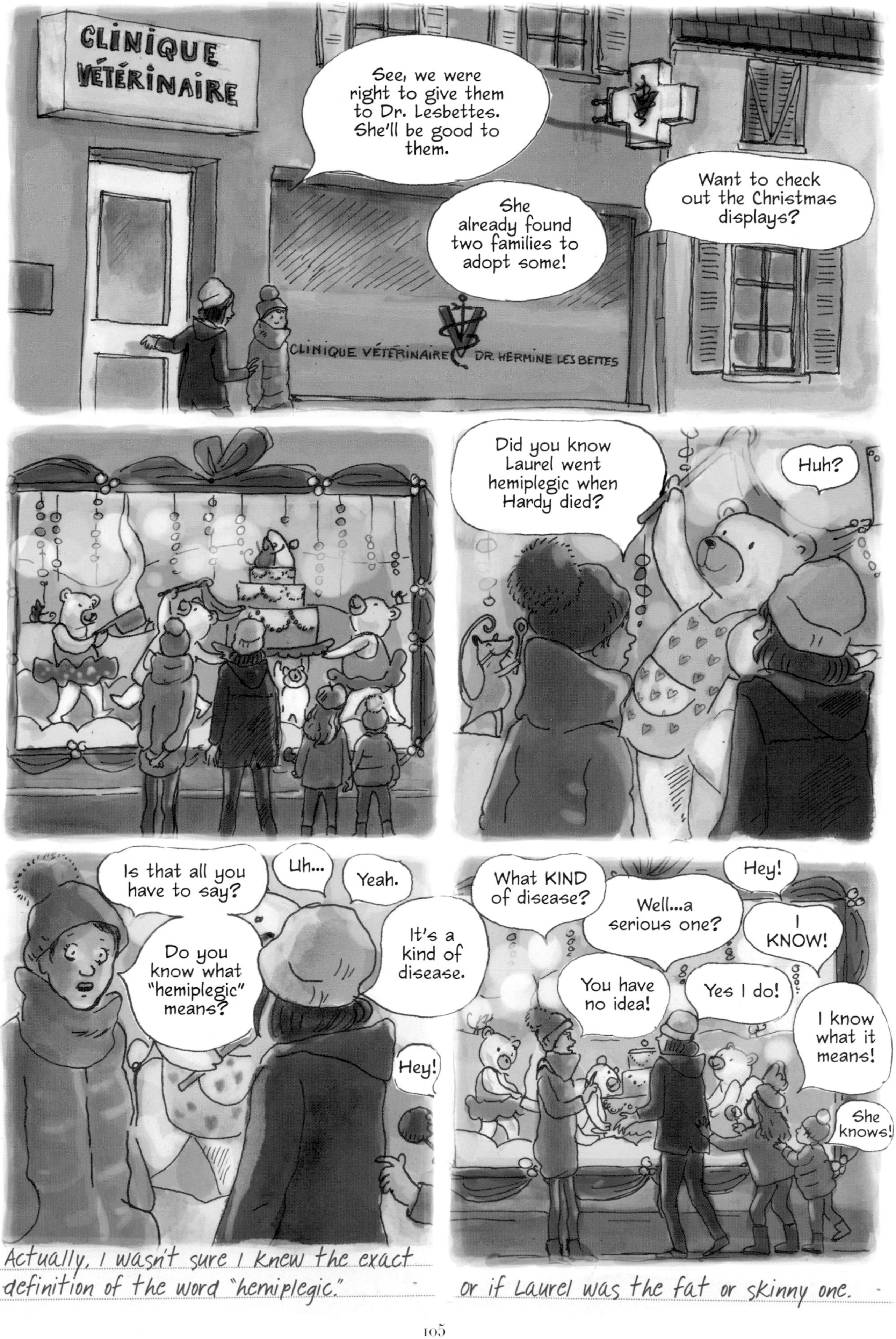
CLINIQUE VÉTÉRINAIRE
See, we were right to give them to Dr. Lesbettes. She'll be good to them.
She already found two families to adopt some!
Want to check out the Christmas displays?
CLINIQUE VÉTÉRINAIRE DR. HERMINE LES BETTES
Did you know Laurel went hemiplegic when Hardy died?
Huh?
Is that all you have to say?
Uh...
Yeah.
Do you know what "hemiplegic" means?
It's a kind of disease.
Hey!
What KIND of disease?
Hey!
Well...a serious one?
I KNOW!
You have no idea!
Yes I do!
I know what it means!
She knows!

Actually, I wasn't sure I knew the exact definition of the word "hemiplegic."

or if Laurel was the fat or skinny one.

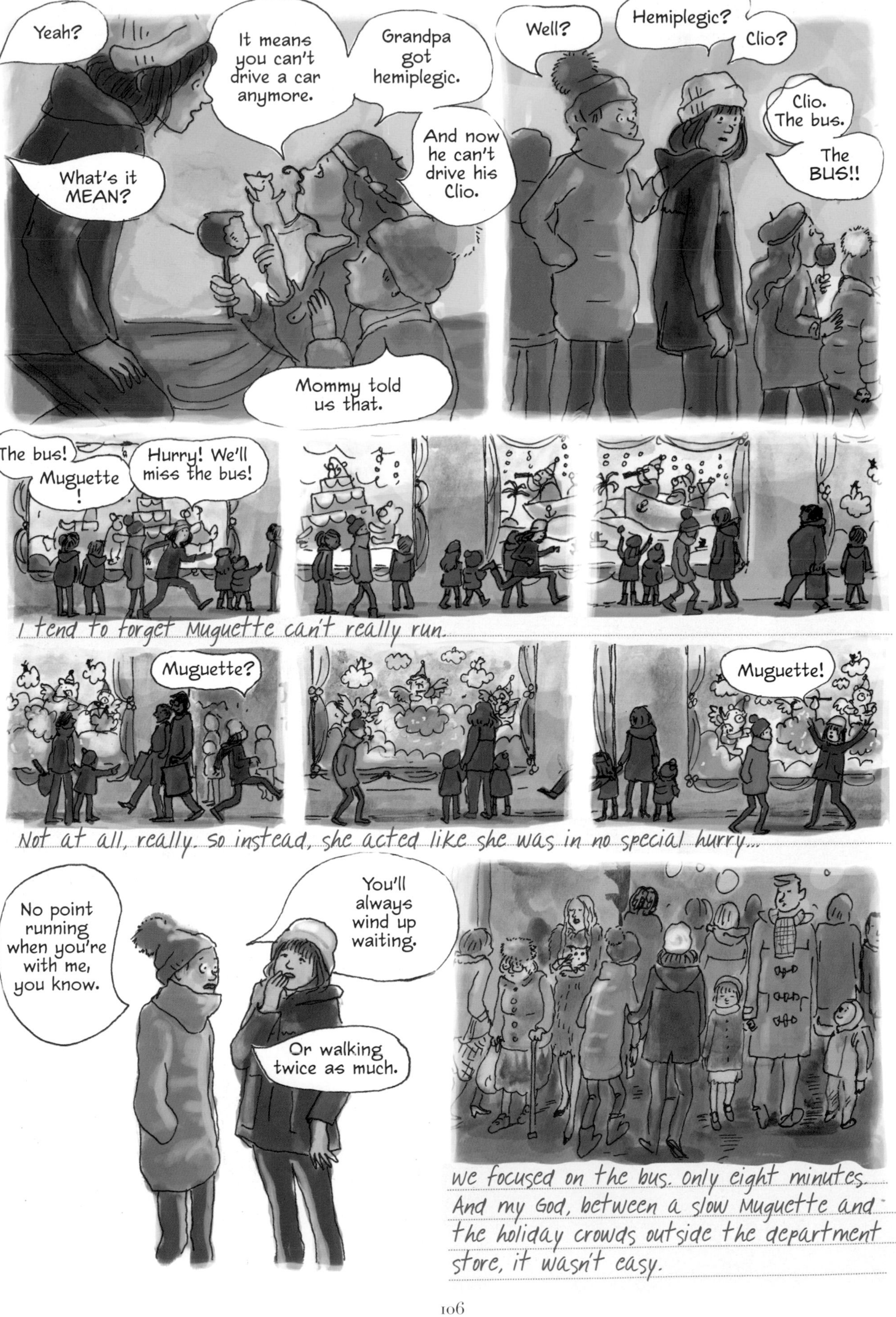
Grandpa got hemiplegic.
Yeah?
What's it MEAN?
It means you can't drive a car anymore.
And now he can't drive his Clio.
Mommy told us that.
Well?
Hemiplegic?
Clio?
Clio. The bus.
The BUS!!
The bus!
Muguette!
Hurry! We'll miss the bus!
I tend to forget Muguette can't really run.
Muguette?
Muguette!
Not at all, really. So instead, she acted like she was in no special hurry...
No point running when you're with me, you know.
You'll always wind up waiting.
Or walking twice as much.
We focused on the bus. Only eight minutes. And my God, between a slow Muguette and the holiday crowds outside the department store, it wasn't easy.

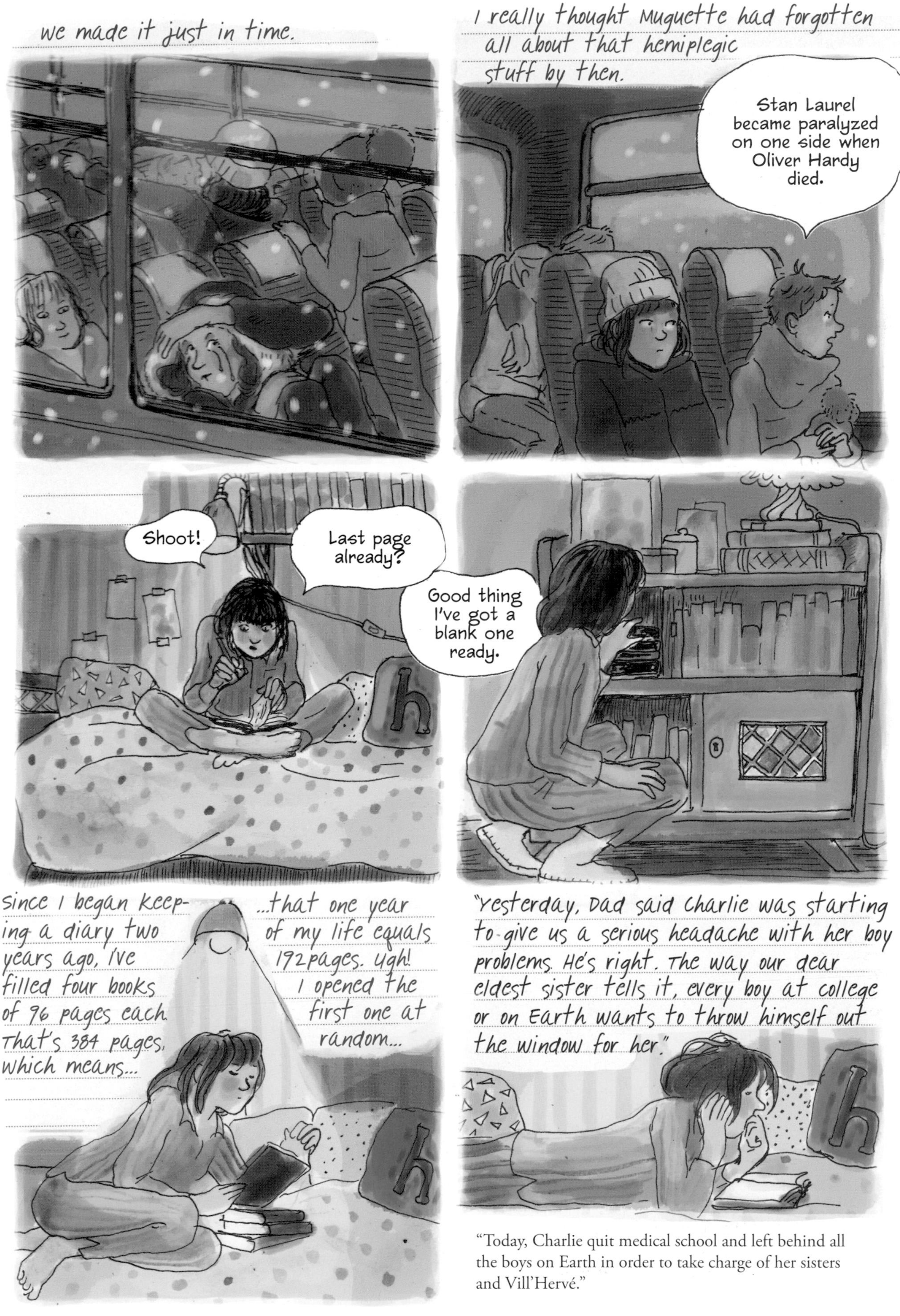
we made it just in time.
I really thought Muguette had forgotten all about that hemiplegic stuff by then.
Stan Laurel became paralyzed on one side when Oliver Hardy died.
Shoot!
Last page already?
Good thing I've got a blank one ready.
Since I began keeping a diary two years ago, I've filled four books of 96 pages each. That's 384 pages, which means...
...that one year of my life equals 192 pages. Ugh! I opened the first one at random...
"Yesterday, Dad said Charlie was starting to give us a serious headache with her boy problems. He's right. The way our dear eldest sister tells it, every boy at college or on Earth wants to throw himself out the window for her."
"Today, Charlie quit medical school and left behind all the boys on Earth in order to take charge of her sisters and Vill'Hervé."

Mom and Dad are dead. I'm writing these words and they mean nothing, nothing at all. Mom and Dad died on Friday, and I...

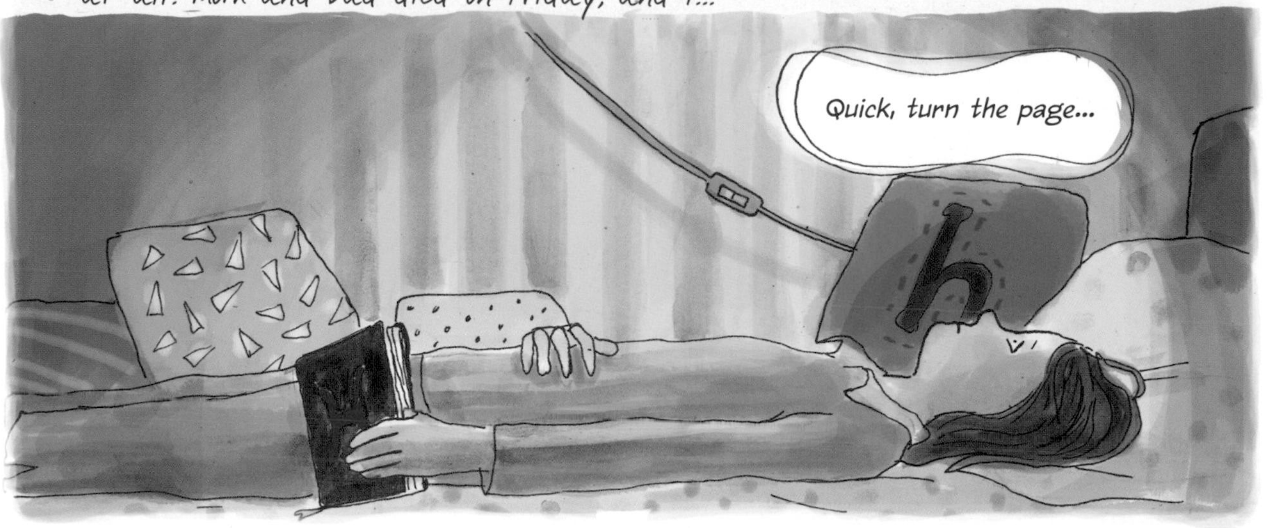
Quick, turn the page...

While Hortense was swallowed up by the past parading by in thin violet lines across her first diary...

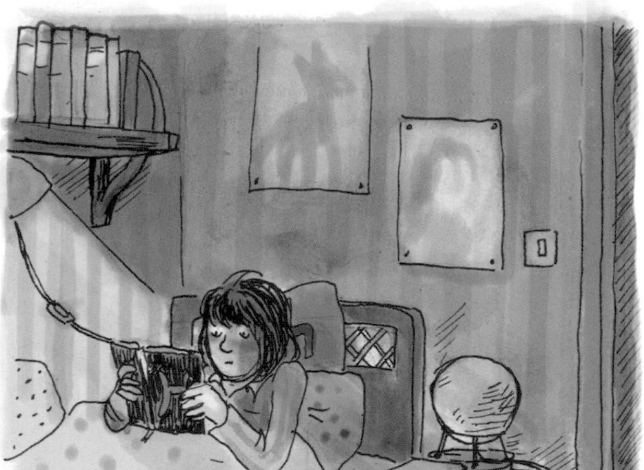

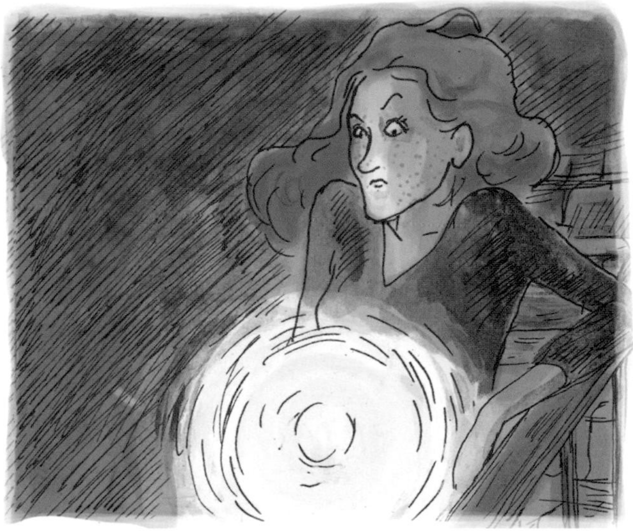

...in the silence of a slumbering Vill'Hervé, Bettina was preparing for a mysterious expedition.

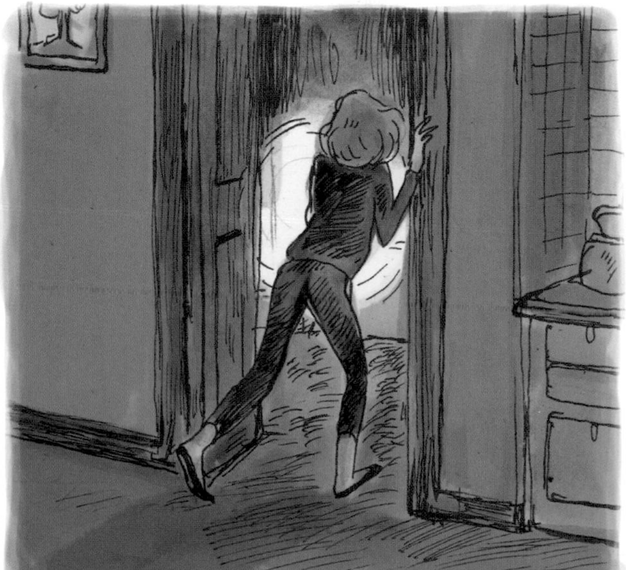

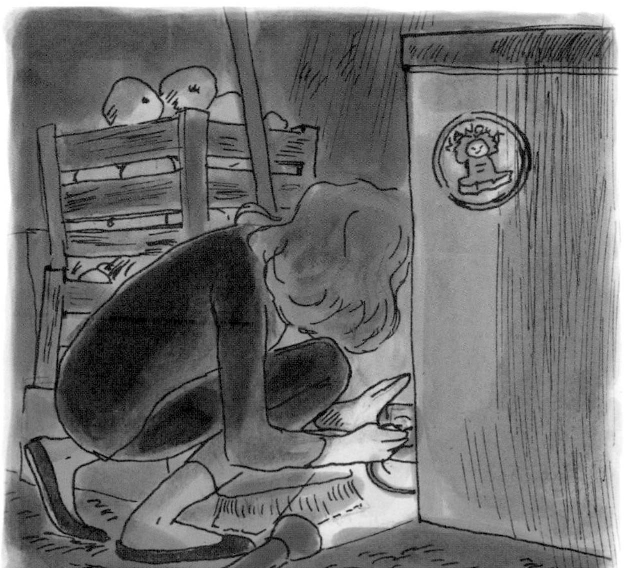

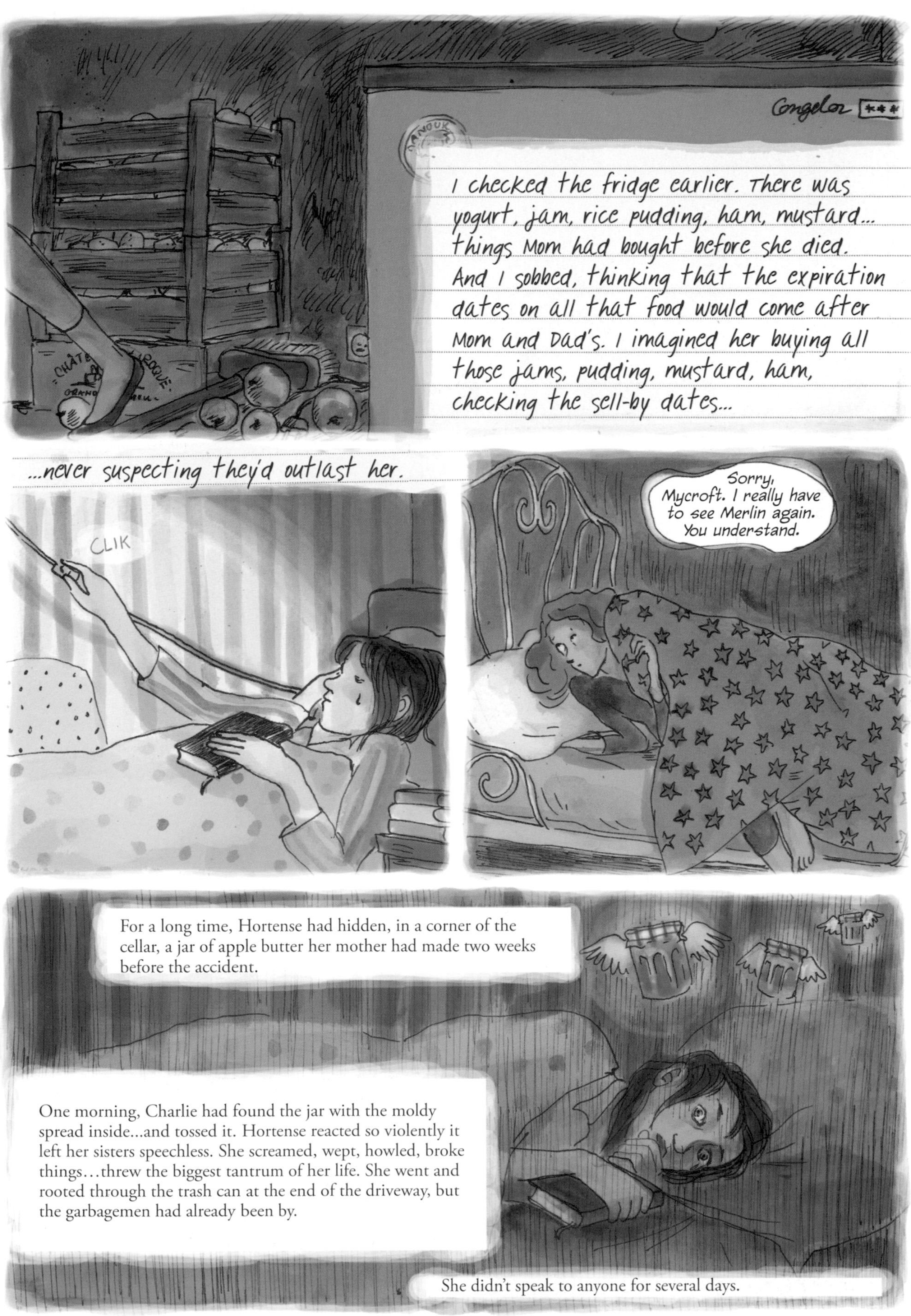
I checked the fridge earlier. There was yogurt, jam, rice pudding, ham, mustard... things Mom had bought before she died. And I sobbed, thinking that the expiration dates on all that food would come after Mom and Dad's. I imagined her buying all those jams, pudding, mustard, ham, checking the sell-by dates...
...never suspecting they'd outlast her.
CLIK
Sorry, Mycroft. I really have to see Merlin again. You understand.
For a long time, Hortense had hidden, in a corner of the cellar, a jar of apple butter her mother had made two weeks before the accident.
One morning, Charlie had found the jar with the moldy spread inside...and tossed it. Hortense reacted so violently it left her sisters speechless. She screamed, wept, howled, broke things...threw the biggest tantrum of her life. She went and rooted through the trash can at the end of the driveway, but the garbagemen had already been by.
She didn't speak to anyone for several days.

Brrr, it's freezing!

I need to figure a way to fix Madame Boiler once and for all...

It's like she's gotten Seasonal Affective Disorder.

No one left me any bread?!?

I'll go look in the freezer.

AAAAAAAARGH

Charlie?!!

THAT GODDAMN RODENT!! sonofabitch rot in hell! you rip tail   MYCROFT!

My-croft!

That pest unplugged the freezer!

Eew!

Looks like a dump!

Or Gargantua's stomach!

...when he's having a bad case of indigestion.

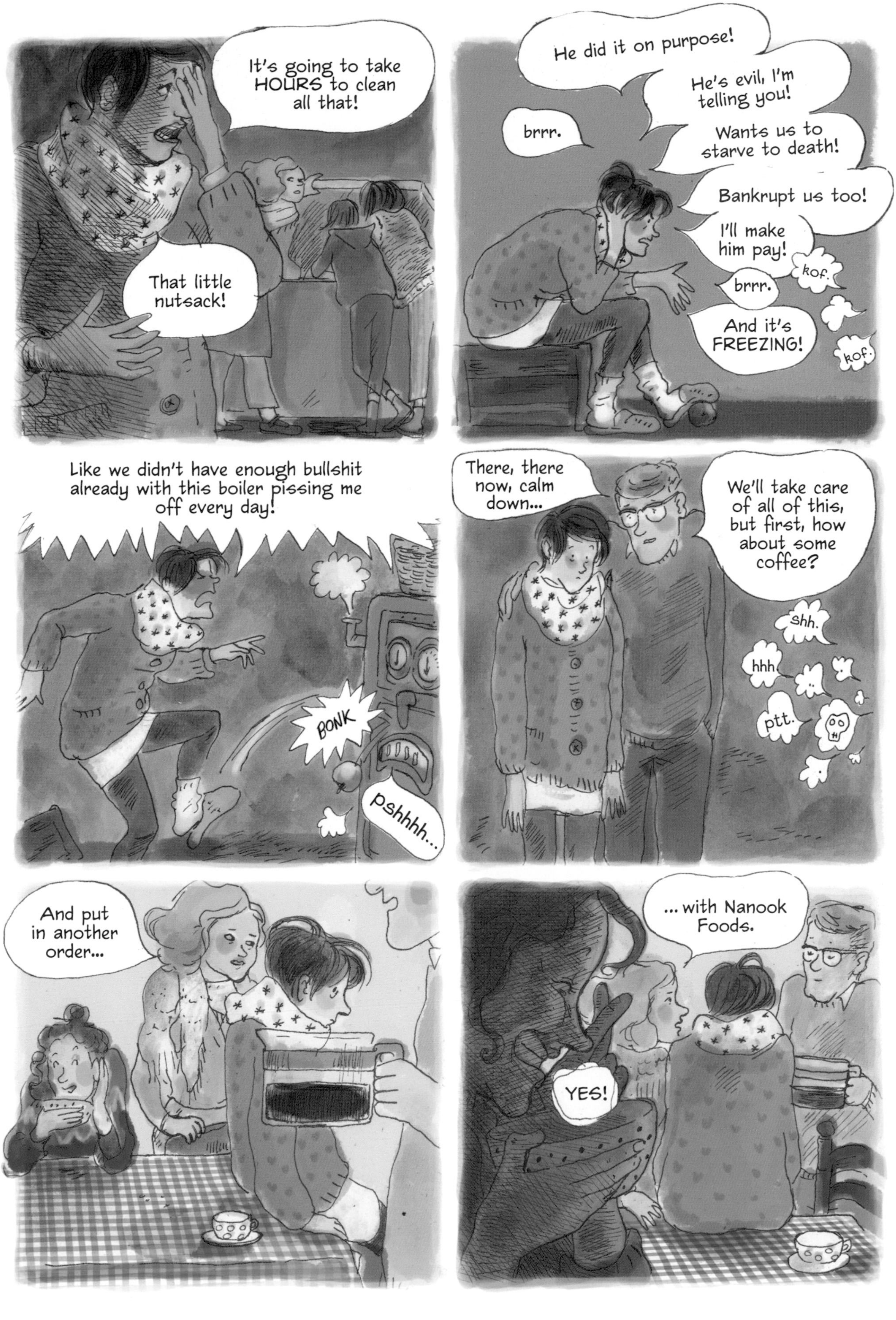
It's going to take HOURS to clean all that!
That little nutsack!
He did it on purpose!
He's evil, I'm telling you!
brrr.
Wants us to starve to death!
Bankrupt us too!
I'll make him pay!
kof.
brrr.
And it's FREEZING!
kof.
Like we didn't have enough bullshit already with this boiler pissing me off every day!
BONK
pshhhh...
There, there now, calm down...
We'll take care of all of this, but first, how about some coffee?
shh.
hhh
ptt.
And put in another order...
...with Nanook Foods.
YES!

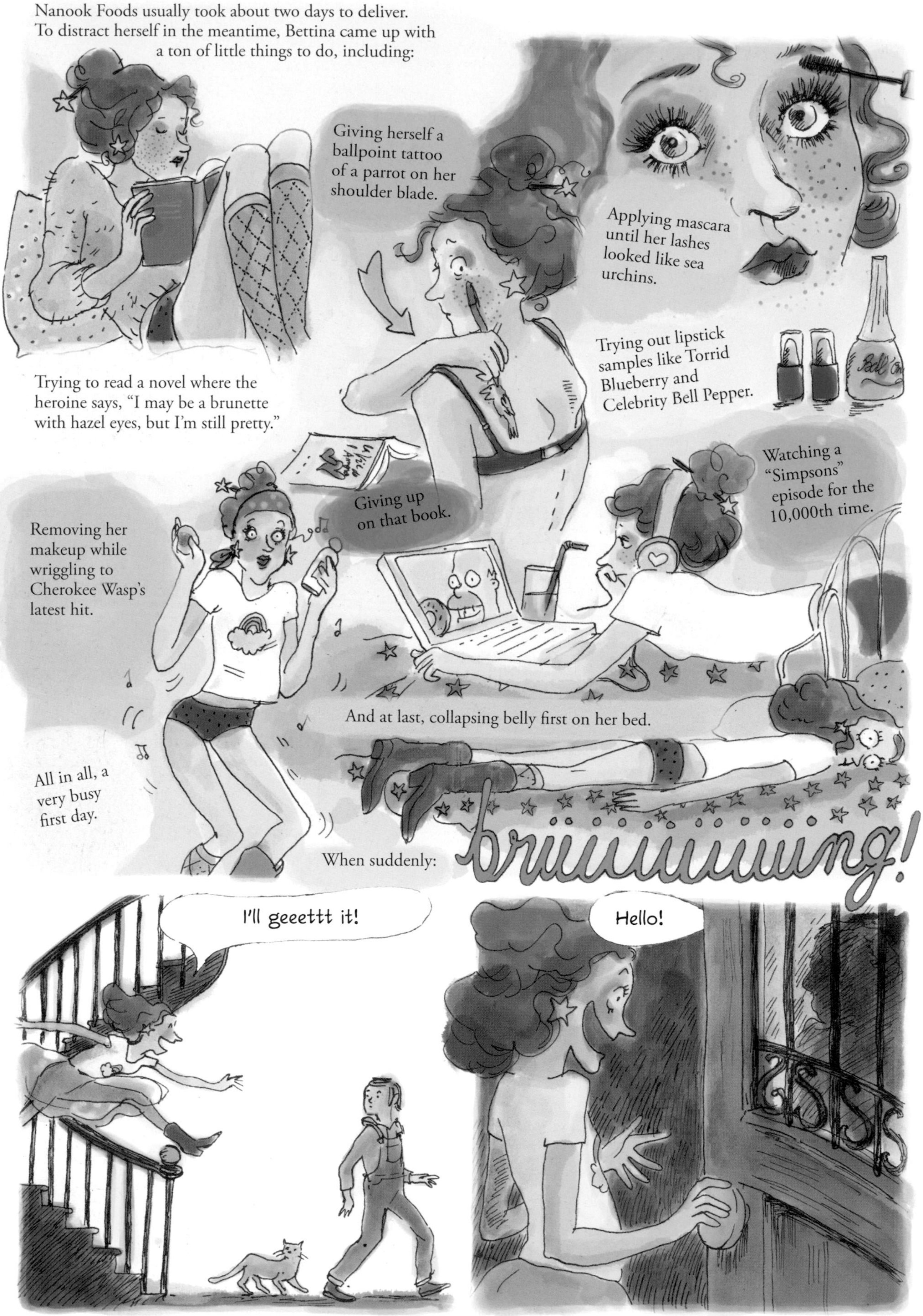
Nanook Foods usually took about two days to deliver. To distract herself in the meantime, Bettina came up with a ton of little things to do, including:
Trying to read a novel where the heroine says, "I may be a brunette with hazel eyes, but I'm still pretty."
Giving herself a ballpoint tattoo of a parrot on her shoulder blade.
Applying mascara until her lashes looked like sea urchins.
Trying out lipstick samples like Torrid Blueberry and Celebrity Bell Pepper.
Giving up on that book.
Removing her makeup while wriggling to Cherokee Wasp's latest hit.
Watching a "Simpsons" episode for the 10,000th time.
And at last, collapsing belly first on her bed.
All in all, a very busy first day.
When suddenly:
bruuuuuuuing!
I'll geeettt it!
Hello!

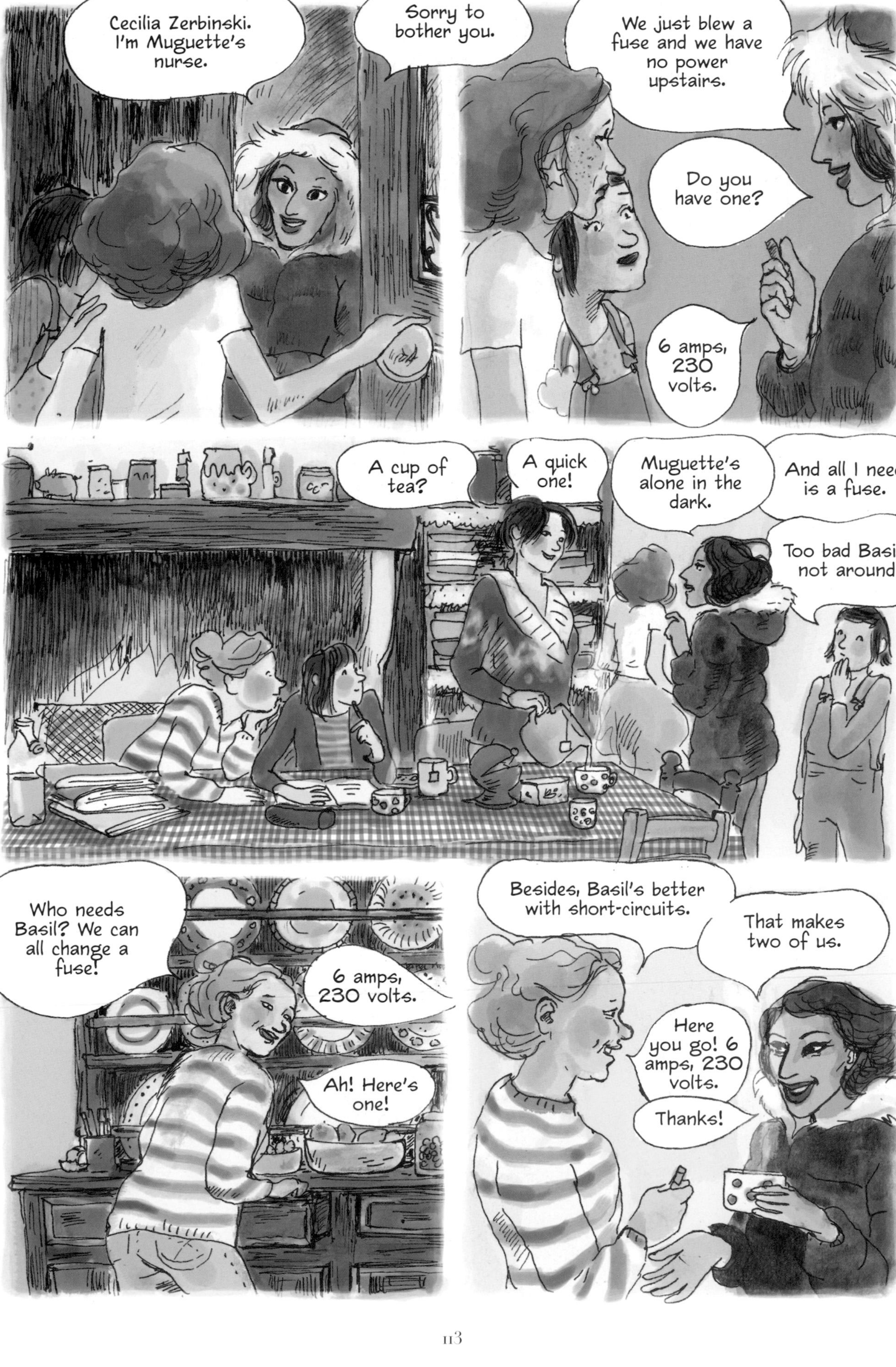
Cecilia Zerbinski. I'm Muguette's nurse.
Sorry to bother you.
We just blew a fuse and we have no power upstairs.
Do you have one?
6 amps, 230 volts.
A cup of tea?
A quick one!
Muguette's alone in the dark.
And all I need is a fuse.
Too bad Basil's not around!
Who needs Basil? We can all change a fuse!
6 amps, 230 volts.
Ah! Here's one!
Besides, Basil's better with short-circuits.
That makes two of us.
Here you go! 6 amps, 230 volts.
Thanks!

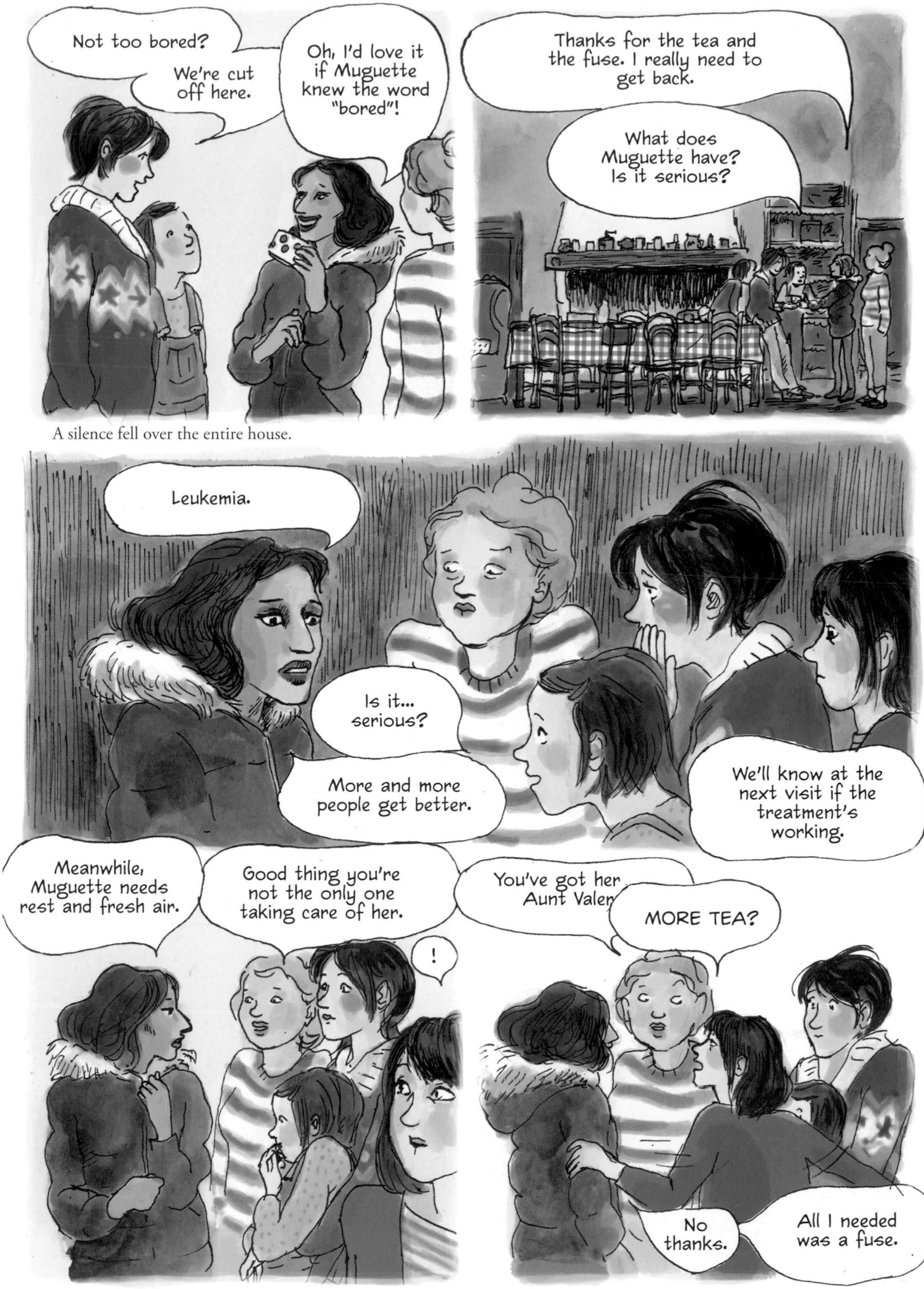
Not too bored?
We're cut off here.
Oh, I'd love it if Muguette knew the word "bored"!
Thanks for the tea and the fuse. I really need to get back.
What does Muguette have? Is it serious?
A silence fell over the entire house.
Leukemia.
Is it... serious?
More and more people get better.
We'll know at the next visit if the treatment's working.
Meanwhile, Muguette needs rest and fresh air.
Good thing you're not the only one taking care of her.
!
You've got her Aunt Valen
MORE TEA?
No thanks.
All I needed was a fuse.

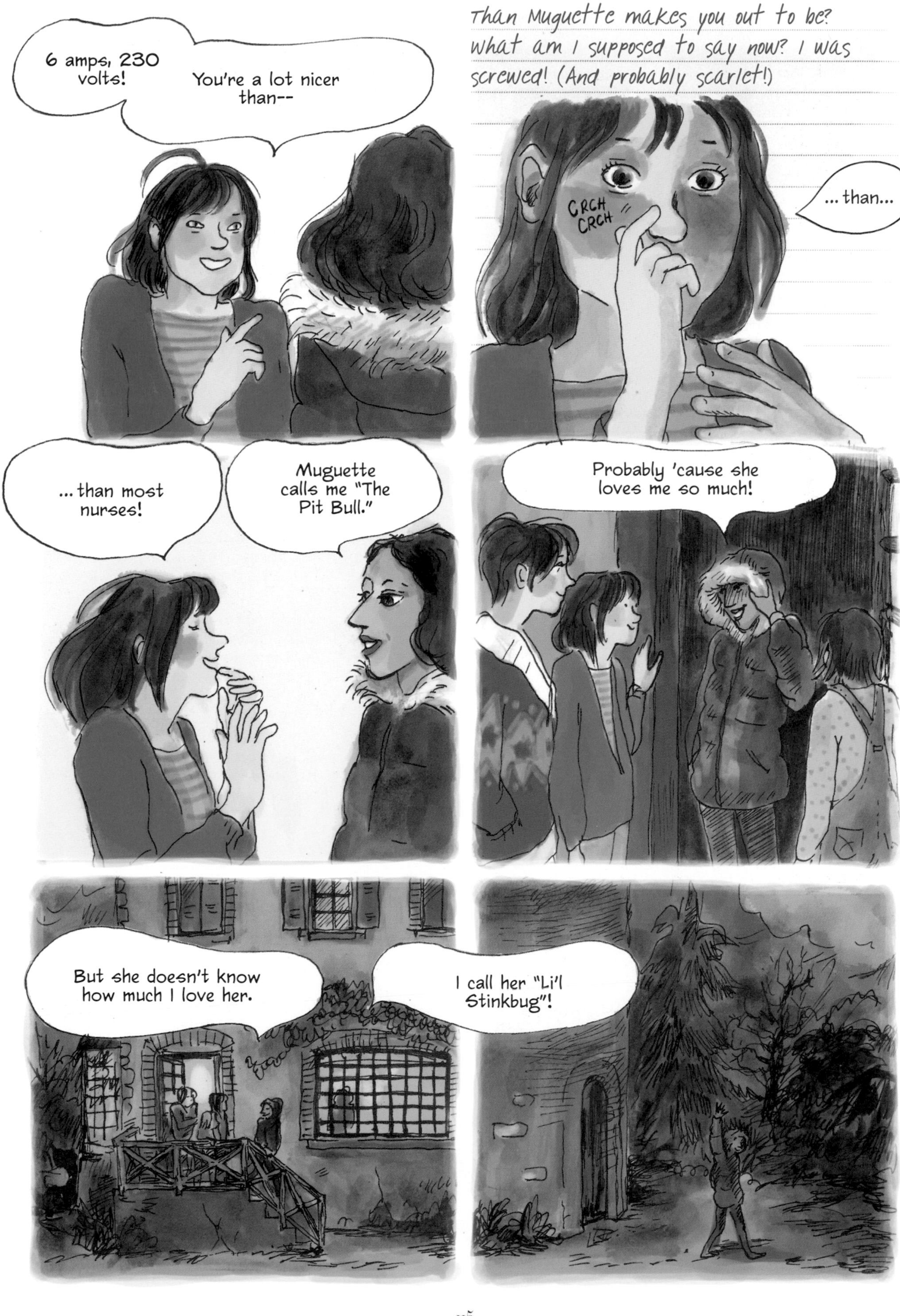
6 amps, 230 volts!
You're a lot nicer than--
Than Muguette makes you out to be? What am I supposed to say now? I was screwed! (And probably scarlet!)
CRCH CRCH
... than...
... than most nurses!
Muguette calls me "The Pit Bull."
Probably 'cause she loves me so much!
But she doesn't know how much I love her.
I call her "Li'l Stinkbug"!

Sometimes, Enid would lock herself in the bathroom to pee and chat with her friend, Flush the Gnome. She'd tell him whatever was on her mind, and he'd answer with gentle taps on the tank. To her it was a real conversation.

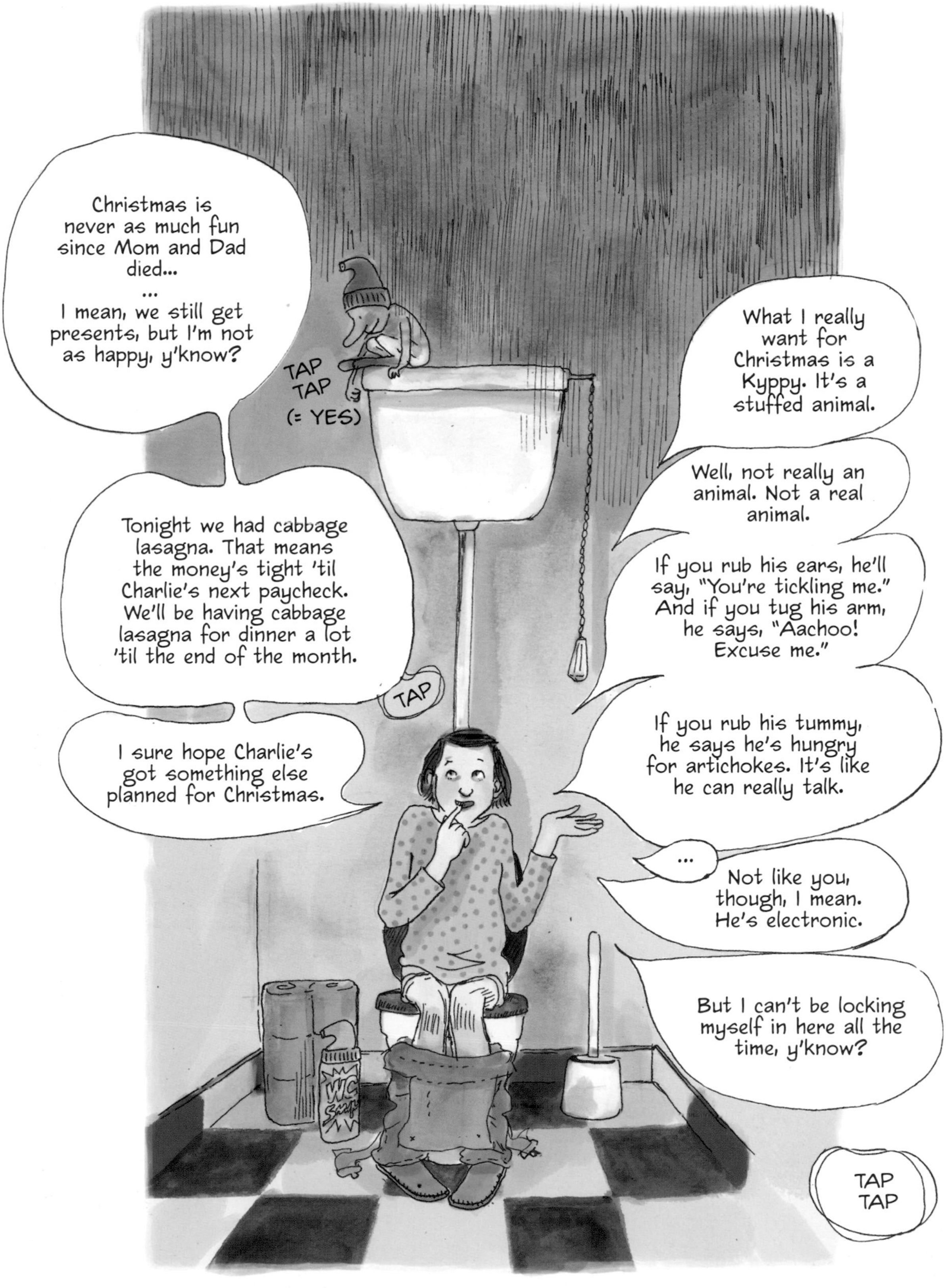
Christmas is never as much fun since Mom and Dad died... ... I mean, we still get presents, but I'm not as happy, y'know?
TAP TAP (= YES)
What I really want for Christmas is a Kyppy. It's a stuffed animal.
Well, not really an animal. Not a real animal.
Tonight we had cabbage lasagna. That means the money's tight 'til Charlie's next paycheck. We'll be having cabbage lasagna for dinner a lot 'til the end of the month.
If you rub his ears, he'll say, "You're tickling me." And if you tug his arm, he says, "Aachoo! Excuse me."
TAP
I sure hope Charlie's got something else planned for Christmas.
If you rub his tummy, he says he's hungry for artichokes. It's like he can really talk.
...
Not like you, though, I mean. He's electronic.
But I can't be locking myself in here all the time, y'know?
TAP TAP

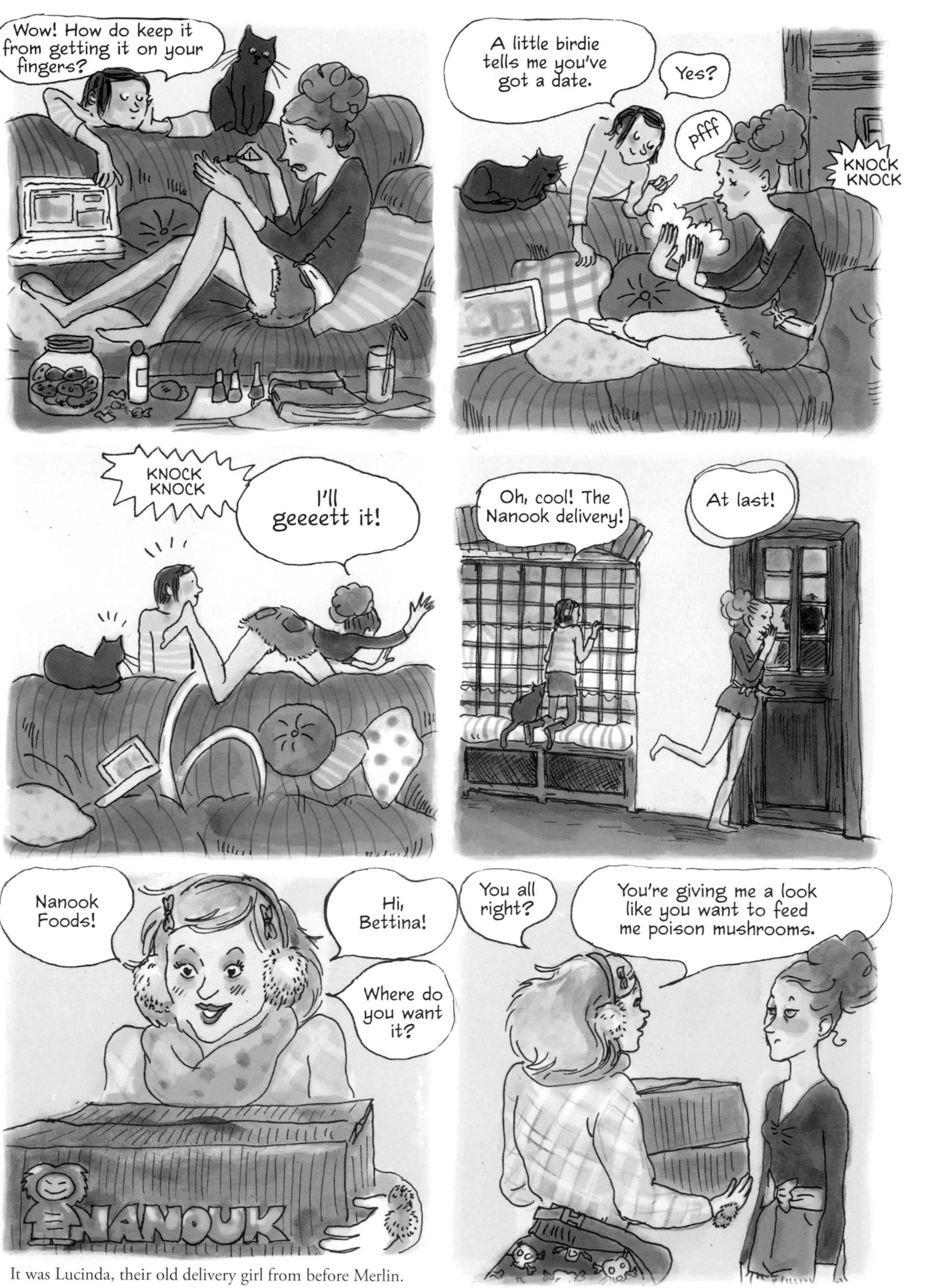
Wow! How do keep it from getting it on your fingers?
A little birdie tells me you've got a date.
Yes?
pfff
KNOCK KNOCK
KNOCK KNOCK
I'll geeeett it!
Oh, cool! The Nanook delivery!
At last!
Nanook Foods!
Hi, Bettina!
Where do you want it?
NANOUK
You all right?
You're giving me a look like you want to feed me poison mushrooms.

It was Lucinda, their old delivery girl from before Merlin.

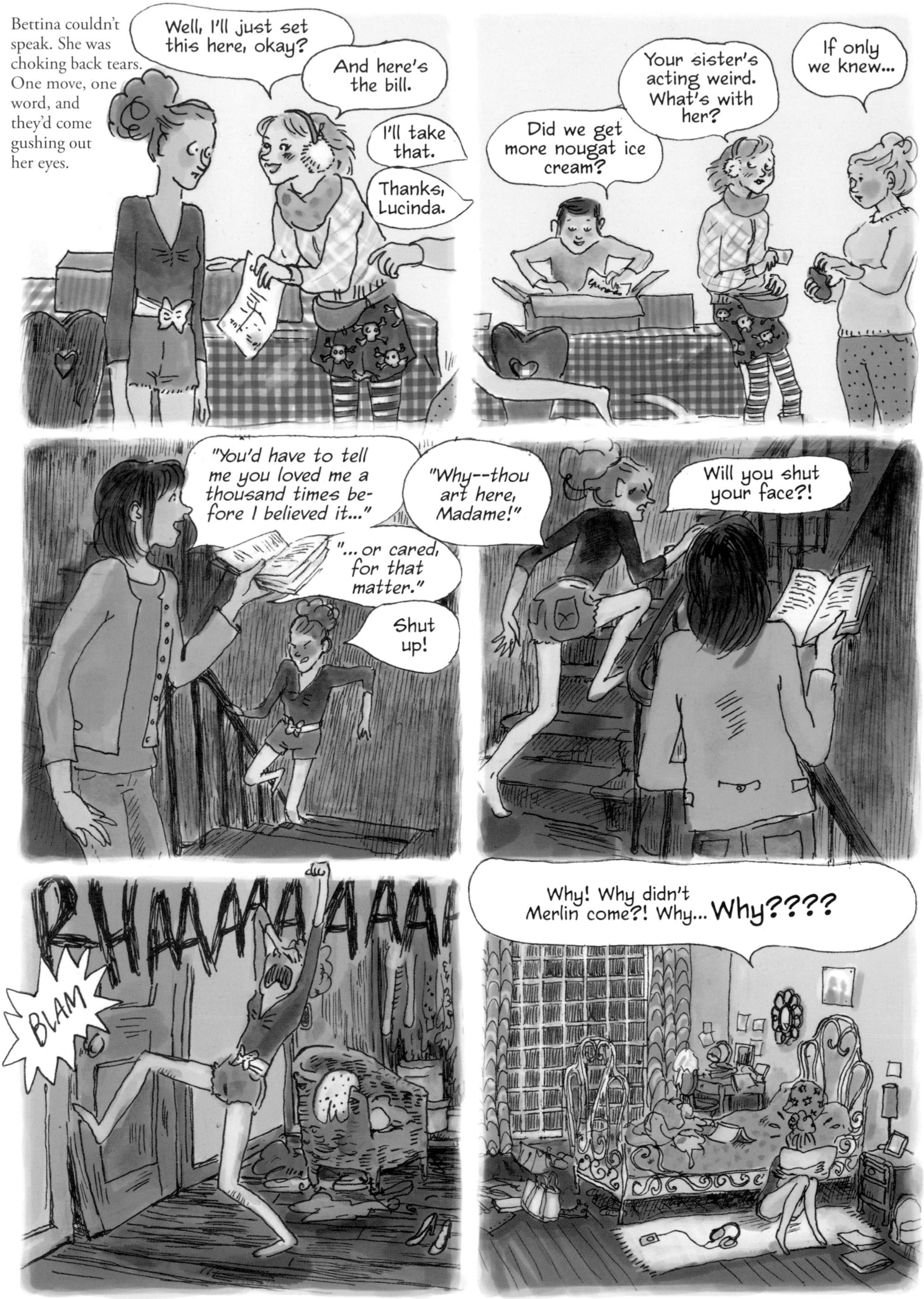
Bettina couldn't speak. She was choking back tears. One move, one word, and they'd come gushing out her eyes.
Well, I'll just set this here, okay?
And here's the bill.
I'll take that.
Thanks, Lucinda.
Did we get more nougat ice cream?
Your sister's acting weird. What's with her?
If only we knew...
"You'd have to tell me you loved me a thousand times before I believed it..."
"...or cared, for that matter."
Shut up!
"Why--thou art here, Madame!"
Will you shut your face?!
RHAAAAAAAA
BLAM
Why! Why didn't Merlin come?! Why... Why????

The air had become blue as glass. An Anatolian wind had covered all Western Europe with frost, and Madame Boiler had to work twice as hard. But none of this disheartened the grasshoppers. It was open bar now in Hortense's belly, liver, spleen, and ribcage, with a trampoline on every floor, even at night.

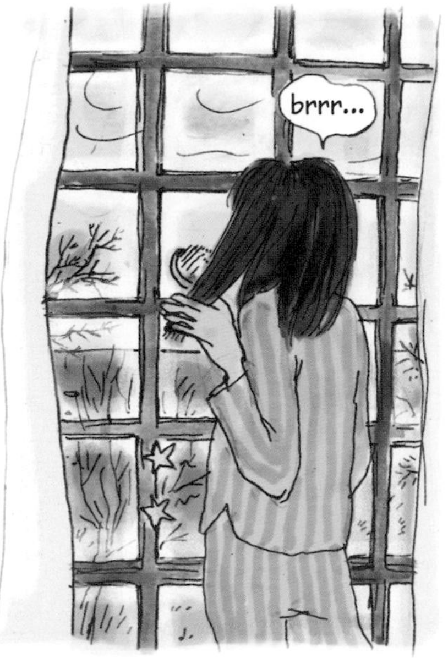
brrr...

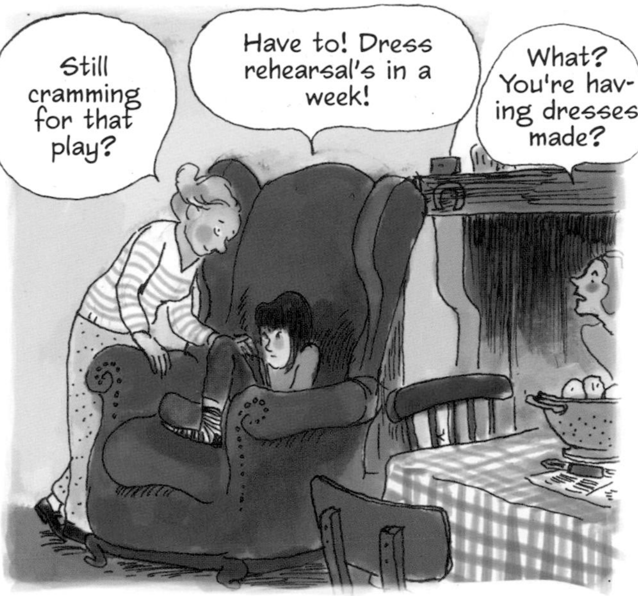
Still cramming for that play?
Have to! Dress rehearsal's in a week!
What? You're having dresses made?

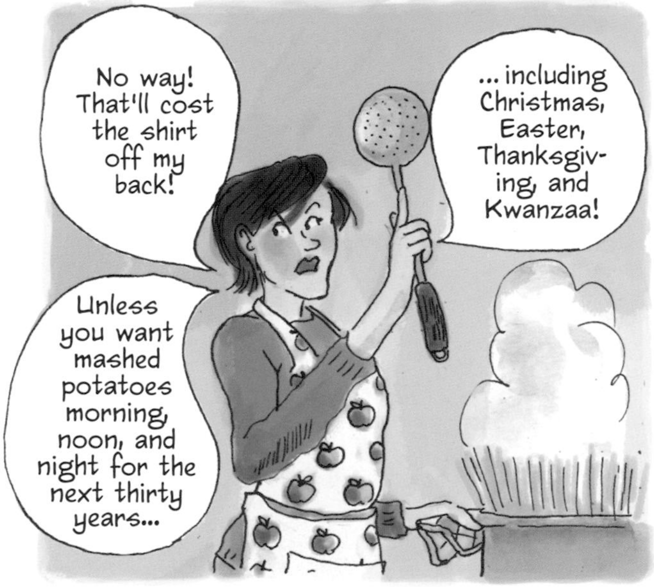
No way! That'll cost the shirt off my back!
Unless you want mashed potatoes morning, noon, and night for the next thirty years...
...including Christmas, Easter, Thanksgiving, and Kwanzaa!

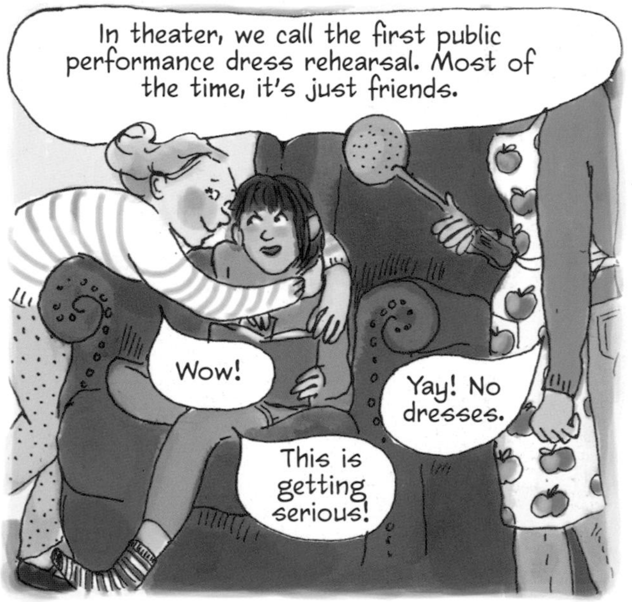
In theater, we call the first public performance dress rehearsal. Most of the time, it's just friends.
Wow!
Yay! No dresses.
This is getting serious!

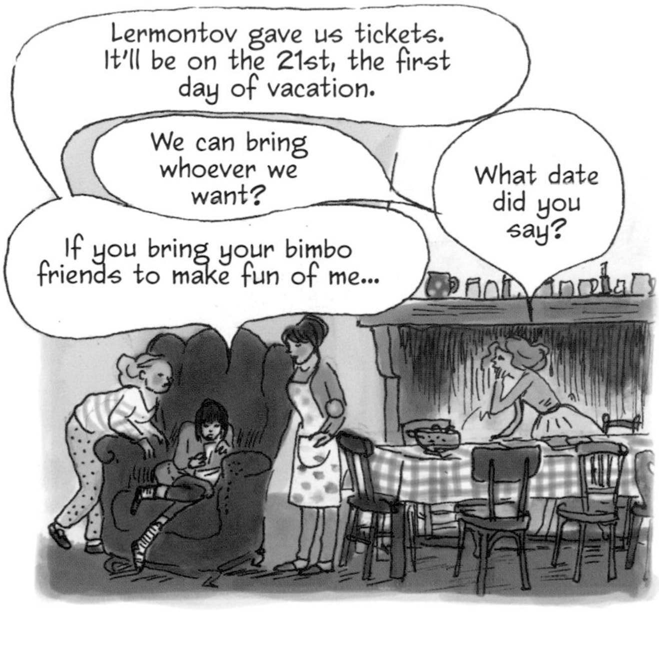
Lermontov gave us tickets. It'll be on the 21st, the first day of vacation.
We can bring whoever we want?
If you bring your bimbo friends to make fun of me...
What date did you say?

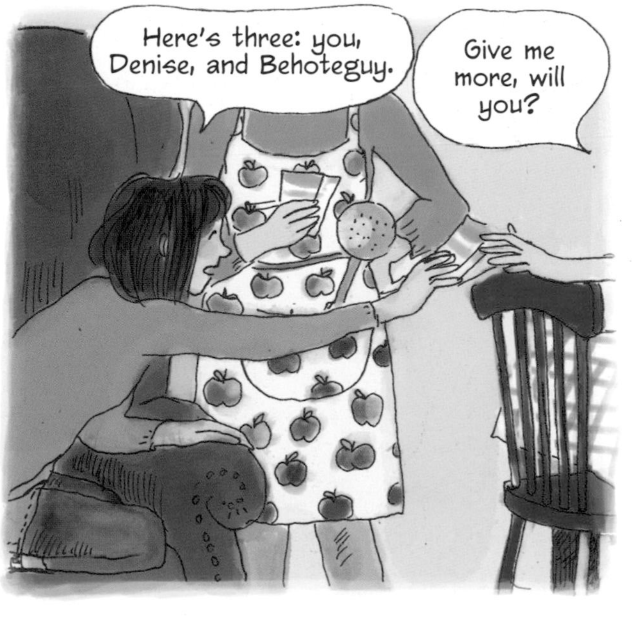
Here's three: you, Denise, and Behoteguy.
Give me more, will you?

For their parents--
Nuh-uh! Liar! She wants one for her loverboy, the one who--
HOP!
Heeeeey!
No I don't, you little runt!
Merlin Merlin mmm-mm-mm-mm.
Merlin Gillepsie
c/o NANOUK

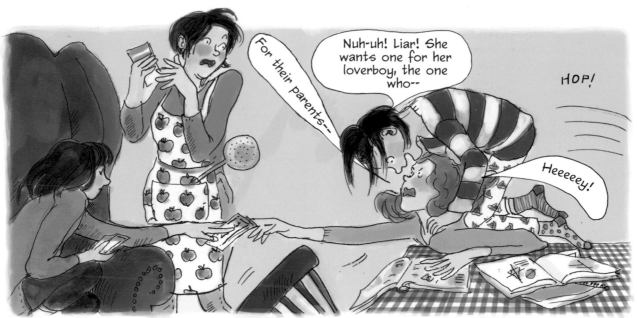

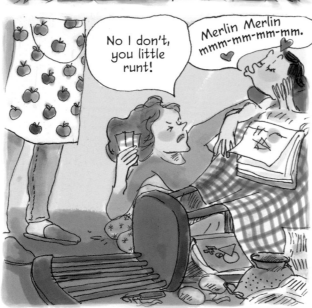

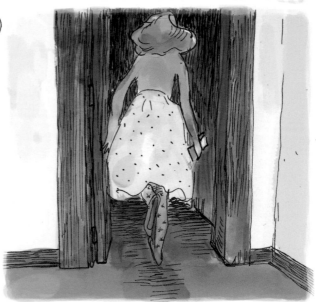

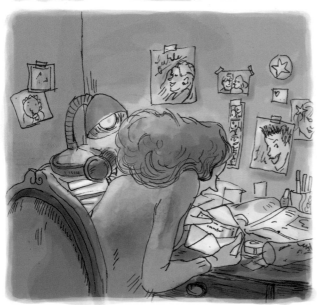

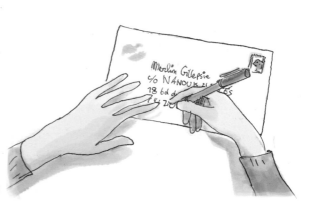

People were starting to hide Christmas gifts around the house. They tried not to be seen with presents, locking themselves away to wrap them and sticking them in places where they were never supposed to be found. The season was afoot.

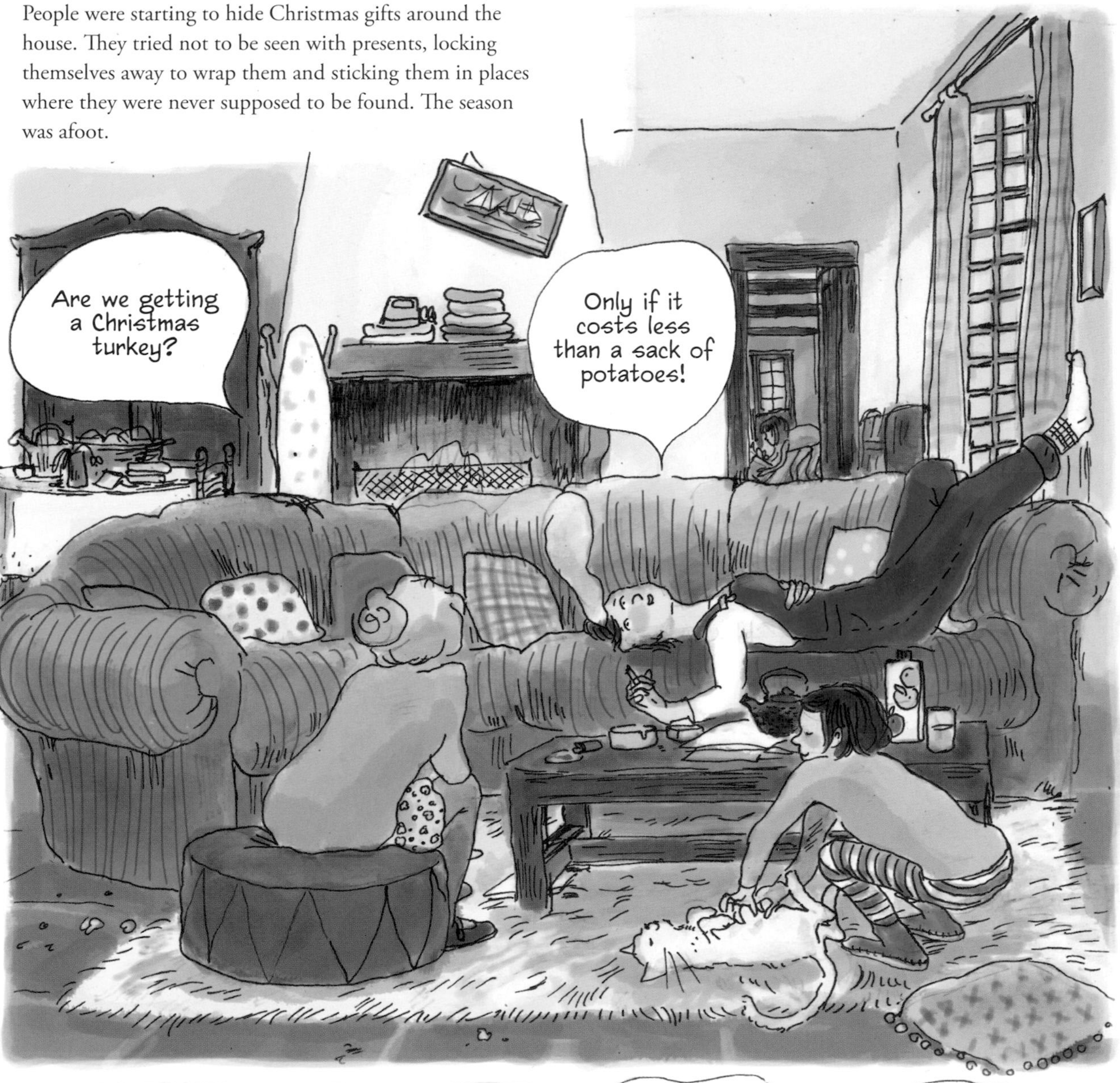
Are we getting a Christmas turkey?
Only if it costs less than a sack of potatoes!

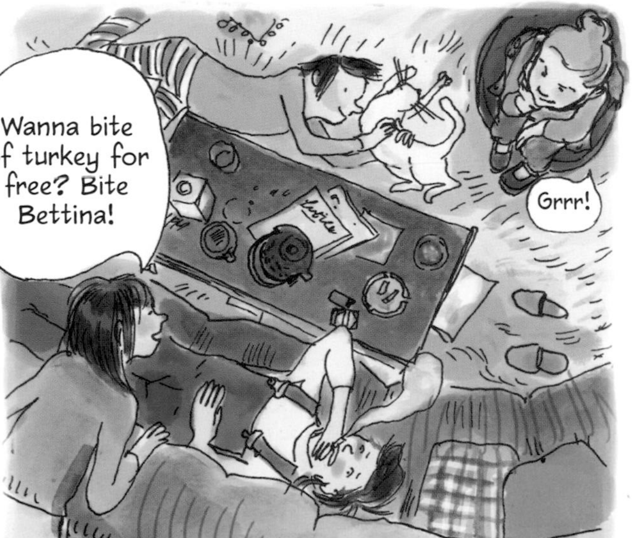
Wanna bite of turkey for free? Bite Bettina!
Grrr!

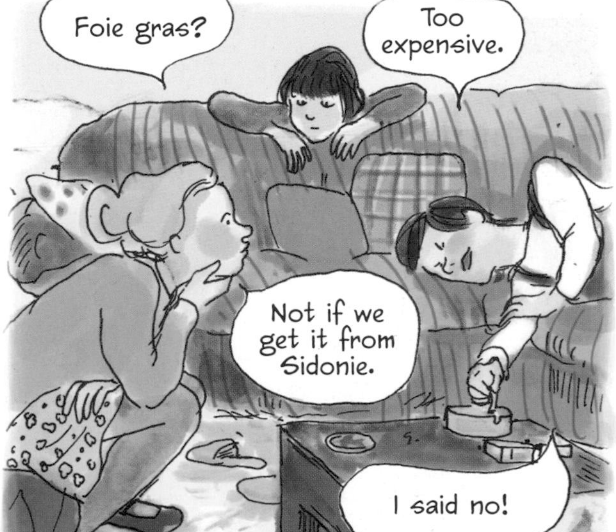
Foie gras?
Too expensive.
Not if we get it from Sidonie.
I said no!

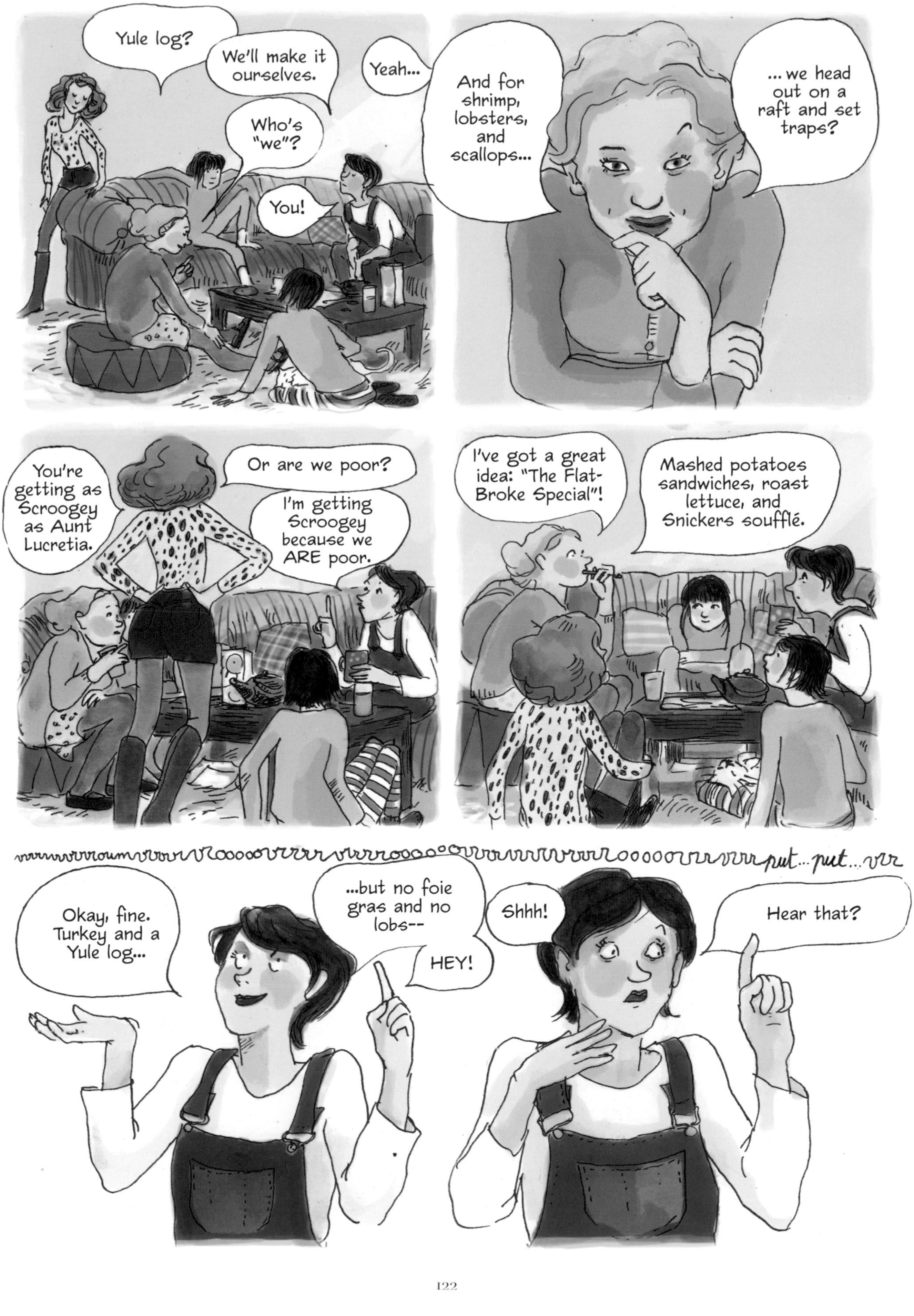
Yule log?
We'll make it ourselves.
Yeah...
Who's "we"?
You!
And for shrimp, lobsters, and scallops...
...we head out on a raft and set traps?
You're getting as Scroogey as Aunt Lucretia.
Or are we poor?
I'm getting Scroogey because we ARE poor.
I've got a great idea: "The Flat-Broke Special"!
Mashed potatoes sandwiches, roast lettuce, and Snickers soufflé.
vvvvvvvvroumvvvvvVVooooovvvvvvvvvvooooOvvvvvvvvvvvvvooooovvvvvvvput...put...vvv
Okay, fine. Turkey and a Yule log...
...but no foie gras and no lobs--
HEY!
Shhh!
Hear that?

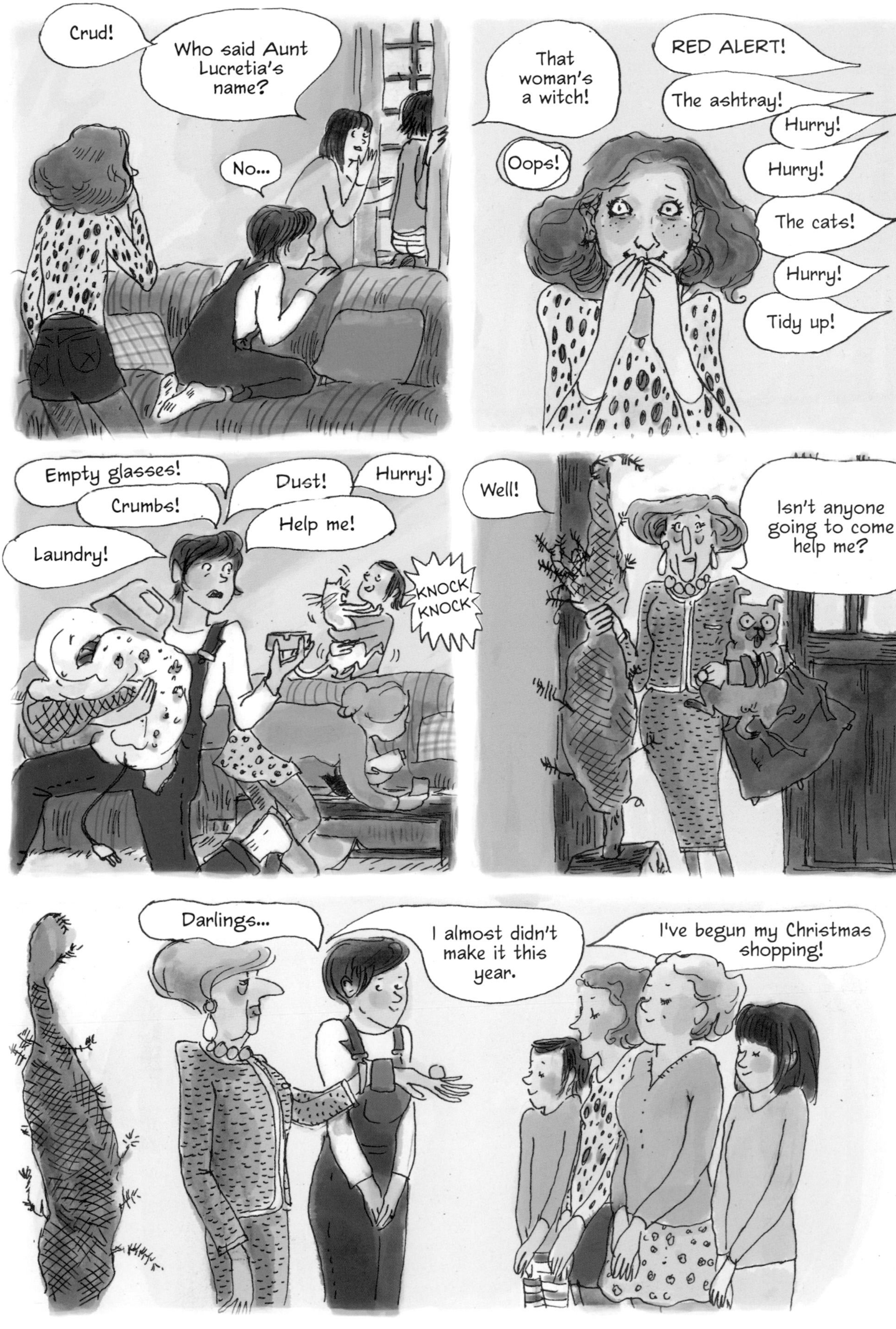
Crud!
Who said Aunt Lucretia's name?
No...
That woman's a witch!
Oops!
RED ALERT!
The ashtray!
Hurry!
Hurry!
The cats!
Hurry!
Tidy up!
Empty glasses!
Crumbs!
Laundry!
Dust!
Hurry!
Help me!
KNOCK KNOCK
Well!
Isn't anyone going to come help me?
Darlings...
I almost didn't make it this year.
I've begun my Christmas shopping!

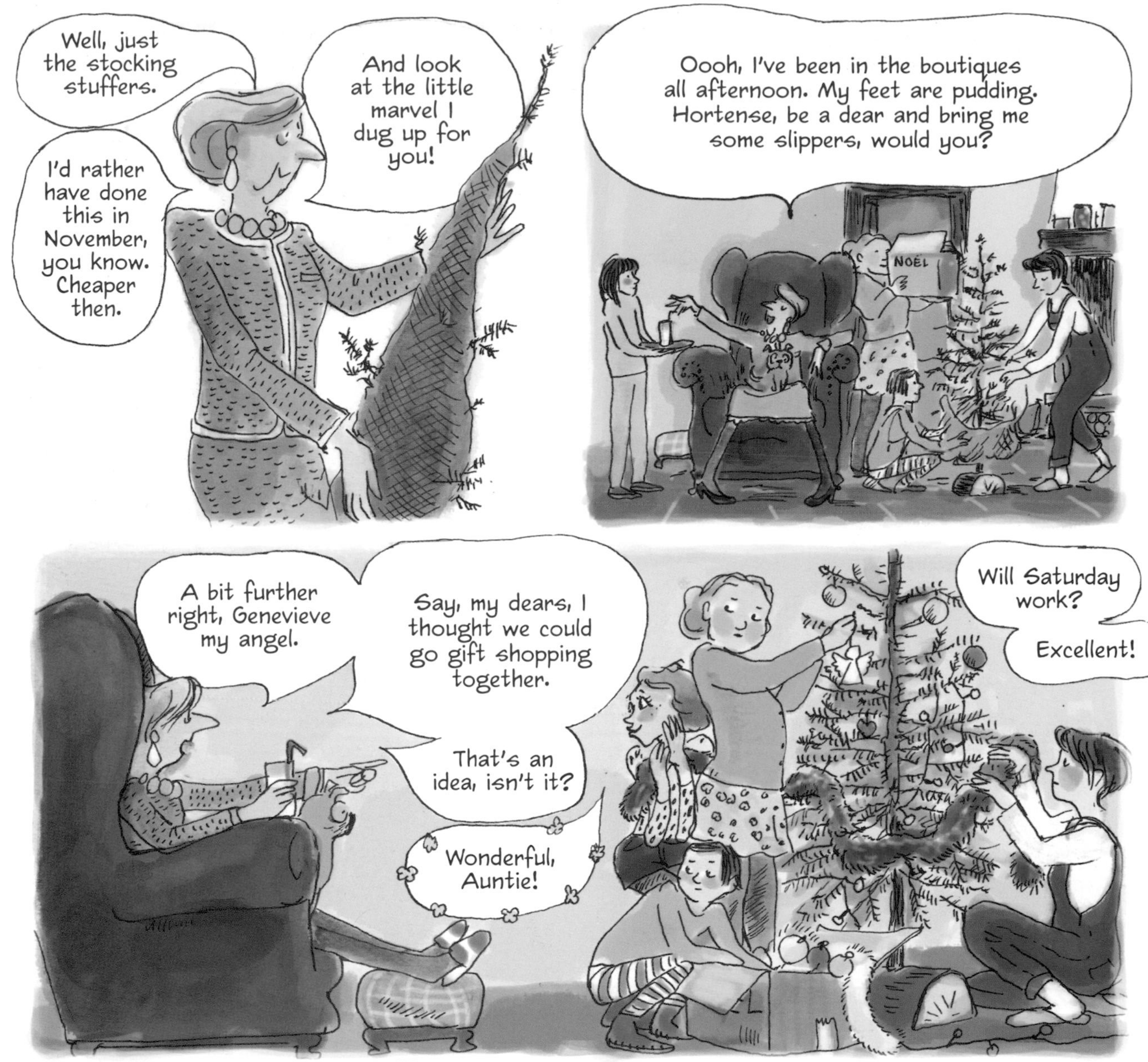
Well, just the stocking stuffers.
I'd rather have done this in November, you know. Cheaper then.
And look at the little marvel I dug up for you!
Oooh, I've been in the boutiques all afternoon. My feet are pudding. Hortense, be a dear and bring me some slippers, would you?
NOËL
A bit further right, Genevieve my angel.
Say, my dears, I thought we could go gift shopping together.
That's an idea, isn't it?
Wonderful, Auntie!
Will Saturday work?
Excellent!

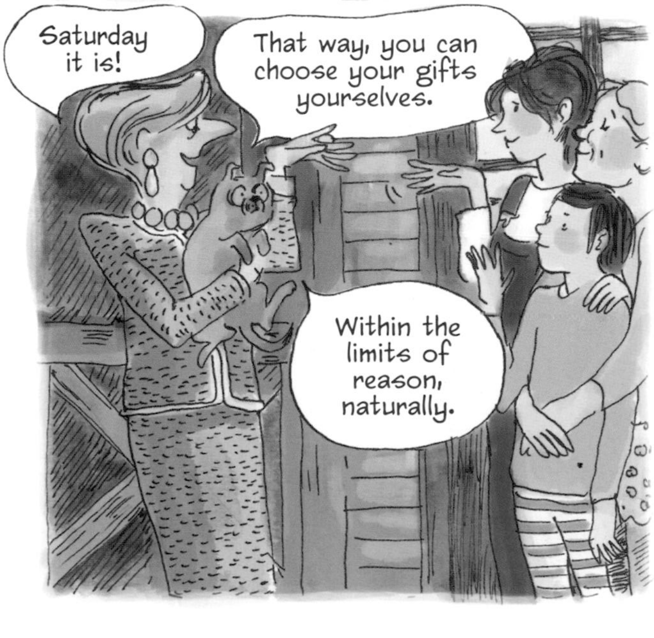
Saturday it is!
That way, you can choose your gifts yourselves.
Within the limits of reason, naturally.

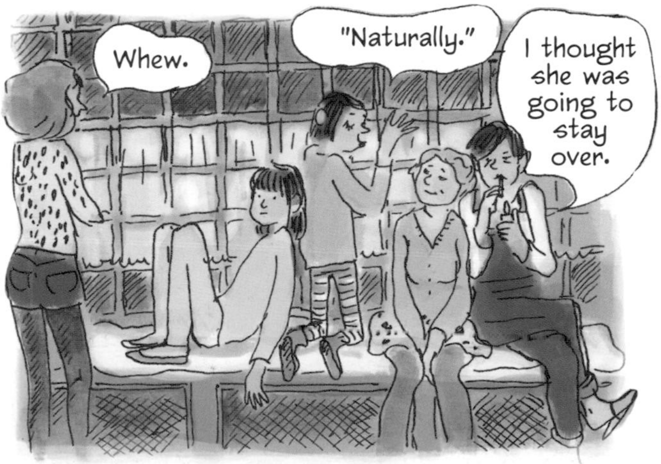
Whew.
"Naturally."
I thought she was going to stay over.

As after every visit from their Aunt Lucretia, the sisters were worn out. Relieved. And unfathomably sad. Because, through no fault of Aunt Lucretia's, the death of their parents became a palpable ache once more, dreadful as the carcass of a drowned animal floating back up to the surface of a lake.

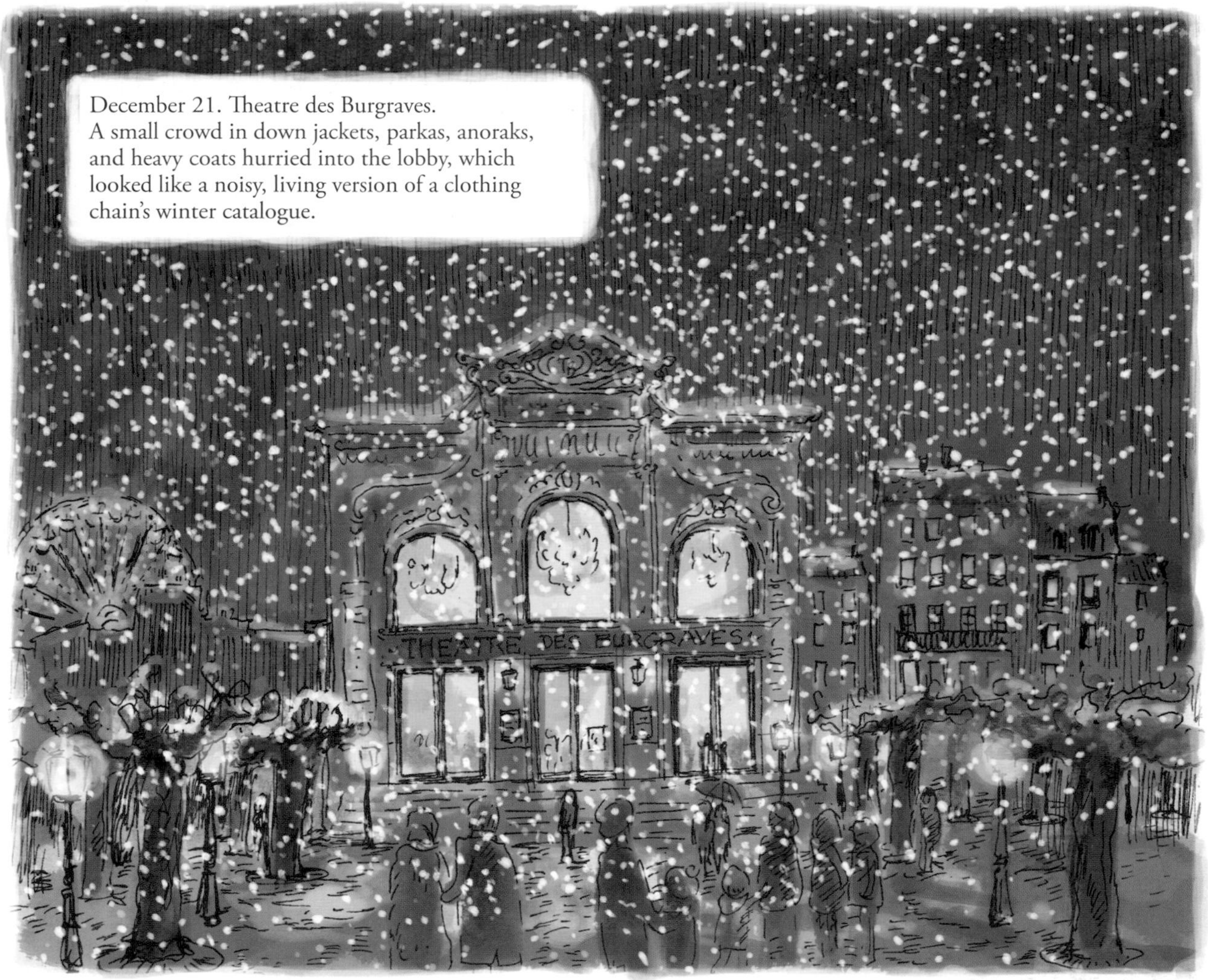
December 21. Theatre des Burgraves.
A small crowd in down jackets, parkas, anoraks, and heavy coats hurried into the lobby, which looked like a noisy, living version of a clothing chain's winter catalogue.
THEATRE DES BURGRAVES

Charlie thought Cecilia Zerbinski looked quite chic in her Russian Princess coat. She thought that maybe Basil would like her to trade her old fraying sheepskin in for a prettier, more feminine coat. If only she had the money...

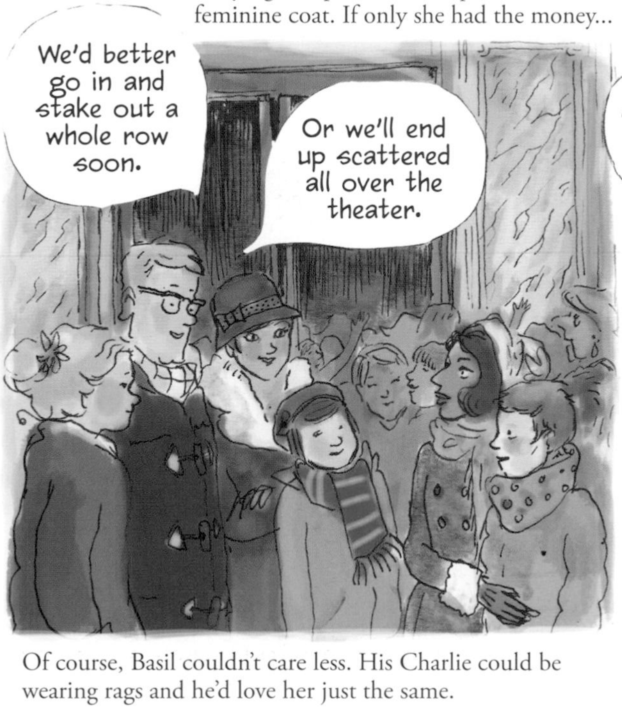
We'd better go in and stake out a whole row soon.
Or we'll end up scattered all over the theater.

Of course, Basil couldn't care less. His Charlie could be wearing rags and he'd love her just the same.

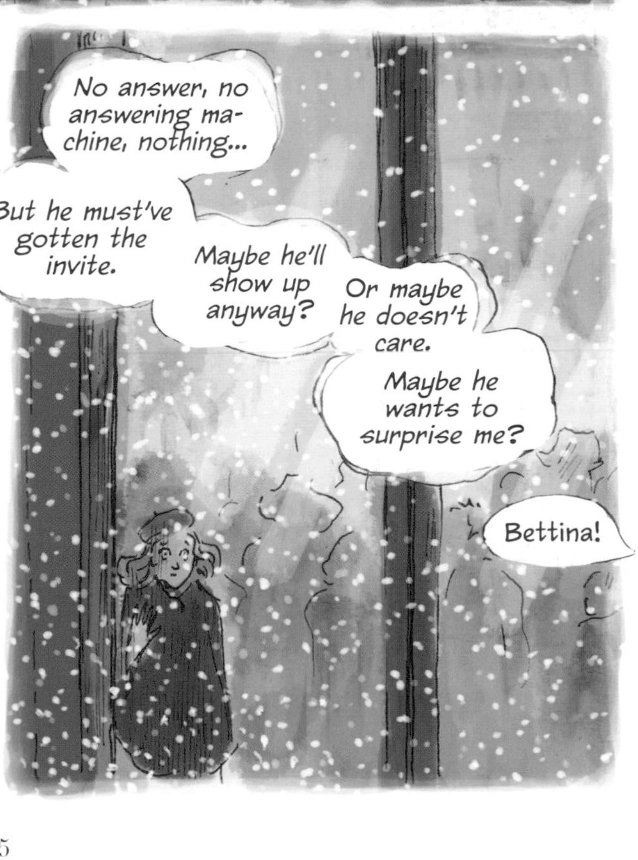
No answer, no answering machine, nothing...
But he must've gotten the invite.
Maybe he'll show up anyway?
Or maybe he doesn't care.
Maybe he wants to surprise me?
Bettina!

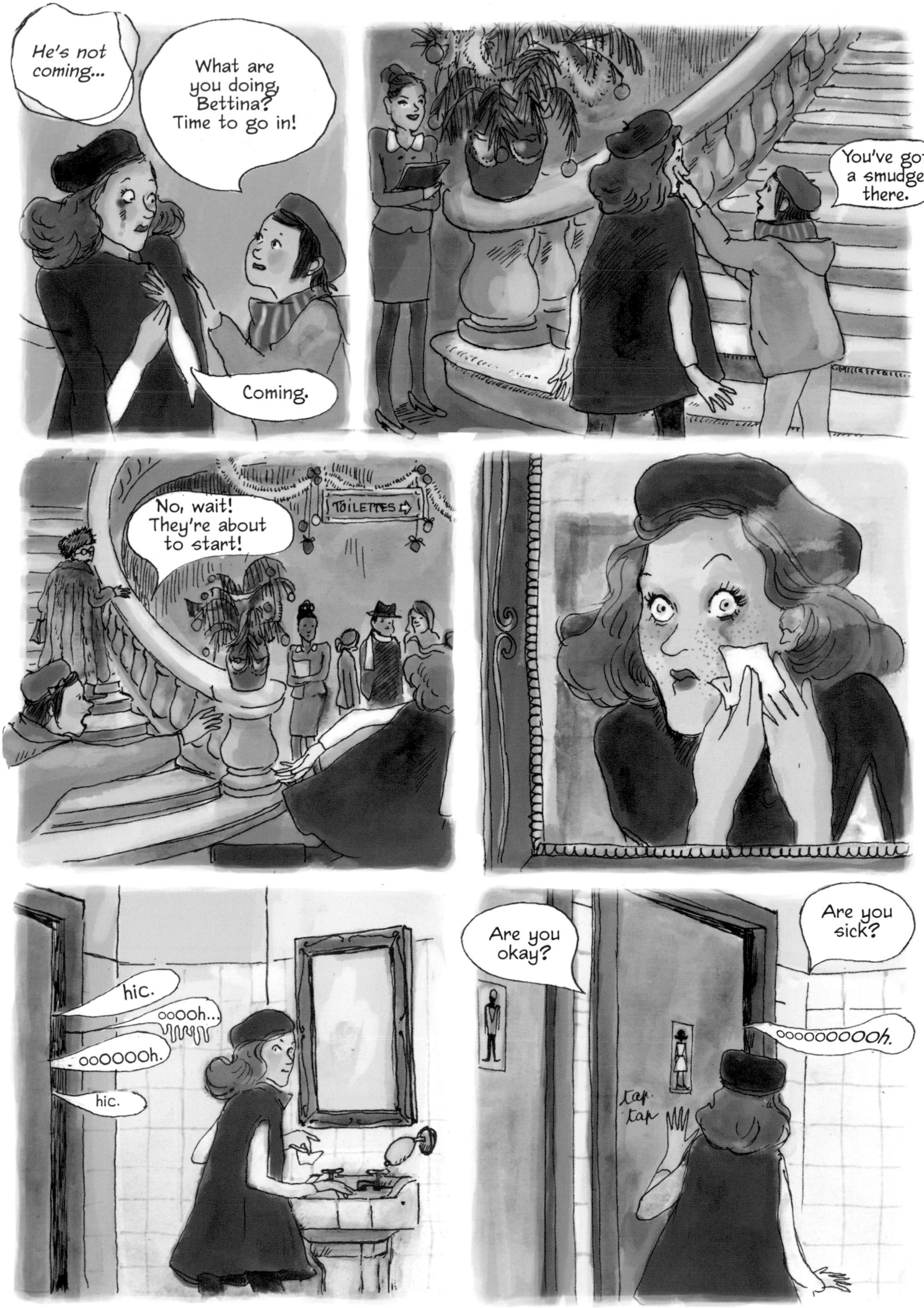
He's not coming...
What are you doing, Bettina? Time to go in!
Coming.
You've got a smudge there.
No, wait! They're about to start!
TOILETTES
hic.
oooh...
oooOOOh.
hic.
Are you okay?
Are you sick?
oooooooOOh.
tap. tap

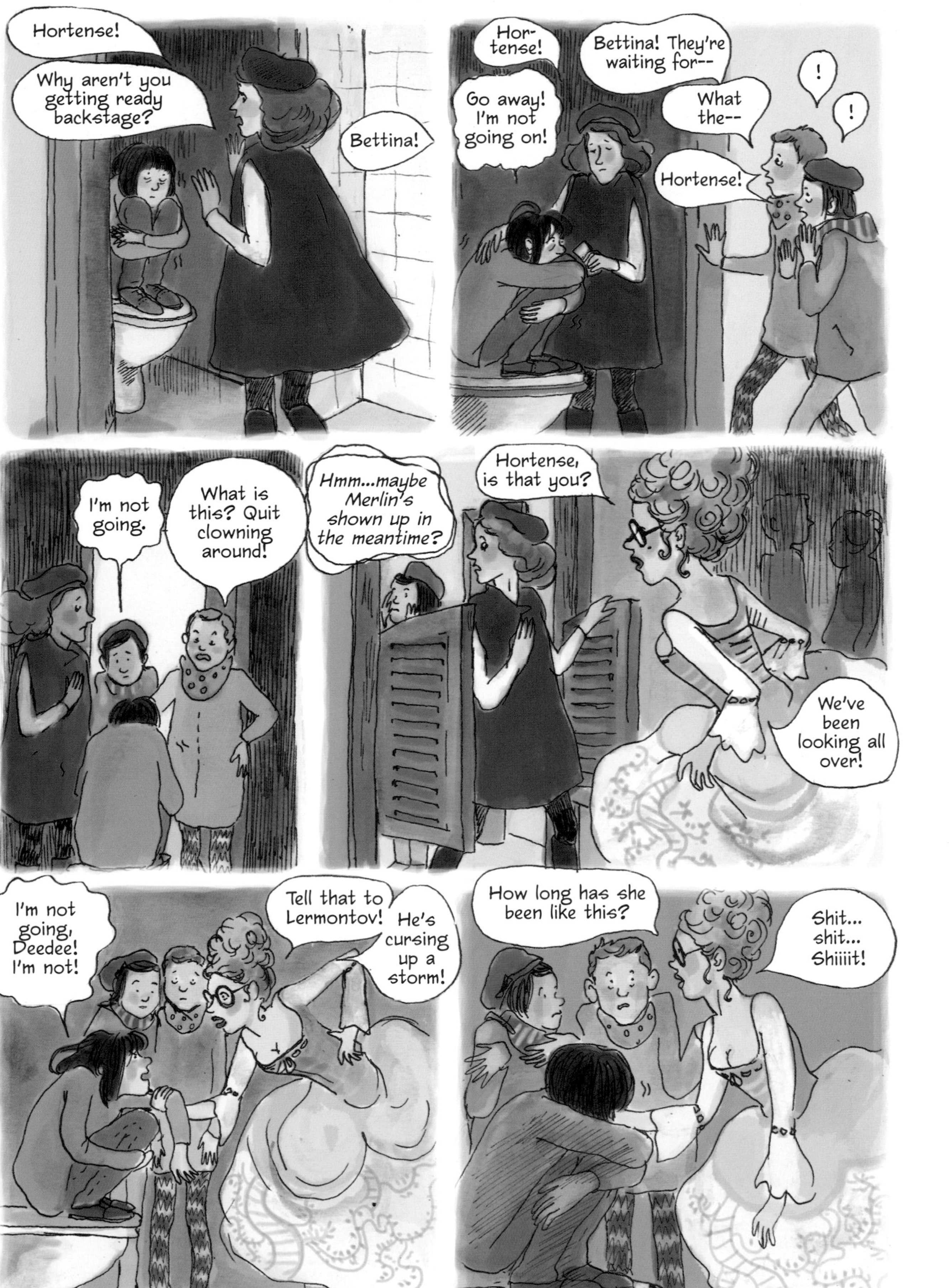

Hortense!
Why aren't you getting ready backstage?
Bettina!
Hortense!
Go away! I'm not going on!
Bettina! They're waiting for--
What the--
!
!
Hortense!
I'm not going.
What is this? Quit clowning around!
Hmm...maybe Merlin's shown up in the meantime?
Hortense, is that you?
We've been looking all over!
I'm not going, Deedee! I'm not!
Tell that to Lermontov!
He's cursing up a storm!
How long has she been like this?
Shit... shit... Shiiiit!

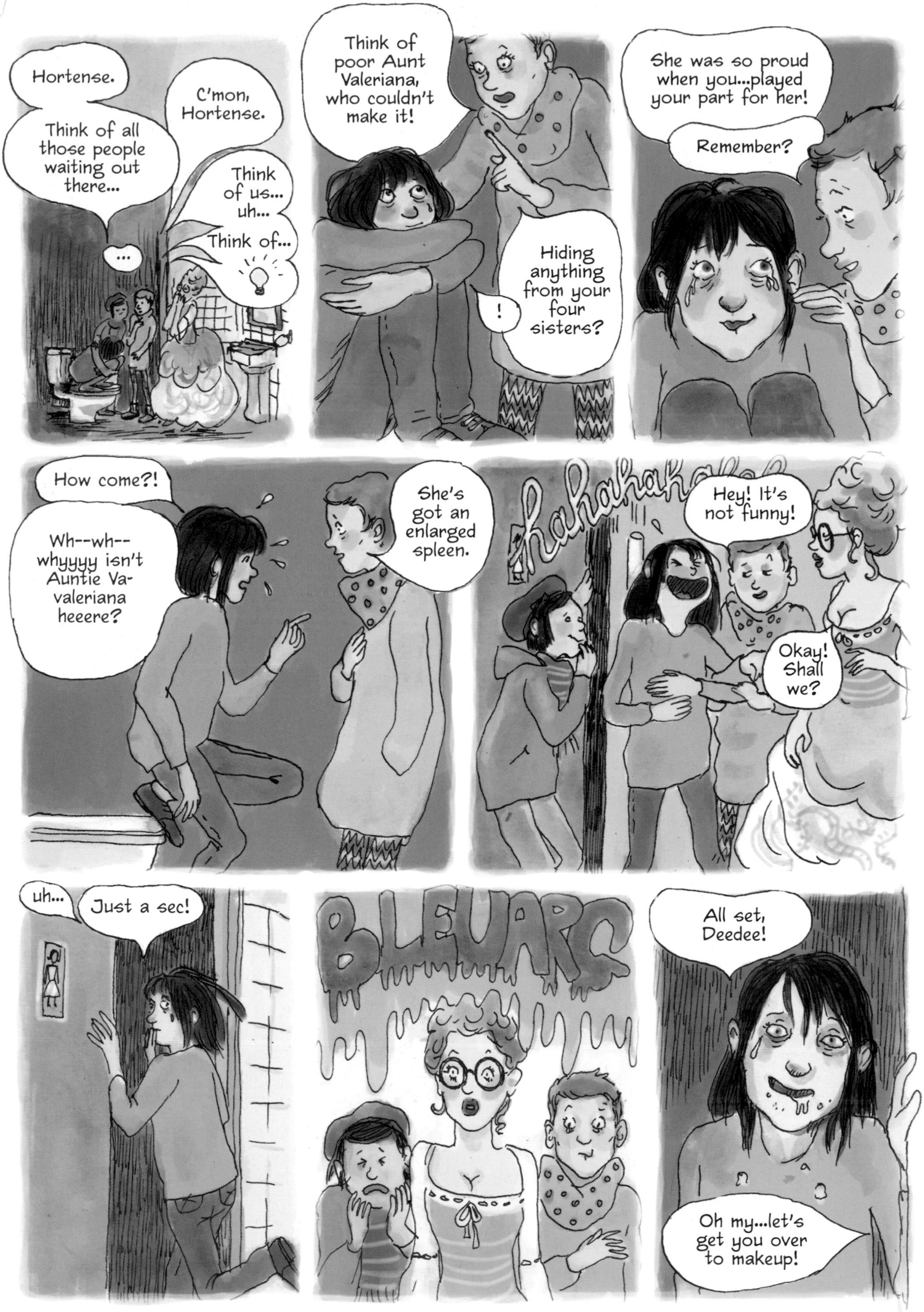
Hortense.
Think of all those people waiting out there...
C'mon, Hortense.
...
Think of us... uh...
Think of...
Think of poor Aunt Valeriana, who couldn't make it!
Hiding anything from your four sisters?
!
She was so proud when you...played your part for her!
Remember?
How come?!
Wh--wh--whyyyy isn't Auntie Va-valeriana heeere?
She's got an enlarged spleen.
hahahaha
Hey! It's not funny!
Okay! Shall we?
uh...
Just a sec!
BLEUARG
All set, Deedee!
Oh my...let's get you over to makeup!

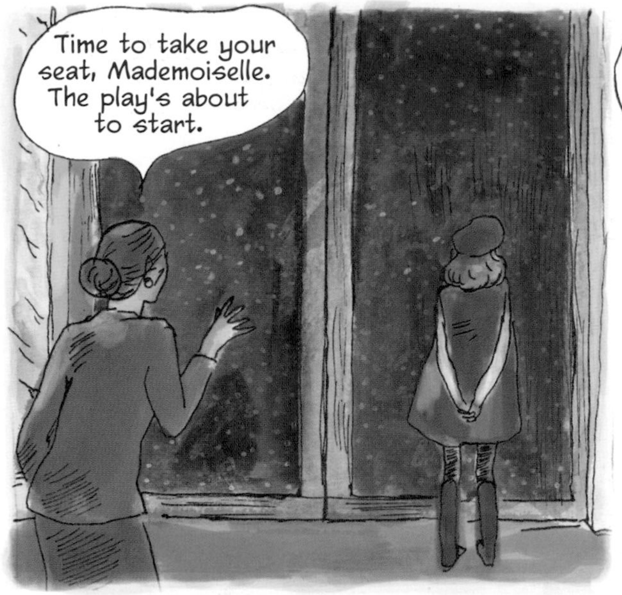
Time to take your seat, Mademoiselle. The play's about to start.

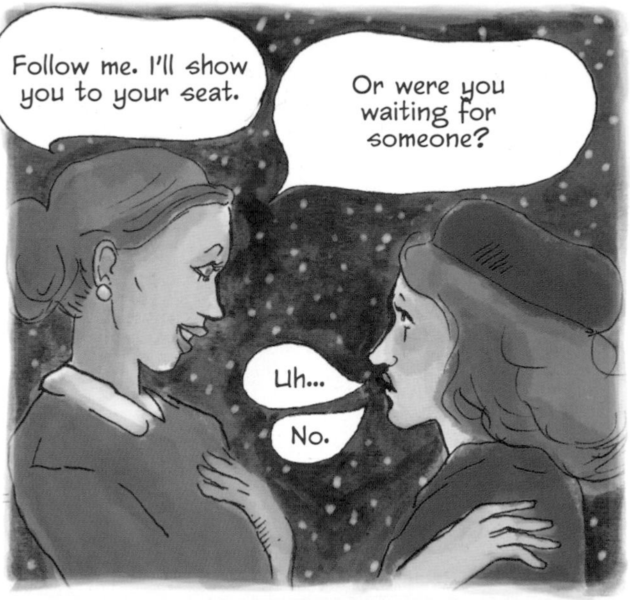
Follow me. I'll show you to your seat.
Or were you waiting for someone?
Uh...
No.

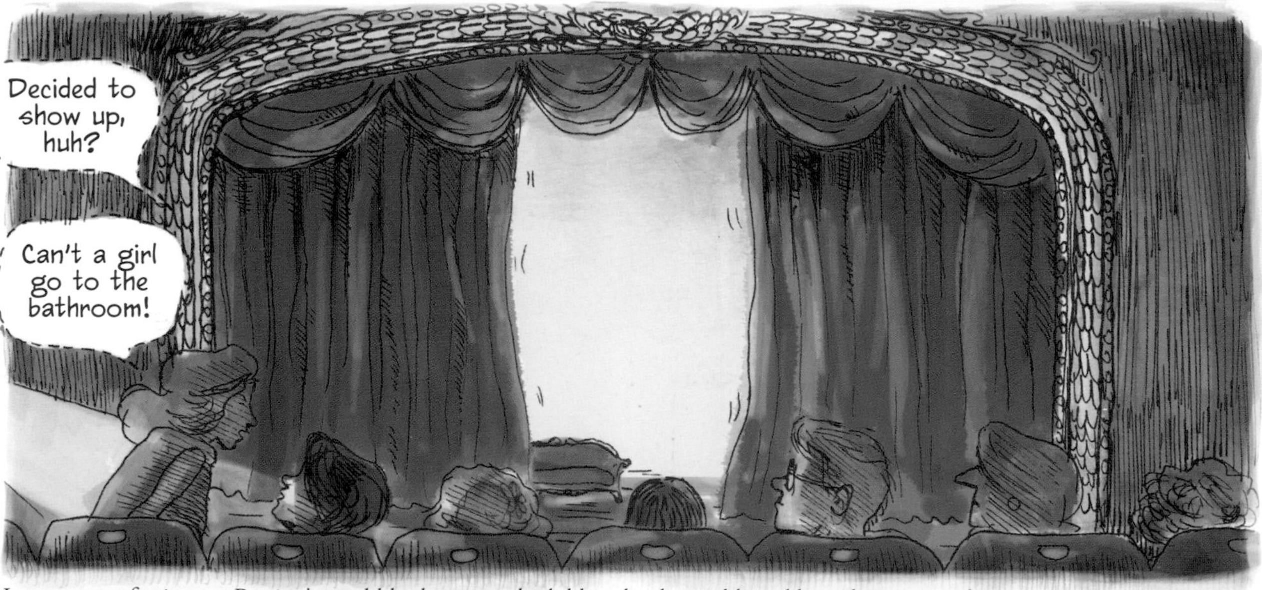
Decided to show up, huh?
Can't a girl go to the bathroom!

In a matter of minutes, Bettina's world had come to look like a landscape blasted by a dozen tornadoes.

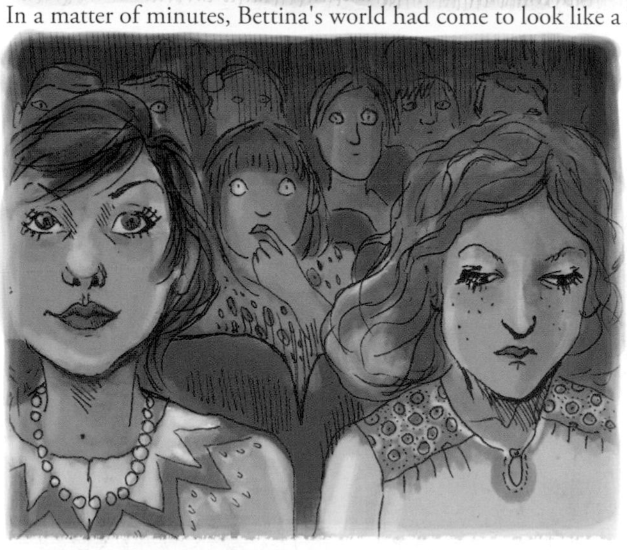

Such that it was a good while before she looked up and recognized, in the sublime young ringleted lady on whose every word the audience hung...

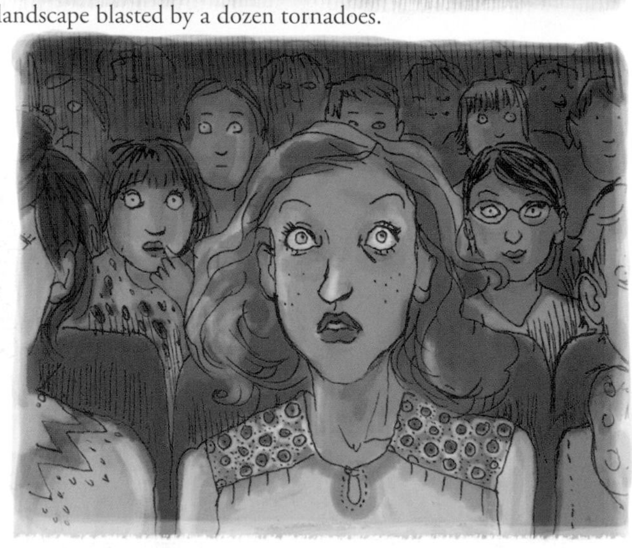

...her very own weird little sister, Hortense. When she realized, Bettina began to listen. For the first time in a long time, she listened to Hortense, and looked at her.

The play's heroine was named Hortense as well. The story was about how a young provincial girl drove her lover, the young Parisian dandy Rosimond—charming, but a poser—to say "I love you."

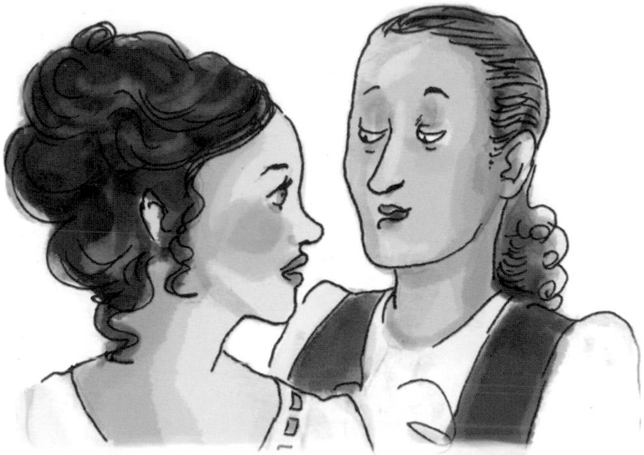

Words he could never utter, convinced they were ridiculous.

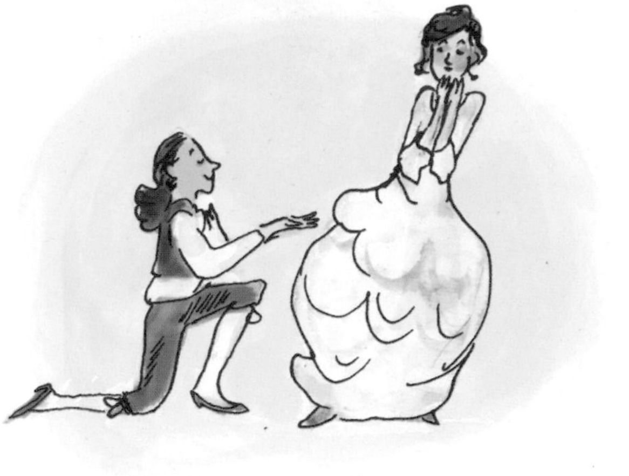

Soon enough, he found out that the only truly ridiculous thing was keeping quiet.

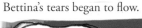

Bettina's tears began to flow.

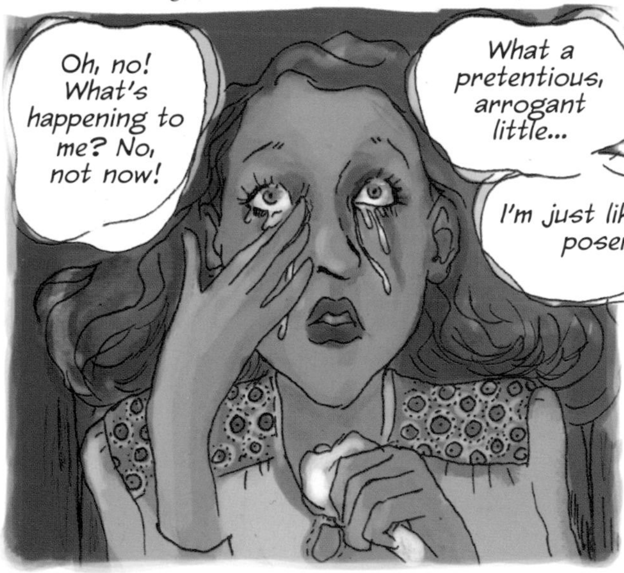
Oh, no! What's happening to me? No, not now!
What a pretentious, arrogant little...
I'm just like that poser!

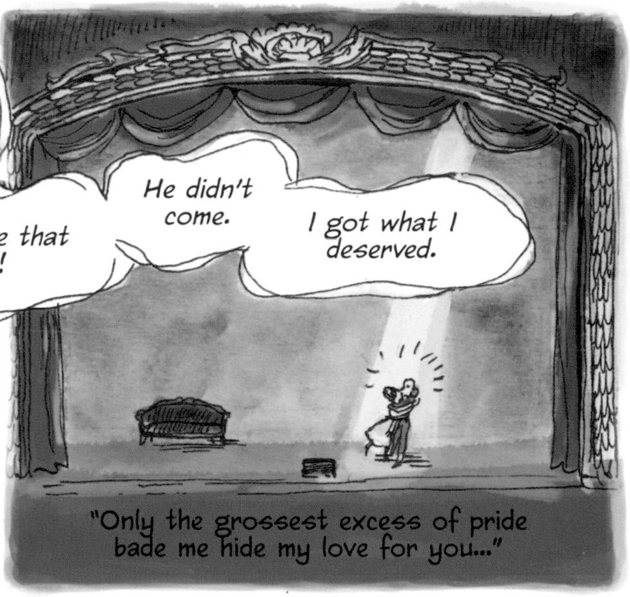
He didn't come.
I got what I deserved.
"Only the grossest excess of pride bade me hide my love for you..."

It was so strange to see Hortense, that odd little creature, getting hugged and kissed by a boy.

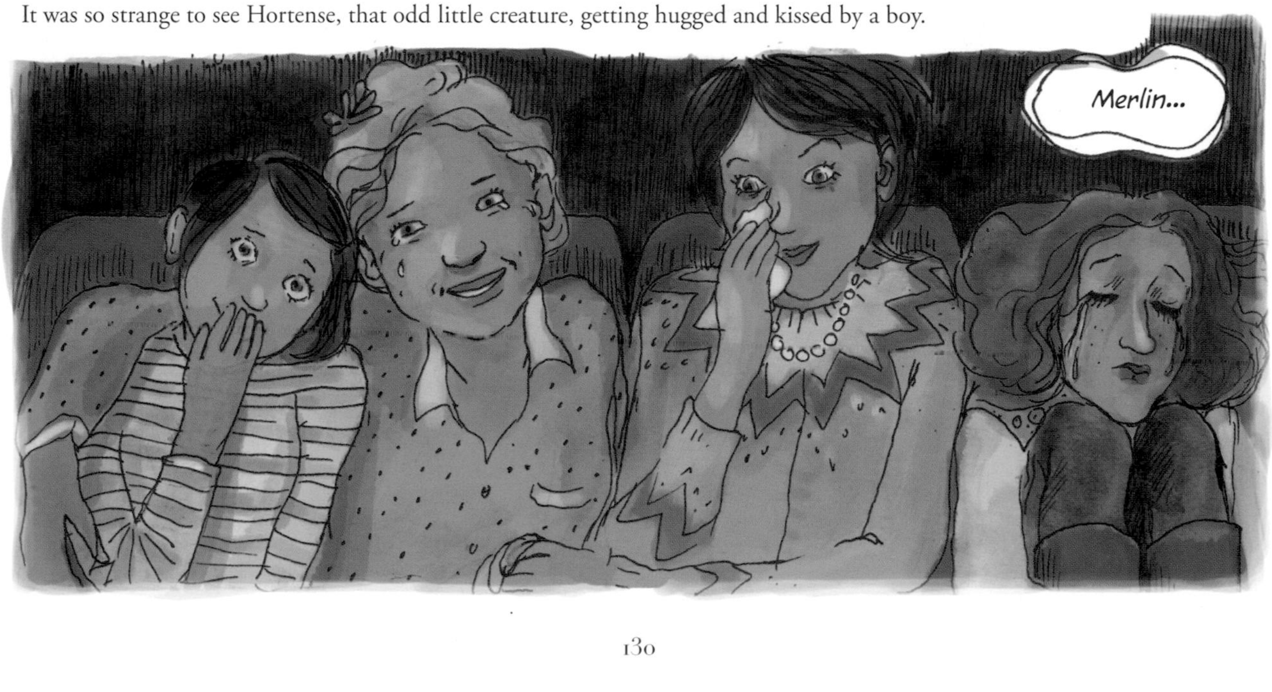
Merlin...

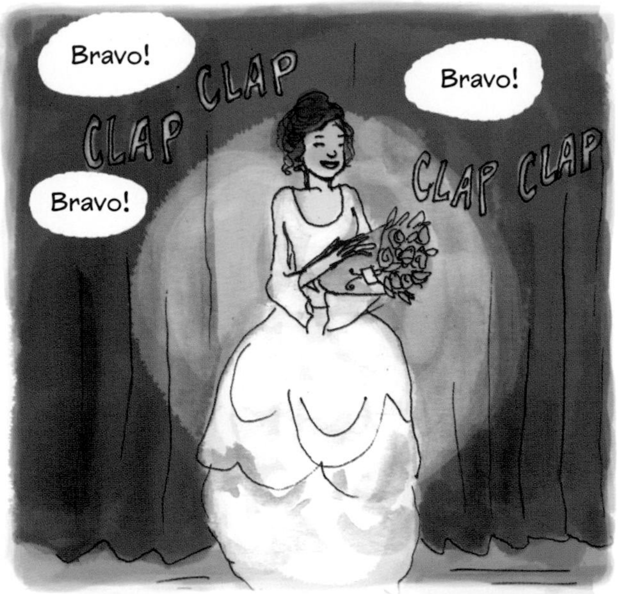
Bravo!
Bravo!
Bravo!
CLAP CLAP
CLAP CLAP

For the next twenty-four hours after the show, Hortense had the heady sensation that the way the world looked at her had changed. The phone kept ringing nonstop.

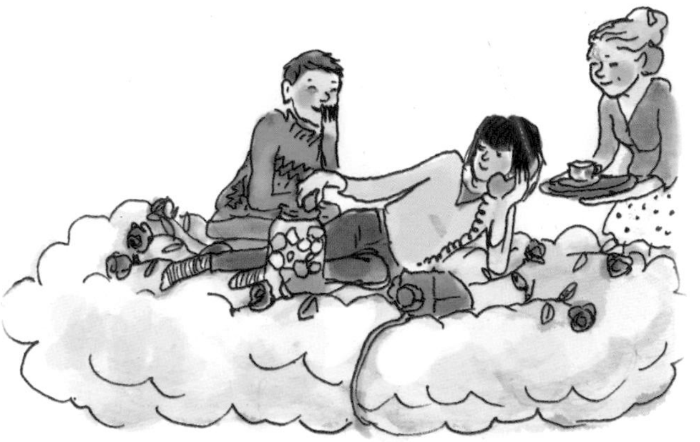

Madame Latour-Destours wanted to speak with her. And Deedee, and Theordore, and Jules. And Ovid. And...

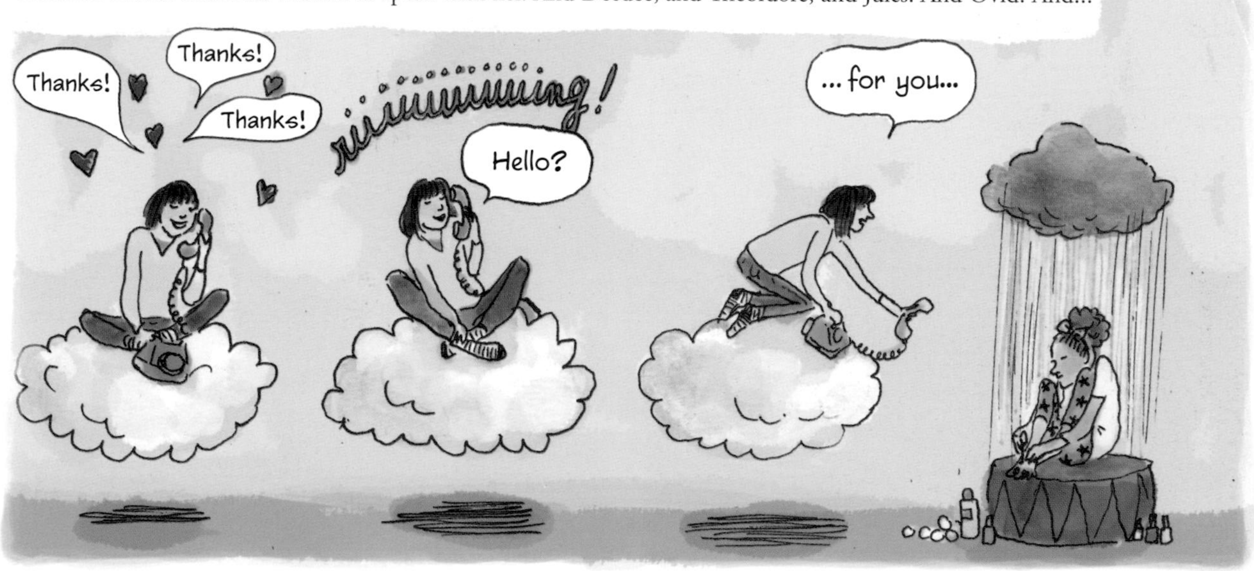
Thanks!
Thanks!
Thanks!
riiiiiiiiiiiing!
Hello?
...for you...

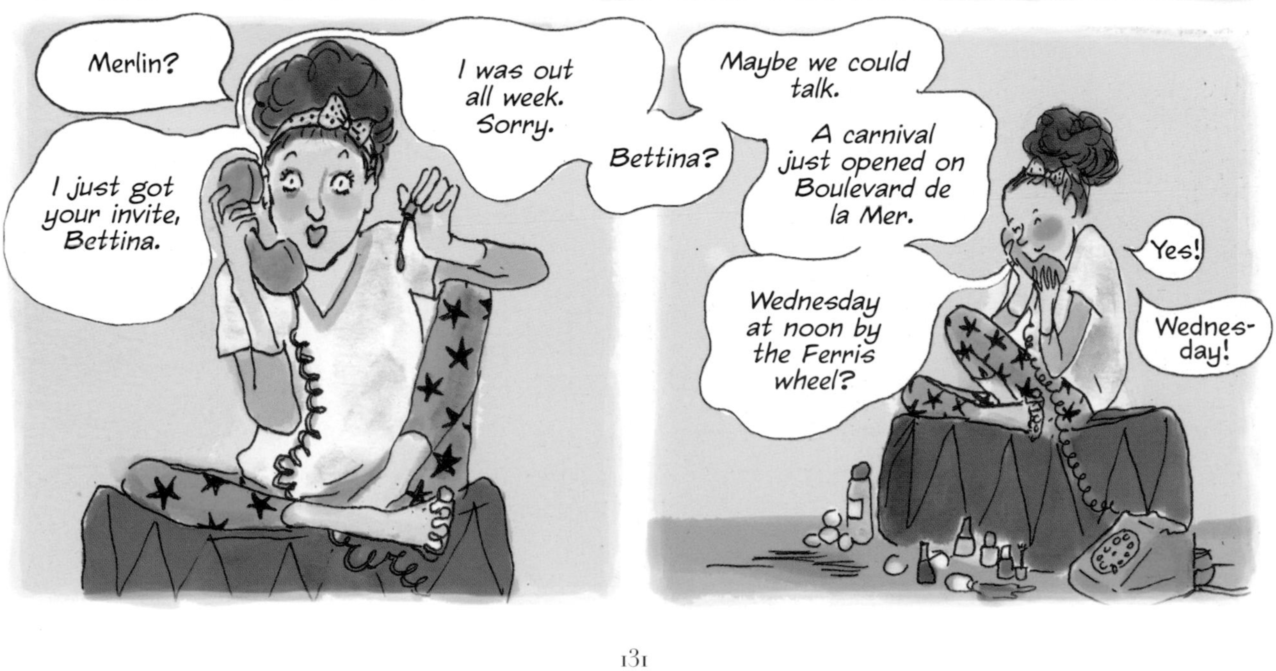
Merlin?
I just got your invite, Bettina.
I was out all week. Sorry.
Bettina?
Maybe we could talk.
A carnival just opened on Boulevard de la Mer.
Wednesday at noon by the Ferris wheel?
Yes!
Wednes-day!

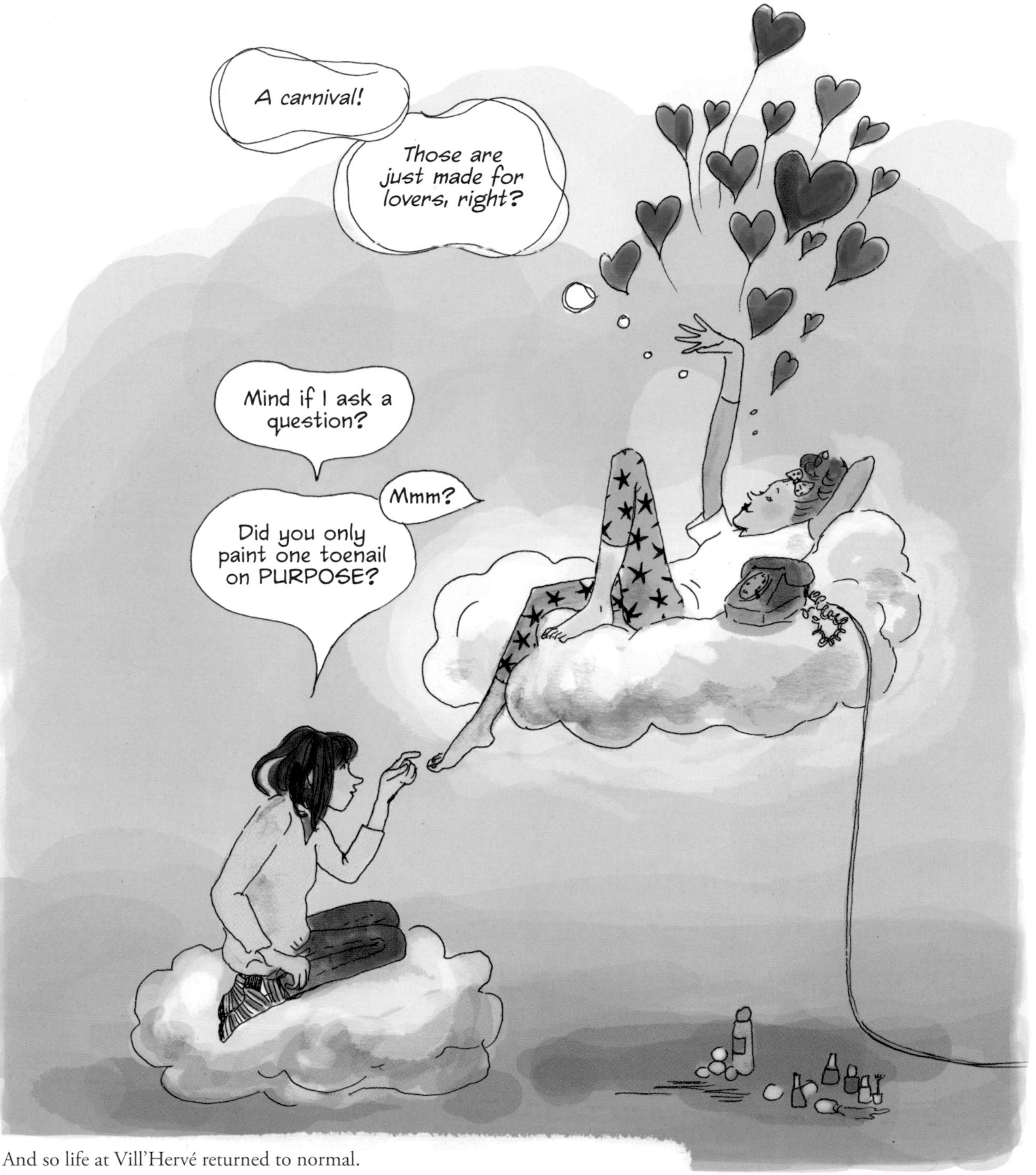
A carnival!
Those are just made for lovers, right?
Mind if I ask a question?
Mmm?
Did you only paint one toenail on PURPOSE?

And so life at Vill'Hervé returned to normal.

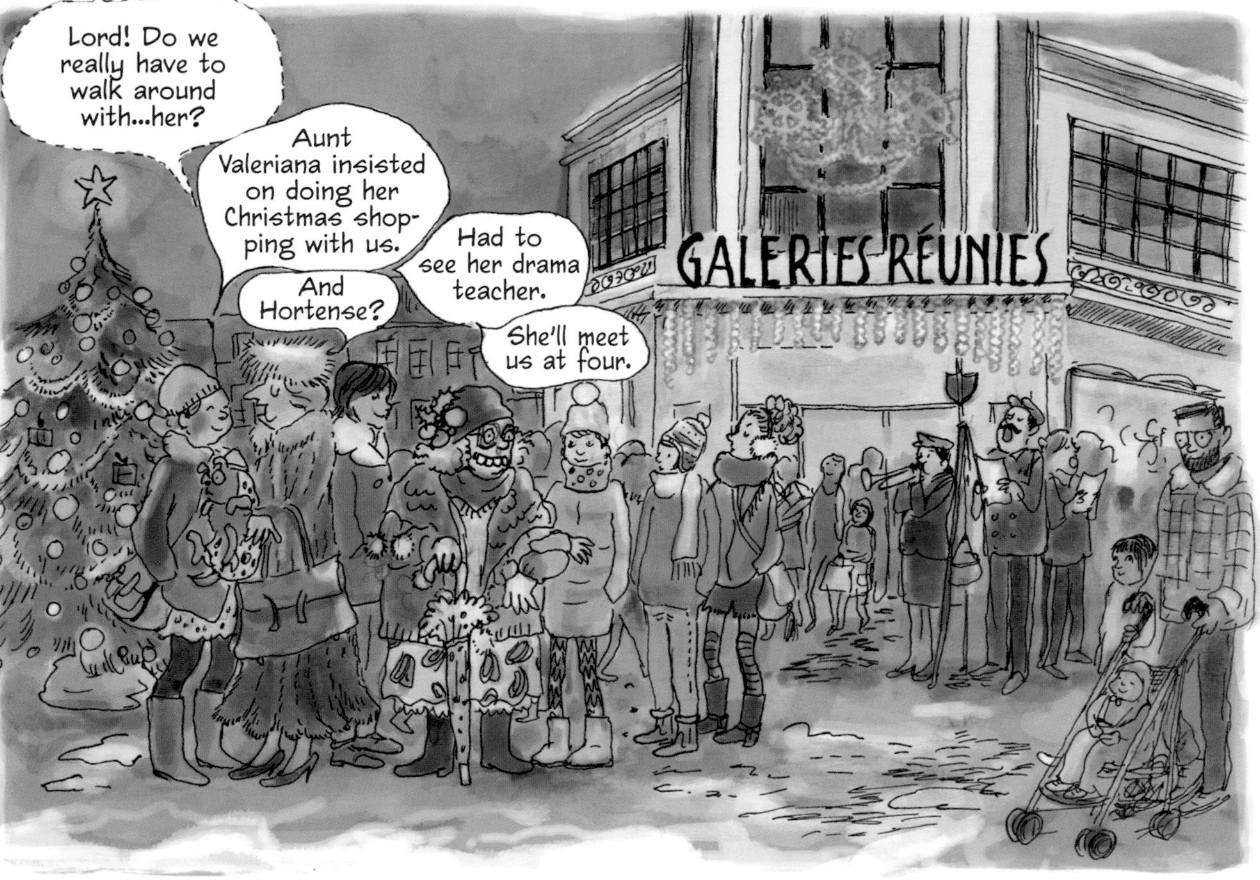
Lord! Do we really have to walk around with...her?
Aunt Valeriana insisted on doing her Christmas shopping with us.
And Hortense?
Had to see her drama teacher.
She'll meet us at four.
GALERIES RÉUNIES

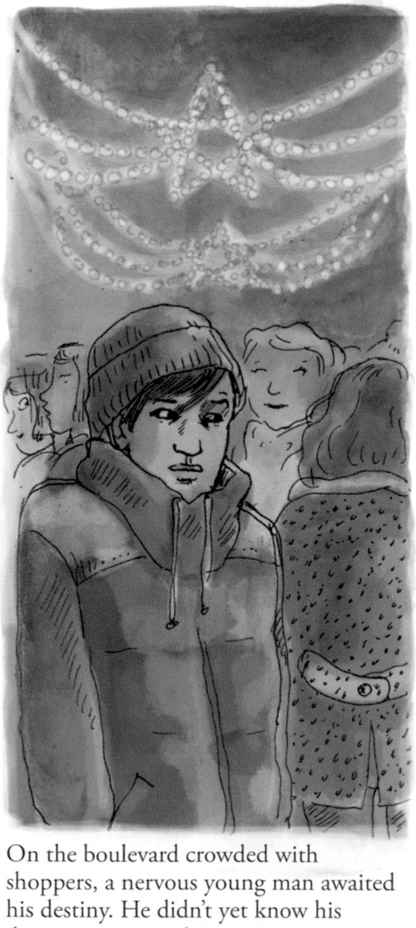

On the boulevard crowded with shoppers, a nervous young man awaited his destiny. He didn't yet know his destiny was named Aunt Lucretia.

The same Lucretia who was railing about Hortense's absence in a stationery shop.

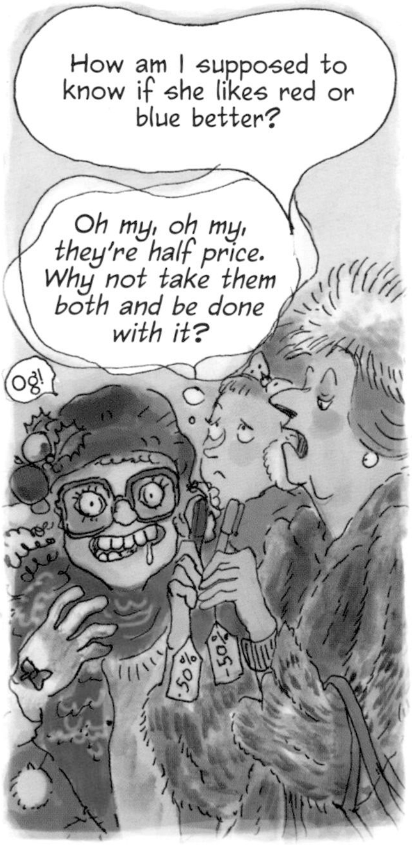
How am I supposed to know if she likes red or blue better?
Oh my, oh my, they're half price. Why not take them both and be done with it?
Og!
-50%
-50%

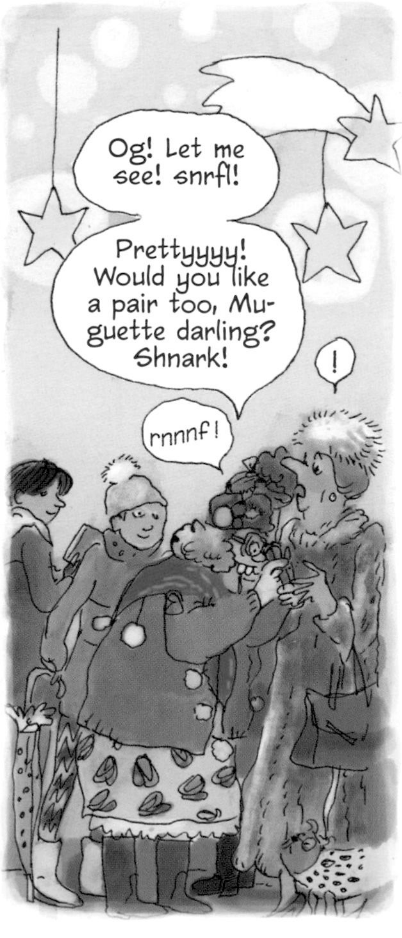
Og! Let me see! snrfl!
Prettyyyy! Would you like a pair too, Muguette darling? Shnark!
!
rnnnf!

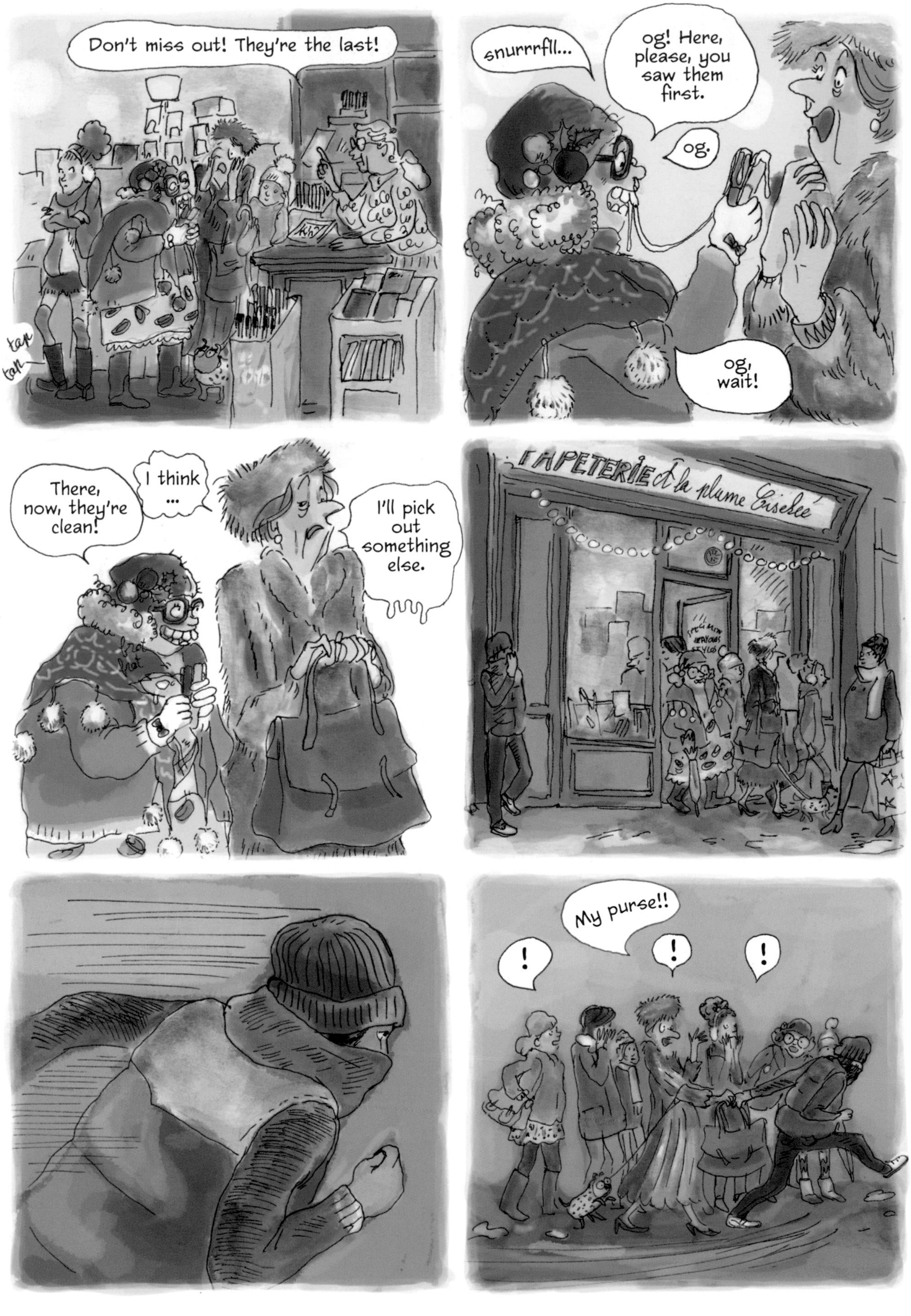
Don't miss out! They're the last!
tap tap
snurrrfll...
og! Here, please, you saw them first.
og.
og, wait!
There, now, they're clean!
I think ...
I'll pick out something else.
PAPETERIE A la plume Ciselée
My purse!!
!
!
!

DIMINU 'TIFF
HOMMES
FEMMES
Hold this for a sec!
?
MY PURSE! My puuurrse! Thief!
GNNNN
WOOF WOOF!
THIEF! Let me go!
WOOF WOOF!
Police! Call the police!
It's okay!
POW!
Poliiiiice!
You have your purse. That's what matters.
Quick, run!

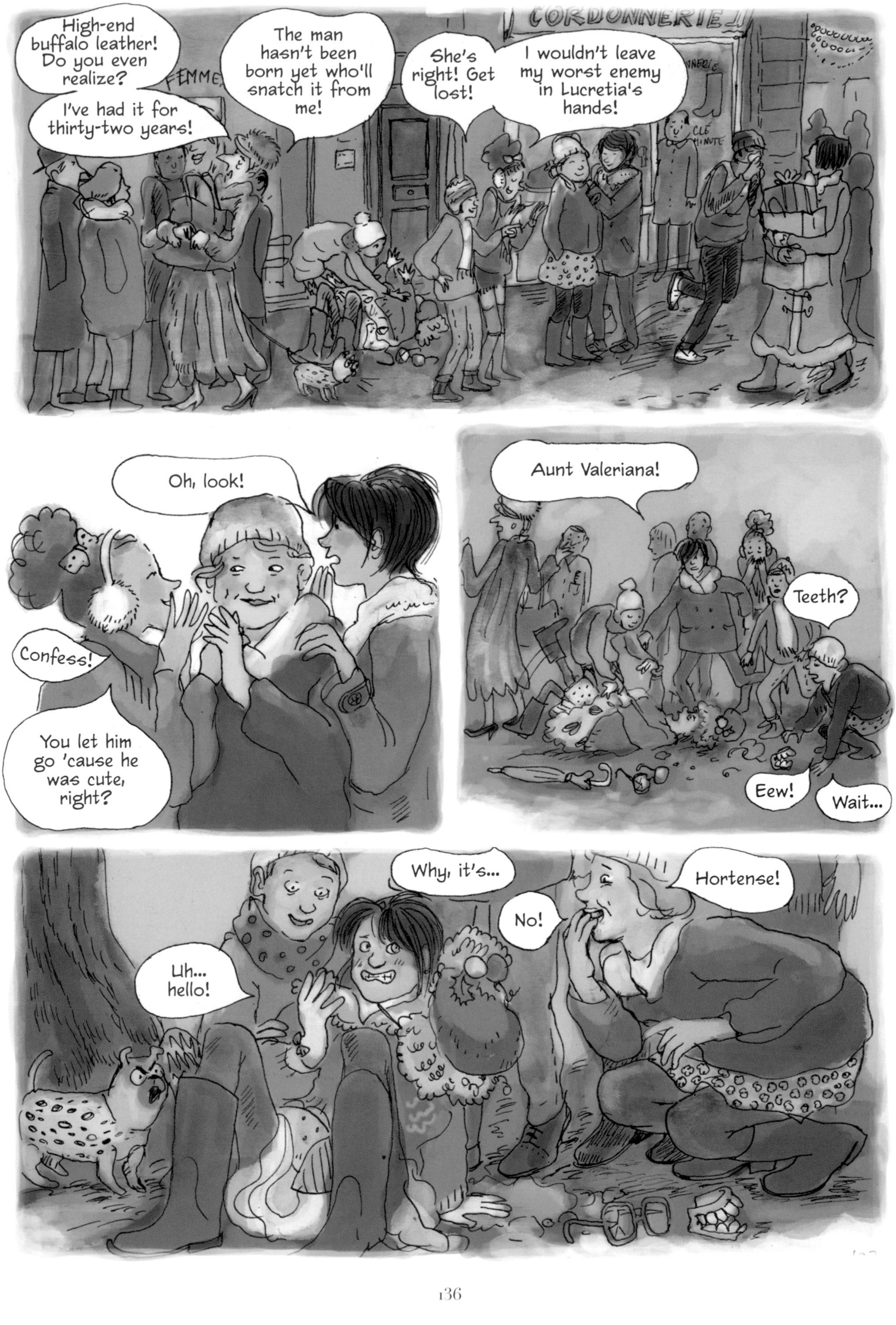

CORDONNERIE
High-end buffalo leather! Do you even realize?
I've had it for thirty-two years!
The man hasn't been born yet who'll snatch it from me!
She's right! Get lost!
I wouldn't leave my worst enemy in Lucretia's hands!
Oh, look!
Confess!
You let him go 'cause he was cute, right?
Aunt Valeriana!
Teeth?
Eew!
Wait...
Why, it's...
Hortense!
No!
Uh... hello!

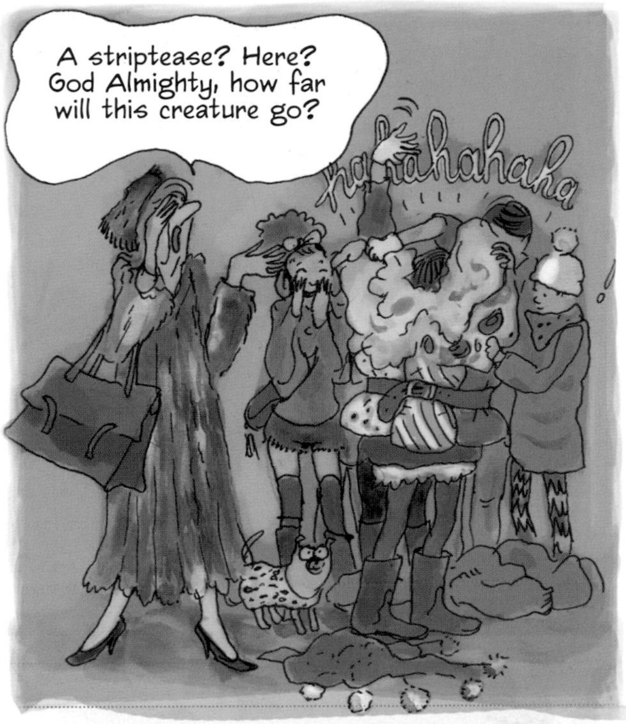
A striptease? Here? God Almighty, how far will this creature go?
hahahahaha

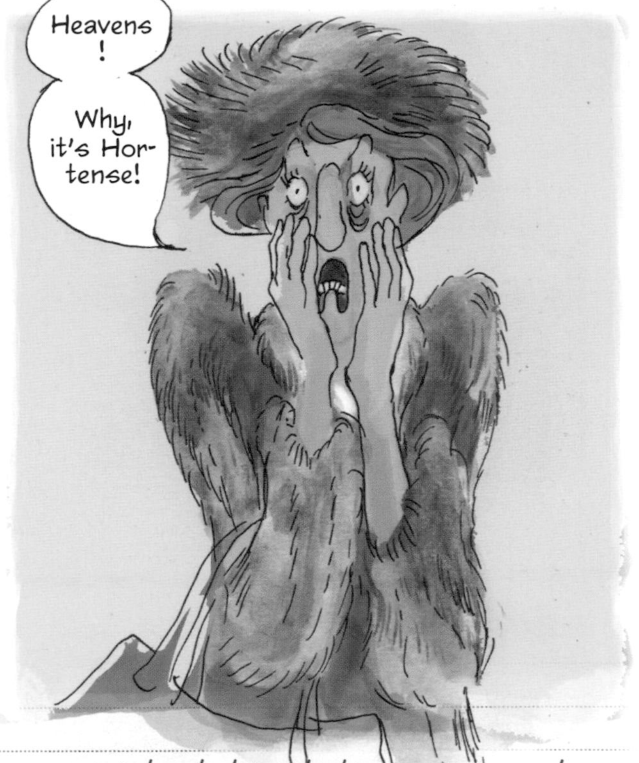
Heavens!
Why, it's Hortense!

Aunt Lucretia absolutely insisted on filing a complaint at the station, which wasted more time...especially since we gave them ten different descriptions of the thief. Afterwards, we tossed Auntie and her bags into her Renault with a promise to see her for dinner on Christmas Eve. And, victory! I (Aunt Valeriana, I mean) kept her from buying me that stupid pen!

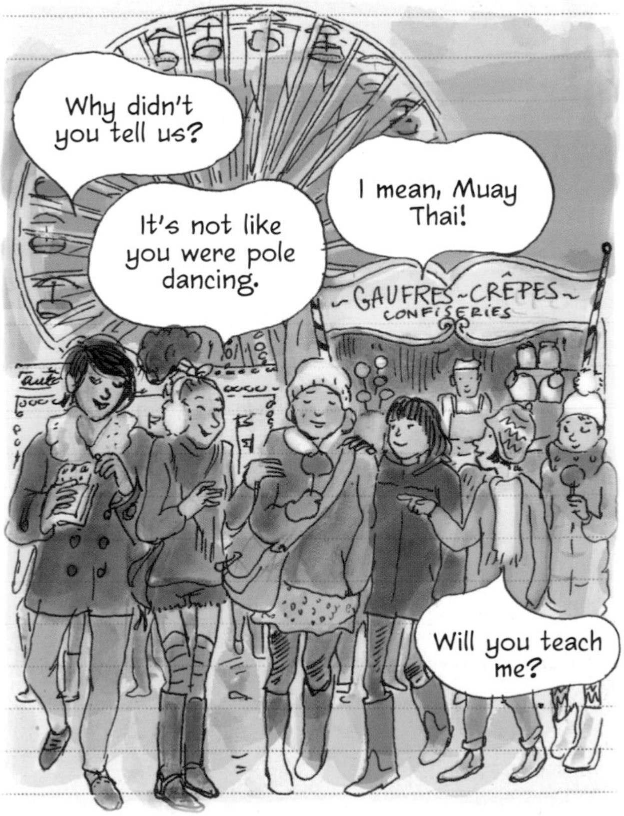
Why didn't you tell us?
It's not like you were pole dancing.
I mean, Muay Thai!
GAUFRES~CRÊPES~
CONFISERIES
Will you teach me?

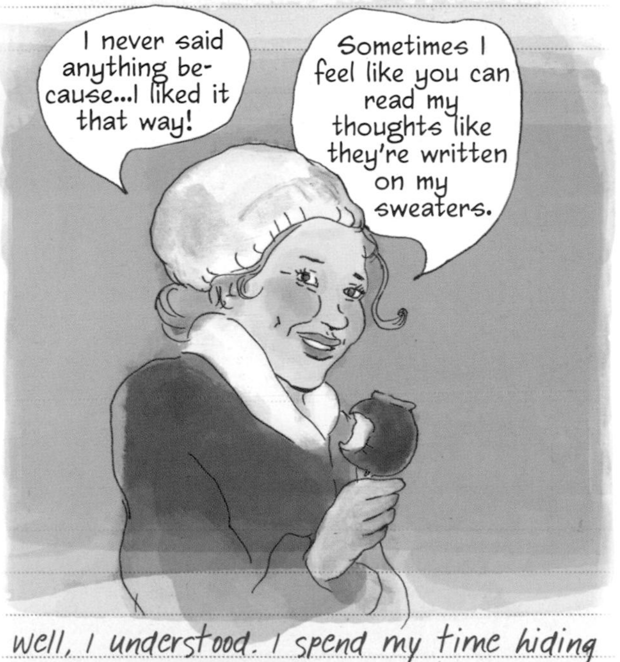
I never said anything because...I liked it that way!
Sometimes I feel like you can read my thoughts like they're written on my sweaters.

Well, I understood. I spend my time hiding anything and everything, even when I buy a stamp. But it'll be hard for her to find another secret!

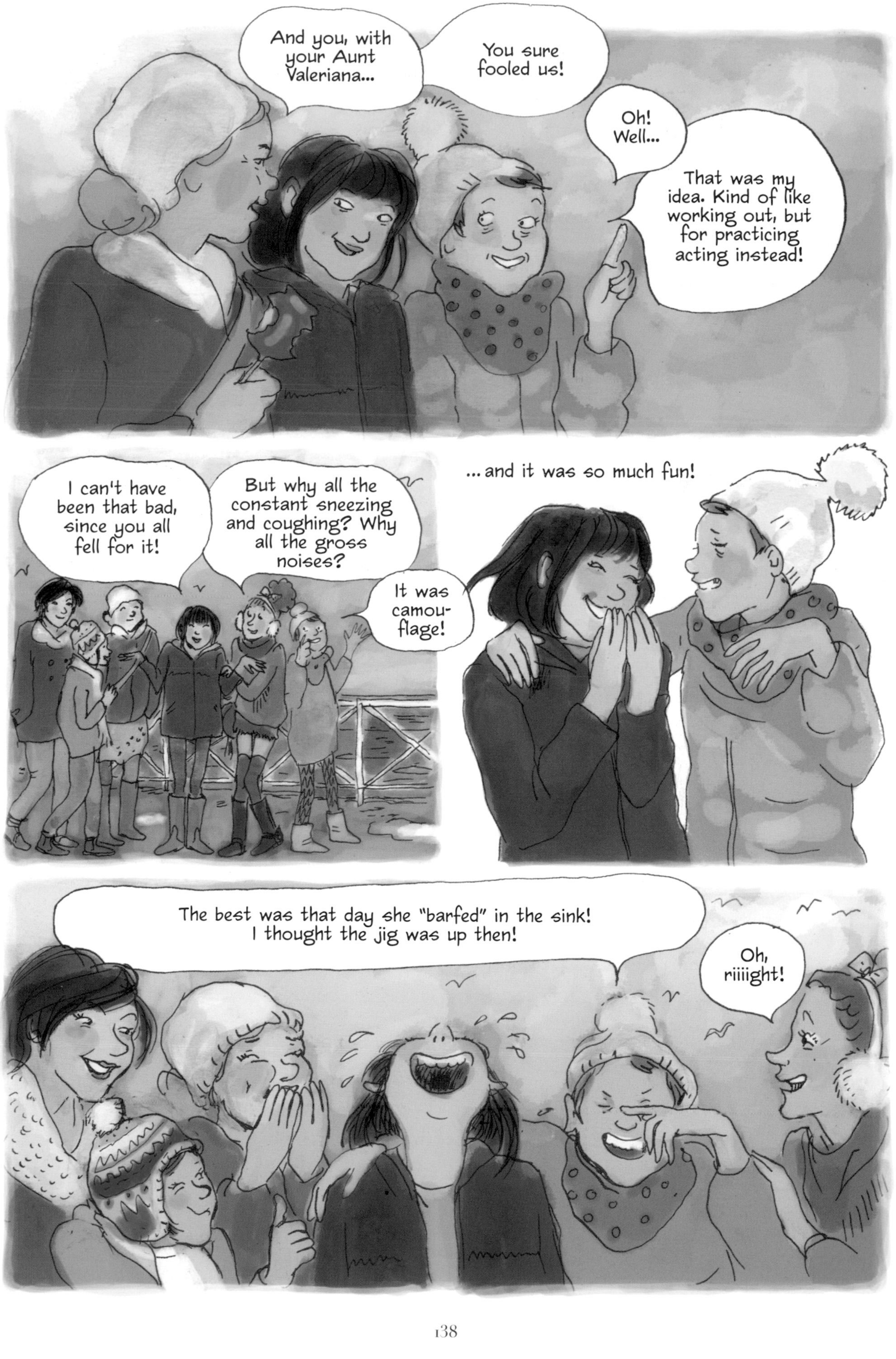
And you, with your Aunt Valeriana...
You sure fooled us!
Oh! Well...
That was my idea. Kind of like working out, but for practicing acting instead!
I can't have been that bad, since you all fell for it!
But why all the constant sneezing and coughing? Why all the gross noises?
It was camou-flage!
...and it was so much fun!
The best was that day she "barfed" in the sink! I thought the jig was up then!
Oh, riiiight!

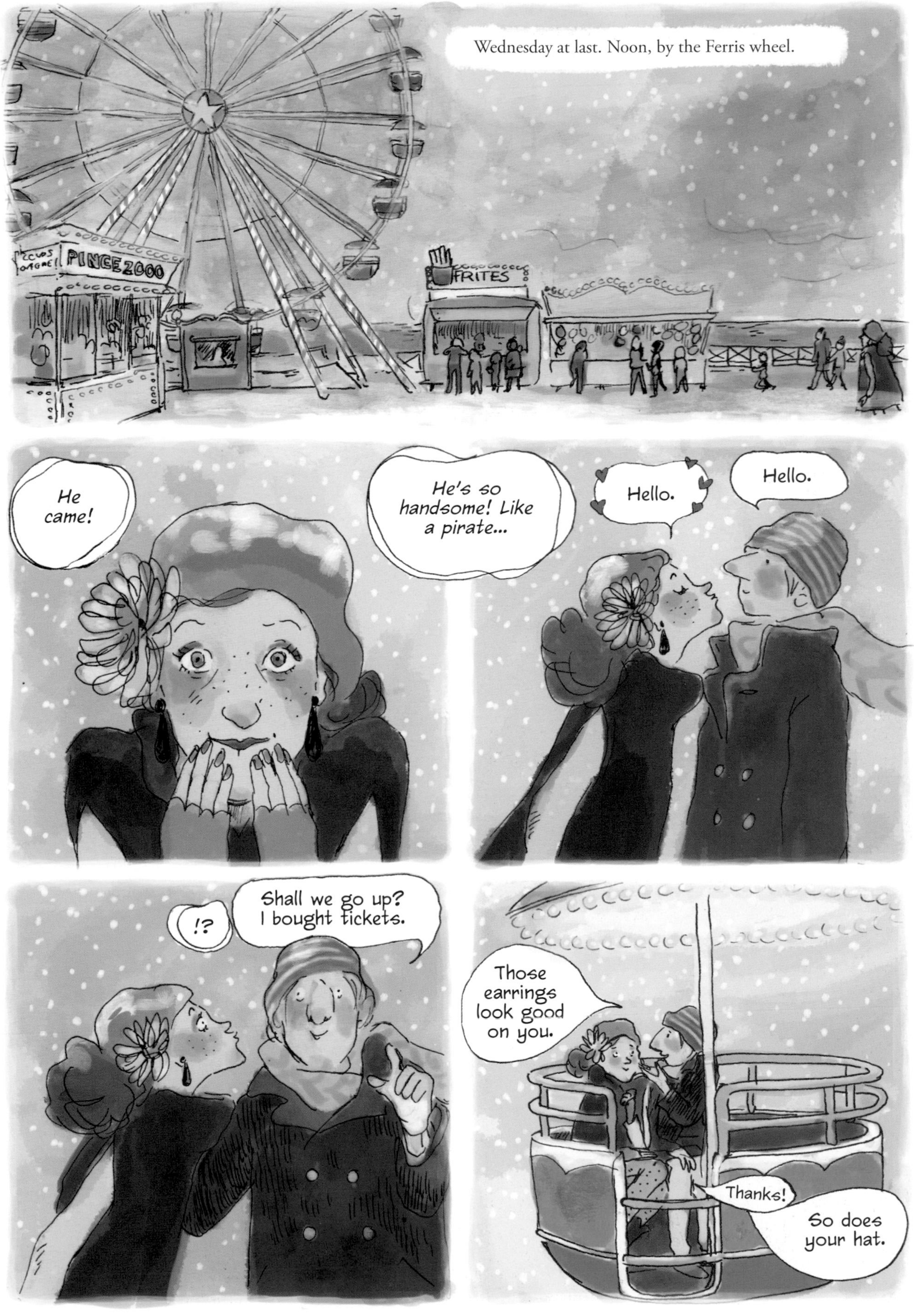
Wednesday at last. Noon, by the Ferris wheel.
PINCE2000
FRITES
He came!
He's so handsome! Like a pirate...
Hello.
Hello.
!?
Shall we go up? I bought tickets.
Those earrings look good on you.
Thanks!
So does your hat.

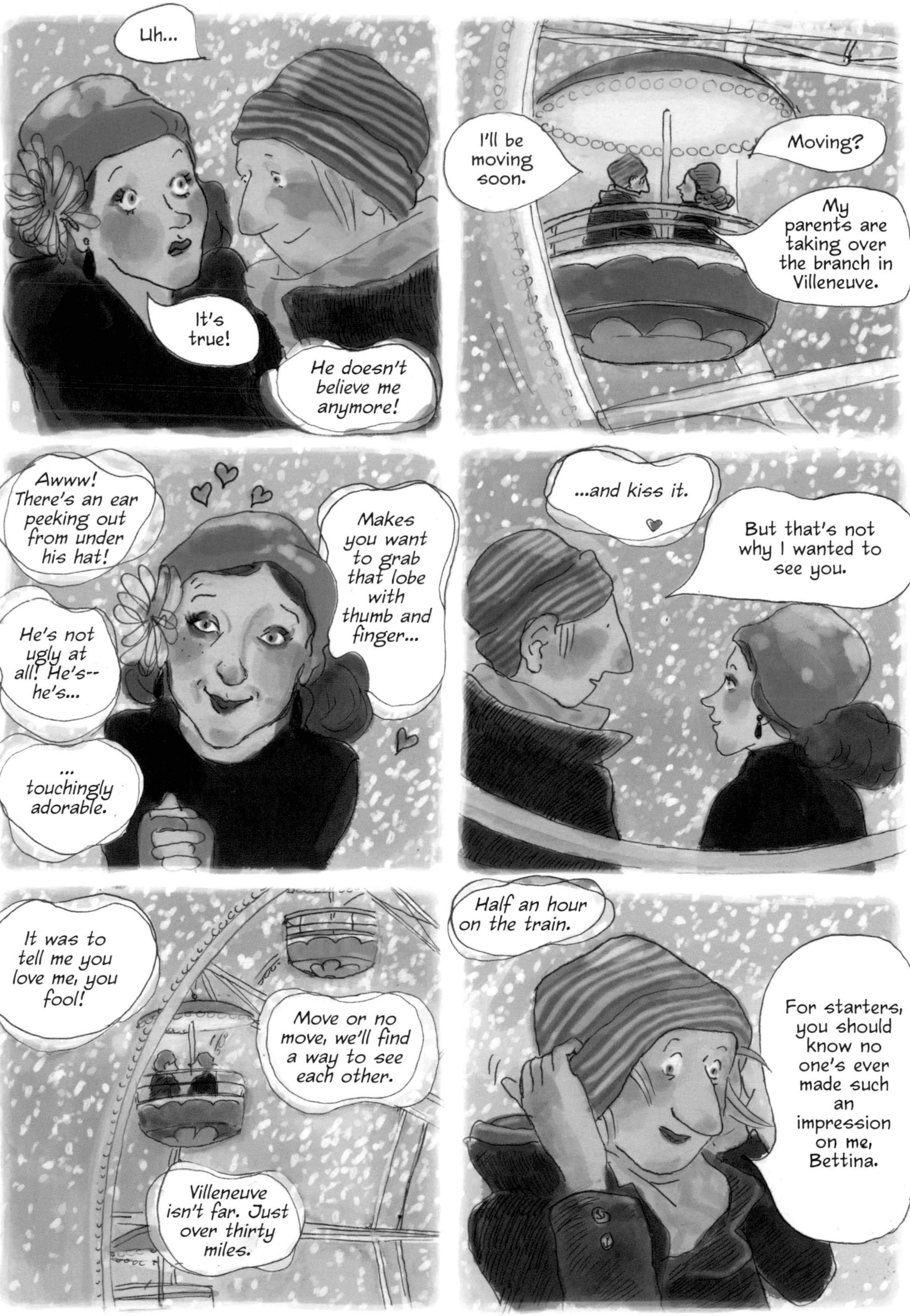

Uh...
It's true!
He doesn't believe me anymore!
I'll be moving soon.
Moving?
My parents are taking over the branch in Villeneuve.
Awww! There's an ear peeking out from under his hat!
He's not ugly at all! He's-- he's...
... touchingly adorable.
Makes you want to grab that lobe with thumb and finger...
...and kiss it.
But that's not why I wanted to see you.
It was to tell me you love me, you fool!
Move or no move, we'll find a way to see each other.
Villeneuve isn't far. Just over thirty miles.
Half an hour on the train.
For starters, you should know no one's ever made such an impression on me, Bettina.

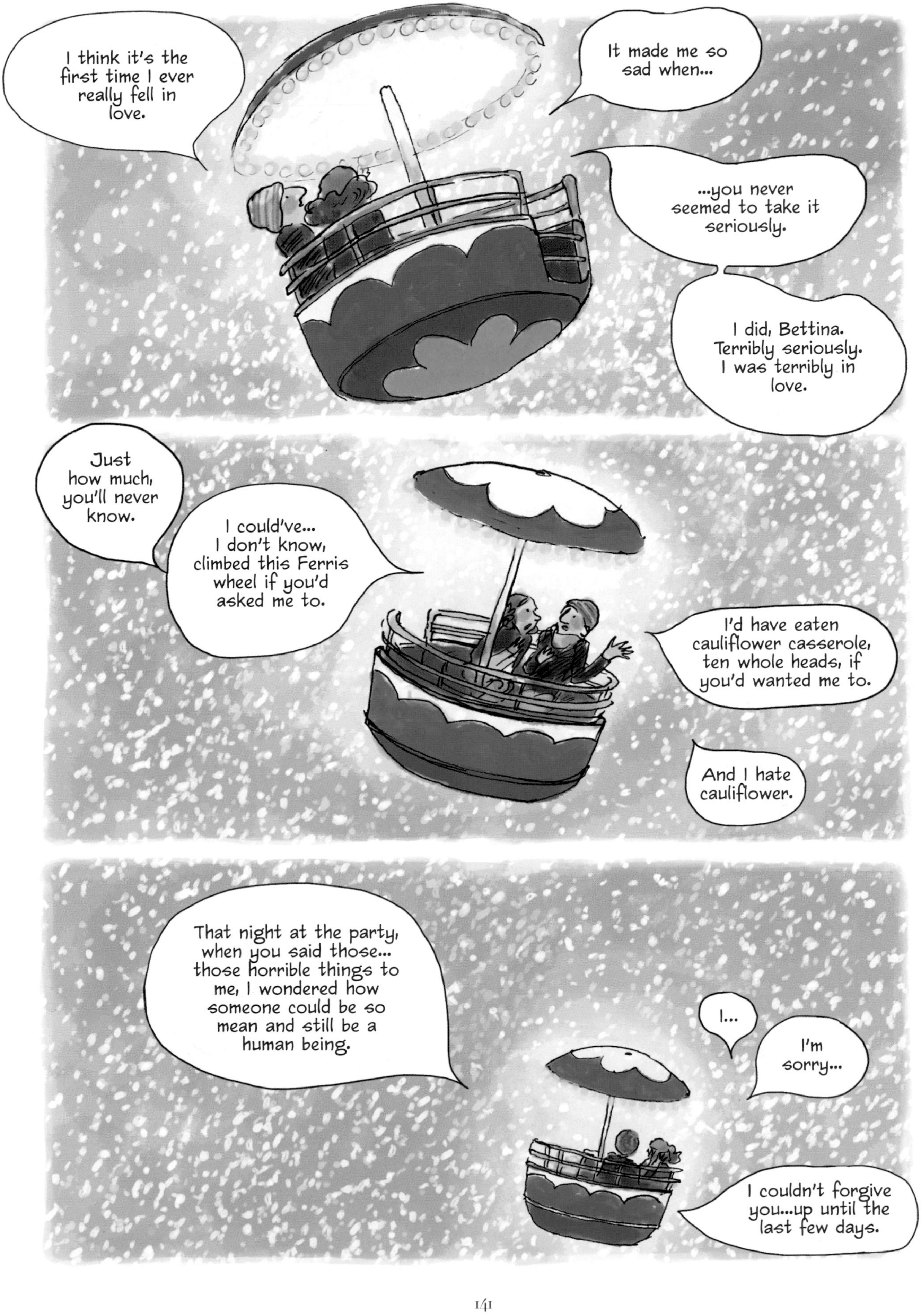

I think it's the first time I ever really fell in love.
It made me so sad when...
...you never seemed to take it seriously.
I did, Bettina. Terribly seriously. I was terribly in love.
Just how much, you'll never know.
I could've... I don't know, climbed this Ferris wheel if you'd asked me to.
I'd have eaten cauliflower casserole, ten whole heads, if you'd wanted me to.
And I hate cauliflower.
That night at the party, when you said those... those horrible things to me, I wondered how someone could be so mean and still be a human being.
I...
I'm sorry...
I couldn't forgive you...up until the last few days.

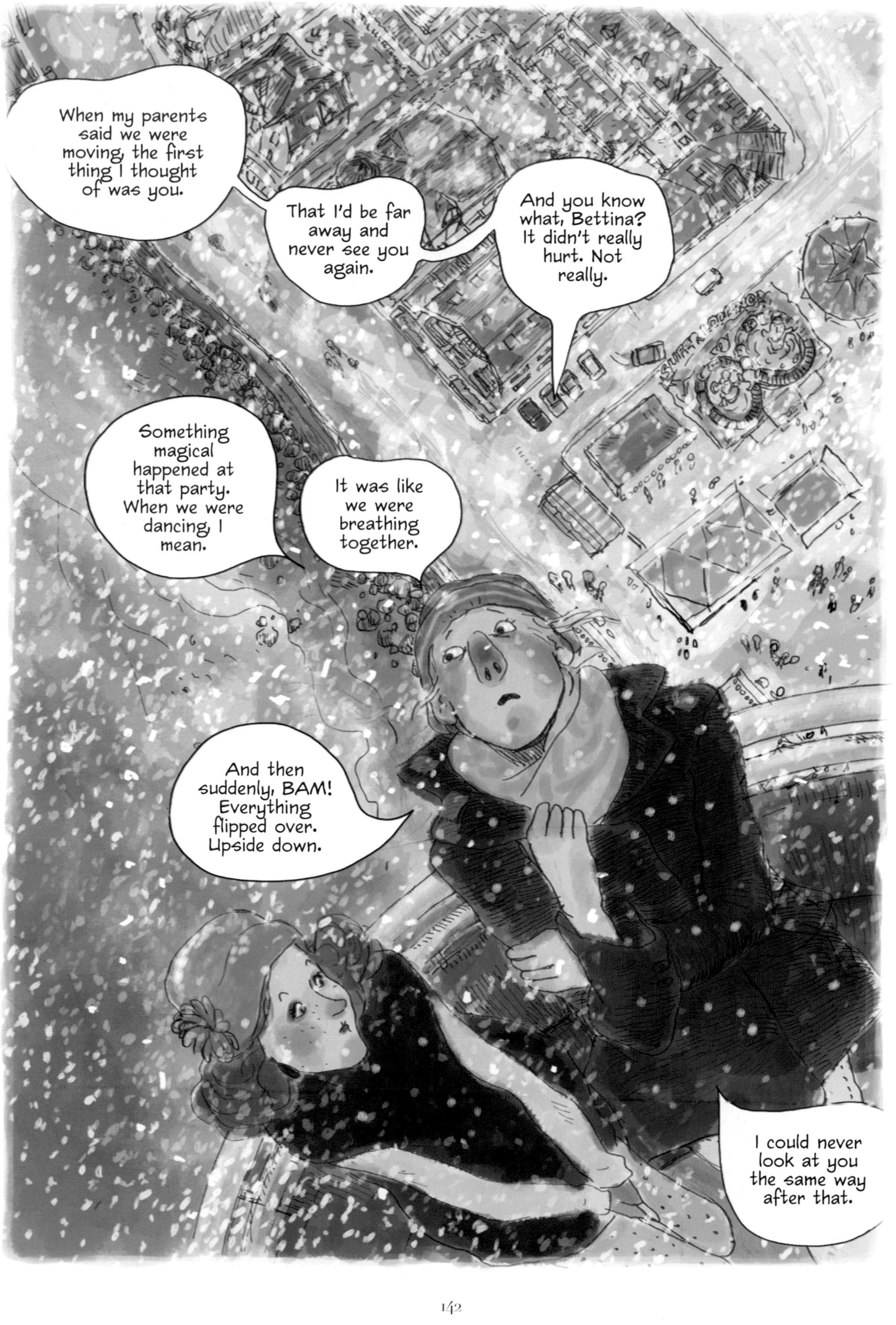
When my parents said we were moving, the first thing I thought of was you.
That I'd be far away and never see you again.
And you know what, Bettina? It didn't really hurt. Not really.
Something magical happened at that party. When we were dancing, I mean.
It was like we were breathing together.
And then suddenly, BAM! Everything flipped over. Upside down.
I could never look at you the same way after that.

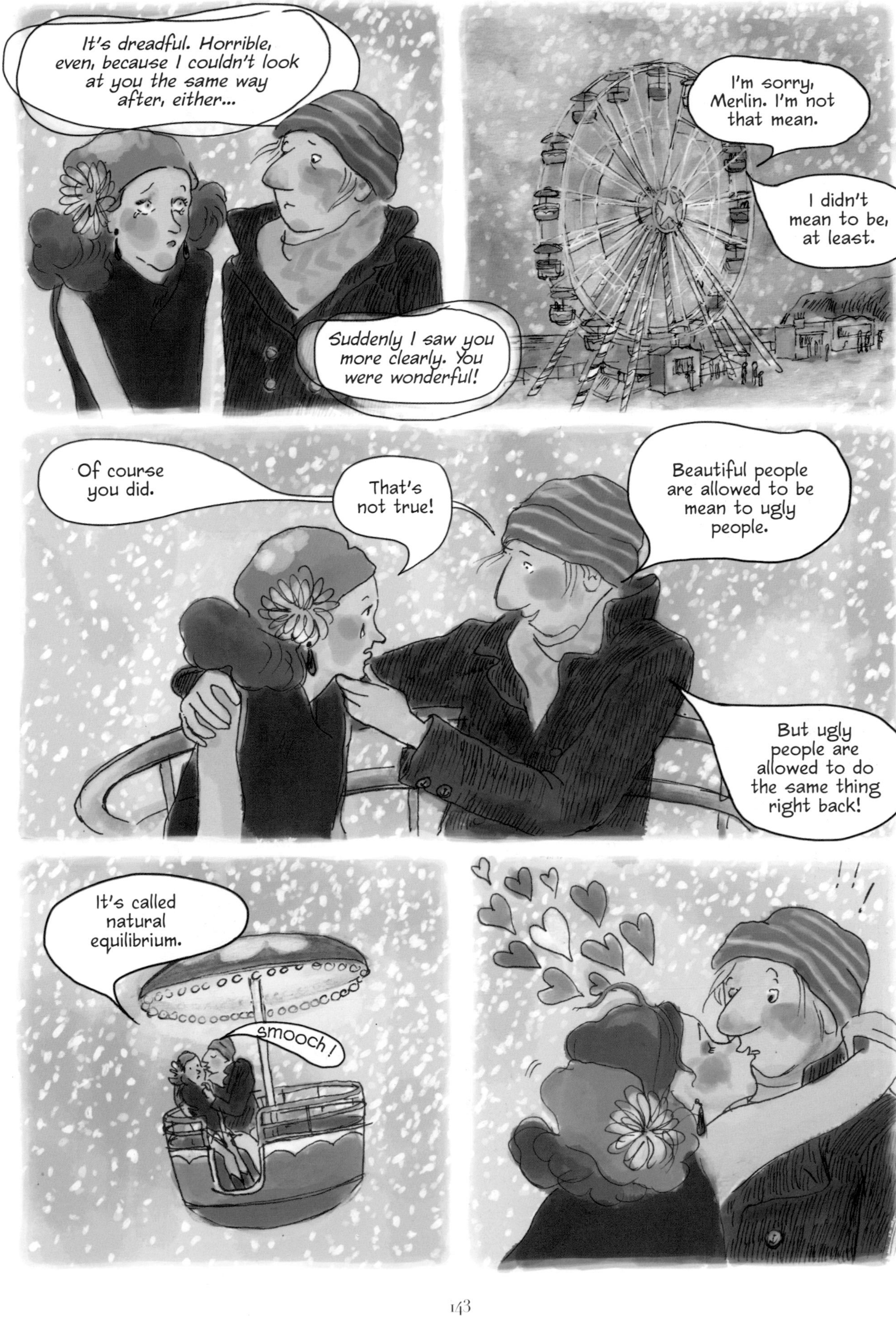
It's dreadful. Horrible, even, because I couldn't look at you the same way after, either...
Suddenly I saw you more clearly. You were wonderful!
I'm sorry, Merlin. I'm not that mean.
I didn't mean to be, at least.
Of course you did.
That's not true!
Beautiful people are allowed to be mean to ugly people.
But ugly people are allowed to do the same thing right back!
It's called natural equilibrium.
smooch!
!!!

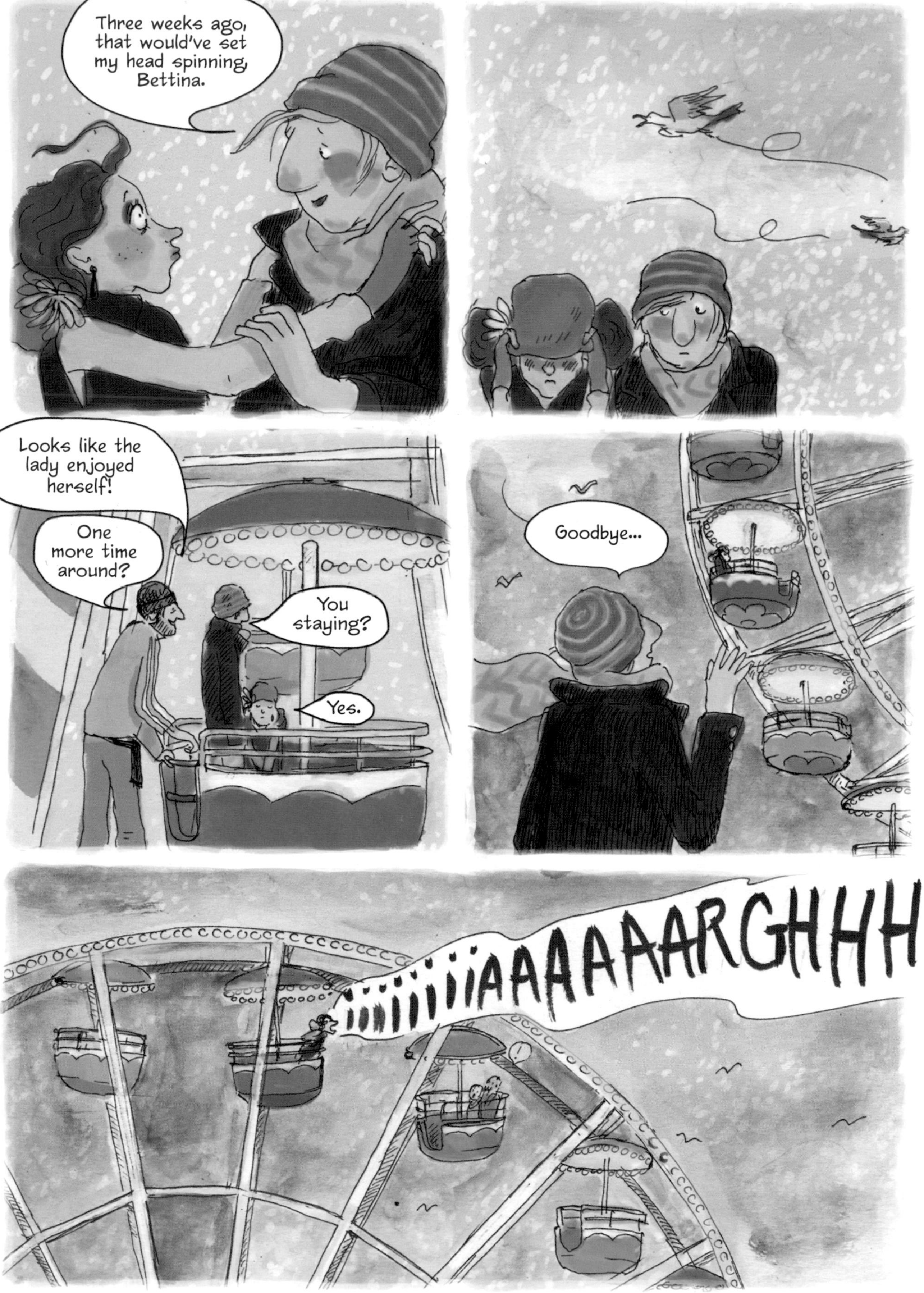
Three weeks ago, that would've set my head spinning, Bettina.
Looks like the lady enjoyed herself!
One more time around?
You staying?
Yes.
Goodbye...
iiiiiiiAAAAAARGHHH

Up there, on top of the world, with the long snowy boulevard below looking like a well-ironed shirtsleeve, Bettina wasn't crying anymore.
She had too many tears inside to know where to start.
Things couldn't have changed so much since Gersende's party! Not in so short a time!
And yet, if everything had changed so much for her, why not him too?
And then, Bettina saw the truth.
The truth was that she'd always loved Merlin without noticing. Was that even possible?
She had to do something. It couldn't end like this, before it even began.

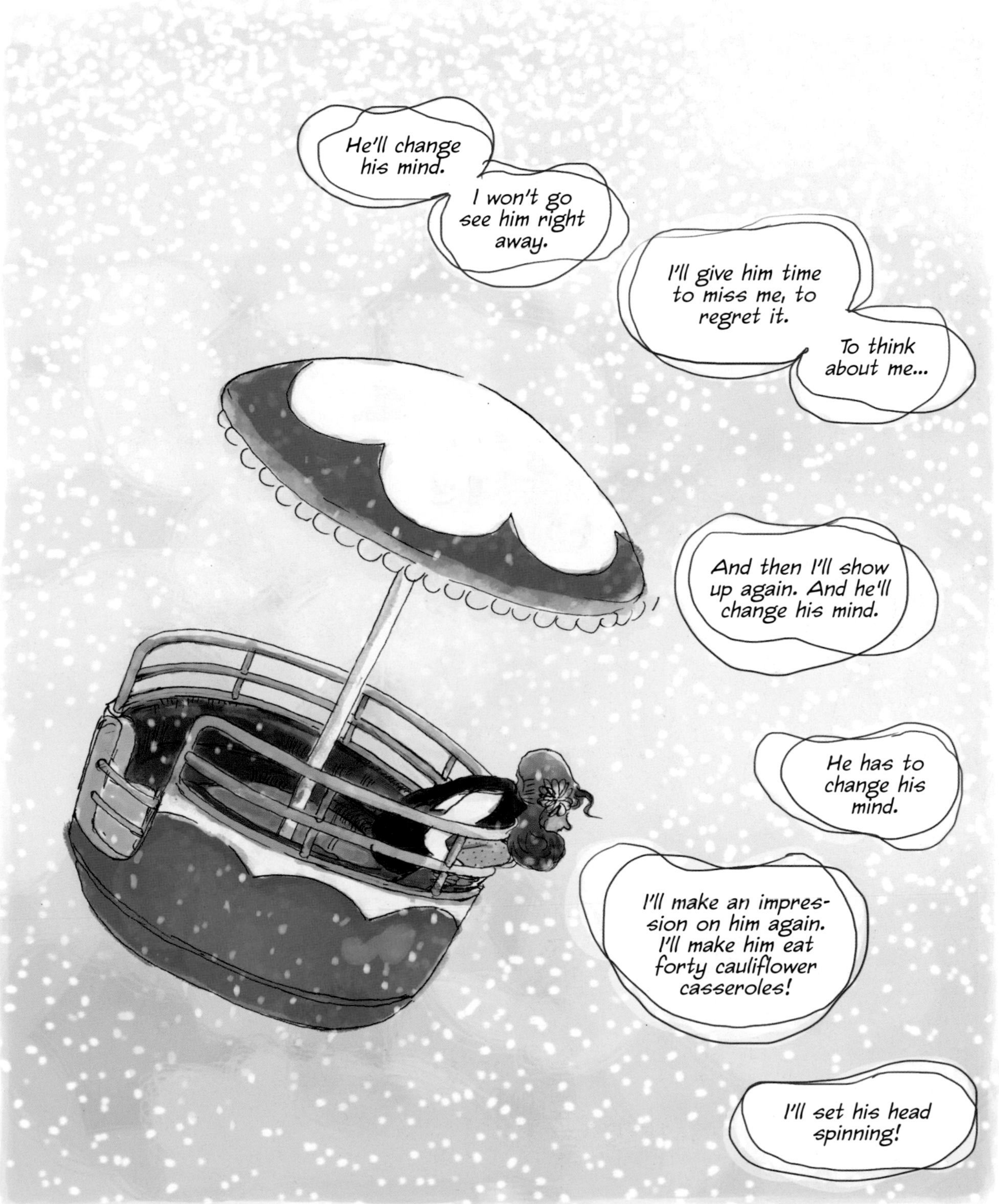
He'll change his mind.
I won't go see him right away.
I'll give him time to miss me, to regret it.
To think about me...
And then I'll show up again. And he'll change his mind.
He has to change his mind.
I'll make an impression on him again. I'll make him eat forty cauliflower casseroles!
I'll set his head spinning!

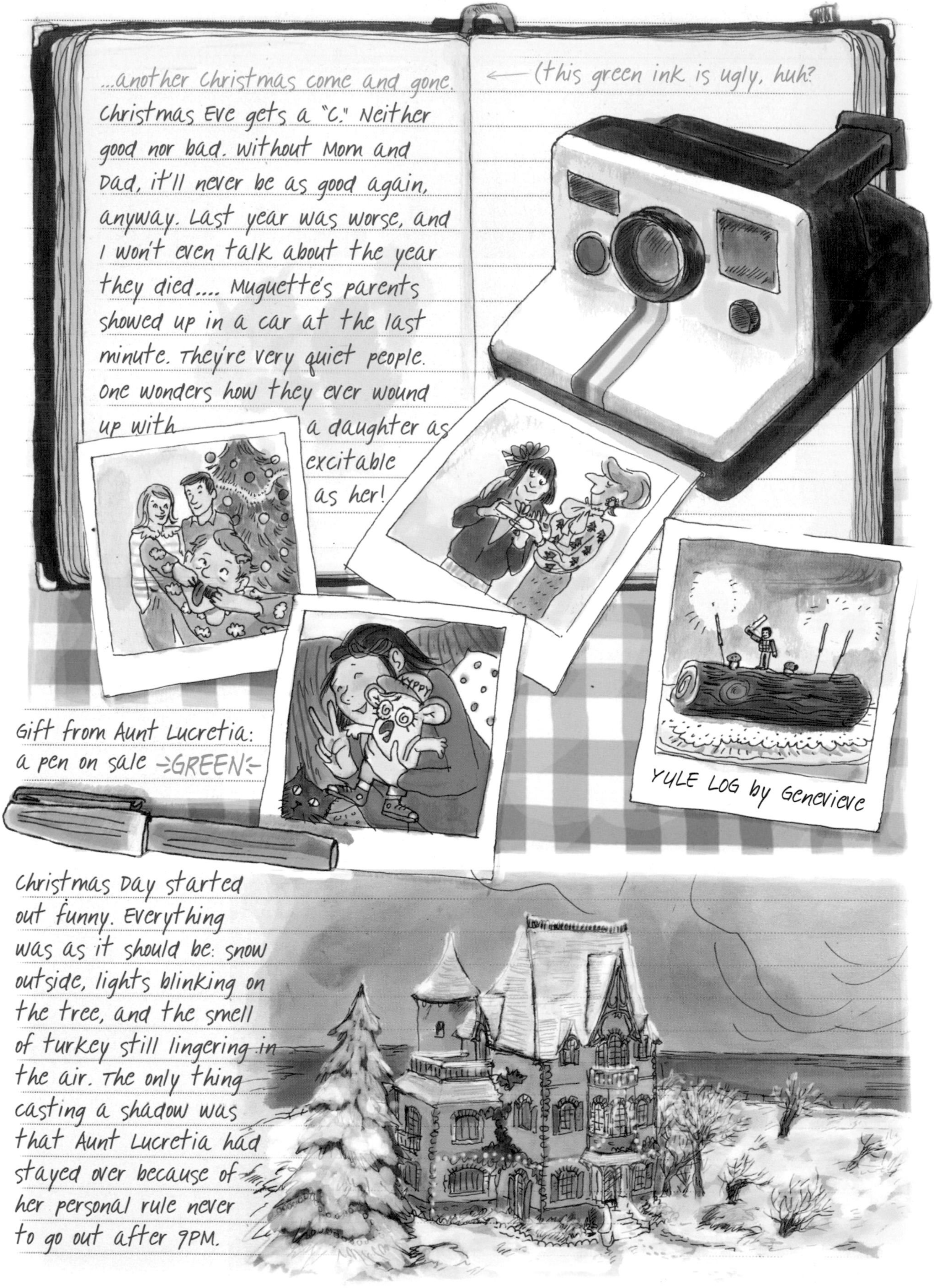
...another Christmas come and gone.
← (this green ink is ugly, huh?
Christmas Eve gets a "C." Neither good nor bad. Without Mom and Dad, it'll never be as good again, anyway. Last year was worse, and I won't even talk about the year they died.... Muguette's parents showed up in a car at the last minute. They're very quiet people. One wonders how they ever wound up with a daughter as excitable as her!
Gift from Aunt Lucretia: a pen on sale =GREEN=
YULE LOG by Genevieve
Christmas Day started out funny. Everything was as it should be: snow outside, lights blinking on the tree, and the smell of turkey still lingering in the air. The only thing casting a shadow was that Aunt Lucretia had stayed over because of her personal rule never to go out after 9PM.

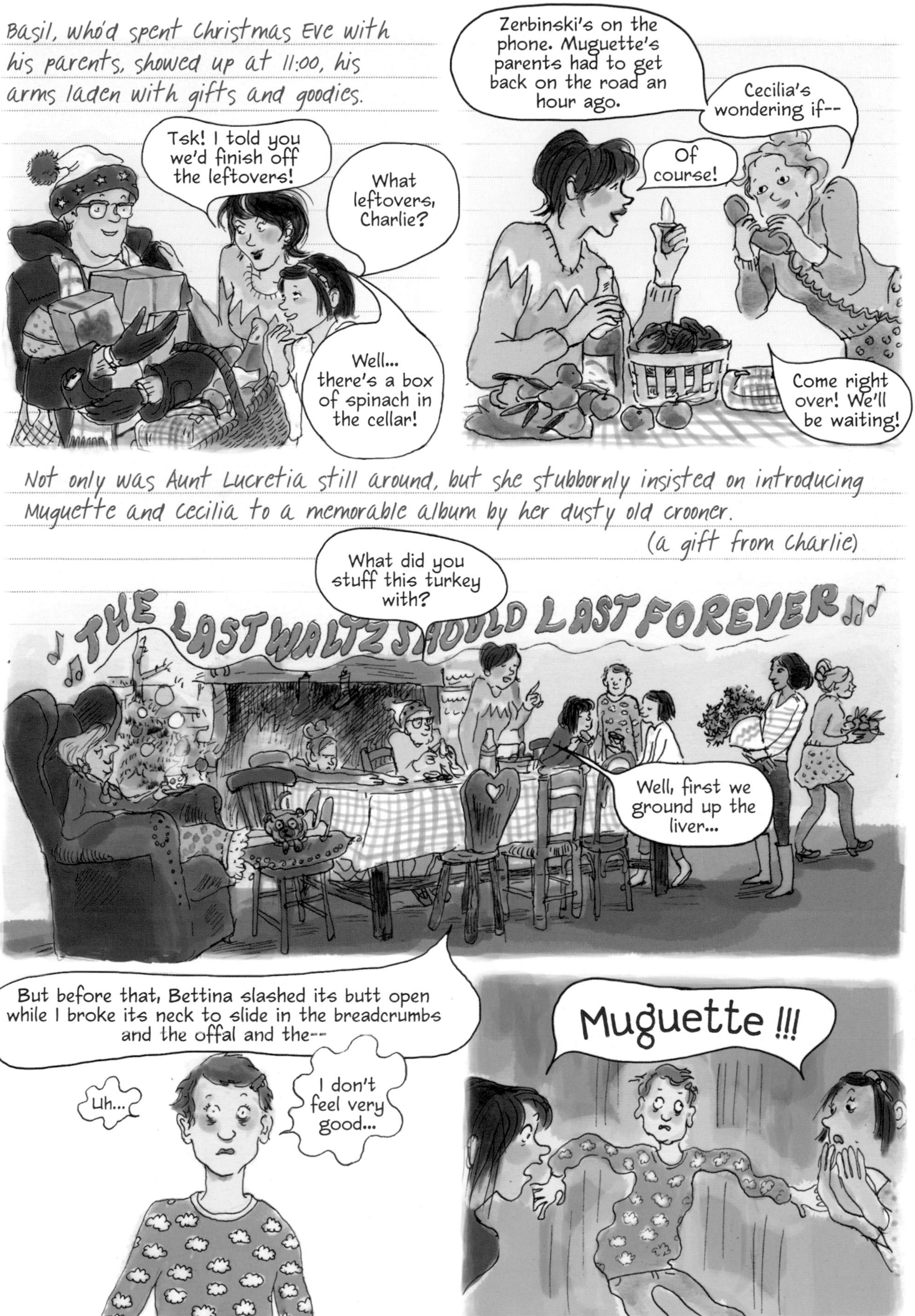
Basil, who'd spent Christmas Eve with his parents, showed up at 11:00, his arms laden with gifts and goodies.
Tsk! I told you we'd finish off the leftovers!
What leftovers, Charlie?
Well... there's a box of spinach in the cellar!
Zerbinski's on the phone. Muguette's parents had to get back on the road an hour ago.
Cecilia's wondering if--
Of course!
Come right over! We'll be waiting!
Not only was Aunt Lucretia still around, but she stubbornly insisted on introducing Muguette and Cecilia to a memorable album by her dusty old crooner.
(a gift from Charlie)
What did you stuff this turkey with?
THE LAST WALTZ SHOULD LAST FOREVER
Well, first we ground up the liver...
But before that, Bettina slashed its butt open while I broke its neck to slide in the breadcrumbs and the offal and the--
Uh...
I don't feel very good...
Muguette !!!

Honking madly, Basil and Zerbinski whisked Muguette away to the ER at Florence-Cor Hospital in Villeneuve. I wanted to go with them so badly...but Charlie wouldn't hear of it. It wasn't my place, end of story. Next came a long, gloomy wait.

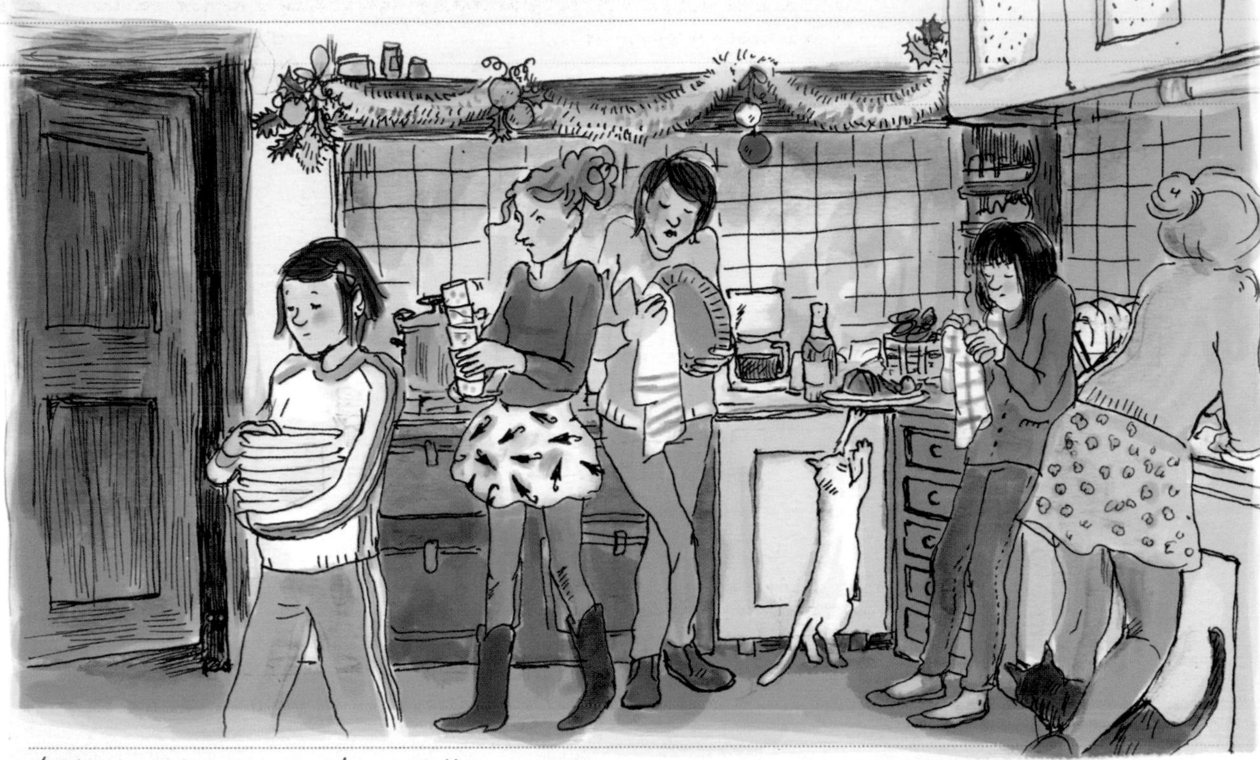

And around 3 PM, a phone call.

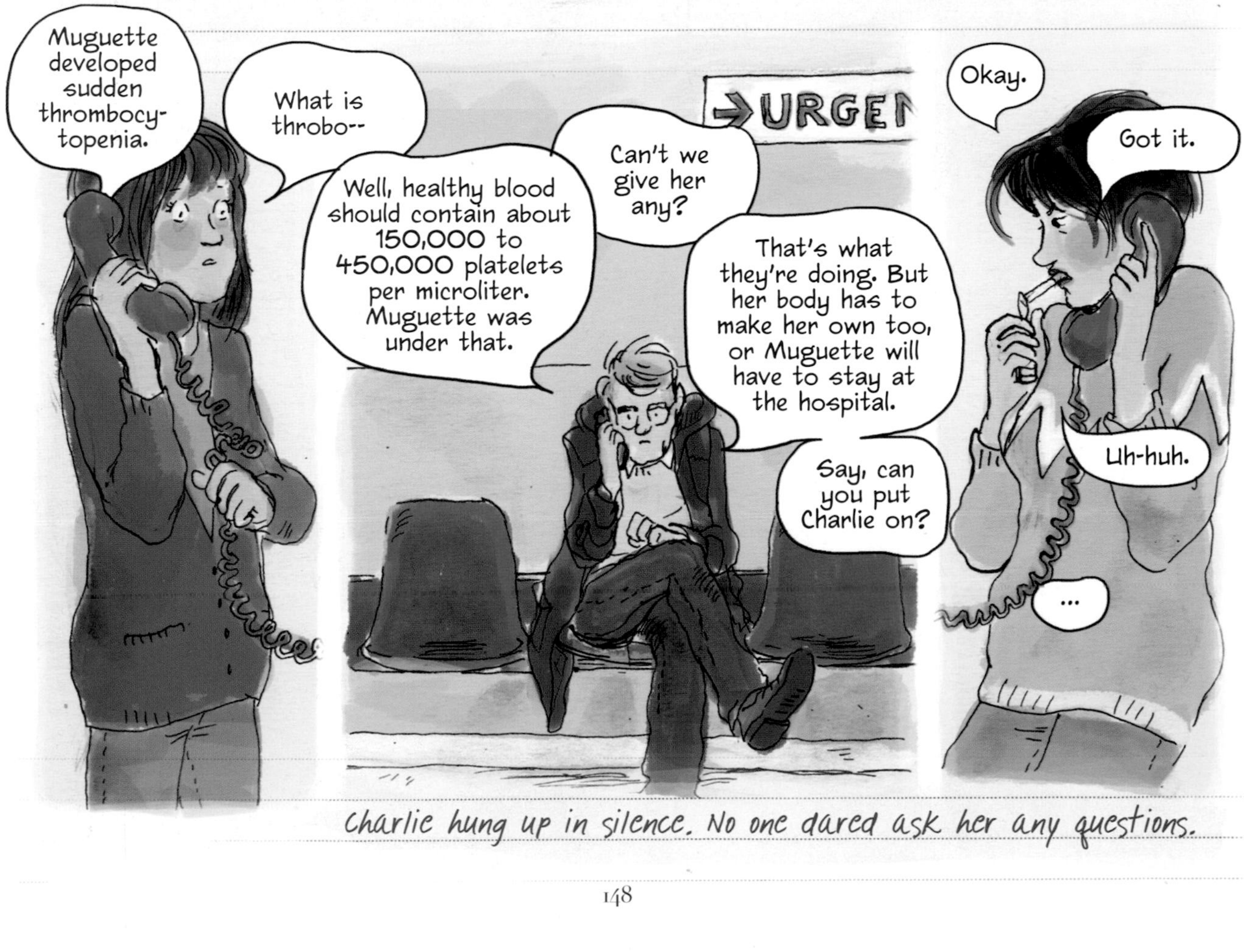
Muguette developed sudden thrombocy-topenia.
What is throbo--
Well, healthy blood should contain about 150,000 to 450,000 platelets per microliter. Muguette was under that.
Can't we give her any?
That's what they're doing. But her body has to make her own too, or Muguette will have to stay at the hospital.
Say, can you put Charlie on?
→URGEN
Okay.
Got it.
Uh-huh.
...

Charlie hung up in silence. No one dared ask her any questions.

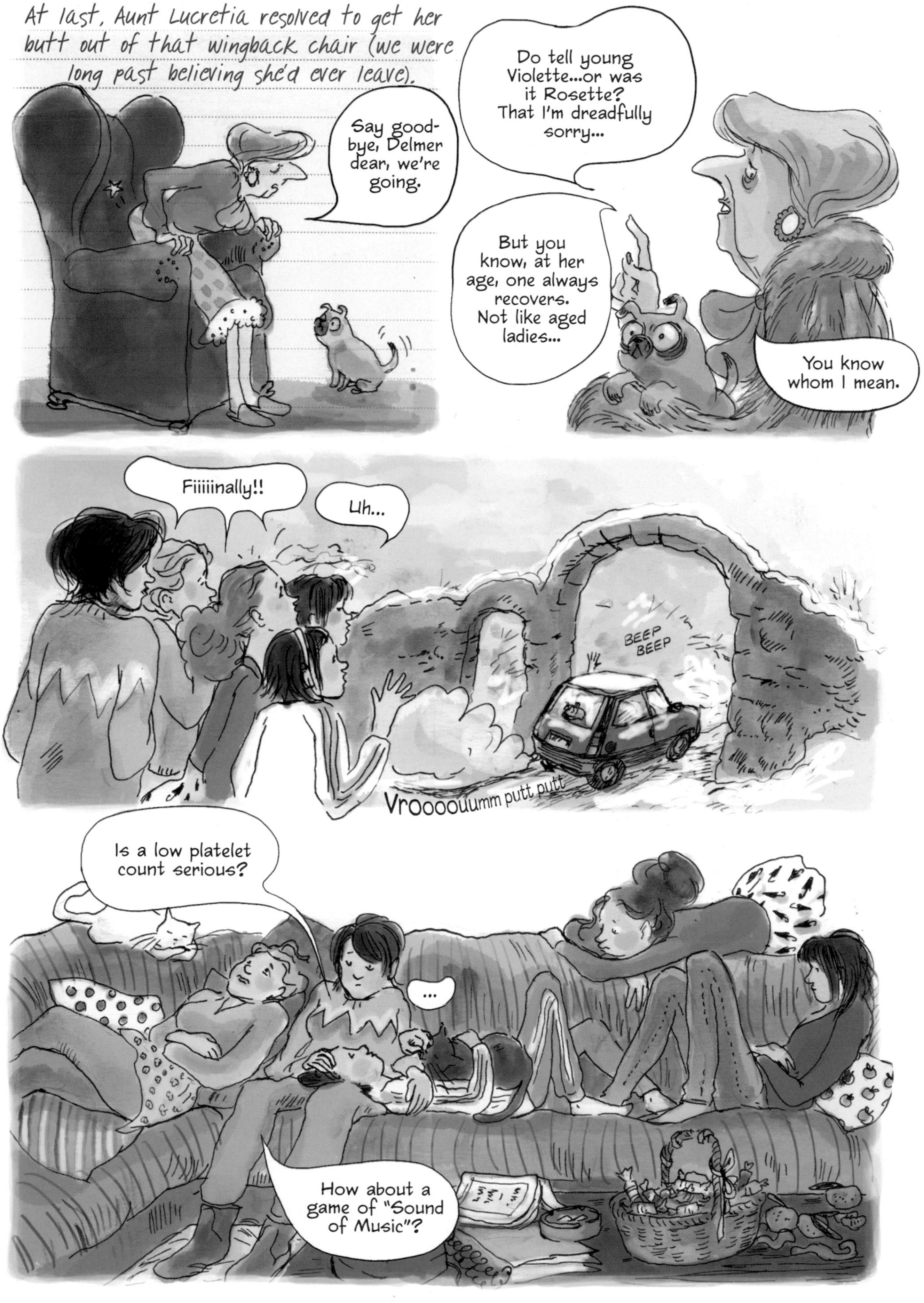
At last, Aunt Lucretia resolved to get her butt out of that wingback chair (we were long past believing she'd ever leave).
Say good-bye, Delmer dear, we're going.
Do tell young Violette...or was it Rosette? That I'm dreadfully sorry...
But you know, at her age, one always recovers. Not like aged ladies...
You know whom I mean.
Fiiiiinally!!
Uh...
BEEP BEEP
Vroooouumm putt putt
Is a low platelet count serious?
...
How about a game of "Sound of Music"?

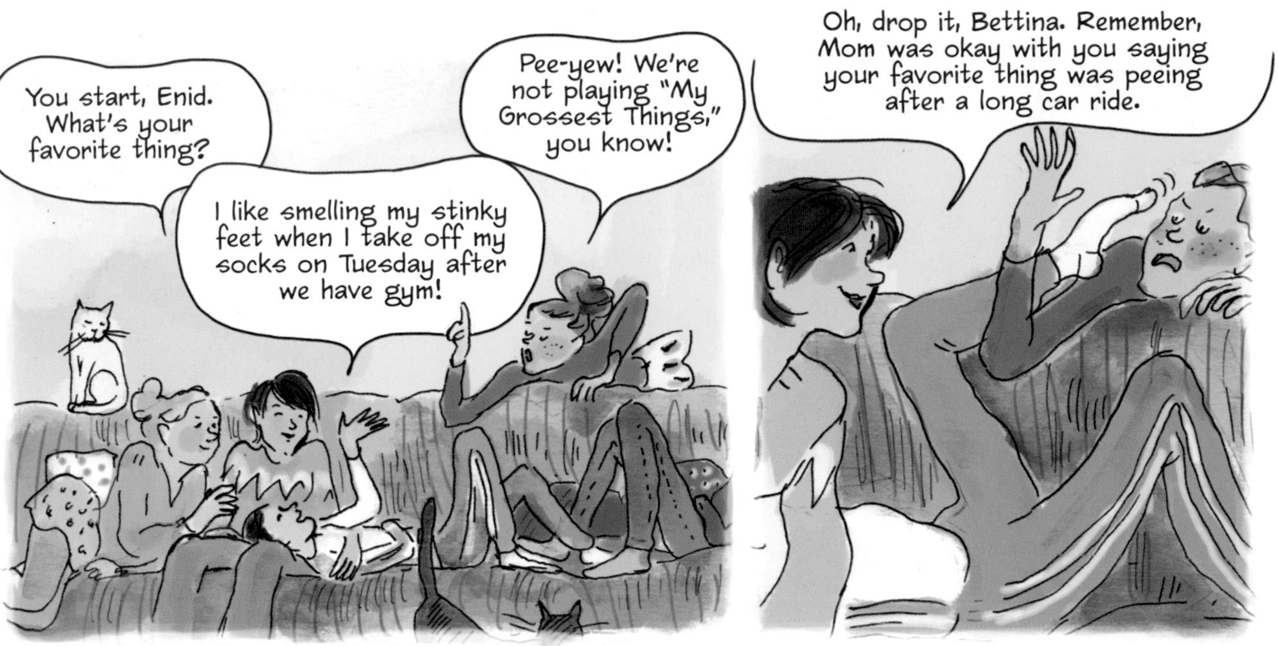

You start, Enid. What's your favorite thing?
I like smelling my stinky feet when I take off my socks on Tuesday after we have gym!
Pee-yew! We're not playing "My Grossest Things," you know!
Oh, drop it, Bettina. Remember, Mom was okay with you saying your favorite thing was peeing after a long car ride.

The "Sound of Music" game was a Verdelaine household tradition for cheering each other up by thinking about things they liked.

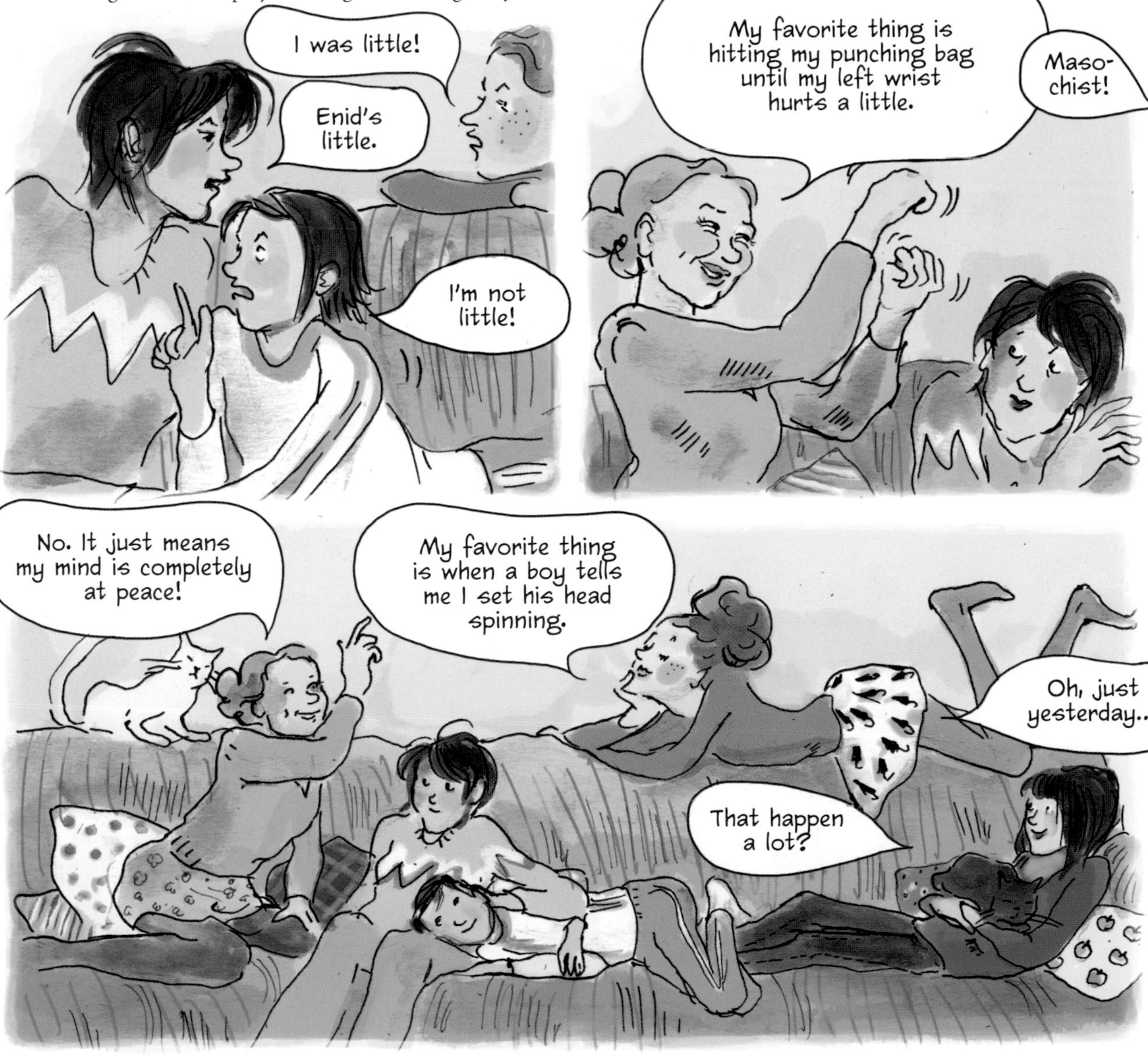

I was little!
Enid's little.
I'm not little!
My favorite thing is hitting my punching bag until my left wrist hurts a little.
Maso-chist!
No. It just means my mind is completely at peace!
My favorite thing is when a boy tells me I set his head spinning.
That happen a lot?
Oh, just yesterday...

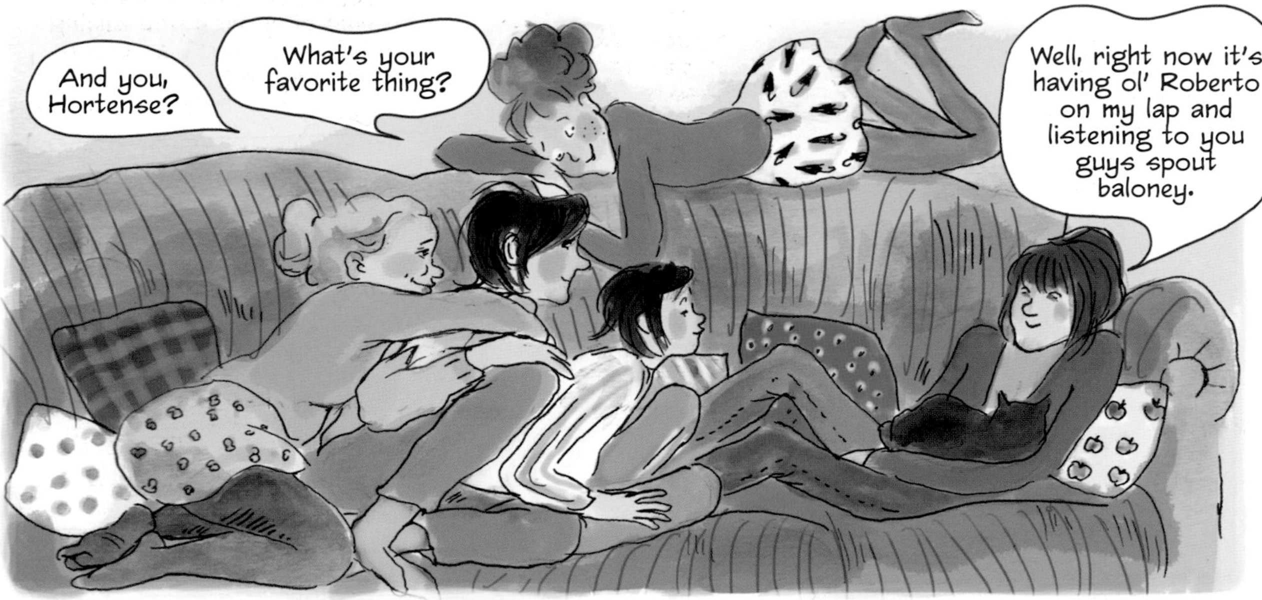
And you, Hortense?
What's your favorite thing?
Well, right now it's having ol' Roberto on my lap and listening to you guys spout baloney.

In the gentle warmth from the fire and the late afternoon light, Hortense felt like nothing terrible could happen. Muguette just had to get better. She HAD to.

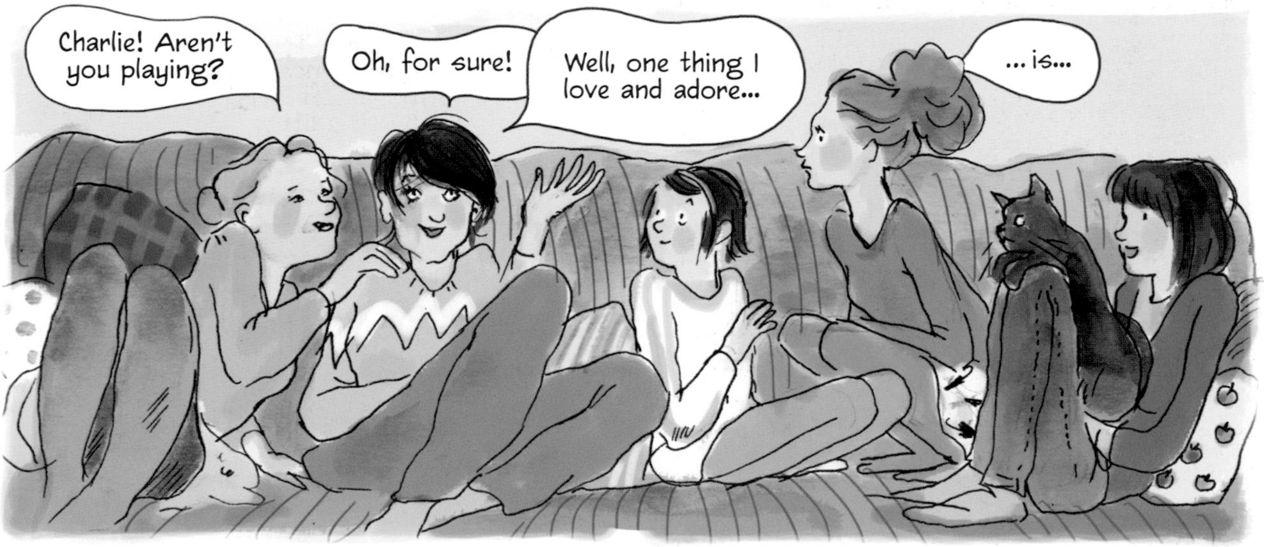
Charlie! Aren't you playing?
Oh, for sure!
Well, one thing I love and adore...
...is...

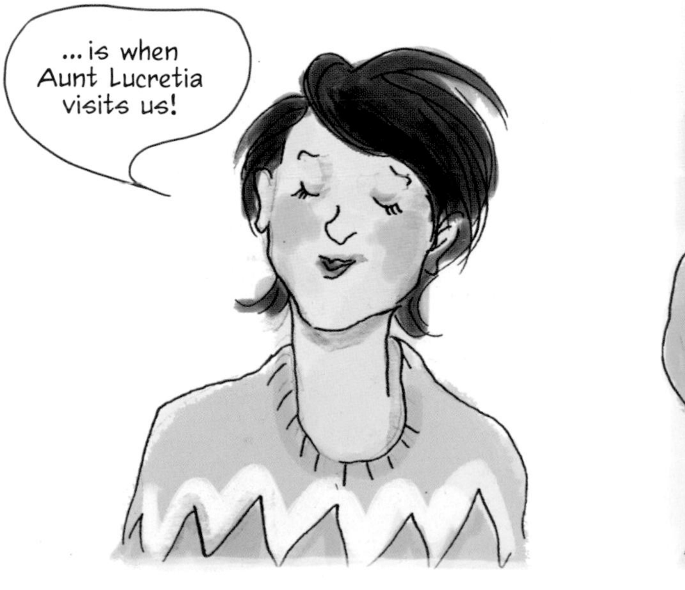
...is when Aunt Lucretia visits us!

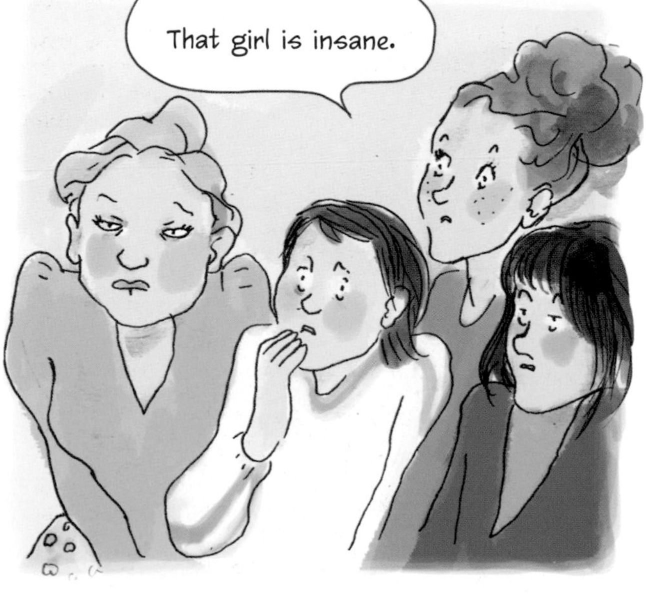
That girl is insane.

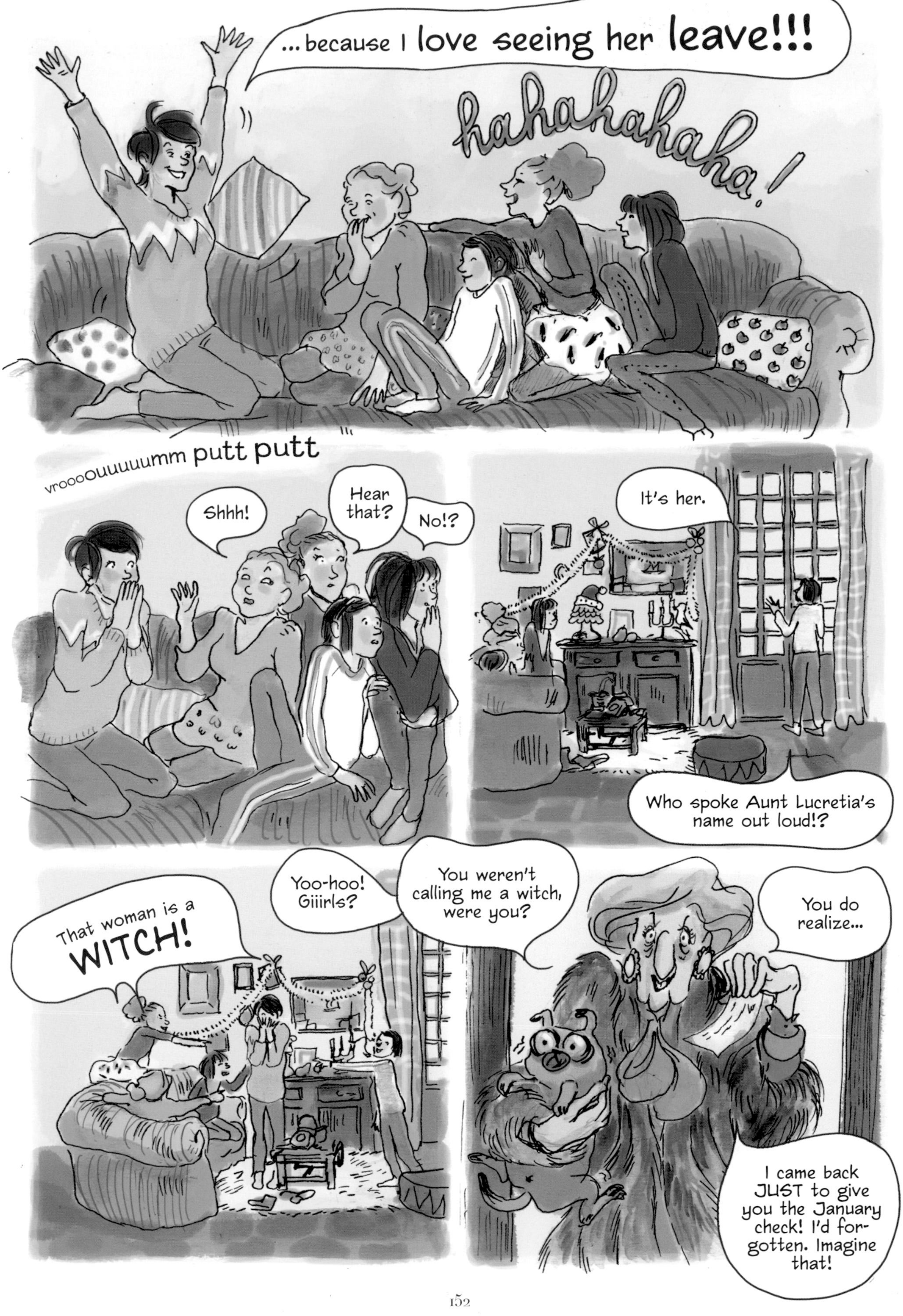

...because I love seeing her leave!!!
hahahahaha!
vroooOuuuuumm putt putt
Shhh!
Hear that?
No!?
It's her.
Who spoke Aunt Lucretia's name out loud!?
That woman is a WITCH!
Yoo-hoo! Giiirls?
You weren't calling me a witch, were you?
You do realize...
I came back JUST to give you the January check! I'd for-gotten. Imagine that!

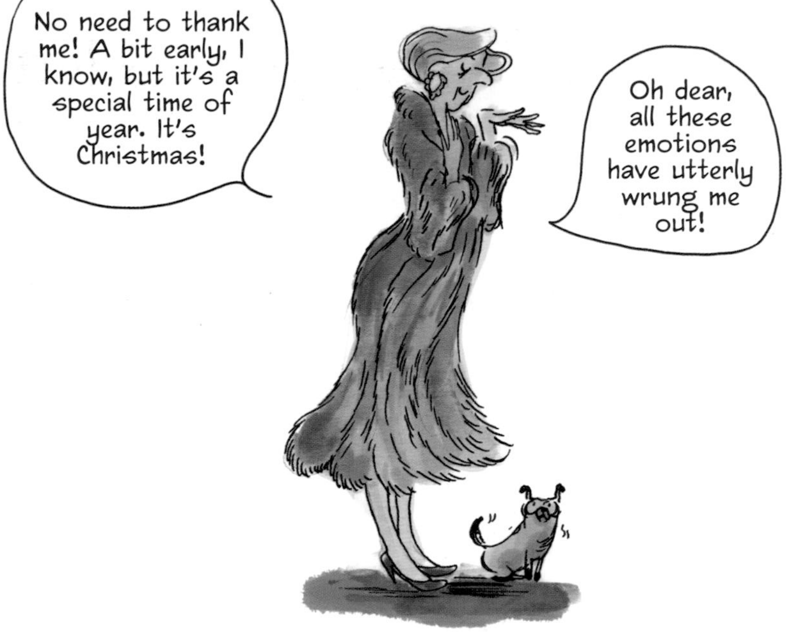
No need to thank me! A bit early, I know, but it's a special time of year. It's Christmas!
Oh dear, all these emotions have utterly wrung me out!

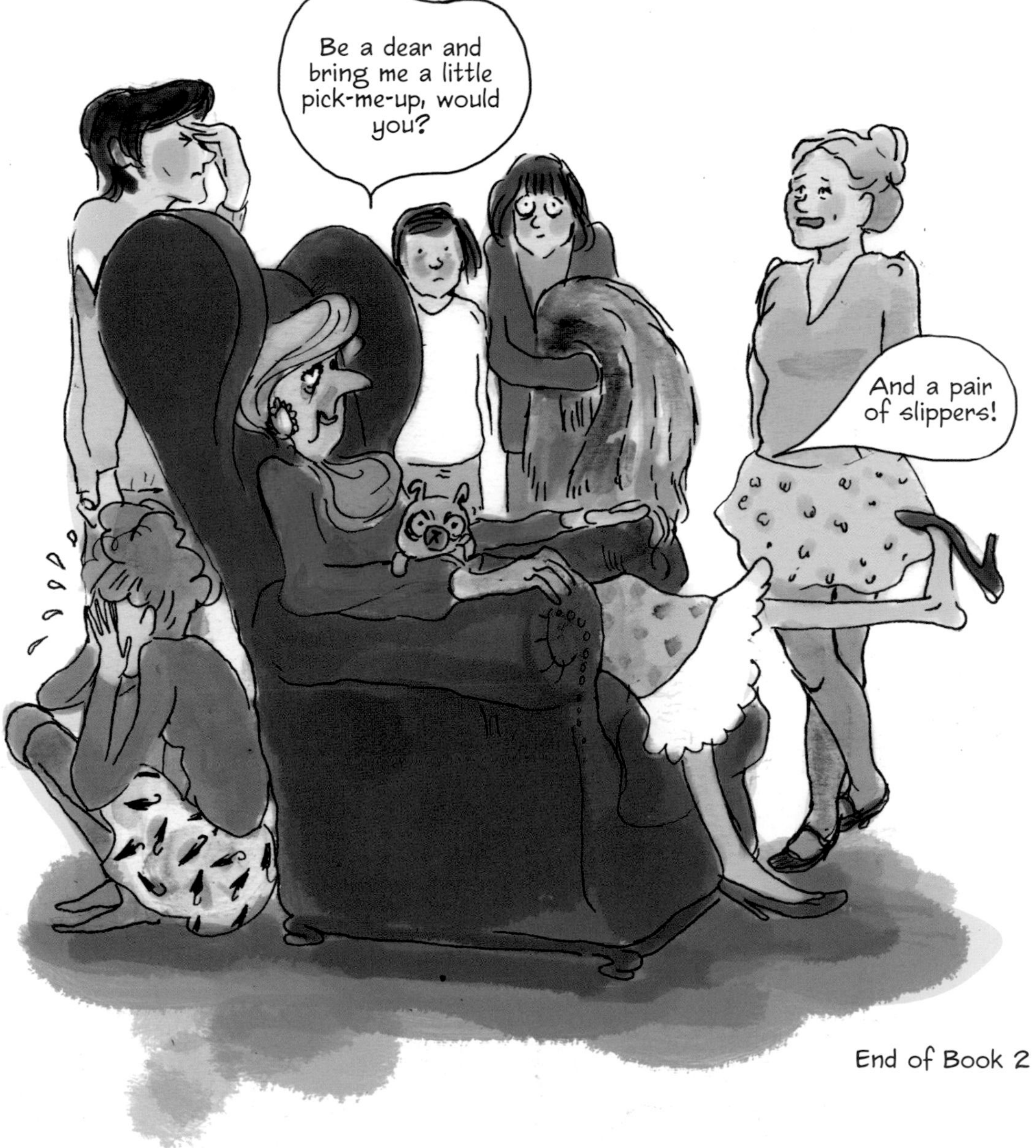
Be a dear and bring me a little pick-me-up, would you?
And a pair of slippers!

End of Book 2

Volume 3:
Bettina

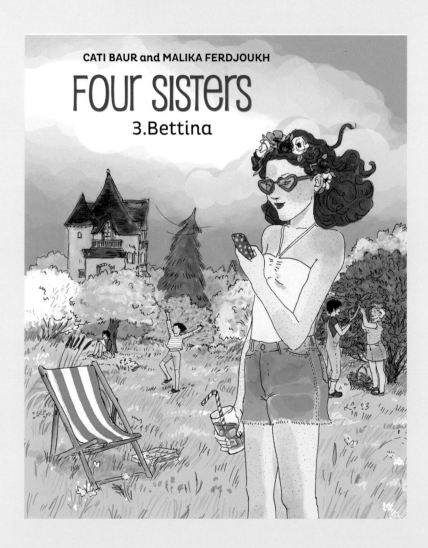

CATI BAUR and MALIKA FERDJOUKH

FOUR SISTERS

3.Bettina

OTHER BOOKS FROM EUROCOMICS/IDW

VIOLETTE
BY TERESA RADICE & STEFANO TURCONI

ENOLA HOLMES
BY NANCY SPRINGER & SERENA BLASCO

THE QUEST OF EWILAN
BY PIERRE BOTTERO, LYLIAN,
AND LAURENCE BALDETTI

CORTO MALTESE BY HUGO PRATT

THE ADVENTURES OF DIETER LUMPEN
BY JORGE ZENTNER & RUBÉN PELLEJERO

THE SILENCE OF MALKA
BY JORGE ZENTNER & RUBÉN PELLEJERO

PARACUELLOS BY CARLOS GIMÉNEZ

FLIGHT OF THE RAVEN BY JEAN-PIERRE GIBRAT

THE REPRIEVE BY JEAN-PIERRE GIBRAT

MATTÉO BY JEAN-PIERRE GIBRAT

ALACK SINNER BY CARLOS SAMPAYO & JOSÉ MUÑOZ

JEROME K. JEROME BLOCHE BY ALAIN DODIER

LIGHTS OF THE AMALOU
BY CHRISTOPHE GIBELIN & CLAIRE WENDLING

ONE MAN, ONE ADVENTURE:
THE MAN FROM THE GREAT NORTH
BY HUGO PRATT

TALES FROM THE AGE OF THE COBRA
BY ENRIQUE FERNÁNDEZ